A KILLING SNOW

A KILLING SNOW

a novel by

Dave Hoing & Roger Hileman

www.penmorepress.com

ISBN-13: 978-1-942756-88-0(Paperback)
ISBN :-978-1-942756-89-7(e-book)

BISAC Subject Headings:

FIC033000 FICTION / Westerns
FIC031010 FICTION / Thrillers / Crime
FIC027100 FICTION / Romance / Western

Cover Illustration by Christine Horner
Portraits by Diane House
Address all correspondence to:

Penmore Press LLC
920 N Javelina Pl
Tucson AZ 85748

DEDICATION

For two remarkable men, a century apart:

Michael Hileman, Jr.
(1820-1915)

and

Dave Glime
(1945-2016)

Table of Contents

OBITUARY

TRIAL

STORM

ACKNOWLEDGMENTS

AFTERWARD

OBITUARY
AN OLD FEUD FUELED BY DRINK

On this first Thursday of the new century, Mariel Erickson, sole reporter, editor, and typesetter for the *Goss Valley Sentinel*, wasn't wearing her wooden leg. She propped herself up with her crutches and clattered down the steps to the printing press in the cellar of the post office. Outside, the temperature was below zero, with a northwest wind that made the air feel twenty degrees colder.

Mariel hated winter. She didn't remove her wraps until she had scooped a shovelful of coal into the stove, splashed kerosene over them, and dropped a match into the metal potbelly. The lumps took the flame on the first attempt. She held her hands above the stove, luxuriating in its heat. When she could no longer see her breath, she hobbled to the press, dragging a stool with her.

She had actual news to print this week: the obituary of Clyde Hartwig. Although she was determined to be professional about it, Hartwig was a man against whom she harbored strong resentment. In the spring of '87, in full view of five witnesses, he used a baseball bat to bludgeon a man to death. He didn't go to trial until January of 1888. With such overwhelming evidence, he should have been hanged. Instead, the jury voted to acquit. In dismissing the incident as "an old feud fueled by drink," they gifted him with twelve extra years of life he didn't deserve.

Last night she'd set the types for her usual recipes and sewing tips, as well as the week's weather forecast from her husband Randall. Unsure what to write about Hartwig, she'd left ten column inches blank for his obituary, then had gone home to mull the wording. She worked out a draft sometime after midnight, and was back here at the post office by seven.

Mariel felt a twinge in her back as she lifted the tray of types next to the press. She was going on sixty-two, and every day seemed to bring a new bodily complaint. Arthritis in her hands made the meticulous task of handling individual letters clumsy and painful. It didn't help that the device was an old-fashioned screw press that must be over a hundred years old. It didn't even run on steam, let alone electricity, and its devil's tail had to be cranked by hand.

She balled and opened her fists, stretching the ligaments until she had achieved some degree of flexibility in her fingers. After measuring the blank space again, she reached into her tray of types and set the text.

PROMINENT CITIZEN DIES

It is this correspondent's duty to report the passing of Goss Valley resident Clyde Hartwig. Mr. Hartwig was forty-four years of age when he expired in his sleep on Tuesday, 2 January 1900, at approximately four o'clock in the morning. Dr. Allen Brandon has ruled his death the result of a previously unsuspected heart ailment.

Clyde Eugene Hartwig was born to Werner and Kathryn Nolan Hartwig on 19 April 1855 in Franklin County Pennsylvania. He was joined in matrimony with Louisa Ottomeier in that state in August 1876.

Mrs. Hartwig bore him two children. The family immigrated to Dakota Territory some years later, and has resided in Goss Valley since its founding in 1883.

A long-time employee of the Koeperich Livery, at one time Mr. Hartwig supplemented his occupation by selling Turkish red wheat seed to the farmers of the area. For many years he invested in the Chicago grain markets. Initially this venture proved unprofitable, but in the fall of 1888 there was an upturn in the markets, and he rapidly accumulated one of the largest fortunes in the Mid-west.

Such was the status accorded him by his new wealth that in November 1889 he was invited to join the delegation sent to Washington to witness President Harrison's historic proclamation of statehood for North and South Dakota.

From 1894-1895 Mr. Hartwig acted as mayor pro tempore of this city when Herbert Goss resigned for health reasons. He did not seek the office in the subsequent election.

Sometime after this he purchased the old Michael Hammon property and further increased his income from land rental.

Mr. Hartwig was predeceased by his parents, his young son Wayne, and, it is believed, a brother. He is survived by his wife and a daughter, Jeannette.

The date, time, and place of Mr. Hartwig's internment have yet to be announced.

A typesetter for years, Mariel could read blocks of text backwards as well as forward. As she proofread the article, she massaged the stump of her left leg just below the knee. There was still a phantom tingling in the area where her limb had been, an itch that could not be scratched. She wondered how such a sensation was possible after all this time. Or ever.

Whatever the source of her discomfort, it was worse when she wore the prosthetic. Then the itch seemed to emanate from the wood itself, a most unnerving sensation indeed.

She concentrated on her wording. She was sorely tempted to print what she really thought of Hartwig. His death was utterly unsatisfying. It elicited not a peep from his lips, not a twinge of distress, not a word of repentance. He simply closed his eyes and did not awaken, flouting justice and dooming his victim to lie unavenged in his grave for all eternity.

She inked the letters, placed a folio sheet of paper onto the press, and printed the entire issue on one side, like a broadsheet. When the ink was dry, she cranked out fifty copies of the paper for distribution tomorrow, then removed the copy and swept the types into the cleaning bucket.

The obituary was real news, a commodity she often lacked, but in her mind Hartwig's belated death was a waste of ten column inches of perfectly good blank space.

ARRIVAL

CHAPTER ONE
SHADOWS OF THE MOON
Friday, July 23, 1886

Bruno perked up his ears and wagged his stumpy tail as the train swayed to a halt at the Kimball station. There'd been several other stops between Chicago and here, but somehow he knew, in ways only dogs did, that this time they'd be departing the cramped car for good. He sprang over Randall and thudded onto Mariel's lap like a sack of cannonballs. Whining impatiently, he pressed his nose and front paws against the window. His nails dug into Mariel's thighs even through several layers of clothing.

She scratched the scruff of his neck to calm him. Part bulldog, part God-knew-what, Bruno was quite possibly the ugliest dog she had ever seen. He possessed a flat snout, a bloated belly, a mouth two sizes too big, and a tongue that oozed slime. But he had a kindly disposition, and their daughter Ellie and son Alex had loved him through their adolescent years. Following in his father's footsteps, Alex went off to West Point, and Ellie's beau Everett was allergic to dogs, or maybe it was only to Bruno, so they couldn't take him into their new home after the wedding. Mariel suspected Everett's complaint had less to do with allergies than with Bruno's unfortunate tendency to slobber from one end and emit disagreeable vapors from the other.

Nevertheless, the old dog had galumphed his way into their hearts, and when Randall procured a transfer to Dakota Territory, there was no thought of leaving him behind.

The train's whistle sounded to confirm its arrival. Mariel clipped a leash to Bruno's collar, picked up her bag, and rose from her seat. It felt good to stretch her legs. Although she had reached the age when her body required no reason whatsoever to hurt, she had reason aplenty after their journey. Randall had chosen not to spend the extra money for a sleeping booth, and these five days of heat, humidity, and inactivity had taken their toll.

Not to mention that the incessant clacking of the rails nearly drove her mad.

Randall was aching, too. His shoulders slumped in exhaustion. He wore a neatly clipped mustache, having given up the waxed twirls and sideburns of his youth, but was otherwise clean-shaven. However, for the past two days he'd been too tired to bother with his razor. Graying stubble shadowed his cheeks and chin, making him appear older than his fifty-one years.

"Almost there," he sighed. He stepped into the aisle between rows of seats, creating space among the other passengers for Mariel to get out. "Don't let the dog make a nuisance of himself."

"When was he ever anything but?" she said, shortening up on Bruno's leash.

Randall adjusted his spectacles and smiled wearily. They followed their fellow travelers out the exit and down the steps onto the platform. As they made their way to the baggage car, Mariel looked out over the plains of Dakota. Heat shimmered above the prairie grass. Although their final destination was said to be in a valley, the land was featureless, with not a rise or dip to impede the view to the horizon. The late afternoon sky was as deep and blue as any she'd seen, intimidating in its incomprehensible vastness.

But so, so beautiful. She had always loved poetry, and wondered what magic Keats or Wordsworth might weave about this landscape. She herself aspired to write, but she had no gift for rhyming. Prose would not do it justice.

Entire families poured from the cars onto the platform. Some were Easterners moving here for cheap land to homestead and some ex-soldiers taking advantage of a government program, but most were European immigrants. By their threadbare look, they'd spent their entire savings for the passage to and across America. Mariel heard at least half a dozen languages spoken as they fussed over their meager belongings and made their way into the station.

She felt fortunate indeed. Unlike these newcomers, whose futures were cobbled together by dreams, she and Randall wouldn't be trying to build a life from nothing. They arrived in Dakota to assured circumstances. When Randall had expressed disillusionment with his position in Chicago, his old war friend Mike Hammon helped arrange for his transfer to this post. His guarantee of employment spared them the hardships of breaking sod and raising crops.

Randall handed his claim ticket to the baggage clerk and rewarded him with a nickel when he delivered their suitcase and two trunks. Mariel took the suitcase as Randall struggled to maneuver the cumbersome trunks through the crowd.

They'd expected Mr. Hammon, but he was nowhere to be seen. Instead, a young fellow with a thin neck and narrow forehead was accosting all the men as they left the station, saying, "Lieutenant Erickson?" He had long black hair and patchy whiskers that sprouted more from his neck than his cheeks and chin. He was wearing, as Randall would put it, a "beat-to-hell" Stetson and dusty denims, with a six-shooter on his hip, like the cowboys in the dime novels so popular out east. Mariel smiled into her hand. He did have a feral appearance, but he looked more like a caricature of an outlaw than a real hombre, a poor man's Wild Bill.

Bruno growled as the man approached Randall. Mariel tugged on his leash and told him to sit. The man looked at her, then at Randall. "Lieutenant Erickson?"

Randall nodded. "And you are?"

"Mr. Hammon sent me. Name's Clyde Hartwig. Maybe you heard the slogan, 'Hartwig wheat, can't be beat'? That's me."

"Afraid not."

"Well, it don't matter. I'm mostly a drayman now. Work at Koerperich's Livery. Welcome to Dakota." He eyed their luggage. "I thought there'd be a lot more. Ain't much to start a life with."

"This is just to get us through the first week," Randall said. "The rest will be coming after we get established."

Hartwig took the trunks from Randall, who then took the suitcase from Mariel. "Mike says some kind of science contraptions?"

"Weather instruments. I'm with the Army Signal Corps."

Mariel could see that meant nothing to Hartwig. He had a peculiar odor of dill weed about him. His wife must have recently pickled cucumbers. The smell reminded her of canning fruits and vegetables for her father in Ohio. She'd never enjoyed canning, then or now, although she still did it as need arose.

"Nearest fort still in business is Lookout, here in Brule County," Hartwig said.

"I won't need a fort for what I'll be doing. Just a flat roof and a good view."

"Whatever you say," Hartwig said. "My wagon's right over

there."

The men walked toward a flatbed with a four-horse team waiting at the north side of the station.

Bruno resisted as Mariel tried to follow them, refusing to budge regardless of how insistently she jerked on his leash.

Hartwig glanced back. "No offense intended, ma'am, but the daylight won't keep. We got twenty miles to go yet."

Randall returned and scooped up Bruno under his free arm. As he and Mariel caught up with Hartwig, Bruno growled again and chose that moment to unleash an ill wind. Mariel's eyes watered.

Hartwig plugged his nose. "Whew-ee! You got yourself a dog-shaped skunk there. It can ride in the back with the luggage."

"I do apologize," Mariel said. "He doesn't usually behave like this. I fear he doesn't like you, Mr. Hartwig."

None of the other travelers were bound for Goss Valley. Once those wagons had gone their separate ways, Mariel, Randall, and Hartwig had this stretch of prairie to themselves. The flatbed was wide enough for all three to sit abreast in the front, Hartwig holding the reins on the left, Randall in the middle, and Mariel on the right. Bruno rode in the back. The land that had looked so featureless from the station was surprisingly bumpy. Just outside Kimball Hartwig turned north onto what he called a trail, but Mariel called two ruts in the grass. A rolling expanse of bluestem, coneflowers, and goldenrod rose on either side of them, high enough to brush against their legs. Meadowlarks perched on slender stalks and warbled a sweet song. Three red-tailed hawks circled overhead, perhaps with dreams of feasting on a corpulent bulldog.

Bruno was oblivious to danger. With so little luggage in back, he had room to bound from side to side, woofing his excitement as he tried to take in every sight and scent.

"Bruno, hush," Randall said, and was ignored. The dog was as clever or as dimwitted as he needed to be in order to get what he wanted. Since there was no food involved, today he was dumb.

Mariel loosened the strings on her bonnet and drew in a breath of fresh air. It was a hot but grand afternoon, filled with promise. "Mr. Hartwig, would you be offended if I were to remove my hat to enjoy the sunshine on my face?"

"I've seen gals wearing a good deal less than that."

"You're a young man, Hartwig," Randall chided. "Maybe your generation speaks to ladies this way, but mine doesn't."

"Beg pardon, Lieutenant. I meant my wife, of course."

Mariel left her bonnet on. Bruno was not alone in taking a dislike to the man. "I lived in Ohio when I was a child," she said. "It was flat, but it didn't seem quite so *infinite*. It's like gazing into forever."

"Don't fret none, ma'am, the accommodations will make you feel right at home."

"I'm not fretting, Mr. Hartwig. Dakota is truly quite beautiful."

"Where will we be staying?" Randall said. "I understand our house isn't finished?"

"The widow Bohnet's hotel in Goss Valley. You know who's running the place, don't you, Lieutenant?"

Randall smiled. "It'll be good to see Mike again."

"How long you been in the Army, if you don't mind me asking?"

"Over thirty years."

Hartwig gave Randall an odd look. Mariel had seen it before: Thirty years and you're only a lieutenant? Fortunately, Hartwig had enough sense not to comment.

"A man needs a change of pace sometimes," Randall explained, which was true enough. Mariel knew his lack of promotion weighed heavily upon him sometimes, but it didn't particularly bother her. She wasn't the kind of woman who insisted upon driving ambition in her husband. They were living well enough on the wages of his present position.

The sun was on its downward arc when the wagon topped a hill, then dipped into a shallow valley, neither of which had been visible from the train station. At the bottom of the hill stood an old shanty, its walls charred by fire, its roof collapsed into the structure. The fields around it showed signs of new growth over blackened roots.

"Is this the work of Indians?" Randall said.

"Ten years ago it might've been," Hartwig said. "This was the Liljegren place. He probably did it himself 'cause he couldn't make enough to live. Damn immigrants come here thinking it's gonna be easy."

"What about the Indians, Mr. Hartwig?" Mariel said. "They'd been chased out of Ohio by the time my father and I arrived there. I don't believe I've ever seen one, other than in a medicine show. Have you?"

"Well, sure, but we don't pay them much mind. After Custer, the Army rounded up all the Injuns and put them in Crow Creek Reservation. It ain't too far from Goss Valley, but they don't hardly come out, except to trade for food or horses. Or whiskey. Them Crows like our whiskey."

"Does anybody ever visit the reservation?"

"You mean white men?" He shrugged. "Dakota's Injun Affairs fella, and maybe some soldiers, but otherwise, why would we?"

"Curiosity. I should very much like to see how they live one day."

"Nothing to see. They're just Crows. My wife's sewing circle makes noises every now and again how they're gonna donate clothes to them, but they ain't done it so far."

"Then it's time they did."

"Forgive her," Randall said, "she has romantic notions about the noble savage."

"Takes all kinds," Hartwig said.

The wagon passed the shanty, leaving nothing ahead of them but prairie and two parallel ruts that converged on the horizon. After an indeterminable time of unchanging scenery, Mariel found herself mesmerized by the grass as it swayed in a southwest breeze. Lengthening evening shadows created the effect of ripples, with furrows of darkness undulating beneath crests of color. It was very much like she imagined the sea to be, green replacing blue, but waves nonetheless, rolling and breaking on distant shores.

How the natives must have loved this land.

She closed her eyes and tried to call the lines of verse the image evoked. "*On such a full sea are we now afloat,*" she murmured. "*And we must take the current when it serves, or lose our ventures.*"

"Beg pardon?" Hartwig said.

"Shakespeare."

"You one of them educated females?"

"Elmira College, class of fifty-eight."

"What you just said, that was Shakespeare? 'Cause that shit don't even rhyme."

"It's not supposed to rhyme, Mr. Hartwig," she said. "Tell me, do you not pity the Indians being cooped up in a reservation after having once had all this?"

"It's where they belong, Mrs. Erickson. Can't just have them running around free."

"Why not?"

"They're savages, ma'am. Or were, till we corralled them."

"How so?"

"You folks got a daughter?"

"Her name is Ellie."

"Injuns're almost as fond of white gals as they are of whiskey. How'd you like one of them ravishing your Ellie?"

"I shouldn't like *anyone* ravishing her, Mr. Hartwig."

"Anyway, you got no cause to worry about them no more. They ain't got any fight left in them. Your worst enemy out here's gonna be the weather. It can turn on you faster than a dollar-short whore, pardon my French. Don't let this nice day fool you."

"Looks like you're going to need my services," Randall said, removing his hat and staring into the fathomless sky.

Moments later Bruno started barking. Without warning he launched himself from the back of the wagon and disappeared into the tall grass. Mariel heard the agitated squawks and clucks of unseen birds. They sounded like the chickens her father raised. Dog and fowl alike were invisible, but she could see the grass move in their wake. Lines of disturbance radiated out like the spokes of a wheel as the birds scattered. Occasionally one would appear above the grass flapping ineffectual wings, before falling back to earth. Bruno was hot in pursuit.

"Bruno, no!" she cried. "Oh, Mr. Hartwig, stop the wagon."

Hartwig pulled up on the reins. Laughing, he said, "Prairie chickens. Got a gamey taste, but they're pretty good eating."

"I'm going to shoot that damned dog," Randall said. He hopped down from the wagon and chased after Bruno.

"You'll do no such thing," Mariel said.

The grass was more or less the same height, obscuring the uneven ground below. Randall tripped and went down, but popped back up immediately, apparently unhurt. He resumed his search at a walk. Mariel could hear Bruno's growls and an unfortunate chicken's death squawks.

"Buffalo wallows," Hartwig said. "Used to come through

here by the thousands. It was so hot in summer, they'd lay on their backs and take dirt baths to cool themselves off. Carved these ruts all over the place."

"You might have warned him," Mariel said.

"You never know where they're gonna be, ma'am, till you step in them."

A few moments later Randall stormed back, lugging a most unhappy Bruno by the scruff of his neck. The dog had blood on his muzzle and feathers in his mouth.

"Idiot animal," he said.

"It's just learning the ways of the prairie, Lieutenant," Hartwig said.

****

Bruno slept curled up between the trunks, yipping at dog dreams. One end of his leash was attached to his collar, the other secured to the handle of a trunk.

The sun was beneath the horizon when they arrived at Crow Creek, but the sky wasn't fully dark. The creek looked to be forty feet wide, with no bridge in sight. Wagon ruts went right down into the water.

"Oh, dear," Mariel said. "Goss Valley is on the other side of the river?"

"Don't worry, Mrs. Erickson. Ain't rained much since June, so the creek's no more than knee deep here. You could wade across it if you had to."

"*Do* I have to, Mr. Hartwig?"

"No, ma'am. I come this way all the time. Horses don't mind getting wet."

He clicked his tongue and shook the reins, and the wagon lurched out into Crow Creek. The crossing was smoother than Mariel expected. Once across Hartwig had to negotiate an area of smelly muck thick as a bog, which he called gumbo flats. Luckily, the flats were narrow, and by dark they were immersed in grasses and wildflowers again.

A half-moon in Dakota gave off nearly as much light as a full moon in Chicago. Its glow washed over the prairie, transforming green stalks and blue flowers to silver and shadow. The air was cooling quickly. The day's benign songs of larks were replaced by keening coyotes and screeching hawks, chirping crickets and lovesick toads.

Bruno awoke and whined, his bravery limited to flightless birds. Mariel understood his distress. She'd always had a vivid imagination, and it was getting the better of her. If these animal cries had been present this afternoon, she hadn't noticed. Tonight she did.

"How much farther, Mr. Hartwig?" she said.

"Not far, ma'am."

The moon was on her right, still low in the sky. It threw their shadows to the west, their bodies stretching like grotesque stick figures upon the illusory snow. Hartwig, being the tallest, cast the most prominent outline, his wide Stetson a disturbing contrast with his elongated head and neck.

The keening abated somewhat. Silence was more alarming than the noise. Mariel sensed the coyotes were closer, perhaps pacing the wagon. Every now and again she saw eye shine in the shadows of the moon. She huddled into her dress. "Do hasten, Mr. Hartwig."

CHAPTER TWO
PRO PATRIA VIGILANS
Saturday, July 24, 1886

Randall lit a match to check his pocket watch. "After midnight," he said to Hartwig.

"Almost there. Mr. Hammon's gonna have my ass in a sling for being so late."

Mariel objected to his language, but was too tired to protest. She leaned her head against Randall's shoulder, yawned, and tried to stay awake.

"Let me tell you about Mike Hammon," Randall said. "I've never known anyone like him. He was forty-one, I think, when the war broke out. He enlisted right after First Bull Run as an ordinary private, although he'd made sergeant by the time we met. I was a strapping young fellow then, but even fifteen years my senior, Mike would've made short work of me."

The wagon crested another low hill. Beyond that Mariel could see the dark outlines of houses against the stars, only one of which had a light in the windows.

"My father was in the war," Hartwig said. "He never saw fighting, though."

"Mike was captured, and ended up in Andersonville. Ask him about that sometime."

"Never heard of it," Hartwig said. "I was just a kid. That where you met him?"

"No. Andersonville would've killed me. Not Mike. His was one of two platoons from the Illinois Ninety-Second reassigned to courier duty with the Army of the Cumberland's Signal Corps. That's how we met. *Pro patria vigilans.*"

"French?"

"Latin, Mr. Hartwig," Mariel said.

"It's the Signal Corps' motto," Randall added. "It means 'watchful for the country.'"

Hartwig scowled. "Why don't you just say 'watchful for the country,' then?" The prairie grasses thinned as the rutted trail widened into a dirt road. "We're here. And look who's waiting."

As they pulled into the settlement, Mariel saw the silhouette of a man in a hat in the doorway of a two-story house.

Hartwig steered the horses in that direction and stopped in front of the door. He stretched his muscles and popped his joints before coming around to offer Mariel assistance. Her body ached, too, particularly at the juncture where she and the wagon converged. Were Hartwig not so close by, she might have massaged the affected area.

As Randall climbed down, Bruno woke briefly, sniffed the air, and curled up again. "No, you don't," Randall said, unhooking him from the trunk. "Mr. Hartwig will need his rig."

"Perhaps Bruno would appreciate time in the bushes," Mariel suggested.

"He ain't the only one," Hartwig said, which was more than Mariel desired to know—although in that regard she was in sympathy. "I'll take him out back," he said.

"You won't escape that easy," the man in the door bellowed. "I told you ten o'clock. Good thing you're paid by the load, not the hour."

"No offense, Mr. Hammon, but if I don't go now, we're gonna get a load nobody'll wanna pay for."

"Ever the poet, Clyde," Mr. Hammon said. "Go on, git."

Exigency overcoming distrust, Bruno allowed Hartwig to take the leash. As soon as they disappeared behind the hotel, Mr. Hammon motioned Randall and Mariel toward him. Oil lamps inside burned at his back, leaving his face in shadow. Mariel couldn't get a clear view of his features, although she could see he had white hair and a long, unruly beard. He was wearing a brown vest over a stiff white shirt. She could smell the starch.

Randall ascended the three steps to the door. His height was no more than average, yet he towered over Mr. Hammon by a head. "Is it no longer customary for enlisted men to salute superior officers?" he said.

"I'd sooner salute my horse's ass," Mr. Hammon said, breaking into a grin. "Which, in your case, amounts to the same thing." He straightened his back and crisply saluted with his left hand.

"Insubordination," Randall laughed. He returned the sinistral salute.

The two men shook hands.

"You look like hell, Randy. Are you the knucklehead that tossed that bomb in Chicago?"

In May a labor protest in Chicago's Haymarket Square turned violent when a radical threw dynamite at a police officer. "You know me better than that," Randall said. "I'd have thrown it at the protesters."

"So how you been?"

Mariel thought she heard wheezing when Mr. Hammon spoke.

"Same as always, only more so," Randall said.

"You're wearing eyeglasses now. When did you get old?"

"A day at a time. You look the same as you did twenty years ago. That's hardly fair."

Mr. Hammon yawned, then coughed. "I've given it some

thought, and decided against dying."

"Good luck with that. Hartwig says you don't own the hotel?"

"Nah. Fiona Bohnet and her two sons do, but neither of those boys are worth a shit. I got some hope for the older one, Phinny, but Ned's so stupid, he probably ain't gonna live long enough to grow out of it. Fiona hired me and Phoebe to run the place. Speaking of wives...." Randall didn't take the hint, so Mr. Hammon shouldered past him, hopped down the steps, and approached Mariel. He doffed his Panama hat to her, revealing a cowlick that rose straight up from his head like water from a fountain. "Since your husband's still an ill-mannered lout, I'll introduce myself. I'm Mike Hammon. You must be Mariel."

"I am indeed, sir. Honored to meet you. I've heard many a story about your escapades."

"Nothing true, I hope. You are a handsome woman, Mrs. Erickson. What madness made you settle on the likes of *him*?"

Mariel blushed. Randall hadn't told her what a fine liar his old friend could be. She was stout as a barrel of pickles and encrusted in dried perspiration. She probably had bags under her eyes. Still, she lifted her bonnet to primp her hair, trying to stuff the stray strands back into her bun. "Equal parts pity and charity, Mr. Hammon."

"Everyone calls me Mike, except that knucklehead out back." He coughed again, pausing to catch his breath. The wheezing was more pronounced. "Long time since I had my eyes open this side of midnight."

"Are you unwell?" Mariel said.

"Oh, it's just this damned asthma. That's why I left Illinois. Doctors said the climate here would help. I don't know about that, but it's no worse, I guess."

"You should rest. You needn't have waited up for us."

"And delay meeting you? May I escort you into the hotel?"

Mariel took Mike's arm and marched up the steps. She gave Randall a *so there* look. He put his hands on his hips and chuckled.

She heard Bruno barking at some real or imagined nemesis, and then he and Hartwig rounded the corner. Hartwig was still buttoning his trousers. Randall went to take the dog's leash. "Will you retrieve our luggage?" Randall said.

"That's what I get paid for."

Mariel waited while Randall pulled Bruno up the stairs to her. When he handed her the leash, Bruno plopped down on the porch, looked up expectantly, and slobbered. His nostrils were quivering, as if he smelled something appealing inside.

"Somebody hit that dog in the face with a mallet?" Mike said.

"It's the breed," Randall said. "He can't help it."

"He was our daughter's," Mariel said.

"Well, best not let it wander too far. Coyotes are a real nuisance around here."

Mariel was horrified. "Surely coyotes wouldn't eat a dog?"

"Why not? Just another sack of meat to them."

"Why don't you shoot them?"

"We do, but it don't make any difference. If we shot fifty a night till kingdom come, they'd still be out there howling in the dark. Come on in, I'll introduce you to Phoebe."

"Your wife?"

"She'd better be, or we're both going to hell."

Mariel tried to hide her amusement. The same coarse language she found offensive from Hartwig was endearing from Mike's lips.

Whatever aroma was tickling Bruno's olfactory fancy got the better of him, and he suddenly bolted through the door, yanking Mariel with him.

The parlor was spacious and pleasingly decorated. Bruno

strained at his leash in the direction of what must be the kitchen. He sniffed the air, his slimy tongue protruding halfway to the wooden floor. Mariel noticed the planks were planed and varnished. This far into the wilderness, she'd expected a rough-hewn log cabin like she and her father shared in Ohio.

Hartwig thumped and bumped the trunks up the stairs, while simultaneously trying to balance their suitcase on top. "Lieutenant Erickson fell in a buffalo wallow," he said, giggling like a mischievous child. The suitcase tumbled to the floor, nearly striking Bruno and eliciting a warning growl. "You should've seen it—"

"Clyde," Mike said, "if you'd ever bothered to have a brain installed, you'd know when to stop talking. Take their things to the south bedroom. There's a nice breeze through there."

Moments after the drayman dragged the trunks down a hallway, a woman emerged from the direction of Bruno's desire. She appeared considerably younger than Mike, perhaps Mariel's age, but shorter and not as plump. Gray-flecked hair poked out from under a scullery cap. She looked worn out. Apparently she didn't often see this side of midnight, either.

"We've been expecting you," she said. "I made tea and biscuits."

"Mother," Mike said, "this here's Randy Erickson and his wife Mariel."

"How-do," she said with a half-hearted curtsy. "Mike speaks highly of you, Lieutenant Erickson."

"That's only because it's not polite to say what I really think."

"Seeing you again," Randall said, "makes me realize how little I've missed you."

Mike bowed to acknowledge the insult. "Let's have some of that tea. Phoebe makes the best biscuits this side of Deadwood."

Randall looked around, then knocked on a square support beam. "Solid, of fine quality. Where do you find the timber to build all this? We didn't see many trees on the way here."

"There are lumberyards in Mitchell. They bring it in by train from Minnesota."

"That must be expensive."

"Not when the other option is sleeping on the ground." Mike tried to take in a long breath, which only brought on more coughing. "Dammit."

As Mariel, Randall, and Mike sat down at a small table in the parlor, Hartwig returned from the bedroom. Without a word, he tipped his Stetson to them and left.

Phoebe remained standing. Mariel motioned her over. "I just met Mr. Hartwig," she whispered, "but is he as disagreeable as he seems?"

"More so. His wife Louisa's not much better."

"Clyde has his uses," Mike said. "The weather here's so unpredictable most crops can't be depended on every year. But Clyde, he saved the valley with his special wheat seed. It's from Russia or Turkey, some godforsaken place. Cold, heat, drought, or flood, nothing kills the damn stuff. Farmers still plant it today."

"Well, it wasn't *his* seed," Phoebe said. "'Hartwig's wheat can't be beat.' Hmmph. He bought it in Lesterville, over by Yankton. Made a lot of money off it till the farmers found out where it came from, and that he was jacking up the price."

"Still, everyone would've gone bust without him—"

"And then the wheat husks were too hard for our mill to grind. Just so happened Clyde knew people with a more modern mill in Buffalo Prairie, which would grind it for us for a price. Which Clyde got a piece of for sending the business."

"You win," Mike said. "But he did dig out that badger from behind the house for us."

"He did do that," Phoebe said.

Mike turned to Randall. "First thing in the morning we need to get you to the attorney's office. Frank Chamberlain. He's also the Register of Deeds. He'll make sure the paperwork on your lot's in order."

"Is there any question about that?" Randall said.

"Shouldn't be. That Land Commissioner, Sparks, he's giving me all kinds of shit about my veteran's homesteading exemption, but you're not homesteading, so you should be all right. Don't hurt to check, though."

"What kind of shit?"

"Rules about when you mustered out. And then you got to 'prove up' the land so it's better than when you first got it. You were smart to buy in town."

"Mrs. Erickson," Phoebe said, "shall we allow the men to talk about whatever it is men talk about? Perhaps you would consent to assist me in the kitchen?"

"Please, call me Mariel. Before I do anything I need to...."

"Ah. Of course."

"Don't expect anything high-faluting," Mike said. "Fiona don't have any porcelain or flush toilets, just an outhouse in the back."

"I grew up on a farm," Mariel said. "Outhouses are not unknown to me."

"One more thing."

Mariel was just short of squeezing her thighs together.

Phoebe sighed impatiently.

"Randy's letters say you're a schoolmarm. Jerry Hill passed two years back, so Goss Valley has need of a teacher come fall."

"Have you no men or unmarried ladies?"

"None that want the job. The council can pay twenty dollars a month. Interested?"

"I will be in five minutes," Mariel said. She handed Bruno's leash to Randall.

Phoebe led her down a hallway and out the back door, then pushed open the privy door for her. "You must be famished. Would you like tea and biscuits?"

"Not tonight, thank you."

When Phoebe left, Mariel went in and closed the door. The outhouse was a two-holer with a gas lamp hanging from the rafter. The lamp provided light, while the kerosene fumes masked the vapors of the outhouse.

There was an open packet of Gayetty's Medicated Paper on the bench. Having lived for ten years in Chicago, she was familiar with the product. Each sheet was watermarked with Gayetty's name, which seemed a bit silly, considering the paper's purpose. She sat down and examined one of the sheets. It was softer than a corncob or catalog page, but the method of manufacture sometimes failed to remove all the splinters, a hazard which sometimes proved awkward.

CHAPTER THREE
THE DAGUERROTYPE
Monday, August 2, 1886

Thunderstorms overspread Goss Valley in the morning. The rain wasn't heavy nor the thunder particularly rambunctious. It was a welcome relief from the heat.

Mariel stood on the porch beneath the overhang of their new home while she awaited delivery of their possessions from Chicago. She'd been told to expect the wagons by midday, but in her excitement to move in she'd checked out of the hotel early. Just yesterday the builders had finished the house, complete with a shed, barn, and smokehouse in back. She loved the scent of freshly cut oak emanating from inside. Their plot was large and its land rich. In the spring she'd plant flower and vegetable gardens, a little Eden on the prairie.

Randall left her alone with permission to decorate the house however she saw fit, which she would have done anyway. He'd gone with Mike to call on the settlement's namesake and mayor, Herb Goss, who also served as postmaster and publisher of a fledgling newspaper. Goss Valley had been the seat of Buffalo County for the first year after the town's founding in 1883. In November 1884 Buffalo Prairie wrested the county seat away by convincing Governor Pierce that its more modern mill made it more worthy. Certain that skullduggery was afoot, Mike and Mayor Goss were determined to get the honor back.

Mariel didn't know, nor particularly care, why it mattered.

It was nearly one when three wagons turned onto their property. A handsome youth was in the lead. He reined in the horses next to her door.

"You Mrs. Erickson?" he said, brushing blonde hair from his eyes. Even seated he appeared to be tall, with dumpling cheeks and a hairless chin. Although his face would probably always look twelve, his deep voice indicated he was on the other side of puberty. Clearly he had not been in Dakota long, as his accent was strongly Southern.

"I am."

"Pleased to meet you, ma'am. You're gonna be the new schoolmarm?"

Mariel smiled. "I've heard that rumor. Will I see you there?"

"Hell or high water. Won't be till after the harvest, though."

"What's your name?"

"Robert Baughman. Bobby."

"I don't allow such language in my classroom, Master Baughman."

The boy grinned impishly. "Ma don't let me cuss, neither, so I gotta get it in when I can." The other two wagons clattered to a stop beside his. "Where do y'all want your stuff?"

"Y'all" grated on her ears, but she loved the lyrical intonation of his words. "Inside the house would be preferable."

She learned the other two drivers were Ollie Nielson and Danny Koch, both in their teens. Three older men had accompanied them to assist with the heavy lifting. They didn't introduce themselves.

The larger items came in wooden crates, while the dishes, silver, books, lamps, and personal mementos filled several trunks and chests. Bobby and his companions grunted and cursed as they lugged in the crates marked with an X. They left the ones stenciled with *United States Army Signal Corps* in the wagons for later delivery to the post office. Randall had leased a room there for his business. The Army required him to record weather information three times a day, yet even after twenty-nine years of marriage, she still had no idea of the purposes of his equipment, or what the readings meant. But he knew what he was doing, so she didn't need to.

She watched the laborers dismantle the crates with hammer claws. Afterward they collected the bent nails and pounded them straight. Mariel admired their frugality. Nails could be reused.

"Where do you want everything?" said one of the workers, a burly fellow with a beard down to his chest.

She wasn't accustomed to directing grown men, but having been a teacher most of her life, she knew how to give assignments. Good thing, too, for experience had taught her that most males had no inherent sense of décor. Without feminine guidance, they were oblivious to clutter and filth.

First order of business was her rocking chair, which she had them place in the corner of the parlor. From there she sat to direct traffic.

Perhaps excitement made her indecisive, for she changed her mind frequently in the course of the afternoon. The men spent hours moving the furniture from one location to another.

The piano, an upright weighing hundreds of pounds, was most vexing. She thought it looked best against the north wall, but come winter the cold winds would throw it out of tune. Heat had the same effect on strings, so it couldn't be placed near the stove or fireplace, either. In the middle of the parlor it would be an obstacle.

Each time she requested a new arrangement, she made the men lift the piano to avoid scratching the floor, which elicited from them torrents of foul protests. Everyone except Bobby was on the verge of mutiny, forcing her to settle on the bedroom. Of course it couldn't stay there, as that was hardly a proper venue to entertain guests.

"I got hornswoggled into moving the church's new piano," one of the men said. He was a small fellow with sinewy muscles that glistened with rain and sweat. "My mates dropped the goddamn thing on my foot. Broke three toes. To this day they ache every time I hear the sound of a piano."

"Clearly you don't play, then," Mariel said. "Do any of you?"

"Pianos are for girls," Bobby said.

"I shall convey that information to my husband, who plays and is, in fact, not a girl."

The rest of the afternoon went smoothly, but by six o'clock the men had had enough and left to eat supper with their families. They still had to deliver Randall's crates to the post office tonight. At least the rain had passed.

Without being asked, Bobby remained behind to unpack the trunks and chests with her. The first chest was full of toys and knick-knacks Ellie and Alex had cherished when they were younger. Although more than once Randall had urged her to throw the clutter away, Mariel was convinced that they'd want them again someday, if only for their own children. "Just push that one under the bed," she said.

The second chest was almost too heavy for Bobby to lift. "What y'all got in here, gold bars?" "Much better than that, Master Baughman: books."

Some were Randall's newer cloth-bound volumes about weather theories and military matters, some her *MacGuffey Readers*, and the rest old literature bound in leather or vellum. Bobby opened one and looked at the title page. He wrinkled his nose at its mustiness, but there were few things Mariel enjoyed more than the smell of old books.

"Poems," he said. "Keats? Who's he?"

"My father's favorite," she said.

"I like Twain myself. 'Specially that jumping frog."

Mariel didn't know whether or not she approved of Mr. Clemens. He had a fine mind and lively wit, but too often chose vulgarity when elegance would serve him better. If Mariel ever got the chance to publish, she would avoid the crude vernacular. "Good for you for reading," she said. "Leave those in there until my husband can build shelves."

"What about this one?" he said of the third chest, which contained photographs set in wooden frames and covered by glass. "Who're these people?"

Mariel wasn't entirely comfortable with him looking at her more personal affects, but she didn't wish to appear ungrateful for his help. In any case, nothing would harden a boy's resolve to snoop than being told not to.

She took the photograph from him and smiled. Of course she remembered this one: she and Randall in 1867, on the occasion of their tenth wedding anniversary. Infant Alex was bundled in her arms, while six-year-old Ellie stood between them. Ellie had refused to stop squirming, which blurred her image. Randall was resplendent in his Union uniform, his fine black mustaches curling upward over rugged cheekbones. And there was her younger self, bedecked in a frilly dress with full petticoats underneath. Wavy hair cascaded freely over her shoulders, reaching nearly to her waist. How she missed those lovely tresses, and the insouciance of youth that could so blithely defy the convention of hairpins and buns. "Oh, my," she said, handing the photograph back to him. "Who *is* that young woman?"

Bobby studied the photograph, then Mariel. "Why, it's you, Mrs. Erickson. Y'all was right pretty."

"Thank you, Bobby. That's very nice of you to say. We do need to break you of saying *y'all*, however, when addressing one person."

"Yes, ma'am.

"Just unpack the chest for now. I'll decide where to hang them later."

She started to unlatch one of the trunks when a glimpse of the next photograph in Bobby's chest startled her. She must have gasped, because the boy said, "You all right, Mrs. Erickson?"

"Give that one to me, please."

"It's real old."

Indeed it was: a daguerreotype made over forty years ago. Marred by white streaks and splotches, the subject was a beautiful young woman whose eyes never quite met hers, as if she'd been uncertain where the camera's shutter was. It was her mother Claire, who had died before Mariel's eighth birthday. Her father had had the photograph mounted in a frame and protected behind glass. He'd displayed it above the highboy until his own death. After his passing she put it away because she could no longer bear to look at it. She'd been told many stories about her mother, stories of goodness and grace, but had rarely been able to transform those anecdotes into memories of her own. Time was cruel. It stole the living woman and left only a grainy picture in shades of gray, a face peering out, but not at her, never at her. Truth was, Mariel could remember very little about her mother anymore. A warm smile here, a bedtime kiss there, but nothing coherent, nothing substantial, nothing real.

"Maybe I should go," Bobby said.

"Thank you for your kindness."

When he was gone, she put the daguerreotype in the bottom drawer of the highboy. She should stop hiding from those eyes, and someday she would display it again. But not tonight. Her mother had been dead since 1846, a wound that, tonight, was as fresh to Mariel as it had been then.

An hour later, Randall arrived with their trunks and suitcase from the hotel and two sacks of food from the general store. He saw her red eyes but knew enough to let her be until she was ready to tell him.

CHAPTER FOUR
"GATHER UP THE FRAGMENTS"
Tuesday, August 3, 1886

Randall's equipment was ed to the post office last night. He was an early riser, but the postmaster, Mayor Goss, was not. Therefore, they couldn't get in to set up his weather office until after ten a.m. At eight Mariel was frying eggs in her new kitchen when she heard Randall playing the piano in the bedroom and singing "Fountain in the Park."

"'While strolling through the park one day, in the merry, merry month of May....'"

He was a gifted pianist, less so a vocalist. But the song was pleasant, and his voice rose when the tune was supposed to rise and fell when it was supposed to fall. All in all, their life in Dakota was starting much as she envisioned it might. They had a spacious home, at least by comparison to the one in Chicago, a breeze was coming through the window, and her husband was singing.

Randall liked his yolk runny, so Mariel drizzled grease over the eggs until a thin layer of white formed on top. Bruno was stationed at her feet, looking up expectantly. He liked eggs, too. In fact, the next time she fed him something he didn't like would be the first.

As she dropped a piece of bread for him, someone knocked on the door. Bruno barked, but made no move toward the sound. Being a watchdog was fine work unless food was involved. Mariel scooped the eggs onto a plate, put bread in the skillet to make toast, and went to see who was calling at this early hour.

Two women waited on the porch, the older one bearing a pie, the younger one a cantaloupe.

"Mrs. Erickson?" said the pie lady. "I'm Pauline Moehler. Folks call me Peg. We'd like to welcome you and your husband to Goss Valley." Done up in a dress and hat twenty years out of fashion, Peg appeared to be nearing eighty. The other woman's attire was not so anachronistic. She was much younger, perhaps thirty.

"I'm Louisa Hartwig. You've already met Clyde."

"Yes, of course. Thank you. Won't you come in? I was just making breakfast for my husband."

At the sound of voices, the singing and piano playing stopped. "Who's there?" Randall called.

Bruno growled half-heartedly, still torn between ferocity and hunger. The food the ladies brought looked mighty tasty to him.

"We have visitors."

"Let me get dressed."

"Don't bother on our account," Peg said. "We came to speak with your wife."

Mariel put the pie and melon on the table.

"Will you have a seat?" she said. "I'll just be a moment."

She flipped over the bread slices, let them soak up the heat and grease for a few seconds, then plucked them undercooked from the skillet and placed them next to the eggs. Randall hadn't bought butter last night, and she hadn't thought to churn any this morning. "Will you excuse me?"

She took the plate into the bedroom. When she returned, Peg and Louisa were sitting at the kitchen table.

"We're the welcoming committee," Peg said. "Have you found Goss Valley to your liking?"

"This is beautiful country. Randall and I will love it here." To Louisa she said, "I believe I heard you have two children?"

Louisa blushed. "Has Clyde been boasting again? Yes, a boy and a girl. Wayne is eight, Jeannette three." She wore a locket around her neck, which she opened to reveal a small photograph of her offspring.

"Lovely," Mariel said.

"Have you any?"

"Also a boy and a girl, both grown. Ellie recently married, and Alex is at West Point."

"And who is this fellow?" Peg said, nodding toward Bruno. Mariel could tell by the woman's expression that she, too, found his appearance alarming, but was too polite to mention it. "I don't think I know this breed."

"His name is Bruno. I don't think he has a breed. He does have a fine temperament, though."

"I see," Peg said.

As they made small talk about Goss Valley and its people, Mariel suspected they had another reason for calling on her. Eventually they came to it.

"Many of the prosperous ladies in town belong to a sewing circle," Peg said.

"We're a local branch of the Fragment Society," Louisa added. "Clyde said you expressed an interest...?"

Had she? "I'm not familiar with the Fragment Society," Mariel said.

"'Gather up the fragments, that nothing be lost.'"

Mariel knew her Bible—Jesus to his disciples when feeding bread and fish to the multitudes—but she didn't understand what that had to do with a sewing circle.

"Our mission is to clothe the less fortunate in Goss Valley,"

Louisa said.

"We even mean to help the Indians on the reservation," Peg said.

"What's it like there?"

"Well, of course, our branch has only recently been formed, so we haven't actually gone there yet. Our efforts so far have concentrated on the poor immigrants. They came to America with more ambition than skill. While they struggle to find their way, their children go naked in the street."

Mariel recognized the hyperbole in Peg's words. She'd seen it before in the writings of zealots of every cause. "Would you like a contribution?"

"We would like you to *sew*, Mrs. Erickson. Come together with us in fellowship and charity, and bring relief to those who have nothing."

"Amen," Louisa said, her voice a-quiver with fervor.

Mariel was a fair seamstress, and she didn't mind sewing when need arose. But if she were being honest, she simply could not imagine herself cooped up with a group of women, tapping the foot-pedal of a sewing machine and becoming mired in female gossip. She was not unsympathetic to the plight of the immigrants or, especially, of the Indians. Yet if it was as dire as all that, she would rather do her part by writing newspaper articles. It was not her sewing that would clothe the naked, but her words.

Randall momentarily rescued her from an answer when he emerged from the bedroom, fully dressed for the day and carrying the empty plate. "Breakfast was exemplary."

Mariel nodded demurely to acknowledge the compliment. She introduced him to Peg and Louisa, whom he had apparently already met.

"Ladies," he said, tipping an imaginary hat. "I see you brought gifts. That was kind of you."

"We couldn't help but overhear your playing," Peg said. "I must say, Lieutenant, you are the finest pianist we have ever heard."

Randall smiled and bowed. "Then, my dears, you have my deepest condolences."

"May we speak of this matter another time?" Mariel said to the women. "Randall and I, along with young Robert Baughman, are required shortly at the post office to install Randall's weather equipment and ready his office."

"You will consider our proposal?" Peg said. She and Louisa rose from their chairs.

"Of course," Mariel replied, taking their hands in hers and squeezing gently as she escorted them to the door. "You're to be commended for your work."

****

In the early years of Goss Valley, Mayor Goss explained, the post office provided a number of services for the town, also housing the general store, telegraph, and tavern. The printing press for the *Goss Valley Sentinel* occupied the cellar, with somewhat more intimate business transacted in one of the rooms upstairs. As the town expanded, the owners of the general store and tavern departed for their own buildings. Every six months or so the town marshal, John Woolridge, or his deputy Duane Dalton rousted a prostitute named Beryl from her second floor den, but she always paid her fines and came back.

This time it was Randall who displaced Beryl, commandeering the larger of the two rooms as his weather office and relegating her to the smaller one. Beryl made a point to return when she saw the mayor approaching. She expressed her displeasure with epithets Mariel had seldom heard from members of her own sex. Goss was unmoved. Money talked, he explained, nodding at Randall. A woman in her line of business should understand that.

Interested in Randall's work, Bobby had volunteered to help set up his weather equipment on the roof. While he and Randall climbed the fire escape outside, Mariel and Goss were dispatched to arrange his office. Manual labor would seem to be beneath a mayor's dignity, but he didn't complain.

On their way upstairs, Mariel paused to read the bulletin board. It had two wanted posters for minor criminals and a broadside advertising the impending visit of a Professor Josiah Kunkel, who promised to perform a scientific experiment behind the post office on August 14.

"What's this all about?" Mariel said.

Goss shrugged. He was a small, clean-shaven man with spectacles and a scent of whiskey on his breath. He appeared to be a few years younger than she. "No idea. A fellow paid me to post it."

They turned left at the top of the stairs, went to the end of the hall, and stopped at the door on the right. Mariel wanted to ask him about writing for the newspaper, but wasn't sure how to broach the subject.

"There's a cotillion party every Saturday at the Masonic Hall," Goss said as he unlocked the door and pushed it open for her. "Sadie and I like to go when we can. You haven't lived till you've heard old Hank Moehler play the fiddle. You and the mister coming?"

She didn't answer, as her eyes were fixed upon the disaster the draymen had left in their wake. Fortunately, she'd been present yesterday to insure they were more careful with her furniture.

"Mrs. Erickson?"

"What?—oh. Yes, I suspect. I haven't danced in years. Good

Lord. Did a twister come through?"

"Not since eighty-three," Goss said. His face was stricken with terror at the magnitude of the task facing them. "Where do we start?"

Randall's work required a draft table, a desk, file drawers, chairs, a stool, a Remington typewriter, and bookshelves to hold his maps and charts. Tools spilled out of their boxes onto the floor: pliers, wire cutters, a vise, wrenches, lightning arresters, rolls of wire, a compass, and electrical connectors. Randall had also brought the telescope Mariel had inherited from her father, although he preferred binoculars. Finally, there was his Beardslee, a portable telegraph unit the Army once provided in case commercial telegraphs were unavailable. Beardslees were obsolete now, though, so Randall kept his as a memento of the Civil War.

Goss whistled as he examined the typewriter on the floor. "I've been looking into buying one of these. I've got a Scholes and Glidden. Heavy as a bale of hay, and half the letters don't work. The Sears catalog has Remingtons, but I haven't gotten around to ordering one yet."

****

Randall and Bobby finished installing the equipment on the roof before Mariel and Goss had made much progress in the room. When they came down they were drenched with perspiration. It was almost noon on the hottest day they'd yet experienced in Dakota. There was neither shade to block the sun nor breeze to mitigate its heat.

"Forgive my blunt observation," Mariel said, "but you gentlemen stink to high heaven."

"Lieutenant Erickson's thermometer says ninety-six," Bobby said, pronouncing it *nahn-duh SEE-yix*. "I never saw one before, but I sure don't need a tube of glass to tell me it's hot. The tar's melting on the roof."

"That's part of the job," Randall said. "Mike plans to help out when he can, but his asthma gets the better of him sometimes. I'll need another assistant."

Bobby grinned, exposing crooked teeth shading toward green. "Me?"

"You did well up there. I need a hard worker with a sharp mind. Help these layabouts with the furniture and we'll discuss it."

With four people and only one room to arrange, the work went quickly. Through it all, Bobby peppered Randall with questions. Randall had never been a teacher, nor had he ever wanted to be, but he clearly enjoyed sharing his knowledge.

"Will I get paid?" Bobby said.

"I've always had staff below me, but the Army has no plans to send anyone else here, so I'll have to pay you myself. How does two dollars a week sound?"

"*Two dollars*? I could afford to find me a girl!"

Mariel found that charming. "Have you selected your sweetheart?"

"Got a couple in mind." He and Goss moved the drawing table next to the south window, while Mariel and Randall slid the desk to the east window.

"I believe the allowable number is one, Master Baughman," she said.

"Trust me," Randall laughed, "one is more than enough."

Mariel playfully punched his shoulder.

It was normal for a young man to be drawn to the female sex, but today Bobby seemed more interested in this new weather opportunity. "Tell me again, what's the thing with the cups for?"

"Anemometer."

"An-uh-MAH-muh-der?"

Randall nodded. "It measures wind speed and direction."

"I do that by licking my finger. And the ... buh-RAH-muh-der, is it?"

"That measures air pressure. The weight of the air."

"Air don't weigh nothing."

"Of course it does. If the pressure is high—if the air is heavy—the weather is more likely to be fair. If it's low, a storm may be coming."

Bobby looked skeptical. "So if I get a big bucket of air, it'll weigh more than a little bucket?"

Randall shook his head. Mariel had seen this gesture often enough. He wasn't indicating a negative. He was trying to remain patient. "Technically," he said. "Perhaps I used the wrong analogy. The air *pressure* will be the same in both, but.... Never mind. You'll learn as you go."

Goss lifted the typewriter and raised an eyebrow to Randall, who nodded toward the desk. After he set it there, he tapped a few keys. He seemed impressed by the effortless motion of the tiny arms as they struck the roller. "Beautiful," he said.

"That don't make any sense," Bobby said, ignoring Goss. "Even if some air is heavier than other air, how in hell—sorry, Mrs. Erickson—but how in hell can someone use that to figure out a storm is coming?"

"I've got maps and weather charts. I'll take the readings, do some calculations, and compare them to the previous readings. Then I telegraph the results to St. Paul, who telegraphs them to Washington. The experts gather reports from all over the country, and from there issue their indications."

"Indications of what?"

"An indication is their prediction of what the weather is going to be like in the next day or two for a given place."

Mariel could see that Bobby was still having difficulty

grasping the concept. Yet she also recognized the unmistakable spark of curiosity.

"So you can tell us today if a cyclone's coming tomorrow?"

"Not that specifically, no. But I should be able to predict rain."

"Farmers'll like that. How often do y'all have to go up to the roof?"

"*You*," Mariel corrected.

"Washington only requires one a day from eastern Dakota, but I'll do them as I did in Chicago: Six a.m., two p.m., and midnight."

"Y'all won't get much sleep in this job."

"*We* won't," Randall said.

Having lived on a farm, Mariel was accustomed to physical labor, and she didn't mind perspiring when she did it, but when the work was done, she wanted to be clean *now*. She hated the discomfort of sticky clothes and the grime that accumulated in the folds of her skin.

They were two more hours getting the office in order, after which she and Goss were nearly as odiferous as her husband and Bobby. Randall sent the boy away with a shiny new quarter in his pocket, then invited Goss across the street to Duncan's Tavern. Mariel was not included in the invitation, and wouldn't have accepted if she had been. All she could think about was soaking in their big brass bathtub.

She accompanied them out the post office door. Before she turned for home, she risked being considered presumptuous by making a bold request of Mayor Goss. "I have an interest in writing, sir. I'm not a woman who fills my idleness with knitting. With school not set to begin until autumn, I find myself at loose ends. As I've always been imaginative, I would enjoy putting my thoughts into words. Do you need help? I would agree to be an unpaid apprentice."

Which also meant, *Please* rescue me from the ladies' sewing circle.

Goss looked to Randall for permission, but he only shrugged. Fanning his face with his hat, Goss said, "I don't know, Mrs. Erickson. I just started the *Sentinel*, so I can't say there'll be all that much news to print. There might not be enough work for one, let alone two."

"Randall said something about petitioning Governor Pierce to return the county seat to Goss Valley. That would be a good story for me to write."

"I was thinking I'd do that one."

They reached the other side of the street and stepped into the shadow of the tavern, where the temperature was almost bearable. "You could scarcely be considered objective, since you seem to be the one leading the charge."

"Everybody here wants it," Goss said.

"I might also prove useful with setting type."

Goss scratched the top of his head. "I suppose you could write a domestic column if I need filler."

That was not what she had in mind, not at all, so she didn't respond. Instead, she said, "If you'll excuse me, you gentlemen need to be alone to hatch your conspiracies, and I need a bath. Good day to you."

She noticed Goss whisper something to Randall, who replied, "All the time."

CHAPTER FIVE
COTILLION
Saturday, August 7, 1886

Hank Moehler sawed on his fiddle as if he were felling an oak. The notes came so furiously that his fellow musicians found it impossible to keep pace. Theo Parley, the tuba player, had but to oompah in time to the music, but even playing one note for Mr. Moehler's eight, he couldn't match the tempo. And poor Lottie Hammon, Mike and Phoebe's adult daughter, was hopelessly lost on the piano. The score called for her to double the tuba in the left hand. Although she held her own for a few measures, when Theo got off rhythm, so did she, resulting in a muddying of the bass line. Her right hand fared no better. Intending to play chords on beats two and four, she came in instead on one-and-a-half and two-and-three-quarters— virtually everything except two and four. Eventually both gave up and yielded the stage to Mr. Moehler.

Few seemed to notice. Mariel only did because Randall was so dismissive of the players' musical abilities. "Fast doesn't mean *good*," he said, "and those other two are useless."

Kerosene lamps hung from the Masonic Hall's rafters, and torches burned in the corners of the lodge, adding both light and heat to the festivities. Cigar smoke clouded the ceiling. The odor of tobacco blended with kerosene and whale oil. Six couples occupied the center of the floor, whirling and changing partners. The ladies laughed and flirted, contriving to flash a lot of leg, as each new fellow took her hand.

Mariel watched Mr. Moehler in awe. Perspiration dripped from his face. His skin emitted such heat that moisture condensed on his spectacles. What hair he had left was soaked and flew about willy-nilly as he played. He kept time with his square-toed farmer's boots as if he were stomping on spiders. And his hands! His fingers were a blur, his bow hand apoplectic in its swiftness. Rosin rose from the strings like smoke, creating a demonic effect. Inconceivable that a man his age could move like that. "He seems rather good to me," she said. "Do you think you could keep up with him?"

"Of course," he said. He was probably right. He'd studied piano before joining the military.

Clyde and Louisa Hartwig were among the dancers, as were Bobby Baughman and one of the objects of his youthful desire, a pretty red-haired girl in the first bloom of womanhood. Mariel didn't know the other couples.

The song went on for another minute. Afterward Mr. Moehler, clearly exhausted, hobbled to a chair to the left of the stage, upon which he collapsed. Panting, he laid the fiddle across his lap and put his head in his hands. His wife Peg brought him a glass of lemonade as everyone showed their appreciation with applause and hurrahs.

Miss Hammon tapped on the keys while waiting for the excitement to abate. Then she launched into the more sedate "Blue Danube Waltz," acquitting herself quite admirably. The slow one-two-three caused an exodus of the younger people, who obviously preferred Mr. Moehler's blood-pumping rhythm. Many of them used it as an excuse to hurry toward the lodge's lavatories.

Bobby and the red-haired girl parted ways, although Mariel didn't see where they went.

The waltz being unsuitable for a tuba—*everything* was unsuitable for tuba, in Mariel's mind—Mr. Parley also took a break. He went as far as the piano, where he sat next to Miss Hammon. She rewarded him with a radiant smile. Phoebe thought that the two were sweet on one another.

Taking advantage of the slower music, several older couples, including Mariel and Randall, moved to the center of the floor. The men bowed to their partners. The women curtsied. Randall lifted Mariel's right hand in his left, put his right hand on her hip, and kept her at arm's length as they danced. Mariel was grateful for steps that required less energy. Her floral dress and embroidered suede boots were the height of fashion, but the dress's bustle didn't lend itself to wild gyrations, and her boots, being new, still chafed.

She couldn't recall the last time she'd waltzed. Could it have been with Randall at the dance in New York where they'd first met? She was a student at Elmira then, he a soldier at Fort Schuyler. No, it was after that, with her father at their wedding in fifty-seven. In any case, she'd forgotten how much she enjoyed it. She and Randall sometimes had their difficulties, but all of that was set aside in the exhilaration of this moment. It called to mind the days before Ellie and Alex, when they were a young couple with a future made exciting by its uncertainty. How she missed those carefree times! They might not have danced much after they'd wed, but how they had *lived*!

A sense of fondness overcame her. She was tempted to kiss Randall's cheek and request a second dance.

But when Miss Hammon finished, the spell was broken, and Randall was just Randall again. He released her, harrumphed into his fist, and said, "That was pleasant."

By now Mr. Moehler was sufficiently recovered to resume his fiddling. As he approached center stage, Mariel excused herself.

"Are you all right?" Randall asked.

"I just need some air," she sighed.

"Shall I escort you?"

She smiled. "That won't be necessary. I won't be long."

She jostled her way through the young people returning to the hall in anticipation of more frenetic action. A light rain was falling, so she remained in the doorway and looked out at the town. It was dark save for lamps in Duncan's Tavern and the windows of the homes whose occupants weren't here tonight. The Baptists shunned dancing, of course, but she'd been told they were not disagreeable about it, displaying their disapproval not by sanctimony but by their absence.

The rain-cooled air smelled clean, untainted. Cattle lowed from a nearby farm, with coyotes yelping and prairie dogs whistling in the prairie beyond.

Hearing movement to her left, she turned to see a young boy sitting on the edge of the steps and smoking a cigarette in the rain. She recognized Wayne Hartwig from Louisa's photograph. He was only eight years old. "You extinguish that cigarette this instant, young man," she said.

"Mind your own business, hag," the boy said.

Mariel's mouth dropped open. She was so taken aback by his insolence that all she could think to say was, "I'll tell your father."

"Who d'you think gave it to me?"

She tried to control her fury. No child had ever, *ever*, addressed her like that. *Hag*? She wanted to slap his smug little face. But now was not the time. She had no authority over him here. What she did have was a long memory, and if Wayne were in her classroom this fall—*please*, God, let him be in her classroom—she would be happy to remind him of this night.

Mariel stepped into the rain to allow its coolness to wash over her, calm her, ease her angry spirit. She wasn't wearing her hat, and the frizzled forelocks she'd fretted so with earlier lost their Josephine curl. She would look a fright when she returned to the dance, but the rain achieved the desired calming effect, and she no longer had the urge to throttle the miscreant.

"We shall meet again, Master Hartwig."

Mr. Moehler's merry fiddling started up again inside, this time with people clapping in time to the music. As she walked back through the door, she thought she heard the boy laugh.

Bobby's red-haired girl met her coming and going, although Bobby wasn't with her. "It's raining," Mariel said. "You'll get your lovely dress wet."

"Aye," the girl said, and went out anyway.

A boy followed close behind. With hair as fiery as hers, he must be her brother.

Mariel found Randall in the crowd. He looked at her strangely at her damp clothing. "It feels good," she said.

She didn't dance again, even when Mr. Moehler and Miss Hammon were able to coordinate their efforts in a tender version of "Oh, Shenandoah." The song always brought her to tears. But she would need to be held close in order to dance to it, and there was no sense in that. It might encourage certain drives that they'd be too tired to act upon when they got home. That activity was a rare, almost nonexistent, event for them anymore. They could never seem to coordinate their passion.

As the evening drew on, people started to clump together in groups to talk, men with men, women with women, and youngsters with youngsters.

Mariel saw Peg Moehler and Louisa Hartwig approaching. Surely they expected an answer about joining their sewing circle, an answer she didn't want to give and they didn't want to hear. Luckily, fate intervened when someone at the door yelled, "Fight!"

The music stopped as many of the men rushed outside.

A Killing Snow

There was a lot of shouting, although Mariel couldn't make out the words. Whatever it was, it was over in a matter of moments. The men returned, a crimson-faced Clyde Hartwig in the lead, towing his son by the arm. Wayne was sobbing and bleeding from the nose.

Mariel smiled. Hag, indeed.

CHAPTER SIX
LUCK OF THE IRISH
Tuesday, August 10, 1886

Mike and Phoebe Hammon had generously offered their own residence for use as the schoolhouse come fall, as they'd done for Mariel's deceased predecessor, Mr. Hill. Mike and Phoebe were occupied at the widow Bohnet's hotel, and Lottie had long since moved to her own lodging above the tavern. Mike had given Mariel a key to inspect the facilities.

The room in which she would be teaching was spacious, with a double window facing south to catch the winter sunlight. A portable chalkboard rested against the east wall.

Her desk was in front of the double window. She perched on the edge and looked over the room, imagining the children who'd be here in just a few months' time. It was the morning of another hot day. No direct light was coming in yet, but she could see herself standing before the class on a January day, backlit by the cold sun, her shadow tumbling into the room and over her students.

Although she'd brought her *MacGuffey Readers*, she probably wouldn't have enough for the entire class. She also lacked other supplies, such as chalk, slates, pencils, scissors, and paper. The general store in Goss Valley didn't stock many of things she'd need, and delivery time from catalogs was undependable. Happily, the city council approved her request for funding, and Mike had arranged for transportation to Kimball on Saturday to buy what she needed.

Mariel walked around the desk and sat down. She was looking through the drawers when she heard a knock on the door. Without waiting for her to answer, a man, a woman, and a multitude of children filed in.

"Begging your pardon, ma'am," the man said, "but Mr. Hammon told us where to find you. You'd be Mrs. Erickson, the teacher?"

"Yes. And you?"

He extended his hand to her. "Liam Blackford at your service, and me wife Bridget, and our wee ones. We've only just arrived in Goss Valley."

Bridget Blackford curtsied. The children, some of whom weren't all that wee, gathered around behind them, jostling and punching each other. Three of them, two girls and a boy, looked nearly identical in height, age, and appearance.

Oh, dear. How did the Blackfords keep track of them all?

"What can I do for you, Mr. Blackford?"

"If you don't mind me asking, have you been a schoolmarm long, mum?"

Mariel loved his Irish brogue. In Ohio, most folks were second- or third-generation Prussians. Many had never quite lost their old-country accents. Dakota, too, had its share of immigrants of the same hardy stock. Living in America had softened their harsh k's to nasal hisses, but they still sounded as if they were speaking with a mouthful of spit. There was just no way to wax romantic in German. *Ich liebe dich*? Honestly.

Mr. Blackford's lilt, though, carried her away to distant places, places of castles and seacoasts she'd seen only in paintings and tintypes.

"Since I was nineteen years old, Mr. Blackford," she said. "I was fresh out of college—which is to say, a *very* long time ago.

Most places have rules stating female teachers must remain unmarried, but I've always managed to find work. This will be my first term in Goss Valley."

"So you've experience with unruly students?"

Mariel didn't like the sound of that. "Certainly. Why do you ask?"

"Perhaps you heard about the to-do at the lodge on Saturday?"

Mariel eyed the tallest of the Blackford children, a lad of perhaps fourteen. "The incident with the Hartwig boy?" she said. "I was there."

"I see," Mr. Blackford said. "It was our Sean what took the first poke."

Sean, the boy in question, lowered his eyes to the ground. "He was saying unkind things to Megan. Called her a post office special and all of us Catlickers."

Wayne was a scoundrel, no doubt about that. It must not have been much of a fight, though. Sean was several years older and many pounds heavier than Wayne.

Mariel scrutinized the daughters. The oldest of them seemed familiar—perhaps the red-haired girl she saw Bobby dancing with? "I apologize for the behavior of some of our residents, Mr. Blackford."

"You've done nothing that needs apologizing for, mum. It's the Hartwig lad for his words and Sean for his deeds. We hoped for a better beginning."

"Most folks here are good people," Mariel said. "I assume you're Catholic, then?"

"Is that a problem?" Mr. Blackford said.

"Not for me. But to my knowledge there isn't a Catholic church within two hundred miles of Goss Valley. Everyone here is Protestant."

"God forgives you," Mrs. Blackford said, patting her hand.

"We're told the Jesuits built a mission north of the Indian reservation," Mr. Blackford said.

"I hadn't heard that."

"Aye, St. Xavier, it's called. But that's not why we've come to you, ma'am. After the donnybrook, the boy's father said he wouldn't have any bog-jumping micks sharing the same school as his children. Is he someone important? Can he keep our young ones out?"

"No, of course not. Everyone is welcome in my classroom."

"You'll prevent the other children from taunting them?"

"As best I may, Mr. Blackford."

Mr. Blackford gazed at his wife, who nodded solemnly. "How many students have you?"

"As I said, this will be my first term in Goss Valley. But there are a number of young families with children here."

He looked around the room. "And you'll have space enough for ours as well?"

Mariel tried to count over and around Mr. and Mrs. Blackford, but the brood kept changing places, so she didn't know if she was counting some of them twice.

"We've a baker's dozen," Mrs. Blackford said.

Thirteen children? Good heavens, Mariel thought. She'd only had two, and that was more than any woman should be required to bear. She did the math in her head. Thirteen times nine: one hundred seventeen months of pregnancy, almost *ten years*.

"I'll make space," Mariel said.

"Children," Mrs. Blackford said, "introduce yourselves to Mrs. Erickson."

Obviously practiced in introductions, the children lined up tallest to shortest and called out their names.

"Sean."

"Megan."

"Mary."

"Ciara."

"Connor."

"Patrick."

"Frances."

"Aiden."

"Brannon."

"Shannon."

"Rhiannon. We're triplets." She stuck out her tongue: *So there.*

"Caitlin."

"Colm."

"Pleased to meet you," Mariel said with a small grin. "Am I to be tested over this?"

"You'll get to know us soon enough," one of the boys said, which sounded rather ominous.

"I daresay." Mariel had already forgotten his name.

"Is tomorrow morning too soon for them to begin?" Mr. Blackford said. He pronounced "tomorrow morning" *tuhmahduh marnin.*

Lovely.

"Didn't Mr. Hammon tell you? School won't be in session until the harvest is done in autumn."

Mrs. Blackford seemed dismayed. "Joseph and Mary, what will we do with the lot of them till then?"

CHAPTER SEVEN
POG NO THAIN
Friday, August 13, 1886

Randall's first weather indications had assured sunshine, but nature wasn't bound by Signal Corps science, for it was raining. Bruno didn't care. He'd been running in the fields most of the morning. Rain, mud, manure, or animal carcasses, he rolled in them all. He usually returned from his outdoor adventures contented, but not today. Instead of jumping against the door and barking to be let in, he whined until Mariel looked out. He was lying on his belly, filthy, wet, and reeking of skunk.

"Oh, for heaven's sake," she said, holding her nose. "You're not coming into this house, sir, until you've had a bath."

She went inside to retrieve his leash and a jar of vinegar. For some reason Bruno didn't mind rain but hated baths. To prevent his escape she hooked one end of the leash to his collar and tied the other to the pump's pipe. She worked the handle several times before hearing the familiar swelling from below. Water spilled from the spout and drenched his unhappy little self, washing away the grime but not the stench.

For that Mariel covered his eyes and poured vinegar over his body from head to foot. Expecting him to try to squirm away, she was dismayed when he squealed and nipped at her. He shook himself vigorously to remove the offending liquid.

"Why are you carrying on so? You'd think I was beating you."

She set the jar down to examine him. His fur was short, which usually made any injury to his skin easy to find. Nothing was apparent until she touched his rear left flank, just below the tail. He yipped, and she brought back a spot of blood on her fingers.

"Oh, dear, did it bite you?"

Vinegar only masked skunk odor temporarily, so she couldn't bring him into the house yet. But she didn't want to leave him outside, either. After puzzling a moment, she took him to the storm cellar, where it was dark but dry. Since they'd only been in Goss Valley a short while, she hadn't had time to stock the cellar with supplies. That left little mischief for Bruno to get into.

She removed his leash and patted him on the head. The poor thing had never been down here before and peered up at her with a doleful look of betrayal in his eyes.

Mariel climbed the steps and latched the door behind her.

****

"We don't need no spud-niggers in Goss Valley," Hartwig said in an exaggerated whisper to Mariel and Randall. They were standing in line behind Liam and Brigitte Blackford at Lem Smith's General Store. Mariel was getting baking powder and peroxide for Bruno's wound. Randall and Hartwig were buying ammunition for an upcoming coyote hunt.

Mr. Blackford turned to them with a cold expression. "We've a house," he said, "and our own land, bought and paid for from your government."

"Like hell," Hartwig said. "You horse knackers are all the same. Thieves, every one of you. You come near the livery, and

I'll shoot you dead on the spot."

"*Pog no thain*," Mr. Blackford muttered.

"Now, dearie, mind your tongue," his wife scolded gently, touching a finger to his lips.

Mr. Smith rang up the Blackfords' order on his brand new National Cash Register, of which he seemed inordinately proud. "That'll be two bucks even."

Mr. Blackford reached into his vest and produced three coins, two dollars and a nickel. "Oh, and buy me friend Mr. Pogue here a cigar."

"My name ain't Pogue," Hartwig said.

"All well and good," Mr. Blackford said, "seeing as how you ain't me friend, neither."

Wind blew a chilly rain against the window. "It's cold," Mariel said. "Bundle up."

"Thank you, mum." Mr. Blackford tipped his hat to her, then loaded their supplies into a burlap sack and left with his wife.

Randall smirked, tried to hide it by coughing into his shirt cuff, failed, and laughed out loud.

"What's funny?" Mariel said.

"After that," Randall said to Hartwig, "you should accept his offer of the cigar."

"Might as well," Mr. Smith said. "Shame to let a nickel go to waste. Some fine cheroots just come in from N'Orleans on Monday."

"Damn Irish," Hartwig said. "All they do is eat, steal, and shit. Pardon my French, Mrs. Erickson. You know they carve up *horses* for food? And you heard what they done to my boy."

"No offense taken," Mariel politely lied. She didn't care for the man or his son. "I find the Blackfords quite pleasant."

Randall clapped Hartwig on the back. "You forgot coalcracker, mackerel-slapper, turf-cutter, thick Mick, Paddy,

Pavee, shillelagh-hugger, tinker, pikey, and about a hundred others."

Hartwig grinned. "Well, I just ain't got to them yet. So what was funny? What'd he say?"

"I served with many a fine Irishman in the War," Randall said. "Mariel, you might wish to cover your ears. *Pog no thain* means 'kiss my ass.'"

"So why'd he call me Mr. Pogue?"

"Pogue is short for *pog no thain*."

Hartwig thought about that for a moment while Mr. Smith punched buttons on the register. The total popped up on a little window on top of the machine.

When Randall handed him the money, Mr. Smith pushed another button, which caused a bell to ding and its cash drawer to pop open. "Love that sound," he said.

"The mick called me *Mr. Kiss-My-Ass*?"

Mariel took her husband's arm and turned to the door. "He surely did, Mr. Pogue," she said, smiling sweetly.

****

That night she lit a lantern and headed toward the door with the baking powder and peroxide.

Randall looked up from the second issue of the *Sentinel*. "Where are you going?"

"To treat Bruno's wound again. Then if his smell is tolerable, I thought I might bring him into the house."

"No."

"We can't leave him in the storm cellar."

"Mariel, he got bit by a skunk. Skunks carry rabies."

"You don't know this one did."

"No, I don't. The chances are small, but until we know for sure, there he stays."

Mariel blew out the lantern's flame. "How long?"

"Ten days, two weeks. If he hasn't shown symptoms by then, he's probably all right. Until then, don't let him bite or scratch you. He can't even lick you."

Mariel returned slumped down at the kitchen table. "What if he does get rabies?"

Randall folded the newspaper in his lap. "I'll have to shoot him."

CHAPTER EIGHT
DO CHILDREN GROW UP IN HEAVEN?
Saturday, August 14, 1886

Mike Hammon, Mayor Goss, and Goss's wife Sadie accompanied Mariel to Kimball in the Abbot Downing mud wagon. Theo Parley, the tuba player, drove the stage. Since the day was fair, he left the canvas roof rolled up to allow the passengers the benefit of sunshine. Yesterday's rain had softened the ground, slowing their progress but keeping dust to a minimum.

The women sat facing the men. As they bounced out of Goss Valley, Mariel closed her eyes, hoping the clatter of the wheels might take her mind off Bruno. The poor fellow must have howled all night from the storm cellar. He was fussing when she fed him before bedtime and again, or still, at breakfast this morning. Tangling with a skunk certainly hadn't diminished his appetite.

Apparently Mrs. Goss was uncomfortable with silence. She proceeded to fill the void with the latest gossip, some of which included her husband.

Immediately upon hearing her say his name, Goss changed the subject. He nudged Mike, who was staring at the horizon. "How'd you like to be in the *Sentinel*?" he said.

"Fiona already paid for her ad," Mike said.

"I'm not talking hotel business. I'm talking stories of human interest."

"What's interesting about me?"

"You're too modest, Mike. You fought in the War—hell, most men over forty fought in the War—but you were in Andersonville. Everyone's heard of the place, but only you know what it was like on the inside." Goss took a notepad and pencil from his vest pocket. He started scribbling in shorthand. Mariel recognized the script but couldn't read it. "I'll pay you a penny a word and print it in the next issue. What do you say?"

Mike removed his Panama hat and scratched his forehead directly under the cowlick. His gray hair and beard glowed white in the sun. "No," he said.

Goss seemed surprised at the refusal. "If you don't tell your story, who will?"

"Who says anybody's got to?"

Mariel touched Mike's hand. "If it isn't too painful for you, I'd be interested as well."

He nodded and put his hat back on. "I got nothing much to say about me," he said, "but I can tell you about a Tennessee boy name of Tom Beecher. Tried to cross the dead-line. I don't want this in the paper, so put your pencil away, Herb."

"People need to read this, Mike," Goss protested. "*History* needs it."

"Don't go noble on me. You don't care about anything but turning a profit. Nothing wrong with that, but not at Tom's expense. You want to hear the story or not?"

With put-upon theatrics, Goss returned the pencil and pad to his pocket. "Go on. Who was Tom Beecher? A rebel?"

"Nope, he fought for the Union. He never told me why."

Mike paused long enough for Goss to become impatient. "And?"

"In November sixty-three our regiment was captured. We got sent to Danville. On good days we ate wharf rat soup, when we could catch them. And the nights were so cold the whole damn Jim River iced up solid. I lost count of how many of us starved or froze.

"So a couple months later, when we heard we were being transferred down to Georgia, you can probably imagine the cheering. They told us the camp was right in the middle of a beautiful forest. Every prisoner got his own wooden shack and three squares a day. It was like a picnic. That's what they said.

"Tom was no particular friend of mine, but we rode down in the same car. We couldn't wait to get into that warm Southern sun. The minute we stepped off the train we saw what a lie we'd swallowed. Christ Almighty, it was like hell rose up to Georgia. Those poor fellas were covered in all manner of filth. They looked like skeletons. Only thing holding them up was guts and stubbornness. Most had scurvy and the bloody flux and God only knows what else. I heard later there were forty-five thousand souls stuffed onto twenty-six acres.

"'Course there weren't any wooden shacks, and not enough tents for one man in ten, either. Prisoners had to dig holes in the ground to get out of the sun. Nothing they could do about rain but take it as it came. The stream they used for drinking, washing, and relieving themselves was nothing but sewage and flies. For food they got a brick of johnnycake a day and salted pork twice a week. Only the South was short of salt, so they tried preserving with ashes, leaving more maggot than meat.

"The camp's commandant was a vile little foreigner called Henry Wirz. You might've heard of him. After the war the government hung him. Although he did right by me after I escaped, no man ever deserved it more.

"Anyhow, first thing off the train the Rebs marched us Illinois boys into the stockade so Wirz could take roll call. He warned us right off about the dead-line."

"Deadline?" Goss said.

"It was just a plank fence, not even waist high, nailed to posts that circled the camp inside the stockade wall. A man could hop over it easy—except if he did, a Reb sentry shot him down from the pigeon roost. Wirz wouldn't let us bury our dead, or even hold services. If someone died, we had to push him under the fence. A wagon came by every morning to collect the bodies, then took them to a field and threw them in a hole like common beasts. We didn't have room for the living, never mind the dead, but goddammit, we weren't beasts. Even enemies deserve Christian respect."

"What about Tom Beecher?" Mariel said. "You said he crossed the dead-line?"

"Come August he just decided to go home, I guess. Sure enough, soon as he stepped over the fence, a guard put a musket ball in him. He fell back onto the prisoner's side.

"I got a knack for setting bones and binding up wounds, so I was our regiment's medic. When I got to Tom I rolled him on his side to have a look, but the ball had gone in the ribs and out the spine, and I knew it was hopeless. All I could do was take him up in my arms.

"He'd shit himself something awful. Wasn't his fault. 'I can't feel nothing down there,' he said. He must've caught a whiff of himself, because then he said, 'That me?'

"'You dumb jackass,' I said, 'why? You know what happens when we cross the line.'

"He told me to look in his trouser pocket. The Rebs stole our money after Chickamauga—Union greenbacks were worth ten times theirs—but they let us keep most our personal things. I pulled out a watch with a tintype of his sweetheart inside."

Mike exhaled slowly and shook his head. "She might've had the blessed soul of an angel, but Lord, that girl was plainer than an old stump.

"'She's pretty,' I said.

"'Nah, she ain't,' Tom said, and he was smiling with a pride something fierce. 'But she is the light of this world.'

"Then ol' Tom, he left this world for the next. I laid him on his back and palmed his eyelids shut. The sun was just rising, but already the Georgia air was hot and wet as a swamp. I squinted up at the pigeon roost. With some passion I proceeded to inform the sentry of my feelings on the matter.

"'Mind your tongue, sir,'" he shot back. "'Want someone to blame, blame him. Anyone else foolish enough to run, I'll give him the same. Now, send him over. Wagon'll be along directly.'"

"The boy talked tough, but his voice was shaky. I figured he must be new to the War. He stood at his station and lifted his eyes to the sky. I don't know, maybe he was praying.

"There was nothing I could do. I rolled Tom under the fence. Seeing his face in the sun, all handsome and dead, I thought about the news his sweetheart was about to get. That poor gal had waited all this time, loving her Tom. Then one day a letter would come. First she'd think it was from him, and when it wasn't, I could almost see her sink down onto her Daddy's porch and look out at the hills and the crops and maybe a little barn, all the things she and Tom might've had one day, and now wouldn't.

"Made me want to jump the fence myself, climb the roost and teach that sentry what killing meant. But there'd be no sense in that. Plenty of Reb gals had sat down on their porches, too."

"What did you do then?" Mariel said.

"I sang a hymn for him. A quarter-hour later the wagon took him away and dropped him in the hole."

No one spoke. Mike's eyes acquired a far-away look, a man revisiting a place he'd had no desire to visit the first time. Beneath his playful façade must reside a soul in pain.

Finally Goss said, "I couldn't print 'shit' in the paper

anyway."

****

Mrs. Goss had made this journey often enough that Mr. Parley knew exactly where to go first. The coach pulled to a stop in front of Hollingsworth's Fine Millinery. Next door was a boutique for ladies' dresses, and beyond that a haberdashery, no doubt the favorite shop of the Fragment Society. Mariel didn't want to buy a hat, dress, or sewing supplies. She needed a stationer's shop, which was next to a saloon across the street.

Mayor Goss got out of the coach with his eyes fixed on the tavern.

"*Herbert*," his wife warned.

"You know where to find me," he said, and scurried away before she could catch his arm.

Mr. Parley stepped down from the driver's seat, stretched, and yawned. "Believe I'll have a bite to eat," he said. "The restaurant serves a mighty tender beefsteak." His voice carried the deep rhythmic tones of the tuba he played.

"I'll go with you," Mike said. "I'd like to discuss your intentions regarding Lottie."

Mr. Parley looked as if he'd lost his appetite. He gazed at Mariel for help, but she could only shrug. She barely knew the man, and couldn't assist him out of his predicament if she'd wanted to. There were rumors of his romantic entanglements with Lottie, but she didn't know the truth of them.

"What do you mean, sir?" Parley said.

"Oh, for instance," Mike said, "when you see her, just exactly how *much* of her do you see?"

My goodness, Mariel thought, her cheeks burning. She did not envy Mr. Parley's next few minutes. This was not a conversation she needed to hear.

"Shall we shop?" Mrs. Goss said, and her face was also flushed.

To Mariel that seemed like a very good idea indeed. "How does one address the mayor's wife?" she said.

"My name is Sadie."

Inside, Mrs. Goss—Sadie—headed straight for the fanchon bonnets. A number of varieties were on display, arrayed in many colors and adorned with silk tulles, *roses de Mai*, and brides of quilled satin ribbons fastened with bows.

They were stunning, but it was a Kate Greenaway bonnet that caught Mariel's attention. She was partial to green, and this one was a lovely shade of silken emerald, with a frilly brim that encircled the face and radiated outward like the rays of the sun. She removed it from the peg with the intention of trying it on, but came to her senses before doing so and put it back.

If she'd worn it, she would have bought it. If she'd bought it, Randall would have scolded her. Between his salary and her upcoming stipend from teaching, they could afford it. But he was jealous of their pennies, and every expense had to be justified. Even the cost of Bruno's care was a difficult pill for him to swallow, but he allowed it because of Ellie's childhood fondness for the dog.

A male clerk approached her—surprising, in a women's hat store—and asked if she needed help. She said no, but indicated her companion might. The clerk turned to Sadie, who at the moment was trying on a female's stovetop hunting hat.

"*Madame* Mayor!" he said.

"Halloo, Silas. How do I look?"

The clerk laughed. "Like Abraham Lincoln."

"That," Sadie sniffed, "is *not* the proper way to woo a lady." She put the hunting hat down and went back to the franchons.

"You broke my heart when you married Herb."

Sadie touched his arm in the familiar way that old friends

had. "*That* is how to flatter a lady. Mariel, this is our dear friend, Silas Hollingsworth."

"Mr. Hollingsworth," she said.

"*Enchanted*," he said, using the French pronunciation, *ah-shahn-TAY*, dropping some consonants and emphasizing the final syllable. He lifted her hand to kiss her fingers.

As Sadie and Mr. Hollingsworth chatted amiably, Mariel felt herself growing restless. She had no pressing reason to hurry home, but no further desire to gawk at hats she couldn't buy, either. Worse, she was convinced Sadie would insist upon visiting the dress store before the stationer.

Perhaps she was just anxious for the school term to start, even though that wouldn't be for at least six weeks. Goss Valley being a new place, and a new beginning, her excitement was more intense than it had been in Chicago. However, there was no reward in impatience. Buying paper, pencils, protractors, and rulers, whether now or in two hours, would not hasten the first day of class. In any case, Sadie was going to finish shopping when she finished shopping. It would be rude of Mariel to interrupt her when she was clearly enjoying this reunion with her friend.

She gazed out the large window toward the tavern. By now Goss had probably ingested enough whiskey to render him immune from his wife's gossip. Down the street, Mike was setting the unfortunate Mr. Parley upon the path of virtue, insofar as Lottie was concerned.

The clerk addressed them both. "Are you ladies in town for long?"

"Need I remind you that we are both married women?" Sadie said, her eyes bright with mischief. "What have you in mind?"

"I imply nothing improper, madam. I simply meant to say that a spiritualist is giving a reading tonight at Mrs.

Bockhoven's house. I thought you might find it amusing. Her name is Professor Miss Dorothy Bedarius."

Mariel shook her head. "I am not *amused* by chicanery, sir."

"Her placard claims she studied with Cora Hatch Richmond herself," Mr. Hollingsworth said.

Everyone had heard of that famous medium, but Mariel remained unimpressed. "I assure you, 'Professor' Miss Bedarius is a charlatan. If the Lord had intended for the living to converse with the dead, He would not have put a wall of separation between us."

"Perhaps He has given some the gift to see beyond the wall," Sadie said. "Have you never wished to speak one more time with your departed loved ones?"

"What I *wish* is of little consequence."

"Are your mother and father still alive?"

Mariel paused as, uninvited, her old companion melancholy insinuated its way into her awareness. "Mother died when I was a child. Father drowned shortly after my wedding."

"If Miss Bedarius could conjure them now, what would you to say to them?"

"Nothing, because *there is no conjuring*! Please don't tempt me with things that cannot be."

Mr. Hollingsworth patted Mariel's shoulder. "I apologize for mentioning it. I didn't mean to cause you distress."

Sadie lowered herself onto a chair. "It's my only hope," she said, her eyes far away, tears gathering. "Do you suppose children grow up in heaven?"

Mariel knelt next to the distraught woman. "I don't understand."

Mr. Hollingsworth cleared his throat. "Sadie and Herb lost their little girl to scarlet fever when she was two," he said.

"Alma," Sadie said, "I should very much like to look upon her now, woman to woman."

Mariel nodded.

Yes.

Now she understood.

****

After the milliner, Sadie offered no resistance as Mariel led her across the street to the stationers shop. The poor soul had even lost her will to purchase a fanchon bonnet. Goss must have seen them approaching, because he stumbled through the door moments later. He was so pickled Mariel was amazed his feet could find the floor.

She quickly gathered her school materials. The council had been generous. If she was conservative in distributing the supplies, she should be able to stretch them over two terms.

Goss burped and produced a wadded stack of bills from his trouser pocket. "Aren't as many as there were before," he said.

"Oh, wherever *could* the money have gone?" Sadie said. She seemed to have recovered her composure now that she was removed from the aura of Alma.

The coach soon pulled up in front of the stationers. Mr. Parley's demeanor suggested he had been properly chastened, while Mike seemed quite pleased with himself. Mariel guessed that the two had reached an accord on the subject of Lottie, one that did not have Mr. Parley's whole-hearted approval.

Mike had found time after Mr. Parley's life lesson to buy the pump, ropes, winches, and wood for the well. There wasn't room for the bricks, mortar, or lead pipe in the coach, so those were being delivered in the morning.

They loaded Mariel's supplies and headed for home. Goss harangued Mike briefly for another war story for the *Sentinel*, but soon lost his train of thought and fell asleep. His snoring was vexing.

Despite his bothersome exhalations, the ride to Goss Valley seemed to pass quickly. It was nearly dark when Mr. Parley dropped off Goss and his wife, after which he proceeded to Mariel's house. He and Mike carried the supplies inside for her.

They found Randall asleep at the table, head resting on his arms.

"I told you he's getting old," Mike said.

"He probably intends to take the weather measurements at midnight," Mariel said.

"I thought he duped Bobby Baughman into doing the late readings. Oh, hell, let him sleep. Damned officers can't do a thing without us enlisted men. I'll walk over to the post office tonight. I'm going to be up anyway. By the by, where does Bobby put the midnight readings? Army wouldn't take kindly to Randy giving him the key to his office."

"I believe he writes them down and slides them under the door."

"Hope he don't get himself worked up over Beryl's business."

Mariel hadn't thought about the prostitute in the room next to Randall's. "Oh, dear. They do keep the doors closed...?"

"The boy's got ears and an imagination. But he's gotta learn sometime, I suppose."

"Everyone has to learn," Theo said.

Mike gave him a most withering glare. "Not with my daughter, they don't. If that's all you got in mind, young fella, you best find yourself two dollars and get your ass on over to the post office."

Mariel wondered how Mike knew the going rate, but wasn't brave enough to ask.

"That's not what I meant," Theo protested.

"Like hell. Just shut up and take me home, and maybe I won't knock your teeth out."

"Yes, Mr. Hammon," Mr. Parley said. The poor man cringed like a dog that had been beaten too often.

Which reminded Mariel of Bruno. After Mike and Mr. Parley had gone, she lit the lantern and went to check on him. She was greeted at the storm cellar door with the stench of skunk, vinegar, and canine effluvium. The odor was so overpowering, she couldn't bear to descend the steps. Instead, she returned to the house, vowing to clean the filth tomorrow.

CHAPTER NINE
A FLASH OF RED HAIR
Sunday, August 15, 1886

The First Congregational Church was more impressive than Randall had led Mariel to believe a prairie chapel would be. She'd expected a rough-hewn affair on a raised platform, leaving room beneath to dig a cellar when money for it became available. This one was fully finished, with a cellar already in place. The pews were comfortable, as pews went, and the windows were adorned with colorful stained glass that came alive in the sunlight. Someone must have orchestrated quite a fund drive to achieve this.

Yet despite the cheery appearance of the church, something was odd about the mood of the congregation. Nobody would look anyone else in the eyes. The Reverend Quincy Dall delivered his sermon in a subdued voice that was at odds with his fiery reputation. His subject this morning was the Ten Commandments, particularly the injunctions against lying and stealing. Perhaps that was a clue to the problem. Mariel had no idea upon whom he was focusing his rhetoric, but she enjoyed his accent, which she judged to be Bostonian.

She nudged Randall, who had assumed his customary position in the pew of dozing on her shoulder. He'd done that in every church they'd ever attended.

"Are we done?" he said. He'd been up early, as always, to

take his weather readings.

"No," Mariel whispered. "I just want to know why everyone is behaving foolishly."

"Because they're fools," Randall said, yawning and scratching beneath his arm.

"Did something happen while I was in Kimball yesterday?"

"The fine citizens of Goss Valley learned a parable about gullibility."

He inclined his head on her shoulder again, where it remained until services were over.

****

Rain had moved in overnight, but had lessened to a drizzle by the time Mariel went to retrieve Bruno. He must have heard her approaching, because he met her at the top of the stairs. Two days in the storm cellar had transformed him, rendering him more timid than he once was. He cowered when she hooked the leash to his collar, much as Mr. Parley had cringed last night with Mike. Poor man.

Bruno still smelled of skunk. She secured him to the well pump, washed him, then gave him another vinegar bath, careful to avoid irritating the bite wounds this time. The punctures had closed up with no swelling or discharges, making her optimistic that he might be spared the ravages of infection. The healing of an outward injury didn't mean the inside was equally cured, but she could hope. At eleven years old, Bruno wasn't long for the world anyway, but rabies was a dreadful disease.

He thrashed about on his back in a puddle left under the spigot, his stubby legs extended straight into the air, celebrating his freedom. He wagged his tail happily, his tongue lolling from the corner of his mouth and dripping saliva. His incarceration was temporarily forgiven.

Mariel prayed, for Bruno's sake and Randall's, that a bullet would not be his fate.

She patted his head. His bath finished, she left him at the pump and returned to the cellar with a lantern, broom, dustpan, and bucket. She held her breath as she descended the steps. The light revealed how much filth one dog could create in two days. It wasn't just his dung, but his urine, which had soaked into the dirt floor of the cellar. Those vapors, combined with the lingering scents of skunk and vinegar, were nauseating.

Age had weakened her tolerance for unpleasantness. As a child she had shoveled cow manure with her father and thought nothing of it. As a young mother she had changed her children's diapers and called herself blessed.

Now a little canine dirt had her gagging.

It simply wouldn't do. She hardened herself to the task, and did it. In Ohio her father used waste from his cattle to fertilize the fields. She and Randall weren't raising crops, but perhaps they could save the waste for fuel in the winter. He'd already started buying dried cow pies for that purpose. Those were stored in the shed behind the house, so that's where Mariel emptied the bucket.

When she returned to Bruno, he had rolled in the puddle sufficiently to wash away the vinegar and cover himself in mud.

She pumped water over him one more time. As soon as she untied his leash from the pipe and started toward the cellar, he dug in his heels and threw a tantrum.

If she dragged him he would choke. "It's for your own good," she said.

Bruno plopped his fat bottom onto the lawn and refused to budge.

She'd either have to carry him and risk ruining her dress, or give in to his demands. He looked up at her plaintively, his pretty brown eyes a startling contrast to his homely visage. Sometimes she was convinced that he could read her emotions.

The clouds were thinning, the rain done for the time being. "How about a walk first?"

He cocked his head at her and perked up his ears.

"Very well, sir, but when we return it's straight to the cellar with you. Are we agreed?"

Bruno drooled.

The streets of Goss Valley wouldn't be busy, as church was over and most businesses were closed. There'd be few people about for Bruno to annoy. Perhaps she could wave at Randall atop the post office. It was almost time for him to take his weather readings.

"Come along, then."

In the short time it took them to traverse the distance from their house to the center of town, the sun broke through, its crepuscular rays creating irregular patterns of light and shade. Recent raindrops on the grassy areas showed colors like dollops of rainbows. Although the temperature was cool, the air was still moist, so if the sun stayed out, things would quickly turn hot and sticky.

Bruno stopped at every stationary object to leave his calling card for the ladies. He sniffed what he didn't christen to see if anyone had left calling cards for him.

Mariel noticed Hartwig by the livery, probably feeding his teams of horses. As she had no desire to speak with him, she passed by without alerting him to her presence.

The post office was two buildings down. She couldn't see Randall from the street, but he must be there. Yet when a figure approached the edge of the roof, it wasn't her husband, but Bobby.

Randall often had the boy take readings for him, but that was usually at midnight, not in the middle of the afternoon.

They were probably up there together, Randall enlightening Bobby with more wisdom about the intricacies of weather indications.

Then she caught a glimpse of a second person, just the head, just for a moment. But that moment was enough. Sunshine revealed a flash of red hair.

Oh, no.

Oh, Bobby. Please don't do anything foolish.

****

"I invited Bobby to supper," Randall said. A lantern burned on the end table as he lay on the sofa reading the latest *Farmers' Almanac.* He chuckled about its "preposterous and unscientific" weather predictions. For as long as he'd worked for the Signal Corps, he'd been vowing to stage an informal contest to determine which indications were more accurate, his or those of the *Almanac.* He never followed through, though, probably because he'd never hear the end of it if he lost.

"Tonight?" Mariel said, uncomfortable about confronting Bobby so soon. Her maternal instincts would have her scold him, but prudence suggested restraint. Randall would not take kindly to the notion of Bobby bringing a girl to the roof while he was on duty. Still, she hadn't actually witnessed him doing anything immoral. He may simply have been showing off the weather equipment to impress her.

"Does he have Bess's permission?" she said.

"I asked her myself. I have business to talk with him."

"I'll get sausage and bacon from the smokehouse."

By the time Bobby arrived an hour later, she had set the table, fried the meat, and added flour and milk to the grease to make gravy.

Randall answered the door and admitted him.

"Howdy, Lieutenant," Bobby said. "It was nice of y'all to invite me."

"Not *y'all*," Mariel called from the kitchen.

"Come in, son," Randall said. "Have a seat."

They sat at the table while Mariel brought in their meal. Since they were going to be discussing weather matters, she excused herself to eat in the kitchen.

"No, stay," Randall said. "Will you say grace?"

All three folded their hands together as Mariel recited the prayer. "'Come Lord Jesus, be our guest. May this food by thee be blessed. May our souls by thee be fed, ever on the living Bread.'"

"Help yourself," Randall said. He forked two sausages and a slice of bread onto his plate, then lathered gravy over everything. "Mariel," he said, "did you know Bobby was kind enough to take readings for me this afternoon while I had a conversation with Mike and Mr. Goss at the hotel?"

Mariel raised an eyebrow at the boy but didn't respond.

"It wasn't no problem," Bobby said. "I like doing it."

"I daresay you do," she said.

"As to that," Randall said, "I heard a rather alarming story today."

Bobby looked at Mariel, then at Randall. "About me?"

"Now, I understand it's in a young man's nature to be curious about the fair sex. It's also in his nature, perhaps, to take action to satisfy that curiosity. But there are consequences."

Bobby gulped hard. His face reddened. His eyes moistened. "You know about Megan."

"I do indeed. Mr. Hartwig noticed that you weren't alone. Needless to say, I wasn't pleased."

"We didn't do anything wrong! I didn't kiss her or nothing."

Randall smiled, almost kindly, Mariel thought. "Bobby, I'm

not concerned about what you did. I *am* concerned where you did it. The post office is federal property, as are my weather instruments. You allowed unauthorized personnel onto government property."

"What about the lady on the second floor?"

"Beryl? I don't control who Mayor Goss chooses to rent to inside the post office. The roof, however, is mine, and I won't have shenanigans on my watch."

Bobby put his elbows on the table and his face in his hands. "Are you discharging me?"

Randall squeezed his shoulder. "No. I was your age once. The Blackford girl is a pretty little thing. I know how a flirtatious wiggle can raise the fever in a young man's blood. But. It will *never* happen again. Is that understood?"

"I promise, Lieutenant."

"Good. Because a second offense doesn't just mean losing your job. It means going to jail."

Bobby's face paled from beet to chalk. He looked as if he might be sick. "I.... *Jail*? I think maybe I should go home now."

"I expect you at the post office at midnight sharp tonight, Master Baughman."

"I will be."

"*Alone*."

"Yes, sir."

After he had left, Mariel marveled at Randall's calmness. She expected fire-and-brimstone histrionics. Instead, he'd been gentle.

He swallowed the last of his milk and set his glass upon the table just a bit too forcefully. "Now," he said, "let's talk about you."

"What about me?"

"Bobby wasn't the only person Clyde saw today. You were walking the dog in town. He said you looked up and saw Bobby and the girl on the roof."

"How could he know what I saw or didn't see?"

"Did you?"

Mariel didn't know which was the wiser course, the sin of a lie or the foolishness of the truth. It didn't matter. Her delayed response was all the answer he needed.

"Is there a reason," he said, his voice rising with anger, "you chose not to tell me?"

Mariel sighed. This was going to be a disagreeable night.

CHAPTER TEN
THE BROKEN CIRCLE
Saturday, September 18, 1886

Randall warned Mariel that winter often came early in Dakota. There was no snow yet, but it was halfway through September, and the temperature couldn't be too many degrees above freezing. Drizzle from low-hanging clouds was blown to pinpricks on a miserable north wind.

As she approached the schoolhouse, Mariel saw someone already inside. It was a Saturday morning, so there shouldn't be any children, and Mike and Phoebe usually slept at the hotel. She'd hoped to spend a few undisturbed hours writing lesson plans for Monday before going to the church this afternoon to visit the Fragment Society.

A delivery wagon loaded with hay was parked outside. Bobby Baughman met her at the door. "Hey, Mrs. E. She's almost ready for y'all—*you*. Just gotta get a wrench from the wagon."

Inside, another man was attaching a vent pipe from the ceiling to a contraption that at first glance resembled an oversized cook stove. His face was covered in so much soot she wouldn't have recognized him but for his long beard and cowlick.

"What on earth?" she said.

Mike gave the vent's connection a shake. It held firm. "Your new heater."

The device didn't look at all like the wood-burning stoves in use in most of Goss Valley. It was as long in back as it was tall in front, with two metal cylinders beneath and a smaller iron box on top bearing the company's name and the words Hay Burner. "It seems awfully large."

"You think it looks big, try lifting it."

Bobby returned with the wrench. "This what you need?"

Mike shook his head. "Nah, I think it's tight enough."

"How does it work?" Mariel said.

"Burns hay, straw, or slough grass," Bobby said. "You pack cats tight into one of these cylinders underneath while the other one burns," Mike explained. "Each one'll last an hour, and if you dip the cats in water first, they'll burn longer. Then the embers keep giving off heat for maybe another couple of hours."

"Cats?" Mariel visualized an inferno of screaming felines.

"Not real cats, Mrs. E."

"Loose hay's a pain in the ass," Mike said. "Gives off too much smoke, and you gotta keep an eye on the stove all the time. So what you do is twist the stalks into little bundles. When they're compressed like that they don't smoke as much. Who knows why some damn fool decided to call them cats?"

"Don't worry, Mrs. E, I'll show you how to make them."

"First we unload the wagon," Mike said, then turned to Mariel. "There's a shed out back. I'll keep it full of hay for you. Believe me, you'll need it. You ain't felt cold till you've been through a Dakota winter. It'll freeze a man's piss between his pecker and the outhouse hole."

"*Michael Hammon*, there is a child present!"

"Oopsy-daisy." Mike flashed an angelic look of innocence, like a seven-year-old miscreant caught in an act of mischief. The soot on his face made him even more adorable.

"I suppose you use that expression to great effect with

Phoebe. I, however, am not your wife."

Bobby grinned. "It's all right, Mrs. E, I'm a boy. I know what a pecker is."

Mariel could only shake her head. She was fond of Mike. After all, he was installing a heater for her. And he'd volunteered his house as the school. And he'd helped Randall secure his position in Goss Valley. With some people one must simply accept the bad with the good. His qualities so far outweighed his shortcomings that surely a place in heaven awaited the irascible Mr. Hammon. The Lord might have to put a muzzle on him, though....

****

"The Fragment Society uses first names, ladies," Peg Moehler announced. The loose skin under her neck jiggled as she spoke, but her perfect white hair had been bobby-pinned into place with such enthusiasm that a cyclone couldn't dislodge it. "We're all friends here. There's no need to stand on formality."

Mariel had finished her lesson plans, run some errands, and eaten lunch before braving the afternoon cold to meet in the cellar of the First Congregational Church. She had only met about half of the women and knew the rest by sight or reputation, but only as Mrs. or Miss Somebody or other. She didn't *like* being informal with strangers. Then again, she didn't want to be here in the first place.

But Randall suggested, sensibly, that with school about to begin, it might be advantageous to meet some of the mothers of the students she'd be teaching. She agreed to come on a trial basis, knowing that to many of these people, "yes" once meant "yes" always. It wasn't so much Mariel's indifference to sewing —and God knew she believed in helping the less fortunate—but

77

she abhorred the gossip that inevitably arose when a group of flibbertigibbets congregated in the same room.

The cellar was almost as large as the nave above. It was only halfway below ground, with two large sets of double windows on every side to admit as much natural light as possible, which, on a day like this, wasn't a lot. Its floor was constructed of wood, varnished to a deep brown. The varnish imbued the place with the smell of newness.

There was space enough for five rows of six sewing machines each, mostly old Singers, but a few of the new Wilson and Wheelers. These, of course, were appropriated by Peg and Louisa, the unquestioned leaders of the society.

Oil lamps rested on every other sewing table to provide additional lighting. A wood burning stove threw heat from the south wall, but it did little to ease the chill on the north side.

Rolls of denim, satin, wool, and cotton fresh from the drapers shop had been arranged on a counter on the east wall next to the sink, alongside piles of rags and damaged clothing.

"Firstly," Peg said, "let us welcome our new members. Please stand as I call your name. Lucy, Hattie, Gertrude, Mariel, Phyllis, Christina, and Susan. Our work here, ladies, is the labor of the Lord, reaching down through us to enrich the lives of others. There is no assigned seating, so go where—"

"And Bridget, mum," Mrs. Blackford said as she and her daughter also rose. "And me eldest girl Megan." Mrs. Blackford was a wisp of a woman. Her auburn hair had been braided, curled, and wound until it was stacked like nest of serpents upon the top of her head, making her seem half a foot taller. Her youthful appearance was belied only by a hint of gray at her temples.

Megan was already taller than her mother. She chose not to bind that stunning hair of hers, letting its glorious red waves billow down her shoulders.

"Beg pardon?" Peg said.

"We're new, too, mum."

Peg smiled, but not warmly. "Yes, of course. And the Blackfords, our Irish friends." She immediately moved on to business. "We have patterns for the more gifted seamstresses who wish to fashion something new."

"For the rest of you," Louisa added, glaring at Bridget, "there's no shame in patching holes in used clothing."

"As we like to say," Peg said, "an old rag is as good as a queen's gown to those who have nothing. Take what you're most comfortable with, but remember that we have to *buy* the new cloth. The old clothing is donated to us. Please make your choice and find a machine, ladies."

Five minutes of jostling and chaos ensued as the women rushed to the table to claim the best bits. They scrambled and bickered like a troupe of monkeys at the zoo, fighting over the same peanut. Most of them then hurried toward the back where the stove was, leaving the less assertive Mariel, Bridget, Megan, and Sadie at the front. The north wind slipped under the church door and flowed down the steps, bringing the chill and dampness with it.

"Horrid weather," Mariel said. A bundle of torn shirts, trousers, and stockings were all that remained for them.

"I don't mind the cold, Mrs. Erickson," Bridget said. "Reminds me of home. Doesn't it, me love?"

Doonit, may loov? Mariel never tired of the accent.

Megan nodded shyly, keeping her eyes down.

"I think you're supposed to call me Mariel."

"Aye. Mariel it is, then, mum."

"Me, too?" Megan said.

"Perhaps I should remain Mrs. Erickson to you. It's not proper to address one's future teacher by her given name." Mariel studied the girl, her face in profile. No wonder Bobby had taken a shining to her. She was lovely. She reminded Mariel of her own Ellie, a woman grown and married now, but not all that far removed from Megan's age. She thought, too, of Sadie's lost child Alma, who would never get to be Megan's age.

"Holes at the elbows," Sadie said, holding up a woolen plaid shirt. "That I can mend. Herbert falls down so often, he's constantly ripping his sleeves."

"Oh, dear," Megan said. "Has he injured himself?"

"Heavens no. When he falls, he's too drunk to feel pain."

"I've got trousers," Mariel said. "Would you prefer those instead?"

"Thank you, my friend, but Herbert tears trousers as well. And hats. Shoes. Stockings. Undergarments. If he wears it, he tears it, as I like to say. It's all right. Were I given another life, I could come back as a haberdasher, milliner, draper, or cobbler."

Mariel laughed uncomfortably. She felt friendly toward Sadie, but not necessarily friendship with her. Yet there was no doubt that since the journey to Kimball, the woman had often sought out her company. Talk of the spiritualist seemed to have loosed from her an ancient grief. By confiding it to Mariel, she had created some kind of bond between the two women, a bond Mariel could neither embrace nor break.

She, too, had known grief, as a little girl who'd lost her mother, and as a woman who'd loved her father and grandfather to their graves and beyond.

But she'd never had to bury a child.

Do you suppose children grow up in heaven?

She needed to remember those words when she was tempted to feel sorry for herself.

In moments the cellar was a cacophony of pumping foot pedals, spinning gears, whirring needles, and rustling cloth. The women added their voices to hubbub, chewing the rag with gleeful venom. Mariel found that to be especially appropriate slang for gossip in a sewing circle.

"Do you enjoy needlework?" Mariel said. "I haven't much taste for it myself."

"I've thirteen children and a husband," Bridget said. "What must be done must be done. Curse necessity, or bless it, it's all the same."

Mariel had never heard what Mr. Blackford did to support all those hungry mouths, and propriety prevented her from asking. "One would think you get enough of this at home."

"We have," Megan said, then covered her mouth, as if she'd spoken out of turn.

"Indeed." Bridget lowered her voice. "They don't approve of us. They think us Travellers, but we've settled down now. I was hoping if we could join in their activities, they might like us better...."

"Of course you're travelers," Mariel said. "You came from Ireland."

"Travellers with a capital T, mum. They're like gypsies."

Mariel had always thought of gypsies as darker skinned people from central Europe. "Well, I like you anyway," she said.

"*She* doesn't." Bridget nodded toward Louisa. "And I've a feeling that whoever she doesn't like, nobody likes."

"She's not that influential, Bridget," Mariel said. "Her husband is just a drayman."

"I hear Clyde's got more money than he lets on," Sadie said. "He saved money from selling wheat seed and invested in the Chicago grain markets."

"Money doesn't make a man important."

"'Tis the only thing that does," Bridget said. "Sean should not have hit the Hartwig lad."

"He probably deserved it," Mariel said, recalling her own encounter with the hooligan.

"He made unkind remarks to me," Megan said. "Sean only asked that he take them back."

Sadie leaned over to Bridget. "The fight is just an excuse. Clyde's always despised the Irish. He considers you worse than Negroes and Chinese."

"We've done him no harm," Bridget said. "Why does he hate us so?"

Sadie shook her head. "Because he's Clyde Hartwig."

"Has he lived here long?"

"If he'd gotten here any sooner the town might have been called Hartwig Valley."

"I see." Bridget paused. She unwound thread from its spool and wetted the broken end with her lips, then twisted it into a narrow point to fit it more easily through the needle's eye. "Liam signed the papers for a homestead exemption. Am I correct that we must farm the land for five years before it becomes our own?"

"Unless he was in the military," Mariel said. "Then it's three years."

"That's a long while to bear Mr. Hartwig's hate."

"It won't stop then," Sadie said. "He'll never accept you as neighbors."

Mariel poked her finger. "Ouch!"

"Are you hurt, love?" Bridget said.

Mariel sucked blood from the tiny wound. "Just clumsy," she said. "Mr. Hartwig is still a young man. Perhaps age and familiarity will ease his prejudices."

"There's more of us coming," Megan said.

Bridget nodded. "Liam's cousin Carter and his family are set to arrive next spring. His brood's not as large as ours. Liam mailed Carter the application. Soon as he returns it, Liam means to file his claim with Mr. Chamberlain. Mr. Hartwig won't like that."

"You can't do anything about Clyde," Sadie said, "so it's best to simply ignore him."

****

Many of the women seemed determined to make the sewing session an endurance test. Mariel, Sadie, and the Blackfords were not among them. Maybe the husbands of the others didn't need to eat, but Mariel's did. Although it was not yet evening, the clouds had continued to thicken, and little illumination now poured in through the windows. Indeed, it was dark enough outside that the glass became like mirrors, reflecting light from the oil lamps back into the church.

Peg and Louisa huffed when Mariel excused herself, an attitude she found sufficient to justify avoiding the Fragment Society next time.

"The harvest is almost complete," Mariel said to Megan. "I expect to see you in my classroom, Miss Blackford."

"You will, mum. Will Mr. Hartwig's son be there as well?"

"Let me worry about that. I'll not tolerate disrespectful behavior from my students."

The Blackfords turned left as Mariel and Sadie turned right. The clouds had opened up, unleashing a bitter, soul-chilling deluge driven sideways by the wind. Mariel huddled into her coat, but the cold cut through as if she were naked. "Is this what we have to look forward to all winter?"

Sadie laughed, which struck Mariel as rude. "The good news is that in three months this will seem balmy. The bad news is that in three months this will seem balmy."

Mariel lowered her head to keep the rain out of her eyes. She quickened her pace. "Well, isn't that encouraging?"

"At least you're not Randall, atop the post office with his machines."

"He's already taken the afternoon readings, and Bobby Baughman will do it at midnight."

Sadie stopped and put her hand on Mariel's wrist. "Is it true what they say about Bobby and the Blackford girl?"

Mariel pulled away from her. "Sadie, I'm freezing. You shouldn't listen to gossip."

"I don't *participate*, of course, but one can't help overhearing conversations. Is it true?"

"That depends upon what you overheard."

"The girl is beautiful, as surely my Alma would have been. Do you believe any young man could restrain himself with her?"

Mariel didn't answer. Instead, she said, "Is there a dance at the hall tonight?"

"Yes, but Herbert's busy drafting a letter to include with the petition to Governor Pierce. He's pledged to provide a building for the courthouse, and Mr. Chamberlain thirty acres of land."

"Just to get the county seat moved back to Goss Valley? Why is that so important to them?"

"Because Buffalo Prairie has it now."

"And?"

"The scalawags set up the courthouse in a shanty. A *shanty*."

"I still don't understand."

"Forgive my vulgarity, but perhaps it's what Clyde calls a 'pissing contest.'"

Mariel shook her head. If she lived forever, she would never understand men. "Will you attend the dance alone, then? I'm sure there'll be plenty of fellows eager to sign your card."

"Goodness, no! Only a post office special would dare to be seen unescorted. Unless you and Randall will be there, of course. Then I'll go."

"All I want to do is sit in a hot bath for the next week."

Sadie kissed her lightly on the cheek. "Then it's goodnight, my dear."

Home was nearby, but not near enough to prevent every last inch of her bonnet, dress, skin, and hair from receiving a thorough drenching. How bedraggled she must have appeared when she finally arrived at the house.

Randall was nowhere to be seen, but Bruno was seated right inside the door, as if he'd been expecting her. Delivered from his purgatory in the storm cellar two and a half weeks ago, he seemed none the worse for wear, although he wasn't quite as eager to venture onto the prairie anymore.

He looked up at her expectantly.

"No," Mariel said. "Absolutely not. It's pouring. You do *not* need to go outside now."

Bruno cocked his head at her, his tongue dripping drool.

"I hate you," Mariel said, retrieving his leash.

CHAPTER ELEVEN
THE HUNT AND THE HARVEST
Saturday, September 25, 1886

The coyote perched on a small rise, all but its legs exposed in the rifle's sight. It was far enough away not to be frightened off, but close enough to be wary. The creature watched them nervously, ready to bolt at the first sign of danger.

"Aim for the head," Hartwig said. He stood behind Mariel and reached his arms around her, pulling the Winchester tight against her shoulder. His closeness made her skin crawl. She hoped Randall would object to the man's familiarity with her, but he seemed rather amused by the whole business. "I can get a dollar for an undamaged pelt," Hartwig said. "With holes I might get two bits."

The day was comfortably warm—Indian summer, as Mike called it—with a light breeze, ideal for a stroll through the prairie. The flowers were still in bloom, blazing with color and filling the air with their fragrances. It was all quite lovely.

Mariel would rather be anywhere else.

On a challenge from Herb Goss, she'd agreed to accompany Mike, Randall, Hartwig, and Deputy Dalton on a mission to cull the coyote population. She was determined to prove herself fit to be a reporter for the *Sentinel*. Goss wouldn't give her the county seat story, and she didn't want to waste her talents on recipes and sewing tips. "If you don't want to write for ladies,"

Goss had said, "then you'll have to write for men. To do that, go where men go."

One suggestion led to another, and next thing she knew, she was on an expedition of extermination. She planned only to observe in order to write an article. She didn't intend to participate. Yet here she stood with Hartwig's seventeen dollar Winchester in her hands.

Yes, coyotes often attacked calves, piglets, and chickens, threatening people's livelihoods. Normally day hunters, they were adapting to nocturnal raids for their meals, making them harder to see. She understood their proximity to children and horses could also pose a danger, and that shooting them was a preemptive act of self-defense.

But she didn't want to be the one to do it. They looked too much like dogs.

"I'd rather not shoot it at all, Mr. Hartwig."

"Do you want it to eat that ugly hound of yours?"

"Of course not."

"Then aim for the head."

"Suppose the bullet goes astray?" she said.

"Keep shooting till you hit it," Dalton laughed. Mariel had only met the deputy a handful of times, but he seemed a popular fellow. Because his title and both names began with a D, he was known to all as Trippledy. He was a huge man whose stomach storage exceeded his mental capacity.

"Pull the trigger," Randall said. "There are enough coyotes in the world. It won't be missed."

Hartwig rested his chin on her shoulder, his stubbly cheek brushing hers. She could smell his chewing tobacco as his hands engulfed hers, one on the stock, the other on the trigger.

She closed her left eye and looked down the sight with her right. The coyote was in her crosshairs. Its fur was reddish-brown, with flecks of white on the breast and black patches on the haunches. It stood with ears perked and head cocked, sniffing the air. The beast was looking directly at her, its eyes shining like amber in the sun. "My Lord in heaven," she said.

"Let go of her, Clyde," Mike said. "She can do it on her own."

Hartwig released her and backed away.

"You too, Mike?" she said.

"This ain't Chicago, Mariel. Some things you just gotta get used to."

She closed both eyes and held her breath. Her finger twitched as she depressed the smooth metal curve of the trigger. The rifle discharged and kicked simultaneously. An instant later she heard a series of rapid high-pitched yelps. These were immediately followed by the acrid odor of gun smoke. The smoke irritated her eyes, giving her an excuse for her tears. As a child she had helped her father kill chickens for supper, but this was different. They weren't going to eat the coyote. She tried to compose herself, but was overcome with a burst of emotion.

The men chuckled at her reaction. "It's vermin," Randall chided. Mariel opened her eyes and glared at him. She wanted to slap all of them.

The coyote was writhing in the grass. It looked like a dog, and whined like a dog, and suffered like a dog. And she, Mariel Erickson, was the author of its anguish.

"Dammit," Hartwig said, "you gut-shot it. It'll take hours for the thing to die. Come on, put it out of its misery."

"You go," Mariel said. No newspaper story was worth this.

"You shot it," Randall said. "You finish it off. Men's rules."

"Hell, Mrs. Erickson, it's only a coyote," Dalton said. "Someday you'll giggle about this."

"I most certainly will not," she said, suddenly furious. "Well, let's go, then. Come watch the silly woman kill a defenseless animal. Oh, what stories you'll be able to tell!"

The coyote lay thirty yards away. Mariel stormed ahead of the men in the direction of the rise. She heard their snickers, their insufferable condescension, and tightened her grip on the butt of the rifle. How would they like being gut-shot?

The animal writhed on its side in the grass, panting and blinking up at her in terror. Blood matted the fur of its ribcage. Mariel had never knowingly been this close to a coyote. In her scope it appeared big as an alpha wolf, but it was actually quite small and delicate, scarcely larger than a fox.

She knelt beside it, very much wanting to pet it and tell it she was sorry. If she touched it, though, it would surely bite her, and rightfully so.

Then she noticed, partially obscured by the grass, its teats, bursting with milk.

"Oh, no," she said. *You're a mother, too.*

The men came up behind her. "For God's sake, Mariel, get away from it," Randall said.

"You gonna pray for the damn thing, too?" Hartwig said impatiently. "Shoot it. Maybe Reverend Dall will come out later and give it a proper Christian burial."

"Hey, look," Trippledy guffawed, "it's a bitch."

"Good," Hartwig said. "One bullet, and we get her pups, too."

Mariel threw the gun to the ground and fled toward town, covering her ears.

She heard the shot anyway. She knew it was the first of what would be many more, for they hadn't come to shoot just one coyote.

****

The music was performed with such exuberance that it was audible far beyond the walls of the Masonic Hall. This week's dance was an extravagant affair to celebrate the harvest. Musicians from Kimball had been hired to play along with Hank, Lottie, and Theo. A guitarist with a Spanish name received top billing. His entourage included three trumpeters and a man with a kettle drum. Also performing was Goss Valley's own barbershop quartet: tenors Lloyd Koch and Charlie Koerperich, baritone Roy Duncan, and bass Cyde Hartwig—who was, by all accounts, a fine singer.

Afterward, just at midnight, a bonfire was planned in back of the hall. With banners afloat and speeches aplenty, Christians would engage in shenanigans rife with pagan undertones. Rumor had it that someone had even brought May poles, apparently oblivious of the calendar. The town's wives had prepared many fine foods and, most importantly, Mr. Duncan was providing the liquor.

This festival was to be the most stupendous event since the last stupendous event, which was the Fourth of July. Reverend Quincy Dall didn't discourage the merrymaking, so long as every participant, regardless of condition, was present in church in the morning to make amends.

To Mariel it sounded like fun, or would have, if she didn't have blood on her hands.

Randall, rarely one to volunteer for social activities, asked her if she wanted to attend the dance. She declined, with no attempt at civility.

It's only a coyote.

Only a coyote. And her babies, which would now starve to death. And however many more of the poor creatures the men had shot after she left.

They'd laughed at her. Her own husband failed to stop Hartwig's audacious fondling, and then behaved callously when she wept for the animal she'd shot. The last thing she wanted to do was dance. At this moment she didn't care if she never touched a man again.

All she desired was to lock herself into a small room and scream.

But she couldn't.

Randall seemed relieved when she refused to participate in the town's revelry. Without them, the Hammons didn't feel like going, either. Instead, Mike and Phoebe invited them to dinner at their home. That was agreeable to Mariel, for it would allow her to inspect her schoolroom one more time before Monday.

Phoebe set a fine table.

"I told Phinny and Ned Bohnet to look after the hotel tonight," Mike said, gnawing around the bones of a fried chicken wing, "but with free food, booze, and girls to be had at the dance, hell if that was gonna happen. Fiona'll have to do it herself, but she'll be all right. What guests she's got are celebrating with the rest of the town."

Randall took a sip of coffee. "I got a letter from Lucas today," he said.

"The Dakota commander? What's he want?"

"Rounding up delegates for this year's encampment."

"Where's it gonna be?" Mike said. Bits of the meat's breading flaked onto his beard.

Phoebe rolled her eyes. "Well, at least the whiskers protect his shirts."

Mike wiped his face with his sleeve.

"Until he does that."

Mariel managed a smile, despite herself.

"Not gonna, was," Randall said. "It was in San Francisco in August. The letter found me too late to change my plans. It would've been good seeing some of the boys again."

"I couldn't've gone anyway. The hotel keeps me penned up most the time."

Randall turned his eyes toward the north window. Mariel

followed his gaze. The window faced away from town, revealing only darkness. The sky was clear, so she knew the stars would be astonishing, but light from the lamps inside obscured her view of them.

"Interesting choice of words," Randall said.

Mike glared hard at him. "Dammit, Randy, you still gnawing that old bone?"

"If I hadn't dispatched you that day...."

"You wanna blame somebody, blame Pap Thomas. He's the one who sent me to you. Or Rosencrans. Dumb bastard had Beardslees on Lookout Mountain. He could've telegraphed. Hell, even flag signals would've worked. Wonder how many couriers died because of him?"

Randall said nothing. Mariel had heard the tale of their meeting many times, and how it had led to Mike's capture by the Rebels.

"Look, First Lieutenant Shit-head," Mike said, "Andersonville's not your fault. I had to get back to Lookout, whether you sent me or not. I'm the imbecile who got lost."

"That was ill-advised of you," Randall admitted. He was actually a second lieutenant now. Like many officers, he'd been promoted for the duration of the War, then returned to his previous rank afterward.

Mike laughed out loud. "Ill-advised, my hairy butt cheeks! It was plain stupid."

"Your backside is smooth as a babe's," Phoebe said with a naughty twinkle in her eye.

Mariel cleared her throat and lowered her eyes. She could have gone through her whole life without having that image in my mind.

Randall grinned. "All right, it was stupid. Whatever happened to that haversack I gave you?"

Mariel hadn't known Mike long, but he certainly had a

knack for putting people at ease. Trouble was, she didn't want to be put at ease tonight. She looked down at her plate and realized she hadn't touched the food Phoebe had gone to the trouble to cook. It looked good. It smelled good. She would be rude to refuse it.

But when she envisioned those coyote pups crying for their mother's milk, she simply couldn't eat. "I'm not feeling well," she said. "May I be excused?"

"What's the matter, dear?" Phoebe said.

"I suppose I'm just nervous about classes," she said, which was true enough. After tonight she had one day, *one day*, to recover from this trauma before school started. She could not face the hooligans or the angels in such an agitated state. "It happens every year. I'll be fine."

"Would you like me to walk you home?" Randall said.

I would like you to leave me alone, she thought. "No, you two tell your lies. Perhaps I just need to look at the stars. They calm my soul."

"May I come with you?" Phoebe said.

"If you'd like."

Music from the dance overpowered the quietude of the night, but nothing could alter the beauty of the stars. Mariel sat in the grass and removed all the pins from her hair, letting her hair fall to her shoulders. She lay on her back to luxuriate in the magnificent canopy above her, to inhale the fragrance of the earth and its growing things. Detroit, where she had lived until she was seven, had stars, but not like this. Chicago had stars, but not like this. Even the Ohio countryside didn't have stars like this. This land, this Dakota, was so endless that nothing could diminish their power.

Phoebe knelt beside her, resting on her knees. "Do you keep a diary? I've found writing helps me when I'm troubled."

"Words are all we have, and yet they're so insufficient."

"Why does your soul need calming?"

A shooting star burst across the Milky Way. "For my ninth birthday," Mariel said, "my father got out his old telescope and showed me heaven. He pointed the lens at a particular part of the sky and told me to look through the eyepiece. What I saw took my breath away. It was a star—I thought it was a star—with beautiful, shimmering rings around it."

"Saturn," Phoebe said softly.

"Saturn," Mariel said. Tears slid down her cheeks and into her hair. "I had never seen anything like it. I had never imagined it. I thought my father had given me a star of my very own."

"Perhaps he did," Phoebe said.

In the Masonic Hall, the barbershop quartet was singing "Harvest Home" a cappella. Without the blaring instruments to accompany them, their voices were soft and ethereal in the still air.

Beneath the tenors and baritone, Mariel could hear the clear, deep tones of Clyde Hartwig.

She squeezed Phoebe's hand.

"Perhaps," she said.

CHAPTER TWELVE
CHOOSE NOT TO CHOOSE
Monday, September 27, 1886

It was six forty-five in the morning. Mariel paced nervously at the front of the classroom in Mike and Phoebe's house. The children wouldn't arrive for another hour. She looked out the window, which faced south into town. The sun hadn't risen yet, but it was close enough to the horizon to lighten the sky. Randall said the weather would be fine and warm, but this early the temperature was still a few degrees below freezing. She could see the breath of horses and riders as they passed by on their way to begin their day.

At last the harvest was over, the children freed from the fields, their minds hers for the molding. Several women in church yesterday had made it a point to greet her and wish her well for the new term, although the ladies of the Fragment Society avoided her.

Nor were the men overly friendly, not out of spite or meanness, but because they were still in a stupor from Saturday night's debaucheries. All they'd wanted to do was go home and observe the rest of the Sabbath with their eyes closed.

Reverend Dall, who did not imbibe in alcohol, had said a prayer for her—for all of them, really, considering the sorry state of his congregation.

Mariel watched her breath condense on the window. The

stars on Saturday night had calmed her, the church service Sunday morning given her hope, and Reverend's Dall's prayer had restored her strength. Yet she was still jittery beyond all reason. She was forty-eight years old, and had been teaching since she was nineteen. That was twenty-nine years of first days, of introductions, of seat assignments, of high-spirited young ones not quite ready to settle down from the long summer.

Looking over the list, she counted thirty-seven of them. In addition to the Blackfords, there were five other sets of siblings, none of whom she knew outside of church: Daniel and Elaine Koch; Sally and Cynthia Grabin; Belinda and Jeffrey Dalton; Norman and Christopher Wulff; and Hannah, Hailey, and Hope Spencer. Good Lord, she hoped those girls weren't triplets, too!

She'd had larger classrooms with more names to memorize. She'd had siblings before, she'd even had twins. It was all part of the job. So why were her nerves so enflamed on this particular day?

She'd not have to wait long for her answer. At seven-ten Clyde Hartwig and his family approached the door on foot. Wayne huddled between his parents. Three-year-old Jeannette squirmed in Louisa's arms. Mariel had been anticipating Wayne's presence with both eagerness and dread.

Mind your own business, hag.

Had he said that to her in class, she likely would have broken his knuckles with her ruler.

The Hartwigs walked in without knocking.

"Figured you'd be here already," Mr. Hartwig said.

"What can I do for you?"

"I'll make it simple: I don't want no Irish spawn in the same classroom with my boy. What do they need schooling for, anyhow?"

"Is that your wish, too, Louisa?" Mariel said. Louisa nodded.

"I see. What about the Fragment Society's mission to help immigrants?"

"We don't mean the Irish."

"Who do you mean?"

"The mick boy beat Wayne up," Hartwig said.

"Wayne called his sister a prostitute."

"Well, ain't she? I mean, she's a Traveller, right? Louisa heard her mother say so. Everyone knows the Irish rent out their daughters soon as they're old enough."

Wayne peered malevolently from behind his parents. Mariel didn't know if that was because he remembered her rebuke at the dance, or was just naturally spiteful. Jeannette stuck her tongue out. "You don't speak for everyone," she said.

"The whole town hates them."

"Regardless, every child is welcome in my classroom."

"I won't have my Wayne sitting shoulder-to-shoulder with spud-niggers."

"Then I shall surely miss the opportunity to teach him."

Hartwig's face reddened ominously. "You'd choose the Irish over a Hartwig?"

"I'd choose not to choose at all. If it were the Blackfords making demands, I'd tell them the same thing. It's your right to keep Wayne home, but if you do, that decision is yours, not mine."

"I'll go to the council and have you discharged."

Mariel shook her head. "This may surprise you, Mr. Hartwig,"—she *so* wanted to call him Mr. Pogue—"but you are not the first parent to threaten me. Good luck in that endeavor. In the meantime, whether or not Wayne stays, you must leave, and I mean now."

"You haven't heard the end of this," Hartwig said.

Of that she was certain.

As they turned to go, Wayne did an excellent imitation of a

coyote's howl. "Aah-oooo!" he called, followed by the approximation of a rifle shot, and the whining of an animal in pain.

"Yeah," little Jeannette giggled, "Aah-oooo!"

So that story was already being spread. The Hartwigs laughed as they exited. Mariel felt as if they'd driven a stake through her heart. She sat at her desk and forced herself to take deep breaths.

Mike Hammon had the gift of finding the broken places and healing them with humor. Hartwig found the weaknesses and ripped them open with cruelty.

CHAPTER THIRTEEN
NO GOOD DEED
Monday, October 11, 1886

Two weeks into the term, the last child Mariel expected to see in her classroom was Wayne Hartwig. She'd just assigned the younger students a spelling lesson in their *MacGuffey Readers* when Wayne appeared in the back of the room.

The boy was unkempt in his bulky coat and muddy boots. With no hat, his hair stuck out like wires in every direction. His cheeks were red, but not, Mariel thought, from the cold. She could make out a handprint on the left side, perhaps the remnant of an argument lost.

Bearing a sour expression not unlike that of his father, Wayne glanced at the red-headed Blackford children. "Mama changed her mind. Said I gotta come to school, even with *them* here."

Cheeks flushing, Megan Blackford looked down at the floor, while Sean cracked his knuckles.

"Sean," Mariel said, "that will be quite enough of that. It deforms your fingers. If that is intended to threaten Wayne, you'll get my ruler and a seat in the dunce chair."

She understood Sean's anger. She herself had very much wanted to throttle young Master Hartwig at the cotillion in August. If he was truly going to be a student in her classroom, she'd have to resist that urge. Retaliation for a personal insult made outside school was not proper for a teacher, satisfying though it may be.

But just let the delinquent try that buffoonery in class....

"Tell him not to say mean things to my sister, then," Sean said.

"Wayne, don't say mean things to Sean's sister. Now, take your coat off and find a desk." When he settled in next to his friend Emil Klindt, she brought him a *Reader*. "We're spelling today. Can you read?"

"'Course I can," Wayne said, "when I want to."

Emil elbowed him playfully and clapped him on the back. Some of the other children snickered. Mariel silenced them with a glare. "Good," she said. "Today you want to."

"You can't tell me what—"

Before Wayne could finish, Bobby Baughman turned his head in the boy's direction and said softly in his Virginia drawl, "Yeah, she can, Hartwig."

Wayne looked away. "I guess I do."

Mariel was impressed, and Megan positively beamed. Even Sean smiled. The Spencer girls, Hannah, Hailey, and Hope— who thankfully were not triplets—giggled. Mariel suspected that at least one of them were also over the moon for Bobby. Maybe all three.

And why not? He was an intelligent and responsible young man to whom the other students looked up. The body beneath that baby face swelled with muscles attained by lifting and moving heavy objects. Maybe a skinny Irish kid didn't frighten Wayne, but Bobby obviously did. Good.

****

After school she walked to the attorney's office to speak with Frank Chamberlain. Seeing Wayne reminded her of Hartwig's threat of dismissal, and she needed Frank's advice about her legal options, should the scoundrel follow through. Wayne's presence in her classroom argued against it, but better safe than sorry.

A sudden gust blew rain into her face. She pulled her bonnet tighter and bowed her head against the wind. As bad luck would have it, when she looked up, Clyde Hartwig was approaching her from the opposite direction, probably on his way to the stable. As Frank's office was on this side of the street, crossing to avoid Hartwig would not only be rude but obvious.

"Howdy," he said tersely, tapping the brim of his Stetson.

"I was pleased to see Wayne in school today."

"You can thank my wife for that. She says a boy's gotta know his letters, and we can't afford to send him to Kimball every day."

Mariel remembered Sadie's comments about his investment in the grain markets, but didn't challenge him. As he was speaking, Liam Blackford turned a corner and walked toward Frank's office. She desperately didn't want the men to see each other, for her sake as well as theirs, so she kept talking to Hartwig until Mr. Blackford had entered the building.

"Wayne's a bright boy, Mr. Hartwig. He reads quite well for his age."

For a moment Hartwig's sour expression softened, but the scowl quickly returned. "You think I don't already know that? Now, I'm freezing my ass off, and them horses ain't gonna feed themselves, so if you'll excuse me."

"Of course," Mariel said, thinking, thank God. Once they parted, she increased her pace toward the attorney's office. She, too, was freezing her.... She, too, was cold.

Inside, Frank and Liam were seated across a desk from one another, engaging in a lively exchange. Frank was wearing his usual work suit, Liam a tweed coat and tam or beret of some kind.

"*Twelve* dollars?" Liam said.

They both stopped talking and rose when Mariel entered the room. "Afternoon, Mariel," Frank said.

"Mum," Liam said, removing his hat.

"Gentlemen," she said. "It's a chilly one out there."

"In here, too," Liam said, nodding toward Frank.

"I'll be with you in a moment," Frank said. The men sat down and resumed their conversation. "Look here, Liam, there's a ten dollar application fee, plus two for the Register of Deeds, which is me. That's twelve. You just did this for yourself this summer."

"I don't recall the two dollars."

"I didn't charge you?" Frank looked perplexed. "I'm becoming forgetful. Hmmph. I don't know, maybe I felt sorry for you, what with all those kids. Your kind doesn't usually have much money, what with all that moving from place to place."

Liam pounded the desk emphatically. "We are no longer *an lucht siúil*! A Blackford hasn't need of your charity."

Frank took a deep breath and ran his hand over his bald head. "Make up your mind, Liam. Either you want to pay my fee, or you don't."

"So I owe you for Carter *and* meself? Twelve for him and two for me, is it?"

"Let me remind you that I don't have to do this at all. By law, your cousin should be here in person to file the claim. That's how it works."

"He can't come till April."

"My office will still be here then."

"He wants assurance no one else claims the plot next to me own."

"Then it's twelve dollars, and you can keep the two I didn't charge you before."

Liam removed a piece of paper from one pocket and a

handful of coins from another. "Here's Carter's application, signed by him, and your money, you damned Shylock, every penny of it."

He slapped a ten dollar bill and four silver dollars onto the desk.

Frank unfolded the application. "Carter Cowan? That's not an Irish name."

"Could it be 'cause he's from Edinburgh?" *Koodet bay kooze hay's froome Ayddenbuhduh?*

"No reason to get testy. All right, this looks to be in order."

"*Pog no thain,*" Liam said.

"Tsk-tsk, Mr. Blackford," Mariel said.

"Aye," he responded. "Forgive me, mum. I forgot you knew that one. You, too, Mr. Chamberlain."

"What did you say?" Frank asked.

"It's an Irish blessing," Liam said.

"Or something like that," Mariel said.

"Good afternoon to you both," Liam said. He stood up, pulled his hat on, and left.

Frank slid the money into the top drawer of his desk. "Damn people," he said. "Now what can I do for you?"

Mariel had prepared a long explanation in her mind, but discarded it in favor of conciseness. "Clyde Hartwig said he was going to the city council to have me dismissed. Can he do that?"

Frank chuckled. "He went to the council, all right. But he did that with your predecessor Jerry Hill, too. And with Marshal Woolridge. And with just about everyone else he feels did him wrong. He was laughed out of the chambers."

"I've nothing to fear, then?"

"Mariel, Clyde Hartwig is full of hot air and shit, pardon my French, and not much else. Woolridge ought to arrest him as a public nuisance. Anyway, you're a friend of the mayor's wife, and Herb's the one who heads the council. I'd say you're safe."

CHAPTER FOURTEEN
FOWL WEATHER
Wednesday, November 3, 1886

Last Friday, while the elementary children practiced their long division and grammar, Mariel assigned the older students to write an essay about their summer. She'd spiced up the exercise by asking them to pretend they were to be newspaper stories for the *Sentinel*. Although Herb Goss had made no assurances, she hoped he might print the best of the lot if he deemed it worthy.

The papers were due on Monday. She'd graded them over the past two nights. Most were dreadful, which wasn't surprising. The children had received no formal education since Mr. Hill passed away two years ago. Few could read or write well. Grammar seemed as incomprehensible to them as Mr. Pasteur's germs and microbes were to her, and less interesting.

However, Bobby Baughman—when he wasn't making puppy-dog eyes at Megan Blackford—was proving to be an avid pupil. He and his mother Bess had moved to Dakota from Virginia, where he'd attended school for several years. The circumstances of his father's absence were a bit murky, but as that was none of her business, she didn't ask. Whatever his personal history, he wrote passably well, and that was all Mariel cared about. He still sometimes mixed up singular verbs with plural nouns, but overall he was much in advance of the other children.

And she'd succeeded in getting him to stop saying y'all.

His essay was a delightful cautionary tale for Goss Valley's residents. Better still, it answered a little mystery that had been nagging her since her trip to Kimball in August. She'd noticed in church the next day that folks had been behaving strangely, and now she knew why.

****

Special to the Goss Valley Sentinel

FOWL WEATHER

By Robert Baughman
Assistant to Lt. Erickson

Truth is, none of us ever seen a live chicken stripped naked by a cyclone, though of course we all know someone who knows someone who says they have. But last August 14 Professor Josiah S. Kunkel of St. Louis University was a-fixing to test the matter. The Civil War cannon had been rolled back of the post office after the Independence Day celebration, and the professor promised to load five ounces of powder and a chicken into it to determine how much wind velocity was required to suck a living bird's feathers right out of its skin.

Now, there's no doubt twisters do funny things. Lt. Erickson and me take weather readings for the U.S. Army Signal Corps so they can issue their weather indications. We could tell plenty of stories. Paper stuck in fence posts, houses blown apart but crystal not busted, cows in trees, frogs raining out of the sky, and the like.

There was no worries about storms on that day, though. The mercury said ninety-four, the anemometer's cups was standing dead still, and the barometer was steady at thirty inches.

Official readings have to wait until straight-up two, so we could only watch Professor Kunkel and his assistant from atop the post office roof where Lt. Erickson's instruments are set up. A crowd gathered round the men. They was right under us, so we could see and hear everything just fine.

The widow Fiona Bohnet donated a fine Brahma hen to the cause. The chicken paced in a cage at Kunkel's feet. Either way you looked at it, the bird's prospects was dim, as it was slated for the axe that night anyway.

"This is science," Kunkel said. I swear, that man talked smoother than snake oil. "It is my contention that the near vacuum in the center of a cyclone will remove a bird's feathers slicker than any chicken-plucker mother's son. Now, it goes without saying that we cannot duplicate conditions at the center of a cyclone, but what we can do, friends, is duplicate the wind velocity. I estimate the cannon will propel this creature at three hundred miles per hour, which is less than the force mathematicians predict in a cyclone. But the pressure inside the barrel will be higher, owing to its smaller size, so the lesser force times the greater pressure should yield a reliable figure."

What me and Lt. Erickson discussed at the time was how in blazes a chicken could ever get to the center of a cyclone? Winds would blow it away before it ever got inside. Seemed to us that all the good professor was going to do was show that high wind's not healthy for fowls.

"If I am correct," Kunkel said, puffing out his chest and hooking his thumbs into his suspenders, "then this bird will be naked as any Sunday entrée—pardon my language, ladies—but still quite alive."

"You're gonna shoot that chicken out of the cannon?" Hank Moehler said.

"I surely am," responded Kunkel with a keen sparkle in his eye. "I expect it to sail over the plains, then glide to earth squawking its indignation in all its bare-skinned glory."

"How's it gonna glide with no feathers?" Mr. Moehler said. Lt. Erickson and me was in agreement that this was a sensible question.

"Who's the scientist here?" the professor countered. "I tell you, the finest brains in this great land have calculated figures down to the tiniest fraction. There can be no doubt of the result."

"What'll this cost us?" Mr. Moehler said. Old man Moehler sure is a bulldog.

"Not a red cent, friend. I intend to publish a groundbreaking study in which you will all be mentioned by name for your contribution to science. My assistant will take your particulars."

"Well, get to it, then."

As his assistant moved through the crowd with pencil and paper, Professor Kunkel ramrodded a powder pouch down the bore of the cannon. The chicken raised a furious ruckus about being stuffed tail-first on top of the powder.

A hush came over the onlookers. "Anyone have a

match?" the professor said, though I know that was just for show, cause I saw him light up a cigar earlier.

Mr. Moehler gave him one. Professor Kunkle said, "Step back now." He struck the match against the sole of his boot and touched the flame to the fuse.

After a few seconds there was the terrific crack of cannon shot, and that Brahma hen, she arced out over the prairie, trailing plumage and smoke like a falling star.

The crowd applauded with great enthusiasm. The feathers fell out, all right. Course, the blast blew the chicken to smithereens. Me and Lt. Erickson came down to collect the body with the others. We was as surprised as anyone when we got back to find the assistant had picked their pockets clean and Professor Kunkel was long gone.

****

Mariel shared the essay with both Randall and Goss after school.

Goss was impressed, and agreed not only to publish it, but to pay Bobby the tidy sum of one silver dollar for the privilege. That was more than he'd done for Mariel—he was still keeping her at arm's length for failing to write the coyote story—but she didn't begrudge Bobby the honor. She was always happy to see her students rewarded for their accomplishments.

Bobby claimed he'd been so enthralled by the spectacle that he didn't notice the thievery as it was occurring, but Randall had, or so he claimed. He chose not to warn the townspeople because anyone gullible enough to be taken in by such an obvious charlatan deserved what they got.

Mariel was skeptical. True, it was in Randall's nature to

derive satisfaction when the foolishness of others was exposed. It was also in his nature to deny that he himself could have been bamboozled by Kunkel's misdirection. Yet, had he been down among the crowd that day, Mariel suspected that he, too, would have found himself short a pocketbook.

CHAPTER FIFTEEN
WINTER CROW
Sunday, December 12, 1886

Randall returned a little before noon from taking the six a.m. readings, charting his data, and telegraphing his reports to St. Paul. The weather had taken a marked turn for the worst, with little snow but the coldest temperatures of the season so far. His face was red and his mustache frozen with condensed breath and drippings from his nose. His spectacles were frosted over. Mariel wondered how he had been able to see to get home. His fingers were so cold he couldn't bend them.

"I've had enough of this nonsense," Randall said. "I'm installing a hay burner for next winter."

The burner Mike had put in for her heated the classroom wonderfully, but for its size it seemed inefficient to her. Filled with hay "cats," each cylinder only burned for an hour before needing to be fed again. That was all right during a school day, but who wanted to get up every two hours at night to stoke the fire? "How about a boiler? A radiator in every room?"

"Too expensive."

Well, a girl can dream, Mariel thought. "What's the temperature?"

"Eleven below at six, maybe five above now."

She removed his glasses and wiped them off with the hem of her dress, then replaced them on his nose. "You're going to lose your fingers if you don't start wearing gloves."

"Can't when I'm taking readings or writing my charts."

"You could wear them on the way home. I added more wood to the stove. Come, warm yourself."

Bruno was curled up at the base of the stove, sleeping and yipping at dog dreams. He didn't wake up even when Mariel nudged him out of the way with her foot. She helped strip off Randall's frock, waistcoat, and hat, then retrieved a blanket to drape over shoulders.

He rubbed his hands over the heat. "Sometimes," he said, "I question my career choice."

"Mike and Phoebe have invited us and the Gosses for Christmas dinner," Mariel said.

"Phoebe's always feeding us. Why don't you suggest they come here? We have plenty."

Mariel pulled her rocking chair next to the stove and scooped Bruno onto her lap. He still didn't awaken. He was old, his bones a little achier every day. He didn't even tug at his leash anymore when he went outside. The cold didn't help. It was probably easier for him to simply sleep through the pain. Mariel sympathized completely. She scratched him between his ears and said, "Mike and Phoebe are welcome here, of course. But Herb drinks too much and Sadie is too ... I don't know, she seems to want me to be her confidant."

"Is that so bad?"

Bruno drooled on Mariel's dress. "I'm sorry for the loss of their little girl, but I don't know what to say to her. We all lose people."

"That's when Herb started hitting the bottle. When Alma died. Liquor's going to kill him someday, if Sadie doesn't do it first."

Mariel rocked slowly, the floorboards creaking with each forward swing. "We were fortunate with Ellie and Alex."

"They could write more often," Randall said. He coughed into his hands, a spell that lasted for several seconds. "I can't afford to get sick."

Their son had always been a good boy, and continued to excel at West Point. He was near the top of his class and had yet to receive his first demerit. Ellie, however, had had her moments during those tempestuous teen years. She'd outgrown her emotional outbursts by the time Everett had come along, or perhaps because he'd come along. "I was rather hoping Ellie would have news for us."

"News?"

Mariel gave him a *don't-be-thick* look.

Randall nodded. "Ah. *That* news. I'm not ready to be a Grandad."

Although he spoke with his usual stoic reserve, his eyes crinkled and his lips bore a shadow of a smile. It was the expression he affected when he didn't want her to think he was being sentimental.

"Oh, I am," Mariel said. "I am."

"Well, grandma, I feel old today."

"You're shivering. Do you want me to fix you a hot lunch? Tea's good for a cold."

"So is sleep. Wake me in an hour."

****

Randall was bundling up for the two o'clock readings when there was a knock on the door. Bruno suddenly jumped to his feet and started barking.

"Who'd be out on a day like this?" Randall said as he put his frock on.

Mariel rose to answer. She expected one of their neighbors —perhaps Sadie under the pretext of borrowing sugar again—so it took her a moment to register who she was actually seeing. When she did, she screamed and stumbled back into the parlor. Bruno skittered behind her dress.

"Who is it?" Randall said, rushing to steady her.

Standing on their porch were three Indians, an old man, a young woman, and her papoose.

"Get away from here," Randall said. His holster and Colt revolver were hanging on the coat rack next to the door. He grabbed the gun, cocked it, and waved it under the old man's nose. "I'm not afraid to use this. I don't care if you have your squaw with you."

The old man didn't flinch. He simply lifted his hand to his mouth: *We're hungry.*

Despite living only a few miles from their reservation, Mariel had never seen an Indian in Dakota before. They didn't look anything like she thought they would. Yes, they had brown skin and prominent cheekbones, but they weren't wearing the traditional garb she'd seen in books. She expected feathered headdresses, war paint, beads, and buckskin trousers, with buffalo hide draped over their shoulders. Instead, the two adults were clad in the same style clothes white men often wore: woolen trousers, black Wellington boots, and tweed overcoats. The old-timer had a black gambler hat with a white band above the bill, the woman an old Civil War slouch hat.

When Mariel recovered from her shock, she said to Randall, "No, let them stay."

"If you give them food, they'll expect it and keep coming back."

"We can't turn them away at Christmas season."

She approached the old man. His face was crisscrossed with wrinkles and mottled with age spots. He must be at least ninety. That saddened her, because at his age he could surely remember a time when he and his people rode free, before white men had herded them onto reservations.

Whatever pride and vigor he may have had in his youth was long gone. Now he was just an old man dressed in the clothing of his enemy, and he was starving.

"Do you speak English?" Mariel said.

"Little," the young woman responded. Her baby had yet to make a sound. Mariel hoped it was only sleeping, and not dead.

No, she wouldn't let herself believe that. "Come in," she said.

"Oh, for Christ's sake, Mariel, you can't invite Indians into our home."

"I already have, dear. Put your gun away."

Mariel spoke with more assurance than she felt. Although these people were obviously harmless, they were still strange to her. And what if Randall was right? What if they told the other Indians at the reservation where her house was? Maybe some of them wouldn't be so harmless.

Bruno continued to bark from behind Mariel's dress.

"Look at them," Randall said. "They're filthy. I had enough of Indians at Fort Defiance."

"Weren't those Navajos? These are Crow." Mariel knew he'd been in New Mexico Territory in the mid-'fifties, but he'd never mentioned anything particularly traumatic about his time there. In fact, he never talked about it at all.

"Same thing," he said. He checked his pocket watch. "Goddammit, Mariel, don't be pig-headed. I have to take my readings. I don't have time to protect you from these vagabonds."

"Go, then. I'll be fine. Shut the dog in the bedroom first. He's being a nuisance."

Randall holstered the Colt and slung the belt over his shoulder, then snatched Bruno by the nape of his neck and tossed him a little too forcefully onto their bed. When he slammed the door Bruno howled. Mariel wondered if he had memories of the storm cellar.

"Your foolishness is infuriating," Randall said. "If I let them come in, will you stop your nonsense about visiting the reservation?"

"No."

As he stepped onto the porch, he jabbed his index finger into the old man's chest. "Never come back here. I mean it. If I see you again, I'll shoot you."

Randall had been a soldier for thirty years, yet Mariel knew that even duty couldn't pull him away if he truly thought these Crow posed a danger to her.

The Indians stepped aside for him, but otherwise didn't react to his leaving. Mariel scrutinized them. They were dirty, they smelled bad, and their lifestyle and beliefs couldn't be more foreign to her if they'd come from the moon. In all honesty, if she were anywhere but in the comfort of her own home, she would not choose to associate with them.

But these people were hungry, and the woman had a baby.

The Crow remained outside until she made the gesture to enter.

"It's all right," she said, leading them into the kitchen. She opened her cupboards to them. The woman looked at her questioningly. Mariel smiled and nodded. "I'll get you something to carry it in."

The woman said something to the man—her grandfather?— in their language. They took jars of cucumbers and sugar beets, a box of flour, another of salt, a few canned apples.

Mariel brought them a burlap sack. She disliked preserving fruits and vegetables, but Mason jars were valuable, so she didn't want to give them away. She transferred the cucumbers and beets into an empty coffee tin, put the jars back in the cupboards, and placed the lid on the coffee box.

"How about meat?" she said. "We have bacon and beef jerky. Milk? Eggs?"

The woman shook her head. "Enough," she said.

"Follow me," Mariel said. She donned her winter coat and took them outside to the smokehouse. When she opened the door, the cold, delectable smell of meat rushed out to greet them. "Take all you want."

The woman's eyes widened in surprise, but she made no move, so Mariel opened the sack and dropped in enough bacon and jerky to feed them for a few days.

She had heard that Indians rarely showed emotion, and these didn't. Yet the old man said something to the woman, who nodded what may have meant *thank you* toward Mariel.

"You're welcome," she said. Yes, one day she would visit the reservation.

They turned and trudged off into the cold. The baby was still silent, silent as coyote pups.

Aah-oooo, she thought.

CHAPTER SIXTEEN
THE THIRD STAGE OF CHRISTMAS
Saturday, December 25, 1886

Mike had given Mariel and Randall a wild turkey for Christmas, but he and Phoebe already had holiday plans with the Kochs and Koerperichs, so they couldn't accept Mariel's dinner invitation. However, Reverend Quincy Dall could, and did. After his heartfelt and moving sermon, everyone in his congregation hoped he might dine with them. Being Mariel and Randall's first Christmas in Goss Valley, he bestowed that honor upon them.

He was famous for his punctuality, and would arrive momentarily. Mariel set the turkey on the table. Cooking large fowl had always been hit-or-miss with her, but this one smelled delicious.

She handed Randall the carving knife. "I hear Reverend Dall prefers the legs, so leave one intact for him." As she went to the kitchen to retrieve the biscuits and butter, she felt a twinge of melancholy, and wasn't sure why. It was the celebration of the Lord's birth, she had a good home and good friends, and she was employed doing what she loved best, teaching. Her life was overflowing with blessings. She should be happy.

But she wasn't.

Randall opened the front door as she returned to the table. Reverend Dall entered and stamped his feet on the welcome mat. Outside snowflakes wafted through a calm night. Their patina would be beautiful in the morning, frosting the world in sparkles of blue and white. The sky was particularly dark, though, as there was no moon behind the clouds, and the coyotes still howled.

"May I take your coat and hat?" Randall said.

"Thank you, Lieutenant," the Reverend said. "It's a lovely evening. But for the overcast, one can imagine the Star of Bethlehem shining brightly."

"Shall I prepare for three more guests, then?" Mariel said.

Reverend Dall smiled. He caught the reference, although she wasn't sure Randall had. "I'm afraid I'm in a bit of a hurry," Dall said. "The Nielsons have asked me to read to little Constance before bedtime. She's particularly fond of Luke Two."

Randall hung his coat and hat on the hat rack and motioned for everyone to have a seat. "Will you lead us in grace?"

"Of course. Let us bow our heads. O Lord, we thank you for the gifts of your bounty which we enjoy at this table. As you have provided for us in the past, so may you sustain us throughout our lives. While we enjoy your gifts, may we never forget the needy and those in want."

"Amen," Randall and Mariel said together. She thought immediately of the Crow Indians who'd come begging. She wondered if Randall did, too.

"Amen," Dall repeated. "What a fine bird you have here."

"You can thank Mike Hammon for that. He shot it yesterday."

"I shall. Ah, I see my reputation precedes me. You left me a leg. Thank you."

Randall used a pronged fork to lift the limb in its entirety onto Reverend Dall's plate. "How long have you been in Goss Valley, Reverend?"

"No need to be formal. Call me Quincy. Do you mind?" Without waiting for an answer, he picked up the meat with his fingers and took a bite. Appalled was too strong a word, but Mariel was certainly taken aback by his table manners. "Only way to eat a drumstick," he said with his mouth full. "Magnificent. My compliments, Mrs. Erickson."

She nodded her head in acknowledgment as Randall sliced a thin piece from the breast for her. She cut off a small square, holding the knife in her right hand and the fork in her left. When done, she set the knife beside her plate and transferred the fork to her right hand before spearing the square. She made sure to keep her mouth closed and chew several times before swallowing.

"I came with the first farmers," Dall said, "even before the Hartwigs."

He pronounced "farmers" *fahmuhz* and "Hartwigs" *Hahtwigz*. Hot wigs.

"Why isn't the town called Dall Valley?" Randall asked. "You should be mayor."

"Good heavens, no. I'll leave politics to the men with a stomach for that sort of thing."

"Perhaps you mean the liver," Randall said.

Reverend Dall nodded sadly: everybody knew about Herb Goss's drinking. He bit off another chunk of turkey flesh.

"Where did you live before Dakota?" Mariel said.

This time he swallowed before speaking. "Worcester, Massachusetts, originally." *Wooster.*

"I thought I recognized the accent."

"And you?"

"Michigan and Ohio, mostly. I went to college in New York. That's where we met."

Dall raised an eyebrow at Randall. Mariel could almost hear what he was thinking: Your wife went to college? "Do you have children?"

The question took her by surprise, and she looked away.

"I'm sorry," Dall said, "have you lost a child?"

"No, thankfully. We have two, a boy and a girl. Ellie recently married. Alex is at West Point."

"You must be proud."

"Very," Randall said, gazing at Mariel as if to say, *What's wrong?*

She shook her head: *Nothing.* But that wasn't entirely true, for now she knew the source of her melancholy. She had very few authentic memories of her mother, and fewer still of her parents together. One was of a Christmas sometime in the early forties, the briefest fragment of an image, pine burning in the fireplace, meat cooking on the stove, and a stocking hung from the mantle just for her. Mother and Father—Claire and Carl, before she fell, before he drowned—held hands and sang carols to her. How she giggled and clapped.

And then there were the Christmases when her own children were small, squealing with anticipation, no matter how meager the gifts.

"I'm being silly," she said. "Just recalling Christmases past."

Dall placed the drumstick on his plate, and wiped his fingers on the linen napkin. "I understand," he said, taking her hand in his. "What you're feeling is perfectly natural, my dear." *DEE-yah.* She'd never heard "dear" stretched into two syllables before. "You see, there are four stages of Christmas. By this I mean our secular celebrations, not the Lord's birth itself, which is a singular event and the glory of the world. The first stage is when we are ourselves children. Everything is thrilling for us. We often look back at this as the best time of our lives. The second is when we have children of our own. The excitement of Christmas becomes blunted for us as we grow older, but we are able to rekindle it when we share in the joy of our young ones.

In its way, this is the most fulfilling. The third stage is where you find yourself now, Mrs. Erickson. You are not a child, and your children are no longer children. They have left you and Lieutenant Erickson to observe this most blessed of days as adults, no longer filtered through the wonder and innocence of youth."

Mariel realized he was right. It was the unintended and inevitable loss of innocence triggering her sadness. "But I don't love the Lord the less for it. It's just...."

"Of course you don't."

"What's the fourth?" Randall said. "You said there were four stages."

Dall picked up the drumstick again. "The best one of all," he said. "Grandchildren."

MURDER

CHAPTER SEVENTEEN
AN IRISH PAUPER
Monday, January 3, 1887

"How's Theo?" Mariel said to Lottie. They had met by chance outside the post office after Mariel had dismissed class for the day. Lottie was leaving, Mariel entering.

"What Dad doesn't know won't hurt me," Lottie said with a sly smile. Fiona Bohnet had offered her employment at the hotel, but once out of her parents' home and into her own room above the tavern, Lottie had no desire to work with them. She wanted to prove her independence, and good for her. Instead, she played the piano in the saloon at night and served drinks during the day. Neither Mike nor Phoebe approved of that, but Lottie was a grown woman and could do as she pleased.

Except, in Mike's view, when Theo Parley was the author of her pleasure.

"We're still seeing each other, of course," Lottie said. "You won't tell Dad, will you?"

"My lips are sealed," Mariel said, knowing that Mike knew. Despite Mike's bluster, he was a tolerant man—although she wasn't sure she'd care to test the limits of that tolerance.

Lottie squeezed her shoulder. "Mr. Duncan will be expecting me," she said, and hurried across the street.

Inside the post office, Sadie Goss was working at the desk. "Hello, friend," she said. "Coming to see Randall?"

"No," Mariel said. Although she wasn't overly fond of Herb Goss, she would've preferred him to his wife today. Sadie had shared a grief with her, placing the burden upon Mariel to help her bear it. She would've been honored if Sadie were a private woman, withholding her pain from all but her dearest confidants, but she was a gossip who blubbered to anyone who'd stay still long enough to listen. Mariel resented being placed among that group. She reached into her handbag and produced two envelopes. "I just need stamps."

"Two?" Sadie opened a drawer behind the counter. "Ellie and Alex?"

It was none of her business, but she'd see the names and addresses on the envelopes anyway. Hopefully she wouldn't open the letters and read them before mailing them.

"I've been a poor correspondent with my children," she said, affixing the stamps.

"That'll be four cents."

Mariel would have given anyone else a nickel and required no change, but for Sadie she counted out four pennies.

The woman from the room next to Randall's came in and headed for the stairway.

"Howdy, Sadie-lady," the woman said as she passed.

"Hey there, Beryl-girl. Didn't see you go out."

Beryl-girl brushed hair from her eyes and held up a bottle for them to see. "Breakfast."

"It's four o'clock in the afternoon."

Beryl smiled. "Like I said, breakfast."

"Going to be a long night?"

"They're all long nights."

Mariel heard loud voices outside as she watched Beryl climb the steps. "I've always wondered," she said, "and tell me if I'm being impertinent—"

"Do I mind having a whore upstairs?" Sadie smiled and

shrugged.

Mariel nodded.

"Why would I?" Sadie said.

"I mean, with your husband working here, aren't you afraid...?"

"He *drinks*, Mariel. If she can get him to raise anything but a glass, God bless her."

Oh, my, Mariel thought, feeling her cheeks flush. Truth was, Randall worked here, too. To the best of her knowledge he'd never been unfaithful to her. If he hadn't done so when he was younger, why would he start now? He was fifty-one, after all.

What Dad doesn't know won't hurt me, Lottie had said.

What I don't know won't hurt me, Mariel thought. "Well, I should be getting home," she said. She paused, though, as the commotion in the street became cheers and catcalls. These were followed by thunderous footsteps from above and Randall flying down the stairs.

Beryl was right behind him.

"What's happening?" Mariel said.

"Fight," Beryl yelled with a giggle.

"Who?"

"Hartwig and Blackford," Randall said. "I saw them from my window. Those imbeciles."

Randall was out the door in an instant. Mariel, Sadie and Beryl were hard on his heels, but even in that short time the scuffle had ended. Hartwig lay at the center of a small circle of people, flat on his face in the snow, bleeding from the nose and dislodging little puffs of snow with each breath.

Mariel watched from the post office door. The two other women joined the onlookers.

Bobby Baughman restrained Liam Blackford, who looked like he intended to continue the melee. "Don't, Mr. Blackford. He's down."

"Aye, lad. I'm fine now. Let me go."

"You sure?" Bobby said, releasing him.

Liam's right hand was red and swollen. "Arsehole's jaw's as hard as his head. I think I broke me sodding knuckles."

"Good," Randall scowled. "What were you thinking, Liam? Enough folks around here hate the Irish already."

"They can go to hell and be damned," Liam said. "I'm not 'the Irish,' I'm only meself. Whatever I do is me own responsibility, not that of every Irishman who ever drew breath. I've never done this *diabhal* no harm, and I'll not suffer his taunting. This little kerfuffle's just a warning. Next time I'll dynamite the bastard's house."

"Where's an Irish pauper going to get dynamite?" said Roy Duncan, the tavern owner.

"I make it in me cellar," Liam said.

"Like hell."

"Don't you know this is what Hartwig wants?" Randall said.

Liam grinned. "He wants me to dynamite his house?"

"Stop talking nonsense. He means to stir up more feelings against you, and you played right into his hands."

Marshal Woolridge and Trippledy pushed their way through the crowd. They made an odd pair, Mariel thought, the marshal small and wiry, the deputy tall and half a foot beyond rotund. "What's going on here?" Woolridge said.

"Mr. Blackford and Mr. Hartwig were exchanging pleasantries," Randall said.

"The mick cold-cocked Clyde," said Duncan.

"That so?" Dalton said, his jowls jiggling when he spoke.

"One punch," Bobby boasted.

"Who started it?" Woolridge said. "Never mind, that ain't too hard to guess. Someone pick Clyde up before his face freezes to the ground. The rest of you go home."

"You ain't even gonna arrest him?" Beryl said. "You and

Trippledy've tossed me in the hoosegow for less than that."

"And will again," the marshal said.

Duncan and Lem Smith lifted Hartwig to his feet. He groaned and opened his eyes.

Liam held out his wrists to be cuffed. "I present meself to your justice, constables."

"You damn jackass, Blackford," Woolridge said. "You gotta be smarter than him."

"Do your job, boys," Duncan said, and most of the crowd murmured its assent.

"Don't tell us what to do," Dalton said.

"Shut up, Duane." Woolridge stared the townspeople down. "That's how it's gonna be? Well, then. Mr. Blackford, I hereby sentence you to two days in jail and a ten dollar fine for disturbing the public quiet. Sentence suspended. Now get your ass outta here. Have someone look at that hand."

Liam noticed Mariel in the doorway, gave her a wink, and walked away whistling.

Hartwig snatched his arms from the grasp of Duncan and Smith and took a step toward the two lawmen. "What's this shit? That Catlicking son-of-a-bitch attacked me for no reason. Run him out of town. Christ, *shoot* him. My jaw's probably busted."

"Come any closer," Woolridge said, "and I'll make sure it is."

CHAPTER EIGHTEEN
THIEVES OF NEW YORK
Tuesday, January 4, 1887

Mariel's larder was low on supplies, so before school she and Randall went to the hotel for breakfast, where Phoebe immediately put them to work. While Randall helped Mike strip the beds, Mariel assisted in preparing the meal. There were six guests to cook for, plus the four of them. Eggs, sausage, gravy, and bread were on the menu, plus Quaker oatmeal for those with a taste for the bland.

"I heard about that knucklehead Hartwig," Phoebe said. "I don't know why Mike keeps taking him on. The Baughman boy can do everything Clyde does, better, cheaper, and without being vulgar. What started the fight?"

Mariel set plates and bowls on the table. "By the time I got outside, Mr. Hartwig was on his face in the snow." She recalled her conversation with Reverend Dall on Christmas night, and wondered if she'd ever again hear Hartwig's name without thinking of "hot wig."

Phoebe used her spatula to scramble the eggs in the skillet. "I'd've paid good money to see that. For a small man, the mick sure packs a wallop, eh?"

Mariel was surprised by her use of the word *mick*. "I don't know why Mr. Hartwig hates Liam. He seems pleasant enough to me."

"Can't say what Clyde's complaint is, but Mike doesn't care much for the Irish, either."

"Mike? I shouldn't think he dislikes anyone, save perhaps Theo Parley."

Phoebe scooped the eggs into a large dish and dropped sausage in the frying pan. The meat sizzled on the hot metal surface, its aroma wonderful. "Mike don't hate Theo, just wants to make him sweat a little before he gets too cozy with Lottie."

Mariel smiled behind her hand. Mike wasn't mean, but he surely did have the capacity to be ornery when the mood struck him. "Where's the silver?"

"Cabinet to your right."

Mariel counted out ten each of forks, spoons, and knives and placed them next to the plates on the table. "Butter?"

"On your left. I just churned it. Mike milked the cows an hour ago. It's cooling on the porch."

Mariel brought a platter for the meat to Phoebe. "So what's his objection to the Irish? He doesn't like Mr. Blackford?"

"No, he likes Liam fine. It's just…. He don't talk much about the war, so maybe I shouldn't say anything. But Andersonville's why."

"Irishmen fought for the Rebels?"

"The ones he hated were on the Union side, or said they were. Really, they were just bounty hunters who gave themselves officer titles. They came down to Georgia and got themselves captured on purpose. To them prison was just another way to profit. Soon as they were settled in camp, they started taking rations from prisoners too sick to defend themselves. Others they killed outright for anything of value they could steal. Called themselves the Raiders. One of the leaders was a little Irish devil from New York." She glanced around to make sure her husband was still upstairs. "Things got so bad that Mike's regiment asked for a meeting with Captain

Wirz—"

"The prison commandant?"

Phoebe flipped the meat over in the skillet. "A beast of a man if ever there was one. Wirz just cussed them out. It was Yanks killing Yanks, so what did he care? But he finally agreed to let the prisoners put the Raiders on trial. They did, and found them guilty. That gave Wirz more people to hang, so he was happy. 'Cept in the confusion this little Irish fella somehow slipped away."

"Where did he go? Where could he go?"

Phoebe put the sausages onto the platter. "He found a dead man lying in a hole, pushed him aside and crawled into the hole himself, then pulled that stinking corpse over on top of him."

Mariel wasn't as hungry as she'd been a few minutes ago. "He hid under a dead man, and no one saw him do it?"

"You gotta remember there were, what, forty-five thousand prisoners in Andersonville. Anyone could get lost in that. Anyway, it took a couple of hours, but they found him and dragged him right back to the scaffold. That tough ol' Raider begged not to swing. Mike said he was weeping like a baby right till he dropped."

Mariel took the plate to the table, where the guests were starting to congregate. "That would be difficult to erase from one's memory," she said. "But surely Mike doesn't blame all Irishmen—"

"Shhh!"

Randall and Mike came down the stairs, each with an armload of bedding. "Look, dear," Mike said, "piles of laundry."

Phoebe smirked at him. "And I'm sure you'll get them real clean."

The guests laughed, with Mariel and Randall joining in.

"Well, hell," Mike said, "that didn't work out like I had it figured."

CHAPTER NINETEEN
THE BEGINNING OF OLD AGE
Saturday, January 15, 1887

Bruno wasn't as anxious to go for walks anymore. He didn't, in fact, want to do much of anything except sleep. Mariel noticed he'd been slowing down a little more each week since his incarceration in the storm cellar. The rabies scare was long past, but his old age was just beginning. The poor fellow didn't hear or see as well, either. He often failed to respond to her voice. Sometimes he bumped into things directly in front of his stubby snout.

But she couldn't allow him to wallow in his own filth, so she bundled up and attached his leash to his collar. He whined a little, but didn't struggle too much as she pulled him out the door. For once the weather was tolerable, cloudy but above freezing. Water dripped from icicles on the eaves and formed little black puddles in the snow.

Bruno did what was required of him, then trotted inside, letting his nose lead him where his eyes no longer could. Mariel kept a towel on the coat rack next to the door to wipe his feet, but he didn't wait as he'd been trained to do, instead scrabbling to the stove to curl up, his leash still attached.

Without removing her coat she mopped his trail of prints. In the few seconds it took her to get from the door to the stove, he was already asleep. She unhooked his leash and dried his paws, running the towel not only over the pads, but between his toes as well so hidden moisture didn't cause wet rot. Although he never did quite wake up, when she got to his chest and tummy he did manage to roll to his back to enjoy the rubdown. His tongue hung out as he snored.

Mariel looked at him and smiled sadly. His fat little body was failing, but she'd make him as comfortable as she could for as long as possible.

Her own knees and back ached. She wondered, were she to die first, how Randall would treat her in her dwindling moments. Would he cry, would he dote, would he utter sentimental words he rarely spoke now? Or would he remain his usual stoic self, suffering silently, putting on a brave front for her sake?

She almost certainly would die first, as longevity was not a notable trait in her family. Oh, her grandfather Noah, on her mother's side, had lived well into his sixties, but her father Carl died before he was fifty, and her mother Claire while only in her late twenties.

Claire's death was murky, even now. Her father had always maintained it was an accident—she fell and hit her head—but Noah's demeanor hinted her ending was more nefarious. Yet even in her adult years no one would tell her. Both her father and grandfather had been protective and infuriatingly brave. What they had considered an act of kindness had haunted her ever since.

Mariel found herself becoming angry with Randall. If he tried to be brave when her time came, she'd rise from her death bed and throttle him. Didn't the end of a long companionship deserve honest tears?

Even in his sleep Bruno could perform certain functions. A villainous vapor rippled outward from him and quickly engulfed the entire room.

Mariel plugged her nose and, laughing at her own silliness, gazed again upon his homely face. "Thank you, little friend," she said. "I was getting a bit morose."

****

Mike's asthma was acting up, so he and Phoebe decided not to go to the cotillion at the Masonic hall. Truth was, they rarely went anyway, but tonight Randall had promised to play the piano. Herb Goss had shamed him into proving he could keep up with Hank Moehler's fiddle. Goss intended to write a story about the competition for the *Sentinel*.

"You scoundrel," Mariel said to Mike, "I've had you on my dance card since we arrived in Dakota, and you still haven't danced with me."

"Been meaning to," Mike said, "but your husband'll shoot me if I do."

"I didn't say that," Randall countered. "I said I'd shoot you if you dance better than I do."

"Like I said." Mike laughed, a sound which soon became wheezing. He mopped his mouth and beard with a handkerchief. "Phoebe can go, though. What do you think, Mother?"

"Not if he dances worse than you," Phoebe said. "I still have bruises from last time."

"Just sit and listen to him mangle the piano, then. Randy can play as well as anyone, long as it don't matter what order the notes come in. He'll break his fingers trying to match Hank."

"If you weren't such a sick old man," Randall said, "I'd knock you on your tailbone."

"A Reb said that to me once."

"What happened?"

Mike grinned, his crow's feet crinkling and his eyes

twinkling. "He knocked me on my tailbone. But that was him. They'll be singing hosannas in hell before you could do it."

"Show some respect, sergeant. I could have you court-martialed."

"Good luck with that. I mustered out in 'sixty-five."

"I'll make it retroactive."

"You can't even spell retroactive."

Randall sighed. He was beat, and he knew it. "Come along, Mariel," he said. "Herb and Sadie are meeting us there. If he's sober."

"We've plenty of time."

"I'd like to practice a few times with Hank beforehand."

"Go, then. I want to ask Mike something."

"I don't want you to walk alone."

"I walk farther than that every day to and from school. Button your coat."

When Randall left, Mike said, "This sounds ominous."

"Should I leave?" Phoebe said.

"It doesn't matter," Mariel said. She folded her hands in front of her. "I just have a favor to ask of Mike."

"Which is?"

"You probably know I'm interested in writing for the *Sentinel*, but so far Mr. Goss has been resistant, other than a women's page. I don't want to write about recipes and sewing, I want to write about important things. I spoke to him last week, and...."

"I know where this is going," Mike said. "The thing about Tom and the dead-line? Goss's been trying to pry war stories out of me since he started that damn rag."

"I know it's difficult, but it's the only way he'll—"

"I'm real fond of you, Mariel, and that husband of yours, too, but the war was personal. I saw shit people shouldn't have to see and did shit people shouldn't have to do. I don't even like thinking about it, never mind putting it on display for everyone in town to read. The war's over. Time to let the son-of-a-bitch *be* over." He held out his hand. "We still friends?"

"Of course." Mariel cupped his hand in both of hers. This wasn't what she hoped for, but it was what she expected. "I'm the one who should be sorry."

"Nah. Maybe someday we'll talk, just you and me and Randy. Meantime, keep nagging Goss. Something'll come along. How about a story on the Temperance Society? He'd love to read what those folks are up to these days."

Mariel hid a smile behind the pretext of scratching her nose. "You're evil."

****

"It's not really supposed to be played in a minute!" Randall complained to Hank.

"It's *The Minute Waltz*, ain't it?" Hank said. He, Randall, and Mariel were in front of the stage at the piano. The dance was still a half hour away, and few people were in the hall. The Gosses hadn't arrived yet.

"No," Randall said in his *I'm-smarter-than-you* voice. "It's pronounced my-NYOOT, as in small, not MIN-uht." He pointed out the front page of the piano score. "But the title is actually *Waltz in D-flat Major, Opus Sixty-Four, Number One*."

"Well, la-de-damn-dah. That's a whole lot of numbers for such a short song." Hank flew through the opening few measures again, his bow stroking impossibly fast.

"Chopin himself nicknamed it *Valse du Petit Chien*."

"That's worse than all the numbers."

"It means *Little Dog Waltz*."

"Well, find me a dog that can play piano, and it can take as long as it wants. I play the song in a minute. And, by the way, you can't."

Randall's face reddened. "It's not a difficult piece. I simply play it was the way it was intended."

"If whatever-his-name-was meant for people to fall asleep during it, he could've just as well wrote this."

Hank's fiddle magically transformed itself into a concert violin as he performed a lovely, slow and resonant version of *Brahm's Lullaby*, replete with vibrato.

"Lullaby, and good night," Mariel sang, but Randall shushed her.

"Who did you study with?" he said.

"Didn't study with nobody," Hank said. "I hear it, I play it. Don't need to look at no paper with squiggles and dots."

Voices started to drown out their conversation as people wandered into the hall. Lottie was in the crowd, along with Theo and his tuba. Herb and Sadie Goss weren't far behind, and toward the back, arm-in-arm, Bobby and Megan followed, trying so hard to look grown up.

Mariel was still concerned about nature getting the better of them, but she had to admit that, in their youthful innocence and beauty, they did look sweet together.

"Can you even read music?" Randall demanded.

"Why should I?" Hank said. "I can play it, so why in hell would I need to know how to read it?"

"I speak English, too, but I still learned how to read."

"You're just afraid to lose to a hick."

"You're not a hick," Mariel said. "You're... What's the term I'm looking for, Randall?"

"*Musician*." Randall spit out the word. He'd gone a bit green. "I studied for *years*."

"Ah, quit your bellyaching. You said you could keep up with me, so keep up with me. If you can't do it, just say so. You can skip your whupping and go dance like everyone else."

Lottie and Theo wound through the crowd toward them.

"Maybe you'd prefer them?" Randall grumbled.

"They ain't the ones talking big."

When Lottie and Theo arrived, Mariel raised an eyebrow and then gave Lottie a wink.

She smiled back. "Evening, Mr. Moehler, Lieutenant and Mrs. Erickson."

"Are you performing tonight, Mr. Erickson?" Theo said, leaning to starboard as he cradled his tuba in the crook of his right elbow. "I've heard you're quite the pianist."

Randall gazed forlornly at Hank and said, "That rumor has been somewhat exaggerated, Mr. Parley. I'll leave the music to the experts. Excuse us, please."

He took Mariel's arm and led her to the table where the Gosses were sitting. Mariel heard Hank laugh, and by the way his body stiffened, so did Randall.

"You haven't won many battles tonight," she whispered.

He shrugged as if he didn't care, but Mariel knew he was embarrassed. "There are days like that," he said.

Goss rose for Mariel.

"Sit down, Herb," Randall said.

"Give up on Hank already?" Herb giggled, the stink of whiskey already strong on his breath. "That won't be much of a story."

CHAPTER TWENTY
BLOW THE MAN DOWN
Thursday, February 24, 1887

"We got all we needed," Herb Goss said in an agitated manner, pounding on the table and grinning. He waved a piece of paper over his head.

Mariel didn't care for saloons, but Duncan's was cleaner than most. At Randall's insistence she'd come after school to hear the momentous news Goss promised. Most of the town had gathered. She and Randall, Mike and Phoebe, and Frank Chamberlain and his wife Pearl joined Herb and Sadie at their table.

Hank and Peg Moehler sat with the Duncans and Clyde Hartwig. Louisa wasn't present, probably home caring for the children.

Lottie played the piano while Theo sang. His voice was better than his tuba playing, but only a little. For reasons only he knew, he'd chosen a sailor's shanty.

> "As I was a-walking down Paradise Street,
> Sing, weigh, hey, blow the man down.
> A pretty young damsel I chanced for to meet.
> Give me some time to blow the man down."

Mariel tapped her toes. Although she'd never seen an ocean,

she had fond memories of the song. Her grandfather Noah, a whaler for some thirty years before he made his way inland, loved it. He'd often sung it to her when she was a child, making silly faces as he puffed his cheeks out to "blow the man down." He made her giggle every time.

While she enjoyed the music, it was apparent that Mike and Phoebe didn't. Mike was pointedly not looking at his daughter and her beau, and Phoebe was not looking at Mike.

"Quiet!" Goss shouted. For once he didn't appear drunk.

Lottie stopped playing, Theo stopped singing, and the people in the tavern stopped talking. A delicious air of anticipation followed.

Finally Hank Moehler broke the silence. "What's this about, Mayor?" he said.

"What I've got here," Goss said, "is a petition for Governor Pierce. His office told me that if we wanted to get the county seat back, we'd have to get the signatures of at least a hundred voters."

"What's that got to do with us women?" said Beryl. Mariel thought she had a good point.

Goss ignored her. "Took us a while—hell, there's not that many voters in the whole Valley—so what I did, what Clyde and I did, was to go to other towns. Clyde got almost every white man in Lesterville to sign, and I even got some in Buffalo Prairie itself. What this means is that with a stroke of the pen Governor Pierce can give us the county seat."

To Mariel's mind this was not momentous news. It changed nothing, it solved nothing. Many folks seemed to agree. A few men applauded, but many of them looked annoyed at having been summoned away from more important activities. The women didn't react one way or the other. None of their names was on the petition, so what did they care?

"Is that all?" Hank said. "I thought you was gonna tell us

gold was found in Crow Creek."

"We'd have the richest damn Injuns in the whole country," Marshal Woolridge said.

"Maybe they could buy their own land back," Roy Duncan said.

"Who'd sell it to them?" Hartwig said, and everybody laughed.

"I'm telling you," Goss said, "there are advantages to being the county seat. I plan to deliver the petition to the governor myself once the snow melts and the roads open up. You'll see."

"Fine," Hank said, "but why not just print it in that rag of yours and be done with it?"

"If you don't care, why did you sign the petition?" Goss said, his facing going red as his nose when he was on a bender.

"To shut you up, mostly," Woolridge said, which was followed by another round of laughter.

"What the hell?" Goss said. "What the *hell*."

Mike cleared his throat. ""Come on, folks. Having the county seat brings in jobs and revenue from the government. Not to mention that the people coming to town for county business'll need food and lodging, whiskey, horse care. We all like money, don't we?"

"When you see those folks," Duncan said, "send them here. They can buy me a drink."

Sadie leaned toward Mariel and whispered in her ear, "Herb had hoped they'd be more enthusiastic. Good lord, he's going to get drunker than usual tonight."

"I heard that," Goss said.

"Good," Sadie said.

Mariel suppressed a smile. "Upon further reflection, Mayor Goss, I withdraw my offer to write this story for the *Sentinel*. I'm sure you'll do an admirable job." She looked at Mike. "Surely something else will come along for me."

"Nothing gets printed without my say so." Goss got up and stomped out of the tavern. Sadie followed behind.

In his wake a mixture of gaiety and grumbling ensued. Many of the women left, but the men seemed to adopt the attitude that as long as they were at the tavern, they might as well drink.

"It's too quiet in here," someone yelled to Lottie. "Play something."

Mike still wouldn't look at her. "Randall," he said, "how about you play instead? I hear your duet with Hank didn't go well."

"It didn't go at all," Randall said.

"Well, Hank doesn't have his fiddle now. I'm sure everyone'd love to hear what they missed out at the dance that night."

Lottie, who couldn't have overheard any of their conversation, resumed playing "Blow the Man Down." As soon as the accompaniment came around to the verse again Theo took up where he left off.

> "She was round in the counter and bluff in the bow,
> Sing, weigh, hey, blow the man down.
> So I took in all sail and cried, 'Way enough now.'
> Give me some time to blow the man down.
>
> "I hailed her in English, she answered me clear,
> Sing, weigh, hey, blow the man down.
> 'I'm from the *Black Arrow* bound to the *Shakespeare*.'
> Give me some time to blow the man down."

Now that they were paying attention, the tavern's customers booed. Hartwig went to the piano and nudged Theo out of the way.

"Stick to the tuba, Parley," he said loudly enough for all to hear. "Let me show you how it's done. You just keep on tickling them keys, Miss Hammon."

Mariel could see that Theo's feelings were hurt, but he didn't resist. He lowered his eyes and walked out the back of the tavern. Lottie shook her head at Hartwig. She stood up, looked at Mariel and motioned for her to follow, placing prayerful hands together as if to say, *Please?*

"Well, someone's gotta play," Hartwig said.

"Now you got no excuse," Mike said to Randall. "Get up there, lieutenant, and show them what you're made of."

"Nobody wants to hear my inept fumblings."

"Like hell." Mike had the same mischievous look in his eyes that he always did when he teased Randall, but there was a harder edge this time. Mariel thought it might have more to do with Lottie than with Randall. He raised his voice to address the group. "This man here's a soldier, folks, a gen-u-ine lieutenant in the Army of these United States, and he's fixing to play the piano for you."

"Michael, don't be irksome," Phoebe whispered.

The crowd applauded.

"Sergeant," Randall said, "the devil has a special place in hell for you."

"Already been there."

Randall pushed away from the table.

"May I be excused?" Mariel said. She put her coat on.

"My own wife doesn't want to listen to me."

"It isn't that."

Mike tugged Mariel's sleeve. "Say hello to her for me, won't you?" So he'd been watching Lottie after all.

"Of course."

Phoebe nodded. She looked so sad.

Mariel escorted Randall to the piano, but kept going when

he sat down.

"Let's hear it for Lieutenant Erickson," Hartwig said.

"Same song?" Randall said. Without waiting for an answer, he started in. He usually didn't do as well when he had to play from memory, but this song was so famous, Mariel could probably have performed it herself. Hartwig came in on the next verse. Mariel paused for a moment. She didn't like the man, but his singing voice was magnificent. His bass tones resonated in her soul, even when performing such frivolous music.

> "So I tailed her my flipper and took her in tow,
> Sing weigh, hey, blow the man down.
> And yardarm to yardarm away we did go.
> Give me some time to blow the man down."

People have such diverse natures, Mariel thought. That such beauty could flow from the throat of evil must be one of the Lord's little jokes.

No, she told herself. Hartwig wasn't evil. Certainly he was crude, hateful, and bursting with the arrogance that so often paired with stupidity. But he wasn't evil.

As she exited into the cold night air, pinpricks of freezing drizzle stung her face. She found Lottie and Theo leaning side-by-side against the tavern wall, foreheads touching.

"We're leaving, Mrs. Erickson," Lottie said without preliminaries. She wasn't wearing a hat, and her hair was already flattened by a thin glaze of ice. Her cheeks were red and streaked with unfrozen tears.

"You'll catch your death," Mariel said. She heard perfectly well what Lottie had said, but her mouth was simply working to give her brain time to process the words.

"We're to be married," Theo said.

A hundred questions came to mind, but the only one she managed to articulate was, "Are you with child?"

Lottie looked stricken, as if Mariel had just told her God had died. "Do you think so little of us, Mrs. Erickson?" she said.

"Forgive me," Mariel said. She stepped forward to embrace them both. "Where will you go?"

"Theo has relatives in Cedar Rapids," Lottie said, gently pulling away from her. "We'll lodge with them until he finds employment."

She could hear Hartwig singing inside, or perhaps it was only the memory of his voice. "There's no joy for you here?" she said.

"Don't we deserve to be happy?" Lottie said.

Mariel knew Mike had made it difficult for the couple, but until now hadn't realized the extent of his pressure upon them. She felt panic rising. Lottie wasn't particularly close to her, Theo not at all. She wanted to scream and didn't know why. They did deserve happiness. "Your parents say hello," she said.

"May all your days be blessed," Lottie said, "and theirs."

She took Theo's arm, and they walked away on a street slick with ice.

As Mariel watched them turn the corner, she thought about Mike. *Weigh, hey, blow the man down.*

CHAPTER TWENTY-ONE
BLOOMING IN WINTER
Friday, February 25, 1887

Bobby was unable to take the midnight readings, so Randall had to do it himself. Because he was required at the post office again at six a.m., he went straight to bed upon his arrival home. He didn't snore often, except when utterly exhausted. Tonight, it was a ragged, strangulating sound that Mariel found so disruptive she couldn't be in the same room with him. She retrieved a clean blanket from her trunk, and moved to the rocking chair next to the stove. At her feet Bruno snored, too, but his breathing was soft and steady, unlike the clanking locomotive that was her husband.

She pulled the blanket over her shoulders and settled in for the night, enjoying the slight blow back of wood smoke as she listened to the crackling in the stove and the rain on the window. The droplets sounded as if they instantly transformed into ice pellets upon contact with the glass. She'd never understood how it could rain when the temperature was below freezing. Randall had explained it once, but his scientific jargon was lost on her.

Getting to school in the morning would be horrid, especially if snow blew in behind the rain and covered the ice. But that was a worry for tomorrow. Tonight the tapping rhythm was comforting in its way: tears from heaven to match the tears in her heart.

What should she tell Mike and Phoebe? Should she tell them anything at all? They didn't see Lottie often, so they likely wouldn't notice her absence for some while. Should she let her friends go on in ignorance until they discovered their daughter was no longer occupying her room above the tavern? That would not only be cruel, but detrimental to Mariel's relations with them, should they later learn she'd known all along. She couldn't bear losing Mike and Phoebe's friendship.

Yet if she spoke up now, Mike might still find a way to stop them, to interfere with their dash toward happiness. That would be a betrayal, not only of Lottie and Theo, but of love itself.

She remembered the breathless flutter in her stomach when she'd first seen Randall at that dance in New York, she in the modest attire of a college student and he resplendent in his second lieutenant's uniform. His rugged face was gentled by spectacles and a crisp black mustache. Passion overwhelmed them both then, and if had it cooled in the intervening years, was that a reason to deny Lottie and Theo those feelings now?

Mariel folded her hands in her lap as if in prayer. Why didn't they simply disappear and leave her as confused as the rest? "I don't want this burden," she said to Bruno.

The old fellow's hearing was failing, and he didn't awaken. If there was an answer in his silence, she couldn't find it.

Randall didn't snore when he was young. After their first night together, it seemed to her smitten heart that he would always be that dashing young soldier, brave, strong, flawless. She closed her eyes and brushed her hands across her thighs. Her fingers lingered. Perhaps this was spurred by a deep memory, perhaps to offset the sadness of the moment, or perhaps to remind herself she was still alive, could still feel. Whatever the guiding force, the sensation was pleasant.

Wood popped in the stove. The rain on the window was heavier and harder, no longer in the form of liquid, but sleet. She couldn't look at her husband's instruments and predict the weather, but she'd lived long enough to know that freezing rain followed by sleet inevitably ended in snow.

Good. If there was enough of it to block the roads, nobody would be going anywhere for a few days, delaying the necessity of a decision. Her breathing came a bit faster now, and for the moment Lottie and Theo were forgotten.

Randall had been so handsome in that uniform....

****

She was asleep in the chair when Bruno's whining woke her at four a.m. She bundled up and took him out into a bitter, snowy morning. Disliking the cold as much as she, he finished his business quickly. She brought him in, unbundled, and returned to the rocker.

Randall got up an hour later and woke her again to fix his breakfast. "Was I snoring?"

"Tornadoes are quieter."

"Sorry. Bobby had to work on an assignment for you. He put it off until the last minute."

"That's not like him."

"Two words: Megan Blackford."

Mariel smiled. Or winced. Or both. Bobby and Megan, Lottie and Theo. Love, blooming in the desolate winter, while she and Randall went about their lives as if they had forgotten they'd ever been young.

"If he's late, I'll sit him in the dunce chair," she said, sounding harsher than she felt. She actually found the young people's romance charming.

"In which case, I hope she was worth it. Just toast today."

Randall yawned. "Four hours of sleep used to be plenty. When did I get old?"

Right after Alex was born, Mariel thought. Me, too.

The bread was no longer fresh, but the skillet would compensate. She retrieved a knife and sliced what remained of the loaf. "How many?"

"Two. And some coffee. I'm dressed, I'll get the water. Has the dog been out?"

"About an hour ago." Mariel added wood to the fire and set the pan on top of the stove. She cut two slices of bread. Toast did sound good, so she cut a slice for herself as well and dropped all three pieces onto the skillet. "It's cold out there."

Randall put on his coat and took a pail outside to the pump. Although he returned within moments, frost had already formed in his mustache. "What a fine morning," he said.

"I told you," Mariel said.

"At least you don't have to stand in the wind on top of the post office."

"Don't be stubborn. Wear your gloves."

He removed his coat and shook off the snow. "If we'd stayed in Chicago, winter would be almost over now."

"You wanted to come."

He replaced the coat on the rack. "A change of scenery was necessary."

What he meant was: Thirty years in the Army and still a second lieutenant. He'd been promoted to first lieutenant during the War, but that commission ended when the war did, and he was reduced to second again. His rank didn't rise when they moved to Chicago, and it hadn't risen in Dakota. However, relocating to the plains removed him from direct contact with the superiors he felt were persecuting him. The surprise was that it took him so long to realize that the only avenues open to him in Chicago went sideways or down.

"I like Goss Valley," Mariel said. "And Mike and Phoebe are here."

As were, for the time being, Lottie and Theo.

Randall filled the coffeepot with water. "Don't burn the toast."

Mariel flipped the bread over with a spatula. She preferred her toast blackened, especially when it was dunked in milk. The backs of the slices were done within a minute. She took them out, and brought them to him on a plate, along with a brick of butter and a table knife.

As she retrieved the coffee from the cupboard, she debated whether or not to tell him about Lottie and Theo's intentions, but decided against it. Surely the weather would delay their departure long enough for her to decide between their love and her friendship with the Hammons.

She measured out the coffee, strong the way he liked it, and broached a different topic. "Peg Moehler said that the Fragment Society intends to mend clothing for the Indians. I thought I might go to their meeting at the church tomorrow. Do you suppose the weather will improve by then?"

"Won't know that until I see the reports from out west. I thought you didn't like those ladies."

"It's the gossip I dislike."

"What do you expect with a group of women together in one room?"

"Do you remember last summer," she said, "when Mr. Hartwig came for us in Kimball?"

Randall nibbled at his toast, eating from the side rather than either end. That always annoyed Mariel, in a petty, peevish way. "Why?" he said.

"When I told him I should like to visit the Indian reservation? I haven't changed my mind."

He stopped eating and studied her. "Then it's time you did.

Do you have some silly notion about writing about Indians for Goss's paper? Nobody cares about them. Your only hope with Goss is to get Mike to talk about the war."

"I want to see a reservation." And to learn if the papoose of that Crow woman who'd come begging was alive or dead....

"It's just a town. No tepees, no wigwams. Their buildings are made of wood, like ours."

"But how do they live? Have they adapted to our ways? Are they Christians?"

Randall's face reddened as he finished his first piece of toast. "Mariel, you are not going to the reservation. I forbid it."

Forbid?

"I see."

"Don't use that tone with me. It was bad enough that you gave those beggars food."

"You said they'd return, but they never did."

"Which is as it should be. There's no reason for you to go. It isn't safe. *They* don't want you there. Leave them alone and they'll leave us alone."

The coffee was boiling. She poured Randall a cup and set it too forcefully on the table. Some of the hot liquid sloshed out onto his lap. "Dammit!" he said.

"Are you hurt?" she said, trying to sound contrite.

He brushed off the coffee that hadn't yet soaked into his denim trousers. "I'm fine. I've got my long johns on underneath. What is the *matter* with you?"

"I'll wash those."

Randall pulled out his pocket watch. "No time. Now, forget this foolishness. You aren't going, and that's all there is to it."

"What if I find someone to escort me?"

"Who'd do that?" He walked to the door and removed his coat from the rack.

As he left, Mariel stomped her foot, then sat at the table and stared at the door. She dropped her toast on the floor for Bruno to eat. He opened one eye, apparently weighing the virtue of food against sleep. Sleep won.

Surely it was anger clouding her judgment, but she realized that not only was her husband no longer the dashing soldier of their youth, but perhaps he never had been.

It did no good to pout. The weather would probably keep most students home from school, but she felt obligated to be there for those who made the effort to come.

CHAPTER TWENTY-TWO
LAUGH AT THE SKY
Saturday, February 26, 1887

"What is it, exactly, that you want from us, Mrs. Erickson?" Peg Moehler said. "You avoid us for months, and now you think you have the right to make demands?"

As usual, Peg and Louisa Hartwig were seated in the warmest part of the church basement, next to the stove on the south wall. The chugging of foot pedals and whirring of presser bars and bobbins stopped while everybody listened in on their conversation.

Sadie had come in with Mariel, but now took a step away.

"I'm not demanding anything," Mariel said. "When you recruited me last summer, you claimed that you also helped the Indians on the reservation. I think that's an excellent idea."

"Did I say that?" Peg said, glancing at Louisa. Louisa shook her head with a look of disdain.

"That's how it's going to be?" Mariel said.

"First those Irish friends of yours," Louisa said, "now the filthy Crows. I'm having second thoughts about allowing Wayne in your classroom."

Many possible rebukes occurred to Mariel involving bad, Lord's-name-in-vain kind of words. Instead, she took a deep breath. "How dare you," she finally said. "*Gather up the fragments, that nothing be lost.*' You boast of your charity. You claim to clothe the poor, but where is your good work? Who's benefitted? Certainly not the immigrants. This Fragment Society of yours is no charity, it's an excuse for you hens to get together and cluck your gossip. Mrs. Moehler, you *told* me you help the Indians, or intended to. Those people are starving and cold. *Do* what you say. Help them."

"But, Mariel," Sadie said, apparently torn between retaining their friendship, such as it was, and offending the most powerful women in town, "it's nearly spring. The snow will be gone in a few weeks. They needed us in December, not now."

"And where was the Fragment Society in December?"

"We will not be interrogated," Peg said, "nor have our integrity questioned. You, madam, are no longer welcome in our group."

Thank heavens, Mariel thought. "If you were in my class, I would teach you how to spell the word 'hypocrite'."

"I already know how," Louisa said. "It's P-I-S-S O-F-F."

"How very clever. Are you coming, Sadie?"

Sadie looked at the floor. "I'd rather stay."

"As you wish."

Mariel felt the glares of the women as she ascended the steps. She wouldn't give them the satisfaction of reacting to their scorn. Outside, the snow and wind continued, as they had since last night, The sun was higher in the sky this time of the season, which, according to Randall, made cold snaps shorter, fewer, and further between. This was small consolation on a day like today.

She lifted her dress to protect it from the drifts. However, her boots weren't tall enough nor her woolen leggings thick enough to keep the snow and cold out. From the knees down she felt as if she had turned to ice.

These women would provide her neither the escort nor the excuse she needed to visit the reservation. The more serious problem was Louisa Hartwig's none-too-subtle threat: She wasn't the only one who had a child in her classroom. If Louisa pulled Wayne, perhaps the other mothers would keep their children home as well.

Clouds raced by above, northwest to southeast. Mariel hummed the tune to a song she'd made up years ago for her students when they were feeling melancholy.

> *When winter comes to call,*
> *and snowflakes start to fall,*
> *Just raise up your voices*
> *And lift up your eyes,*
> *Sing to the heavens*
> *And laugh at the sky.*

The verse often helped to cheer youngsters, but she was not a child, and try as she might, she could find solace in neither melody nor rhyme.

CHAPTER TWENTY-THREE
AFTER THE FALL
Monday, February 28, 1887

Spring wouldn't officially start for another three weeks, but to Mariel March first had always represented the end of winter. That was tomorrow. Melting snow would nourish the blossoming of flowers and budding of leaves. Birds and toads would return with their love songs, bumblebees with their gentle buzz. If Dakota was like Ohio had been, farmers were already sharpening their plows and buying their seed. Once they got into their fields, the planting would fill the senses with colors and smells, and the heart with hope.

Yet it didn't feel like spring. Three days ago nature had dumped a major snowstorm on Goss Valley. Although the snow ended, the clouds had not cleared, nor the wind abated. Mariel's winter doldrums remained firmly entrenched. The men of the town had done what they could to make the streets passable, but that had not been sufficient to bring her students to the classroom.

She sat at her desk and stared at the door, waiting. Try as she might to convince herself otherwise, she knew it wasn't the weather or the roads keeping them away, it was their mothers.

The Blackford youngsters had come, but no others. Apparently even Bess Baughman was riled up, for Bobby wasn't here, either. He was an eager student, all the more because of

Megan's presence. She'd always been an insurance policy against Bobby's truancy, or had been until now.

Mariel couldn't pretend to be disappointed that Wayne Hartwig had stayed home, but she had hoped the other students' mothers would prove less vindictive. If the women of the Fragment Society wanted to be angry with her, so be it, but how could any mother could permit personal indignation to interfere with her children's education? Her own mother had been passionate about learning. Even in death she had cultivated Mariel's mind, leaving books of poetry and, by the power of her aura alone, influencing her father Carl to enroll her in an Ohio classroom. This, despite the fact that he himself had been illiterate and saw little value in schooling.

"Where's everyone?" said one of the Blackford triplets. The speaker was female, eliminating Brannon.

"I'm afraid I don't know, Miss...?"

"It's Shannon, mum." This meant, of course, that it was probably Rhiannon, as the two girls delighted in pretending to be one another.

"Miss Rhiannon," Mariel said with a knowing smirk and a finger wag.

Rhiannon shrugged: *You caught me—this time.*

Sean raised his hand. "Mrs. Erickson, will we not be having class today, then?"

"You won't get out of it that easily, Master Blackford. We shall start with penmanship."

"Ah, that's for the wee ones," Sean complained.

"Indeed? My dog Bruno has better handwriting than yours, young man. We must continually strive to improve, even as we grow older. One must be able to write clearly and legibly if one wishes to communicate effectively. Now, open your *Readers* to page twenty-seven and copy the first paragraph, in cursive, until each letter is of the proper shape and height. There is lined paper in your desks. You'll be graded on proper form."

"Megan wants to know where Bobby is," little Caitlin blurted.

"She's in love," Ciara said, pronouncing it, *Shayzen loov.*

"Hush," Megan said, which made the rest of the Blackfords giggle. "And his name is Robert."

Mariel touched her fingers to her lips and smiled. Megan's *Robert* came out *raw butt.*

The poor girl likely didn't know about the to-do at the church on Saturday, as her mother wasn't on speaking terms with most of the women in town. Megan would have no idea why her sweetheart wasn't in class.

"I'm sure he's fine," Mariel said. "Now get to work, please, all of you."

While the children practiced their handwriting, she sat in front and opened the cover of *Adventures of Huckleberry Finn,* which Randall had given her on her last birthday. She still considered Twain vulgar, and his use of regional vernacular bordered on obscene. But the book had gotten mostly positive reviews, so she was determined to read it. She hadn't finished three pages when Mike Hammon burst through the door and said, "Mariel, you need to come."

"What happened?"

"I'll tell you on the way."

"What about my students?"

Mike looked at all the red-haired children. "You Blackford kids keep doing what Mrs. Erickson told you. I'll come back with the wagon in a few minutes and take you home."

"You're scaring me, Mike. Has something happened to Randall?"

"I'll see me siblings out, Mr. Hammon," Sean said. "We walked here, we can walk back. You take care of Mrs. Erickson."

"Good lad," Mike said.

Mariel put her coat on and rushed down the aisle between the desks. She followed Mike out the door and climbed onto the buckboard beside him. The wind was still bitter, though the clouds appeared to be thinning. She'd forgotten her hat. "What's wrong, Mike? Tell me."

He shook the reins to start the horses moving. "Your blockhead of a husband lost his grip on the ladder coming off the post office roof. He didn't fall very far, just a few feet, but he clipped his knee on one of the rungs on the way down. Might've dislocated his kneecap. Then he took a good crack to the skull when he landed. Not that Randy's got a brain to damage, but he's woozy as hell. Fool was carrying on like a schoolgirl."

Mariel hadn't forgotten her quarrel with Randall about the Indian reservation, but that seemed trivial now. Goss Valley had no doctor. "Who's tending him?" she said.

"I was, till he sent me after you. Phoebe's looking in on him."

"You shouldn't have left him."

"Be sure and tell him that. Phoebe got his head bandaged up, splinted his leg, and gave him some salicylic acid for the pain."

"That always upsets his stomach so. Laudanum is better."

"Smith was out of it at the store. I mixed the powder in with some tea to calm his gut."

"Where is he?"

"Hotel."

The wind came up hard as they turned west, blowing lacy arcs of snow from the rooftops. Mariel pulled her collar up over her ears. "Please hurry," she said.

"Horses don't like ice any more than Randy. One of them breaks its leg, I'll have to shoot it. Don't s'pose you'll let me shoot Randy?"

"He's not a coyote, Mike."

"Still chewing on that?"

"But he can be a mule...."

"An ass, and I'm stopping one syllable short because you're a lady." Mike pulled the wagon in front of the hotel. "Did you go to the dance Saturday night?"

That seemed like an odd question at a time like this. "We stayed home and read."

"Me and Phoebe didn't go, either. I hear Lottie and Theo didn't show up. Hank says he had to play by himself."

Mariel wasn't ready to talk about that, not now, maybe not ever. In any case, her husband was injured, so it was not a priority. "I'm sure Hank did fine."

Mike hopped off, then helped Mariel down. She hurried inside as he tied the horses to the rail. The air, heated by radiators, bore the pleasant aromas of sausages and wood smoke from the kitchen.

Phoebe met her in the dining area, where several guests were still eating breakfast.

"How is he?" Mariel said.

"He'll live. My first husband was a doctor, so I got plenty of experience in this kind of thing."

She knew Mike had been married before to a woman who'd died of consumption. Amanda, Amelia, something like that. But she'd always assumed, because Phoebe was so much younger, that Mike had been her only spouse. "What room?"

"In the back, same one you two stayed in last summer."

As Mariel strode past the last table before the hallway, her coat brushed a man's plate, knocking a sausage to the floor.

"Hey!"

"It's my husband!" she said, as if that would mean anything to him.

She heard Phoebe say, "I'll bring you another."

The bedroom was murky, with no lamps burning and only

the gray light of morning spilling in under the shade. When her eyes adjusted she saw Randall on the bed, his head wrapped in bloody rags, his right leg propped on several pillows and stabilized by two pieces of wood bound on either side. A sack of ice rested atop his knee. That and the salicylic acid should help reduce the swelling. He was breathing steadily as if asleep, but his eyes glinted at her in the darkness.

Mariel was relieved to find him conscious. "You're bleeding."

"Scalp wound. You know how they bleed. It's nothing."

"How do you feel?"

"Stupid," he said. "I took a tumble."

"So I hear. Would this be a good time to lecture you about being careful?"

"Dammit," he said, "Goss better not write about this in the paper. And who's going to take my readings when Bobby's in school?"

"I will, who do you think?" Mike said, stepping through the door behind Mariel. "Like I don't have enough else to do, now I gotta clean up after you. As usual, the enlisted man does all the work."

"When will I be able to walk?"

"Let's take a look at that knee." Mike lit a lamp, which caused them all to squint. He sat on the bed next to Randall and gently squeezed his leg. "This hurt?"

"Hell, yes, it hurts!"

"Well, it ought to, you jackass. Your kneecap's sitting about two inches too far north. I have to push it back where it belongs. You want some whiskey or something first, Randy? 'Cause you only *think* it hurts now."

Before Randall could answer, Mike forcefully shoved the kneecap with the heel of his hand. Mariel heard a nauseating crunch as the bone slid into place, followed immediately by

Randall's scream. The pain must have been intense, for he lost consciousness.

"At least he didn't puke," Mike said.

"What have you done to him?" Mariel said.

"Let him think too much, he'll get scared and talk himself out of it. Better to just do it quick and get it over with."

Phoebe and a few guests poked their heads in the door.

"We heard hollering," Phoebe said. "You torturing that poor man?"

"Not anymore."

"I told you I'd take care of him when Mariel got here."

"You ain't the only one done any doctoring in your time. See, there was this little war."

Mariel remembered Mike's story about the Tennessee soldier shot trying to escape prison. Mike hadn't been able to help him, but under those circumstances, nobody could have saved the boy.

"What'd you do, use a hammer to reset his knee?" Phoebe said as she examined Randall's leg.

"He'll be all right."

When Phoebe and the others left, Mariel said, "Will he?"

"Long as he didn't tear ligaments, he might only be off his feet a week or two. If he did, well, that's a whole 'nother story. Either way, he won't be climbing that ladder again anytime soon."

****

Randall decided to take up residence in the hotel until the swelling in his knee went down. Since he couldn't even manage the post office steps, the first thing he did when he awoke was to hire men to bring his maps, charts, and typewriter to his room. Goss had arranged for a commercial telegraph unit to be brought to the hotel. Although that would allow Randall to send

160

the reports himself, it would also require splicing new wire into the telegraph pole outside.

Fortunately, Mike was as handy with wire as he was everything else. He and Hartwig were outside stringing it now.

Mariel didn't envy anyone climbing that pole in this cold and wind. She rocked in a chair next to Randall's bed, trying to struggle through Twain by the light of the gas lamp. Once she started a book, she was determined to finish it, regardless how dreadful she found it.

"Why don't you just come home?" she said.

"There's no telegraph pole near our house."

"Do you want me to stay here with you?"

"No need. I'll only be here until I can walk properly."

It was almost three. Mike had delivered the two o'clock readings before enlisting Hartwig's assistance with the wire. Randall was sitting against the headboard, his right leg on the bed, his left on the floor. Phoebe had scrounged up a lap desk for his use.

He scribbled figures onto a chart and said, "When was the dog last out?"

"Before school."

"He's probably pissed all over the floor by now. Go on, there's no reason for you to stay. Phoebe's taking good care of me. I won't heal any faster with you hovering over me."

"I didn't realize I was hovering."

Mariel couldn't decide whether to be offended or relieved. But Bruno probably did need to go out, and she could always use the time to prepare tomorrow's lessons for all the students who wouldn't be in school. She closed her book and put on her coat. "Very well, then. May I return to eat supper with you?"

"If you'd like. That would be nice."

She said goodbye to Phoebe and left through the front door. Perhaps the wind had eased a bit, but it was still frigid. Curious, she walked around to where Mike and Hartwig were working. Mike was at the top of the pole while Hartwig unspooled the wire below.

"Are you going through the window with that?" Mariel said. "It's awfully cold to leave a window open."

"Either that, or I'll have to take it past the shithouse, in the door, and down the hall. That don't make no sense."

"Clyde," Mike called down, "you scratch the paint on the walls and I'll kick your ass. Howdy, Mariel. How's Randy?"

"Irritating."

Mike laughed. "Took you long enough to figure that out."

Hartwig took a step closer to Mariel. "You know that story about your husband falling down the ladder ain't true, right?"

"What are you talking about?"

"I seen it all. He was coming out of the post office with Beryl. You know who *she* is. That woman had herself wrapped all around him. I'm sure he was just being a gentleman so she wouldn't slip on the ice." This was spoken in a way to indicate he thought Randall certainly wasn't being a gentleman. "Then it was him, not her, that fell. That was kinda funny, if you ask me. I mean, too bad he got hurt, but you gotta admit it's hilarious."

"I resent the implication."

"I ain't saying anything bad was going on, just telling you what I saw. Mr. Hammon told me not to say anything."

"Yet you felt the need to do so anyway. You are vile, Mr. Hartwig."

"Maybe, but you won't see *me* keeping company with no whore."

CHAPTER TWENTY-FOUR
THE SNAKE IN THE GARDEN
Sunday, March 13, 1887

After the late February snowstorm, a warm spell settled in, with sunny skies and south winds. By week's end temperatures had climbed into the sixties. "Don't get used to it," Randall warned. "We can still get blizzards in March." But a week later the spring-like weather still held. All the snow had melted, except where it had drifted against buildings. As Mariel, Mike, and Phoebe walked to church, they enjoyed the pleasant morning, but not the quagmire in the streets created by the rapid snow loss.

There was a mat at the church door, but with most of the congregation already here, it was itself covered in mud. The nave looked like a pigsty. Mariel and the Hammons found their usual pew and sat down. Reverend Dall made an announcement before the service began. Herb Goss had heard by telegraph that Governor Pierce had accepted their petition to reclaim the county seat, and would be sending a representative to make an official proclamation on April the twenty-second. While a few men applauded, most of the congregation greeted the news with indifference.

Dall launched into his sermon. He usually started quietly before working himself into a lather of hellfire, blasting sin and sinners alike. Mariel found the preacher to be a curious fellow.

He'd buy a man a drink on Saturday night and then, if the man didn't show up for church on Sunday morning, condemn him to perdition for drinking it. Still, the passion in his voice and his message were familiar, a droning she didn't have to think too much about because she'd heard it all before. She was troubled, and needed the pounding rhythm of his words to render her insensate, to submerge her in a place devoid of consciousness or emotion.

"Damnation," Dall cried after each sin he listed.

Communion was normally offered on the first Sunday of every month, but Dall had been ill last week, so it was postponed until this week. Thus far she and Randall avoided communion, as neither of them had joined the church yet. He wouldn't have come today anyway. His knee was not healing as quickly as anyone had hoped. It continued to swell whenever he tried to get out of bed. Nearly two weeks after his mishap, he was still living at the hotel. Mike fudged the books for a few nights, but when Fiona Bohnet put her foot down, they had to start charging him. As Mariel and Randall each earned a decent wage, this wasn't a finance hardship, but the expense of a hotel room rankled her when he could stay in their home without cost.

"Damnation!"

Several things about Randall had been annoying her lately. He barely had time for her, as he was always either laboring over his weather charts or closeted away with Mike, telling war stories. Those stories were her only hope of writing for Herb Goss's newspaper, yet she was not privy to them. Whenever she appeared, they changed the subject.

Nor had she forgotten his refusal to allow her to visit the Indian Reservation.

"Damnation!"

Of course, she hadn't forgotten Beryl, either. She wouldn't

ask Randall about her, wouldn't give him the satisfaction of a denial, but she clearly remembered Hartwig's words: *That woman had herself wrapped all around him.*

Hartwig could have been lying. Probably was. Or the situation could have been what the scoundrel pretended to suggest, that Randall simply helping her cross the icy street.

Yet how often had he helped *her* cross the street...?

When Goss had written about the accident, he hadn't mentioned Beryl. *LOCAL MAN TAKES A TUMBLE*, the headline had read. The article repeated Randall's official story about falling off the ladder.

"Damnation!"

Can you speak no louder, Reverend Dall? she thought. You're failing to numb my mind. Scream, shout, make me deaf to my own thoughts.

Mike and Phoebe sat next to her in the pew, Mike napping on Phoebe's shoulder as Randall often did on Mariel's. Phoebe looked at her, looked at Mike, then smiled and shrugged.

Sadie and Herb Goss were behind her. Herb was awake, but obviously suffering the effects of recent whiskey. His nose was almost as red as his eyes. Mariel had once asked Sadie if she was worried about Herb dallying with Beryl, but she never thought she'd have to wonder about Randall. True, they rarely—never—found occasion to engage in intimate relations anymore. She still loved him, and wished for his happiness. If he couldn't satisfy his needs with her, should she deny him the opportunity to do so with a more willing partner?

Yes. Marriage was more than sex, maybe even more than love. It was trust.

"Damnation!"

Damnation indeed, Reverend. For it was she who was breaking trust, not Randall. Nearly thirty years of faithful marriage, and she was fretting about a rumor, poisoned words hissed into her ear by that snake-in-the-garden Hartwig. She'd allowed him to put ideas into her head that weren't worthy of her.

Randal *was* helping a lady cross the street.

"Shall we sing the sermon hymn?" Reverend Dall asked. After indicating the congregation should rise, he nodded at the pianist, who was not Lottie Hammon, but Victoria Woolridge. "*I Ought to Love My Savior, Vicky.*"

It was a fairly new hymn, one Mariel didn't particularly care for, but she sang with vigor, hoping the volume of her own voice would drown out the thoughts Dall had been unable to vanquish. She'd never taken communion here, but as the song rounded into the first chorus, she decided she would today.

****

"Your knee shouldn't still be so swelled up," Mike said, grasping Randall's right ankle with one hand and knee joint with the other. He slowly moved the lower leg back and forth while Randall gritted his teeth.

"Why don't you just cut the damn thing off?" Randall said. "It would hurt less."

"Quit your whining." Mike lowered Randall's foot to the bed. "Get your ass over to the Jesuit mission. They've got the closest hospital, if you don't mind a priest doctor. His name is Father Brandon. I hear he's a good man."

"I don't care how good he is. Why do I need a doctor? You and Phoebe are doing fine."

"Because you ripped those ligaments all to hell. Your knee joint's flopping around like an old man's pecker."

"Michael Hammon!" Phoebe said from the doorway.

Mike gave her an impish smile. "Like an old woman's—?"

"Michael!" Phoebe and Mariel said together. Mariel was

seated in a plush chair Mike had brought in for her visits.

"What can a doctor do that you can't?" Randall said.

"Oh, I don't know, shit-head, practice medicine, maybe. Look, Randy, you'll never be able to climb that ladder again with torn ligaments. Sooner or later Bobby's bound to run off with the Irish girl, and I sure as hell don't plan on spending the rest of my life doing your job for you."

"It can't be that bad."

"I'll make it so easy even an officer can understand: Get it fixed or put in for a medical discharge. You know how much an Army pension pays?"

"I agree with Mike," Mariel said. "You need to see a doctor."

Randall raised his leg without Mike's assistance. As long as he kept it bent with the foot on the bed, he didn't seem to have much trouble. But when he tried to straighten it, his face turned red with the effort, and pain forced him to give up. "I am *not* this weak."

"It ain't your muscles," Phoebe said. "The ligaments holding your knee together are broke."

"God damn it," Randall said. "Isn't the mission out past the reservation?"

Mariel's ears, and spirits, perked up.

"Yup," Mike said. "Once the mud dries, I could drive you over there in half a day."

Randall must have recognized the eagerness in Mariel's eyes. "No," he said.

"No, what?" Mike said. "You're going if I have to tie you to the wagon."

"But she's not."

"What are you talking about?"

"I would like to visit the reservation," Mariel said.

"What for?" Mike said.

"No," Randall said.

"Yes," Mariel said.

"Why not?" Phoebe said. "You gotta go right through it to get to the mission anyhow. The Indians won't hurt her. Let her go."

"Mind your own business," Mike said.

"Don't listen to him," Mariel said.

"You are *not* going to the reservation," Randall said.

Mariel stood up and jerked her shawl over her shoulders. "How can you stop me?"

"I'm your husband, and I said no."

"Good for you," she said, tying her bonnet as she stormed toward the door. She excused herself as she stepped around Phoebe into the hallway.

Phoebe followed her out, and Mike followed Phoebe. They all went into the hotel's dining area. "Wait," Phoebe said.

Mariel paused. "I'm not angry with you."

"I know," Phoebe said.

"Randy can be stubborn," Mike said, "but don't be too hard on him. He's just cranky his leg's taking this long to heal."

"That has nothing to do with it. He forbade me to go weeks before he injured his leg."

"I don't see why you're so taken with the Indians," Phoebe said. "But there's another way, if you really want to see the reservation. Might not be till after the ground dries out, but now that it's Lent, the Blackfords will be itching to confess their sins. Catholics gotta do that, you know. Weather kept them away from the mission most of the winter, so I figure they got a lot of confessing to do."

Mariel hadn't thought of that.

"Whoa," Mike said. "I got nothing against the Crow, but Randy'll kick my ass if I go along with this. We been friends over twenty years, Mariel. I don't want that to end here."

"Then get back there and convince him to go to the doctor,"

Phoebe said. "Just keep your mouth shut about the Blackfords."

"Yes, Mother." Mike nodded *so long* to Mariel and returned to Randall's room.

"Liam and Bridget like you," Phoebe said. "I'm sure they won't mind if you ride along. But if you want more company than that red-haired brood, I'll go with you one of these days."

"You are a dear friend," Mariel said, thinking, But I am not.

Sooner or later Bobby's bound to run off with the Irish girl. As Theo had run off with Lottie. Now would be the time to speak out. But self-interest clouded her perspective. Would her motive for betraying their secret be for the Hammons' benefit, or her own?

She said nothing about the young lovers.

Phoebe stepped outside with her, shielding her eyes against the sun. "I been to the reservation, once. Pretty sure you'll be disappointed. It's nothing special."

A journey there would involve disobeying Randall. A wife was expected to submit to her husband's will. Mariel had to admit that the prospect of flouting convention was titillating, but it risked irreparable harm to their marriage. Was curiosity worth the repercussions? "I'd still like to see for myself," she said. "Perhaps I'll call on the Blackfords this afternoon."

"Did you know they used to cut up horses for leather and pig food."

"Surely you don't believe Liam would do that?"

"Not in Goss Valley, or I'd've heard about it." Voices inside caught Phoebe's attention. She peered in the door. "Couple of kids fighting over a biscuit. You ain't thinking of walking all the way out there, are you? I'd drive you, but these natives are restless enough."

"It doesn't have to be today."

"Mrs. Hammon," someone called from inside.

"Don't worry, we'll get you there somehow," Phoebe said. "If you see Bobby, Mike says to remind him it's his turn to take the two o'clock readings."

She went back into the hotel and closed the door behind her.

A southwest breeze pushed the ribbons on Mariel's bonnet from her shoulders. She wished spring were here to stay, but Randall was right, there could still be plenty of winter to come. For several moments she stood in the street, thinking and enjoying the warmth. If Liam wasn't knackering horses now, how did he make his living? The family arrived too late in the summer to plant crops, and he didn't have enough land to profit from cattle or sheep. None of the children smelled of manure when they came to school, so it wasn't hogs, either. Could it be the markets, borrowed money, an inheritance— doubtful, considering the condition of the clothes they wore— gambling, bartering, or, if they truly had been Irish Travellers, thievery...?

There was no way to know without asking the Blackfords outright, which was rude. Perhaps someday one of them would volunteer the information. Or Bobby might let something slip, if the conversation was manipulated just so.

The road out of town was a morass of mud and ruts. Liam's farm was a fair distance into the country. Although the Blackford children regularly walked to class, Mariel would be mortified to visit the family attired in a wet dress and filthy shoes. Phoebe and Mike were occupied, Randall wouldn't help her, and she dismissed the idea of renting a horse and buckboard from the stable. That would result in a meeting with Hartwig, who would certainly relay the information to Randall before she'd even left town.

Now that Theo had absconded with Lottie, she wondered who was on call to drive the Abbot Downing wagon. Theo's father Glenn, probably. Unless they had a telegraph in their home, she had no way to contact them, and it didn't make sense to walk there, since the Parley farm was nearly as far as the Blackfords'.

It wouldn't be proper etiquette to arrive at their door unannounced anyway.

CHAPTER TWENTY-FIVE
THE CHILD IN THE PHOTOGRAPH
Friday, March 18, 1887

After she dismissed class for the weekend, Mariel was approached by Megan with the alarming news that Marshal Woolridge had arrested her father this morning and thrown him in jail. When Mariel asked why, Megan answered, "You know, mum."

Sean tugged at the girl's sleeve, insisting she walk home with the rest of the children. "You needn't be blabbing Blackford business," he said.

"Is he still there?" Mariel asked.

"The fine is ten dollars," Megan said, and then Sean whisked her out the door.

Mariel erased the blackboard and collected the *MacGuffeys* from the desks, stacking them in the front of the room. The floor needed sweeping, the windows washed, but cleaning could wait until morning. Ten minutes after putting on her coat, she was standing before John Woolridge in the jailhouse, offering to pay Liam's fine.

"Save your money, Mrs. Erickson," the marshal said. He was seated behind his desk, rolling a cigarette. "I only gave him three days."

"What's the charge?"

"Him and Hartwig again. This time Clyde didn't do anything

to deserve it."

"Why do I find that difficult to believe?" she said.

"Well, you know Clyde. But he didn't start it."

Mariel placed a ten-dollar coin on the desk. "I should like him to be released immediately."

Woolridge appraised her as if she'd gone mad, then shrugged. "Wouldn't hurt him to cool off some more, but you want to throw your money away, who am I to argue? I'll get him."

He took the keys from a hook behind his desk and went into the back room, unlit cigarette hanging from his mouth. When he returned, Liam was with him, bedraggled, bruised, and obviously still suffering the effects of drink. He wore a rumpled black overcoat and derby, and smelled as if he'd slept in an outhouse.

"Evening, mum," Liam said. "This is most kind of you...."

"I've something to discuss with you anyway, Mr. Blackford."

"The children's schoolwork?"

"No, they're all excellent. What did you do to him in there, Marshal? Look at him."

Woolridge sat down and lit the cigarette. "Wasn't me that done that. Take him. His buckboard's over in the baseball field behind Duncan's. Clyde being at the livery, I didn't figure that was the best place for his horses, so I got them in my own barn out back."

Liam tipped his hat to Woolridge. "No hard feelings. Obliged for looking after me horses."

The marshal drew in a long breath of smoke. "Word of advice. Stay away from Clyde. I got no idea why he don't like you. I reckon that's just how he is. But he can be a mean bastard when he's riled. Up to now it's just been fists, and you beat him twice. He ain't ever gonna forget that."

"Shall I run and hide, constable?"

Woolridge blew out the smoke. "You got a wife and what, fifty kids? Rumor is, Clyde shot his own brother back in Pennsylvania, or wherever the hell he comes from. Don't know if it's true, but I'd sure hate to see your wife and young'uns crying over your corpse."

"I'm trusting you gave the same advice to Mr. Pogue?"

"Talk some sense into him, Mrs. Erickson," the marshal said as they left.

Mariel walked with Liam to retrieve his horses and buckboard. They made small talk until he mounted the wagon. "What's this about, mum?"

"A whim, really," she said. She told him about her desire to visit the Indians.

"I'll speak with Bridget, but I know what she'll say."

"Is it a problem?"

"No, except if we stop at the reservation, she'll be wanting you to attend Mass with us at the mission as well."

"I'm not Catholic."

"Aye, and that's why. She thinks the only reason everyone's not Catholic already's because they haven't heard a Mass in all its glory."

Mariel thought about it. Although part of her own culture, Catholicism was as mysterious to her as the ways of the Crow Indians, Latin as incomprehensible as their language. "When?"

"Perhaps Palm Sunday? I don't know that we'll go before then."

Reverend Dall would throw a fit if she missed her own church the week before Easter, but she'd think of some excuse. "That'll be fine."

"It's settled, then. If you've no other plans this evening, would you and your husband do us the honor of dining with us?"

"Randall's away seeing a doctor about his injured knee. I

don't expect him back before tomorrow or Sunday." She didn't say where he'd gone for treatment, for fear of being asked why he didn't take her to the reservation himself. If she explained, Liam might come down on Randall's side.

"I read about his accident in the newspaper. Will you come tonight, then? I'll drive you home afterward."

"Perhaps another time. It would be rude to visit your wife unannounced, expecting to be fed."

"We've thirteen children, Mrs. Erickson. She might not even *notice* you."

Mariel smiled. It would a pleasant evening for a ride. "Very well," she said.

****

Liam's house was constructed of the same kind of lumber as Mariel's, with wooden shingles and paint no more than a season old. She'd heard the Blackfords had bought an abandoned homesteader's house, rather than build a new one. The structure was nearly as large as her own—but then, hers only needed to accommodate two adults and a dog. Fifteen people dwelled in this home. *Fifteen.* Where in heaven's name did they put them all?

Liam pulled to a stop next to the door, tethered his horses, and offered Mariel a hand down. "I'll need to bed down the beasties, but I'll show you in first."

As soon as she entered the house, the entire Blackford brood squealed her name with delight. The eleven youngest children charged her and smothered her in knee-to-shoulder embraces. Sean and Megan didn't hug her, but also seemed to approve of her unexpected visit.

"Mariel," Bridget said from the kitchen. "What a pleasure to see you, mum. What have these hooligans done that deserves a special visit from their professor?"

"Not a thing. I wish all of my students were as well-behaved and dedicated as they are."

Liam stepped in behind her. When the children saw their father, they let go of Mariel and rushed to him. Knowing he was incarcerated, they were delighted to see him home so soon.

"A minute, my *Pavee* potato-heads," he said. A small font filled with water was affixed to the wall just inside the door. He dipped the middle finger of his right hand into the water, then touched it in succession to his forehead, his chest, his left shoulder, and his right shoulder. "All right, then. Mrs. Erickson sprung me from the hoosegow."

He tried to pronounce *sprung me from the hoosegow* as an American might, and failed spectacularly. What came out sounded like a mixture of Cockney, Southern swamp, and Yiddish.

Bridget emerged from the kitchen to kiss Liam on the cheek. "She did what from the what?"

"I bailed him out," Mariel said. "Your husband invited me to supper."

"You're always welcome here, mum. I'll just add a bit more vegetables to the stew. Is Lieutenant Erickson coming?"

"He's out of town for a day or two."

Bridget nodded. "Children, where are your manners? Show Mrs. Erickson the house."

"I'll tend the horses," Liam said, and went back outside.

"She's proud we finally have a real home," Megan said.

"Pride is a sin," Bridget said, proudly.

From where she was standing, Mariel saw symbols of their devotion throughout their home: crucifixes above every door, small figurines of Jesus, and what could only be described as a shrine or altar in one corner of the parlor. There a desk was decorated with a large crucifix, a candle, and a porcelain statue of the Virgin Mary, with a Bible on a separate podium.

Noticing her interest, Megan explained, "It's where we worship when we can't go to mass."

"Me and Shannon get to light the candles."

"Shannon, behave," Megan said.

"I'm Rhiannon."

"Bloody hell you are," Sean said, pronouncing it *bluedy hail y'ar*.

"I'm telling Father you cursed," Caitlin said.

"It's all right," Mariel said. "I know their games. And I know which of you is which."

"Do not," Shannon said.

Rhiannon giggled.

"Girls, set the tables," Bridget said. "Boys, go help your father feed the horses and clean the stables. Megan, you escort Mrs. Erickson."

"We want to stay in here with her," Brannon pouted.

"The more of you doing it, the sooner it'll get done. Go."

In a matter of moments all but one of the children had dispersed.

"Follow me," Megan said. "'Tisn't much to see."

Mariel paused before the fireplace. A panoramic series of photographs, glued together and mounted in a frame nearly three feet wide, rested upon the mantel. It depicted all of the children seated on, or standing behind, a large sofa. She leaned in for a closer look. The effect of the separate photographs was seamless, so skillfully arranged they appeared to be a single picture.

Yet something about it seemed wrong. She couldn't put her finger on it, and then Megan tugged her down a hallway. In the back of the house, unseen from the front, were two large bedrooms and a small one, lined up one after the other. Each had a crucifix above the door. The first room, containing seven cots, was in a state of disarray, as one might expect with boys. And, well, it smelled like boys.

The second had six cots, a dresser, and three hope chests. It was immaculate, bedding made, clothes folded, and dainty costume jewelry sparkling in an open box on the dresser. The girls' fastidiousness reminded Mariel of Ellie before those tempestuous teen years descended upon her.

Two rooms, thirteen cots. It must have been bedlam when everyone was present. Somehow Liam and Bridget made it work.

"The last one is Mum and Dah's," Megan said.

"Perhaps I don't need to see that one," Mariel said.

"Don't blame you. I wish we weren't right next to them."

Mariel understood what Megan meant, and her cheeks flushed. "Why don't you and the boys trade rooms?"

"Because then they'd have to traipse through ours to get to theirs."

"You've a barn out back, I assume?"

"Aye, and a smokehouse, and three outhouses. Our own people'd call us 'lace curtain Irish' if they knew all that we now possess."

Mariel assumed that was the term Travellers used for members who had set down roots.

When they returned to the parlor, Liam and the boys were back, both kitchen tables were set, and dinner waiting. Most of the children were seated at the larger rectangular table, while Liam, Bridget, and Sean were at the smaller round one. There were two empty chairs for Megan and Mariel.

"Will you join us in a prayer?" Bridget said.

"Of course."

She and Megan took a seat.

Mariel followed the Blackfords' lead, bowing her head and folding her hands together.

"Bless us, oh Lord," they all chanted, "and these thy gifts, which we are about to receive, from thy bounty, through Christ, Our Lord. Amen."

Their prayer of grace wasn't so very different from her own. But then fifteen hands, precise as a choreographed dance, simultaneously crossed themselves. That *was* different.

From where she was positioned, Mariel had a good view of the panoramic photograph. As Bridget ladled stew into each bowl, she suddenly realized what was wrong. She counted twice to be certain, but there it was: the picture had fourteen children. She was close enough to make out the faces. Though the photograph must be at least two years old, all of the Blackford children's younger selves were recognizable, except for a boy seated at the end of the sofa. About in the middle, age-wise, he appeared to be staring directly at the lens.

"Counting, aren't you?" Brannon said.

"You lost a child?" Megan said.

"Aye," Liam said. "Terence."

"Was it long ago?"

"Before we left Ireland. He was the reason we had the photograph made."

"And why we gave up the old ways," Bridget added.

"Because he was ill?"

"Because he was dead, mum," Liam said.

It took a moment for the statement to sink in. "The boy in the photo...?"

"Yes, mum."

"But his eyes—"

"Were painted on," Sean said.

"We'd not yet had a photograph made of all the children together. It was the only way."

Mariel knew that photographing the dead was common practice, but the thought of it sent a shiver of revulsion through her. Now it was done to commemorate children as they lay in their coffins, but in the past the dead, children and adults, were frequently posed as if they were alive, interacting with surviving siblings or spouses.

My God, she thought, the boy's *eyes*....

They were painted on.

Thirteen living children and a dead one seated among them as if his soul were still present. It was so disturbing, so macabre.

Bridget scooped stew into Mariel's bowl. "Are you all right, mum?"

Mariel recalled the daguerreotype of her mother, that pretty young woman whose eyes could never quite lock on her own.

They were painted on.

They were painted *on.*

Mariel became light-headed. *No, Daddy. No. You didn't, you wouldn't....*

****

She lay awake half the night, staring at the ceiling. The picture of her mother was still in the bottom drawer of the highboy where she'd put it the day her furniture arrived in Goss Valley. Skilled artists could paint directly on the negative, their work indistinguishable from the real thing. Photographers used double exposures or any number of other tricks. Were her mother's eyes real? Were they *real*? Mariel had never thought about it before visiting the Blackfords, never considered the possibility, but she was certain she had but to open that drawer and gaze upon her mother's face, and she would know.

She pushed aside her blankets and went into the parlor. When she brought up the flame on the table lamp, Bruno opened his eyes, wagged his stumpy tail, and went back to sleep. She knelt before the highboy. As she pulled on the knob, the lower part of the picture appeared: the frame, the glass, her mother's dress, hands folded primly in her lap.

Just a few more inches....

Look at me, Mama.

But Mama couldn't look at her, and would never look at her, whether her eyes were those of a living person or the manipulation of a clever deceiver.

"No," Mariel said, pushing the drawer shut and rising to her feet. She didn't want to know. Nothing about a photograph was real. Her mother was once a flesh-and-blood woman, a woman who existed in color, who combed her hair and read her poetry and kissed her skinned knees. That was how Mariel would remember her, not as a two-dimensional image pressed behind glass.

When Randall recovered she would have him mail the photograph to Ellie and Everett. Ellie would enjoy displaying a likeness of her grandmother.

CHAPTER TWENTY-SIX
IN HERE THEY'RE JUST MEN
Saturday, April 2, 1887

"Planting season's coming up," Randall said. He was seated at a table in the dining room of the hotel with Mariel, Mike, and Phoebe, his right leg encased in a plaster cast and propped up on an empty chair. The Hammons had invited Mariel to accompany them to the dance after supper. "School will be ending soon. You're always so restless when you're not teaching."

"I'm aware of that," Mariel said. She took a sip of Phoebe's fine potato porridge.

"I have a proposition for you. You want to write for the *Sentinel*. If you'll forget this nonsense about visiting the reservation, Mike will tell you the story of his escape from Andersonville."

Mariel looked at Mike, who shrugged and nodded. "The devil's deal," she said, without mentioning her planned journey tomorrow with the Blackfords to attend Palm Sunday Mass at the mission via the Crow reservation. "I must give up the one in order to accomplish the other. I shouldn't think the two were mutually exclusive. You've already spoken to Herb Goss about this, I assume?"

"Of course."

"And what assurances did you give him?"

"That you're a reasonable woman who'll compose a fine article to thrill his readers."

Mariel placed her spoon in her bowl. "Mike, you've agreed to this extortion?"

Mike seemed intent on his knife as spread butter onto his bread. "I just want you two to shut up. You're both horses' asses. The only thing worse than the whole town prying into my memories is seeing the way you hack away at each other."

"I know your stories," Phoebe said. "I'll tell them if you don't want to."

"I can do it," Mike said. "But not with Randy here. He'll get his bung in a bunch again about how it was all his fault. With all his whining and carrying on, I won't get a word in. Anyway, Herb don't care how I got my idiot self locked into Andersonville, he's gonna want to know how I got out. And then back in."

"Just tell the damn story." Randall turned to Mariel. "Write for the paper, or visit the Indians. Those are our terms. Choose, dear wife."

"Not our terms," Mike said, "yours."

To listen to the two men bicker, one might believe they had served in the same infantry unit the entire four years. In fact, they had been together for about a week during the war. Their real friendship didn't blossom until after Appomattox Courthouse.

"Why must males be so infuriating?" Mariel said.

Mike guzzled from a mug of Coors, a pilsner beer he'd convinced Fiona Bohnet to ship in from Colorado every month. "You don't gotta decide anything tonight," he said.

"You boys weren't the only ones in the war, you know," Phoebe said.

"Her first husband Jim was killed in 'sixty-three," Mike explained.

"I wasn't talking about him," Phoebe said. "You think it was only men. Well, I got news for you. Women bleed, too."

"Didn't see too many ladies out there getting their backsides shot off," Randall said. "Naturally, there were plenty of widows —"

"Wait here," Phoebe said. "I got a story for you."

She scuttled up the stairs. She and Mike kept a room on the second floor. They slept in the hotel more often than in their own house, especially when school was in session.

"Do you want something to write this down with?" Mike said.

Mariel shook her head. "I'll remember."

Phoebe returned a few moments later cradling a book with worn leather covers. A red ribbon dangled from it, marking her place. "Remember I told you I keep a diary?" she said to Mariel. "I was only twenty-three at Gettysburg. I want you to read this."

"I didn't know you wrote in it that far back," Mike said. "Have I seen it?"

"Only if you were snooping."

Mike affected his best angelic look, but couldn't hold the expression, and his face collapsed into guffaws. "You should see the kind of business she fancies to write about nowadays. Whew! I pull muscles just thinking about some of those positions. That Jim must've been one flexible fella. Not sure I could've done that even when I was a young man."

"Well, you sure as hell can't do it now," Phoebe said.

Mike winked at Mariel. "I've read French novels that made me blush less."

"You read French novels?" she said.

"Everybody hush," Phoebe said. "Take it with you, Mariel. Maybe Herb would like to publish this in his newspaper. I don't care if you look at the rest, but Gettysburg's marked with the ribbon."

"Would it be rude if I open it now?"

"I'd feel funny watching you read."

"Then if you'll excuse me, I'll step into Randall's room. Phoebe, please don't allow them to concoct further conspiracies."

She walked down the hall and closed the bedroom door behind her. The blankets and pillows smelled of Randall. The entire room smelled of him. There was a time the mere scent of him fired her passions.

There was a time. But it had passed, and may not come again once she openly rebelled against Randall's wishes tomorrow.

The sun was setting behind persistent clouds. Light rain plinked against the window pane, like rat feet skittering across an attic floor. Mariel brought up the flame on the lamp and lay back on the bed.

She hadn't known Phoebe before their meeting last summer. She found her to be a pleasant woman, a bit too earthy for her tastes, but a hardy soul nonetheless who had proved to be kind and dependable. The two of them were of a similar age, yet Phoebe seemed older and wiser—immune, or perhaps resigned, to the vicissitudes of the life she'd chosen.

Mariel was tempted to read the diary from the beginning, to learn if the thoughts, feelings, and aspirations of her friend's younger self mirrored her own. What were her dreams and disappointments?

But Phoebe had most wanted Mariel to read about Gettysburg. She lifted the ribbon to open to the pages it marked.

****

I could see the boy was handsome, even screaming as Jim applied the bone saw to his arm. We'd used up the last of our chloroform, and the whiskey hadn't been sufficient for the task. He'd been laying with the dead on the field most of the afternoon, 'til the North's colored gravediggers carried him into our home and put him on the kitchen table. He was in an awful state, white with fever. A musket ball busted his right elbow into splinters, and his forearm hung down at an angle God never intended. He wasn't wearing a uniform, but he must've been a Rebel, because when he cried out to Jesus and Mama and someone named Susannah, it was in a Southern accent.

Even though we'd been cutting soldiers for hours, Jim worked on and on, the teeth of that saw grinding through the boy's arm with a terrible sound. Bone dust clogged air that already stunk of rot, loosened bowels, and vomit. "Tighten that tourniquet," he said. His hard breathing was the only sign of his weariness. His skin was so slimy with sweat that he had to pause often to wipe his hands so they didn't lose their grip.

I did what he said, and soon the arm dropped to the floor. Mercifully, the boy had passed out by then. I had no squeamishness left in me as I picked up the mangled thing by the wrist and took it outside. Our home was full of ailing soldiers, and by now there was a trail of blood across the floor and out the door. I threw the boy's arm onto the pile of severed limbs by the well, where it dislodged a boot with half a leg still inside it.

It was hot that July night. The sun was setting on what, 'til then, was our pretty Pennsylvania countryside. When I was inside I had to steel myself against the moans and the sobbing, or despair would've taken my strength to do what needed doing, but out here at least it was quiet. There were no more cannon and rifle shots, and that awful Reb yell had been silenced by exhaustion, sleep, or death.

Still, I kept my eyes on my feet as I turned back to the door. I dared not look out to the field to see how many more injured and dying might yet come our way.

When I went back in, two Union officers were lifting the boy from the table. They'd spread out their own coats to use as bedding for him. They laid him down tenderly, then brought us the next patient. That poor man had a hole in his gut the size of a teacup. His lungs bubbled like he was breathing underwater.

Jim looked at him and then shook his head at the officers. They set the man aside to wait for his appointment with the everlasting.

"Who's next?" Jim said.

One of the officers placed his hand on Jim's shoulder. "You've done all you can, doc. Rest."

This fight wasn't ours. We were just simple folk caught between two armies. Jim fell into a chair and gazed at the handsome boy. "You gave him your coats. What if he's a Reb?"

"The Rebs are out there," the second officer said, and he pointed to the door. "In here they're just men."

Jim's got strong views against the Confederacy, but he just nodded and leaned his head back against the wall.

While he dozed the officers and I tended to the wounded. I mopped their foreheads and brought them fresh water from the well. Even through all their suffering, the ones who could talk were polite and respectful, calling me ma'am or angel. I'm no angel, but with the respite from fighting, I could open my heart to them. I could hear their cries, and I could hold their hands.

Nothing we did stopped the Lord from taking most of the wounded. The handsome boy had lost too much blood on the battlefield, and when I came to him again, he was awake but slipping away. I thought to ask his name, but I'd learn it soon enough anyway, because men from both sides had taken to sewing their names inside their collars so they wouldn't die unknown.

"Pleased to meet you," I said.

He looked at the bloody stump that used to be his right arm. Then his eyes moved to mine, and I thought I saw anger or reproach in his face. But that lasted only a moment before his expression went soft. With his last breath he said, "Susannah?"

I cradled his head to my bosom as he died and said, "Yes, my dear. It's your Susannah."

✳✳✳✳

Mariel closed the book, dabbed at her tears, and rose from the bed. Her own troubles were nothing, *nothing*. She wondered if Randall had experienced anything like that in the war, and found a new sympathy for him. And what about Mike, caged among those walking corpses of Andersonville?

She lowered the lamp's flame and stared out the window into darkness. The rain was falling more heavily now, streaks of it slithering down the glass and slicing through her reflection. She pulled the curtains, watching her image disappear behind folds of cloth.

Did she really want to write war stories for the *Sentinel*?

She sighed and went to rejoin Randall and the Hammons at the table. Apparently her tears were still evident, because they looked up at her with alarm.

"What's wrong?" Randall said.

"God bless you, Phoebe Hammon."

189

CHAPTER TWENTY-SEVEN
EAGLES LAIR
Palm Sunday, April 3, 1887

"It's not my business," Mariel said, chatting nervously as they approached the Crow Creek Reservation, "but with all these children, how do you make ends meet?"

She sat next to Liam on the driver's seat of the wagon. The nine youngest children rode in the back, while Sean drove the smaller buckboard with Bridget, Megan, Mary, and Ciara on the flatbed behind him.

"We're a different sort of Irish, mum," Liam said. "You've heard we were Travellers. That means gypsies to most, and it's true we've indulged in a fair bit of wandering in our time. In the Irish tongue we were known as *an lucht siúil*. It means 'the walking people.'"

"So you just walked?"

"Aye, walked. No home, no land of our own, nothing holding us to one place. But with so many mouths to feed, we did things the Good Lord mightn't have given His blessing to."

Way ded tangs the gued lard moitent've ginnis bles'n toe. Oh, the music of his words! Snowflakes flitted on a stiff April wind, and Mariel huddled into her winter coat. She could listen to Liam speak all day.

"We'd no ill intent," he continued. "We were just surviving as best we knew how. After many years, I found meself in possession of a few extra handfuls of *punt éireannach*. 'Twas the rare *Pavee* could keep hold of his money a single hour after he gained it, but I think even then Bridget and me knew that we must someday come to rest. Our hearts'd begun to yearn for a true home, and when our dear lad succumbed to the blue death, we took it to be God's sign that it was time. We mean to plant a crop this spring, and make a go of it here as settled folks. Do you understand, mum? We did what we did in *Ériu*, and were hated for it, but we want to do right in America."

"It sounds like a romantic life, simple and free."

"Aye. Like your Indian friends here, before we white devils came a-calling, eh?" Liam removed his hat and scratched the crown of his head. "Surely there'll come a time we'll look back and get misty for the old days. But it was never simple. What man is ever free who's ruled by another man's laws? We were forbidden to squat on private property or on public lands. If we'd had boats we'd've been kept from the sea as well. We were shot at and spat upon and chased out of town. No, mum, to be free is to live alone in a wilderness, unbound by laws or duties to others."

Mariel looked back at the nine children in the wagon, and behind them, in the buckboard, the rest of the clan. She smiled. "You were certainly not alone."

"That we weren't." Liam put his hat back on. "It was no way for our wee ones to live."

They pulled into the outskirts of the Crow Creek Reservation. The remains of Fort Thompson stood at its center. Mike had told her that some years ago the Army turned the fort over to the Bureau of Indian Affairs, after which it had fallen into disrepair. Indeed, it was now no more than a collection of shanties and rundown shops. The main street was rutted and littered with debris. Several Crow Indians, wrapped in blankets, stood in a circle in front of one of the stores. "What about them?" Mariel said. "They were free."

"I can't say, Mrs. Erickson. I don't know their ways."

"May we stop?" she said.

"On our return journey," Liam said. "We daren't be late for Palm Sunday mass."

Mariel scanned the street, determined to take in all she could. There was so much she wanted to learn about this place.

The horses jerked to a halt as some Indians refused to move out of the way. A brave clad in denim trousers and a flannel shirt grabbed the bridle of the lead animal. His braided hair was magnificent, but his eyes bore the dull luster of a defeated man.

"Ah, holy shit-in-the-bed," Liam said.

The buckboard pulled up beside them. "What's happening?" Bridget asked. Even reddened by the raw wind, her cheeks looked pale with fear.

"I've no idea, m'dear."

As the rest of the Crow surrounded the wagons, the youngest of the Blackford children started to fuss and cry.

"It's all right," Mariel said to them. "I don't think they mean us harm."

"Hush, me lovelies," Liam said. To Mariel he whispered, "Don't be wrong, Mrs. Erickson."

A woman wearing a slouch hat emerged from the crowd and approached the big wagon. Mariel wondered if this could be the same woman who, with a child and an old man, had visited her just before Christmas. She recalled the hat, but to her inexperienced eyes, the woman looked identical to every other young female present.

The woman pointed at Mariel and made a beckoning gesture. It was her, then. It must be. "She wants me to come with her," she said.

Liam reached for his Colt. "Begging your pardon, mum, but

that'd be a poor choice."

"Put your gun away, Mr. Blackford. I know her."

The Crow woman nodded and repeated the gesture.

"I'll go as well, then." Liam gave the Colt to Sean. "Only if you have to," he said.

The boy accepted the weapon with grim assurance. In their life as a Traveller, he must have handled guns before. "Aye, sir."

The woman led Mariel and Liam into a store lit by a single candle on the counter. Mariel was appalled at how meagerly supplied the shelves were. In the corner, shrouded in shadow, an old man rocked a papoose. The infant was crying and tugging at his shirt as if it could find its mother's breast there. Mariel's body trembled at the sight, her soul unburdened of a dreadful fear. The child was alive, a condition that wasn't at all apparent in December.

"Thank God," she said to the woman. "I believe you speak English. What is your name?"

"Walks-with-the-Sun."

"How lovely. I'm Mariel."

Pointing first to the child and then to the old man, Walks-with-the-Sun added, "Howling Dog. White Eagle."

"Do you own this store?"

She shook her head. "We... manage?"

"Is White Eagle your grandfather?"

"He is chief."

How sad, Mariel thought. Once a warrior, White Eagle had been reduced in old age to operating a poorly stocked general store owned by his enemies. In winter supplies must be even more difficult to come by.

She introduced Liam and herself. "We're on our way to see the Jesuits. Have you been to the mission?"

"Priests come to us," she said. Then she almost smiled. "With wine."

"It's more than wine, missy," Liam said.

"Shhh," Mariel said, nudging him with her elbow. "When we return from Mass this afternoon, may we visit you again?"

"You are welcome here. This man is not the Angry One?"

Of course that was how she'd remember Randall. He nearly shot them. "No," Mariel said. "My husband stayed home. He hurt his leg."

Walks-with-the-Sun went behind the counter and retrieved a parcel wrapped in cloth. "This will help."

The parcel contained a white poultice. Perhaps it was an old Indian remedy, perhaps no more than salicylic acid powder thickened to a paste. If the latter, it had likely been a gift to the Crow from the Jesuits. But salicylic acid always upset Randall's stomach, so he'd been using laudanum to control the pain instead. She knew enough not to insult her by offering to pay.

White Eagle abruptly stood up and handed Howling Dog to his mother. With a grimace, the old chief pinched his nose shut and scurried into the back room. Mariel could smell the source of his distress. So Crow men were no different than all men everywhere: babies were fine until they needed to be changed. Then they became woman's work.

Mariel fondly recalled when Ellie and Alex were newborns. "May I?"

"You are kind," said Walks-with-the-Sun.

"I am a mother, feeling nostalgic."

Liam looked a little green. "Surely you're not going to...? Here? Now?"

"Good heavens, Mr. Blackford, how can you be squeamish after raising fourteen children?"

"Me and the missus, see, we had an arrangement."

"I'm familiar with such arrangements. Why don't you return to the wagon? I'm perfectly safe here." She gave him the parcel with the powder. "Will you take our friend's gift with you?"

"Be quick about it, if you please. They'll not delay Mass for us."

As soon as Liam had departed, Walks-with-the-Sun brought a rag.

Mariel lifted the child from his blanket and removed the soiled cloth.

"You are kind," the young woman repeated. "We do not forget."

"Nor shall I," said Mariel. Howling Dog had a chubby little face, but his high cheekbones were already evident. He looked at her with eyes nearly black and gurgled happy baby sounds. She cleaned him with the old cloth, wrapped the new one around him, and tied two knots to secure it.

"Thank you," Walks-with-the-Sun said, "Mariel."

"I must go for now, but I'll come back."

"Yes."

Outside, the Indians were gone, and Liam and his family were alone on the street with their horses and wagons. Snow was falling a little heavier now, the wind blowing a little harder. Liam seemed miffed that a child's bottom had taken precedence over a timely arrival at Palm Sunday mass, for he didn't speak again until they were well clear of the reservation.

Mariel, on the other hand, experienced a wave of exhilaration she hadn't felt in years.

CHAPTER TWENTY-EIGHT
THE MISSING AND THE DEAD
Monday, April 4, 1887

Mariel put on her coat as she watched the last of her students file out of the Hammon house. Friday would likely be the last day of school until fall. Although farmers were several weeks away from planting, there were fields to clear, fences to mend, farrowing crates to assemble, and a thousand other preparations necessary in order to grow a successful crop. Any other year Mariel would have lamented the end of classes, but this afternoon her spirits were still high from yesterday's adventures.

Credo in unum Deum, Patrem omnipotentem, factorem coeli et terrae, visibilium omnium et invisibilium, the priest had intoned.

It was the first sentence of the Nicene Creed. Mariel didn't speak Latin, but she owned an English/Latin dictionary, and looked it up when she got home. She loved the sound of the language, loved the idea of it, and those particular words stuck with her. They were accompanied by a half-remembered melody, as if she'd heard them before in a song. Of course she knew the Creed well in English. The entire Mass had been an enjoyable, if somewhat somber, spectacle: the palm fronds, the purple veils, the Stations of the Cross, the chants and responses, the reading of the Passion. She was glad she attended the service, even if the Blackfords hadn't been willing to stop at the reservation again afterward. Little Colm had taken ill, and they were in a hurry to get him home.

That was all right. Her Sunday morning visit with Walks-with-the-Sun had been thrilling enough. Much as she'd loved the Catholic mass, her illicit journey to the reservation had been the highlight of her life in Dakota.

She'd call on the Crow again, sooner rather than later.

Sunday had carried her through Monday as if she'd grown wings. However, now that her day was done and she'd allowed herself to revel in her act of rebellion, she'd face Randall's swift and certain retribution. His wrath would be fearsome. She hadn't seen him since early yesterday, before she left with the Blackfords. He was already furious with her for begging out of Reverend Dall's Palm Sunday service, and surely by now he would have learned what she'd done instead. All it would take was Megan to Bobby, Bobby to Hartwig, and Hartwig to Randall.

Avoiding him wasn't possible, because tonight, of all nights, he was coming home from the hotel. Fiona's guests had had enough of his incessant tapping on the telegraph, and she suggested it was time for him to leave. Mariel decided to postpone the inevitable by stopping at Smith's General Store to buy dog meat for Bruno.

The weather had improved considerably in the past twenty-four hours, a south wind tinged with the promise of blooming things. It was warm enough that she didn't need to button her coat. She unraveled the bun of her hair and let it fall to her shoulders. If loose hair made her look like a post office special, so be it. She was already in trouble anyway.

The only question was how she would respond to Randall's anger. Apologies or more defiance? That was what she was asking herself when she met Sadie coming out of the store. She appeared angry—but then, Sadie was usually in some form of crisis. Before she could ask, Sadie blurted, "Herbert's missing again."

"Again? He's not at the post office?"

"He's not anywhere. Beryl hasn't seen him since this morning."

"Did you look at Duncan's?"

Sadie scowled. "Well, of course. First thing."

"Did he take a horse? Perhaps he's off on this county seat business in Buffalo Prairie."

"That's just it. Governor Pierce's people telegraphed twice today about the ceremony on the twenty-second. They want to know what arrangements are being made. I don't think Herb's done a thing. For God's sake, he's the mayor of Goss Valley. He fought hard for this, and now that it's about to happen, he's off on another drunk. How's it going to look if the mayor can't be bothered to respond to the governor himself?"

Mariel shook her head. "I don't know him well enough to suggest anywhere else. Do you want me to help you find him?"

Sadie's eyes lit up briefly, but her expression quickly drooped. "No. I heard Lieutenant Erickson is going home tonight. You should be there for him. I know it's been a long time since you both slept under the same roof."

Precisely *not* what Mariel wanted to hear, but she smiled and thanked Sadie for her thoughtfulness. "Good luck. I'm sure he'll turn up soon with quite a story to tell."

"He'd *better* have a good story."

****

Randall was on the sofa with both feet on the ground, his left leg bent normally, his right held straight by the cast and balanced on his heel. He wore a shoe on the left foot, and a stocking over the cast to keep his toes warm. A crutch leaned against the armrest.

Mike and Phoebe were seated at the table. Everyone looked grim, although it was an expression of sorrow and worry rather than anger.

Randall glared at her with disgust as she removed her coat and placed Bruno's meat in a cupboard. Their bedroom door was closed, so Randall must have put him in there.

"Sadie says Mr. Goss is missing," Mariel said. "Is that why everyone's so glum?"

"Herb ain't missing," Mike said. "He's over behind the Hartwig's barn, drinking whiskey with Clyde."

"I know where you went yesterday, and what you did," Randall said. "We'll discuss that later. Right now we've got a more pressing problem."

Mariel glanced sideways at Mike and Phoebe. Their faces were a study in misery. Oh, no: Lottie and Theo. The day she dreaded had arrived. She made the decision to tell the truth if they asked her a direct question, but not to volunteer information if they didn't.

"We got a letter from our daughter," Phoebe said.

"After our little falling out, she stayed away from us, so we didn't notice she was gone," Mike said. "Parley, either. Had to be somebody who knew, but nobody said a thing."

"They got *married*," Phoebe said.

Mariel hoped her face didn't look as flushed as it felt. She sat down at the table. "Where?" she said, an honest question, since she truly didn't know, although she suspected, as Lottie had told her they were going.

"Iowa."

"There's a reason I didn't trust that man," Mike said. "If I could get my hands on him...."

"I'll hold him down for you," Randall said, still sneering at

Mariel.

"Did she give any more details in her letter?"

Phoebe shook her head. "Not much. They're in Cedar Rapids now, is all I know. Didn't say whether Theo was working or who they were staying with. Oh, here." She thrust the letter into Mariel's hand. It consisted of four sentences and a signature.

Dear Father and Mother, Theo and I are en route to Cedar Rapids to be among his relations. We were married on March 12 in Sioux City. Please do not be angry with us. We are happy, and we love you both very much.

Your daughter, Mrs. Theodore Parley

"The bastard knocked her up," Mike said. He was clenching his teeth so furiously she could see the movement in his lower jaw even through his thick beard. "She is dead to me."

No, he didn't, Mariel thought, immediately followed by, Please don't ask me about it. She must have looked away too quickly, because everyone noticed her discomfort. "Something you want to tell them?" Randall said.

Since it was her husband asking, not the Hammons, she answered, "As far as I know, Lottie was a virtuous woman. I wasn't well acquainted with her, but I neither heard anything to indicate she was with child. Surely it would have been on the lips of every gossip in town."

"Then why did they run?" Phoebe said, now in full despair, with tears, runny nose, and cracking voice. "Our own daughter didn't invite us to her wedding."

Realizing she was treading dangerous ground, Mariel said, "Would you have gone?"

"Yes," Phoebe said at the same moment Mike spat, "Hell, no!"

After that Mariel didn't need to say more. Their faces took on a sickly hue as they began to comprehend the source of the problem.

Nobody spoke for a full five minutes, although Bruno yipped and whined from the bedroom.

Finally Mike said, softly, "I'm an ass."

They both rose together and gathered their wraps from the coat rack next to the door.

"No," Phoebe said, and she slipped her arm around his waist. "We apologize for burdening you with our troubles."

"Shall I see you out?" Mariel said.

"We know the way."

Randall rose and, using his crutch for support, hobbled toward the door.

"She'll come back," Mariel called as the Hammons walked into the cooling evening air.

They didn't respond.

She closed the door behind them. As she turned back inside, Randall backhanded her with such force she was thrown against the coat rack, knocking both it and her to the floor.

Blood dripped from her nose and lips onto her hands.

"Never disobey me again," Randall said.

Mariel pushed herself to a seated position and pressed the sleeve of her dress against her wounds to staunch the flow of blood. She looked up at him, this raging hulk of a man who was once her ideal of male beauty and chivalry.

She drew in a deep breath.

"You go to hell," she said.

CHAPTER TWENTY-NINE
A SCOTSMAN AND AN IRISHMAN WALK
INTO A SALOON
Thursday, April 21, 1887

Just after noon Mariel was walking Bruno in town when a violent thunderstorm exploded over Goss Valley. The sky transformed from benign overcast to angry black in a matter of moments. Duncan's Tavern being the closest building, she dragged Bruno inside to take shelter there.

Few people were present. Roy Duncan stood behind the bar, where Hartwig and Herb Goss were drinking their lunch. Marshal Woolridge sat in the corner, drenched. He was trying without success to light a wet cigarette. Liam and a man she didn't know were playing a card game. The stranger was wearing a tartan Tam O'Shanter cap. He was rather plump, with graying brown hair and a clean-shaven face, save for bushy sideburns. His skin was wind-burned and rough, making him appear at least a decade Liam's senior.

Liam saw her and waved her to their table. Mariel picked the dog up and joined them.

"Have a game of Maw with us, mum?"

She sat down with Bruno on her lap. He sniffed at the two men without much interest. Old age was rapidly overtaking his poor body. In the space of nine months he'd lost some of his sight, most of his hearing, and an alarming number of pounds.

He was no longer the fat little sack of cannonballs he once was. Skin and bones did not suit him, rendering him even homelier, if that was possible.

"I don't know anything about cards," Mariel said.

"It's better with five anyway," Liam's companion said. His accent was foreign, but not Irish. Scottish, perhaps? "But these other laddies won't play. Perhaps your furry mate'll have a go?"

Mariel scratched Bruno's scruff. "He's more likely to drool on your cards. My name is Mariel Erickson, sir. You must be Mr. Blackford's cousin?"

"Ah, forgive me manners, mum," Liam said. "This is indeed me cousin, Carter Cowan, newly arrived from Edinburgh."

"At your service, ma'am," Cowan said, removing his tam and placing it on the table.

Thunder was carrying on furiously outside, but it wasn't loud enough to drown out Hartwig's voice at the bar. "Well, ain't that just what this town needs, another goddamn spud-nigger?"

"Clyde, don't you start nothing," Woolridge said. He gave up on his cigarette and threw it to the floor.

"I dunnæ mind, constable," Cowan said. "For you see, our friend is mistaken. 'Tisn't true that I'm a spud-nigger. That's my *Pavee* cousin here. The terms for my countrymen are porridge wogs and sheep-shaggers."

"Mr. Pogue's tastes do not run to sheep, I'll wager," Liam said.

"Aye," Cowan said. "He's a cattleman, through and through."

"What the hell's that supposed to mean?"

Hoping to forestall further confrontation, Mariel said, "He means he's from Scotland, Mr. Hartwig, not Ireland." She hugged Bruno a little closer as Hartwig approached their table.

"Same thing."

"Clyde, I'm warning you," Woolridge said. "Herb, walk him back to the stables."

"It's raining," Goss called too loudly. He was seated not twenty feet away, clearly already well on his way to another drunken stupor.

"No worries," Liam said. "Our friend is welcome to remain." He turned to Mariel. "Mrs. Erickson, did you ever hear the one where the Scotsman, the Irishman, and Mr. Pogue here get lost in the jungle?"

"I won't know until you tell it." She watched Hartwig's reaction. His scowl didn't change.

"Seems the three were captured by cannibals. The Chief says, 'We'll eat you for our supper unless you can pass a test.' 'And what is this test?' the Scotsman says. The Chief answers, 'You must each go into the jungle, collect ten of the same kind of fruit, and bring them back here.' Well, that doesn't seem difficult, so the three of them set out. The Scotsman is the first to return, bearing ten limes. 'Now,' says the Chief, 'now you must shove all ten of the fruit straight up your arse without showing any emotion.' The Scotsman gives a mighty effort, but after just three limes he cries out in pain. He is immediately killed by the cannibals. The Irishman is next to return. He has ten very small pomegranate berries. When he hears the challenge, he easily fits the first eight into his arse, but then he starts to laugh on the ninth. He, too, is killed. When the Scotsman and the Irishman meet up in heaven, the Scotsman says, 'Och, man, you could have passed the test. Why did you laugh?' 'Couldn't help meself,' the Irishman says. 'I saw Mr. Pogue coming back with pineapples.'"

All the men save Hartwig guffawed enthusiastically. Mariel thought it crude, but since Hartwig was the, ahem, butt of the joke, she couldn't suppress a little giggle.

"And the Scotsman and the Irishman?" Cowan added. "They

waited in heaven for Mr. Pogue, but he never arrived."

"Think that's funny, do you?" Hartwig snarled. He hooked his left thumb into his belt and rested his right hand on his gun, reinforcing his "poor man's Wild Bill" impression that Mariel recalled from their first meeting in Kimball.

"Aye, lad, I do," Cowan said.

Bruno, though nearly deaf, nevertheless detected the threat in Hartwig's tone. He growled. "Bruno, shhh," Mariel said. "I fear he still doesn't like you, Mr. Hartwig."

"How about I just shoot the old mutt?"

"I wouldn't advise it, Mr. Pogue," Liam said.

"Settle down, Clyde," the marshal said, coming up behind him.

"I don't like it when he calls me that."

"Then pay him no mind. Go back to drinking with Herb."

"Join us in a game of Maw, sir?" Cowan said.

Hartwig patted his six-shooter. "I'll join you out in the street, you son-of-a-bitch."

Cowan laughed so hard his eyes watered. "They really do talk like that in America!"

"'Cause this ol' town ain't big enough fer the two o' us," Liam drawled. His approximation of a cowboy accent was better than the first time Mariel had heard him attempt it.

"Clyde, shut the hell up," Woolridge said. "Nobody's gonna do any shooting in my streets. These folks weren't causing you no trouble, so get your ass to the bar. I'll buy the next round."

"We'll talk again, Blackford," Hartwig said.

Woolridge jabbed a finger at Liam, as if to say—*don't antagonize him*—and escorted Hartwig back to Herb Goss.

Cowan balled his hand into a fist, then opened it quickly in Hartwig's direction as if depicting an explosion. "Boom?" he said.

Liam shrugged. *"Tá sé ina beag bod."*

Cowan smiled and put his cap back on. "*Níos mó oiriúnach do neas bheag ná caorach.*"

Mariel looked back and forth between them. "Do I want to know?"

"No, indeed, mum," Liam said.

****

The thunderstorm ended as quickly as it began, with light hail damage to the shingles and some broken glass in windows that faced south and west. Mariel had feared the weather might turn worse, but she remembered somebody, perhaps Sadie, telling her that this far north twister season didn't start until June.

Even without tornadoes, the deluge was bad enough. Ruts in the street overflowed with water, and the ground in between was a quagmire. There was no way to go anywhere that didn't involve soiling her dress. Nothing she could do about that, but she could carry Bruno to prevent him from dirtying Fiona Bohnet's floors.

Following the incident with Randall, she'd checked into the hotel—as it happened, the same room he'd occupied after his injury. The telegraph unit had been removed, the wire unstrung, and his charts moved back to the post office, but more than two weeks later, the room still bore his scent.

Mike and Phoebe made it clear they stood with her in her grievance against Randall, but they didn't feel compelled to speak with her every time they saw her at the hotel, which was fine with her. Mariel wasn't in a sociable mood and rarely left her room, save for meals and to relieve necessary bodily functions for her and for Bruno.

Randall was already sending her daily notes of apology, and she knew she'd eventually relent and return to him. Although he still wore the plaster cast, his knee was improving, and he could walk with a cane now, rather than the crutch. Mike and Bobby continued to take his weather readings, but Mariel was less inclined to be accommodating. To gain some appreciation for her, she felt he needed to cook his own meals and clean his own clothes for a while, and if that bothered his knee, too bad.

Beryl had offered to look in on Randall, but God help him—*God help him*—if he allowed that woman anywhere near their home. Until Mariel learned the truth about his accident, he would have no more contact with her, thank you very much. Hartwig was a liar, it was true, but Randall had not exactly distinguished himself of late, and as long as she remained angry with him, she was willing to consider any vile possibility.

When she forgave him, *if* she forgave him, she would ask him for his version of the story and do her best to believe him. Until then, she'd stew in the hotel.

Her dress was soaked to mid-shin by the time she arrived at her destination. Bruno fussed briefly, but calmed when she hoisted him to her bosom and carried him like a baby. Inside, Fiona and Phoebe were both scuttling about in a frenzy. When Mariel set Bruno down he ambled down the hall and lay down outside the door to their room.

"That dog better be clean," Fiona said. "I'll not have you messing my floor, either. We got an important guest coming tomorrow, and we just mopped."

"The governor's man?"

"Such a to-do."

Mariel removed her shoes and hoisted her dress and underclothes.

"Not enough." Fiona closed the curtains to the windows on that side of the hotel. "All right, my dear, strip."

"I'll do no such thing."

"All the men are out clucking about the big proclamation,"

Phoebe said. "We've got no children here tonight. Be quick about it. Leave your clothes at the door and go to your room. I'll wash them for you."

Mariel still hesitated. They were women. They didn't care what she looked like.

"Oh, for heaven's sake," Fiona said, "we won't watch."

She removed everything but her barest skivvies and rushed to her bedroom door, nearly kicking Bruno in the process. Once inside he tried and failed to hop onto the foot of her bed. Almost as soon as she lifted him, he curled up and went to sleep.

It was still only mid-afternoon, but Mariel put on her bed clothes anyway. She had nowhere to go the rest of the day, and wasn't hungry. After lighting the lamp she lay down and opened *Huckleberry Finn*, which she still hadn't managed to slog her way through.

Unable to concentrate on Twain's vulgar prose, instead she thought about Carter Cowan and the implications of having more foreigners move to town, particular foreigners who were kin to the Blackfords.

****

Mariel had long since drifted off to sleep when Mike knocked on her door. She knew him by his wheeze even before she got out of bed. She donned her robe and let him in.

"It's after ten. An unusual time for a gentleman to come calling."

He coughed into a handkerchief, bringing up phlegm as white as pus. "First chance I had. My shift just ended."

"This must be important." Mariel returned to bed, sitting upright against the headboard. Expecting him to take the chair, she was surprised when Mike plopped down next to her.

"Let me make this clear," he said, raising the lamp to half flame. "There's no excuse for a man raising his hand to a woman. What Randy did is just plain wrong, and I told him that to his face. If it happens again, I'll knock him on his ass and see how he likes it. But you must know why he didn't want you to go to the reservation."

Mariel leaned forward and hugged her knees to her chest. This was the first time she'd occupied a bed with a man who wasn't her husband. Curiously, she wasn't all that uncomfortable. "I've no idea, Mike, other than Randall's headstrong. His word is Law, with a capital L."

"It wasn't just that. He never told you about New Mexico and the Navajos?"

"I knew he was at Fort Defiance in the 'fifties, before we met, but he never talks about it. What happened?"

Mike looked out the window, and Mariel followed his gaze. The clouds had given way to a lovely starry night. "It ain't my place to speak for him, but if you ever go back home, ask."

"Is that what you came here to tell me?"

"One of them."

"What else?"

"You know Herb Goss's got a drinking problem?"

Mariel smiled. "I believe I've heard that rumor, yes."

"Well, it's bad. So bad I don't see how he's gonna run the post office much longer, let alone be mayor and print a newspaper. Hell, I don't know how the poor bastard's still breathing. His liver's gotta be bloated as a carcass in the sun."

"What has that to do with me?"

"You can't run the post office and you can't be mayor, but some of us think it's important this town's got a paper. I need you to make him show you how to set the type and work the press before it's too late. It's what you want to do. Go do it."

Mariel lowered her head so that her hair fell as a barrier

between herself and Mike. She watched her toes. "We've been through this. If Mr. Goss won't let me write, he surely won't teach me the business."

Following another coughing spell, Mike got off the bed and pulled a chair in front of Mariel. He mopped his nose, mouth, and beard with the handkerchief. "Don't worry, I ain't catching." He turned the lamp's flame up full. "Mind?"

Mariel shook her head.

"I already told you about Tom Beecher," he continued, "and how shitty things was in Andersonville. I didn't tell you how I escaped. Got something to write with?"

Mariel could scarce believe what she was hearing. "But I didn't keep our bargain. I went to the reservation."

"That was Randy's bargain, not mine."

"In the drawer in the nightstand."

Mike retrieved a pencil and some loose sheets of paper and handed them to her, along with *Huckleberry Finn* to give her a solid surface to write on. "There wasn't any other shelter in the camp," he said, "so boys was digging holes in the ground all the time to live in. The Rebs didn't think nothing of it. Well, we dug all right, we dug a tunnel right under the stockade fence. Old Wirz had the bloodhounds on us in less than an hour."

"Slowly, please. I don't know shorthand."

"You gonna write for the paper, you'd best learn it," Mike said, then resumed his narrative, pausing for breath after every few sentences. "I was the only one who made the Flint River. The others were too weak and the dogs ran them down. Soon as I hit the water, I headed downstream. I figured I'd try to meet up with Lincoln's blockade on the Gulf.

"Once the dogs lost my scent, I hid in the greenbelt beside the river. I probably ran ten miles that first night. I slept under a hollow in a tamarack tree down by the riverbank that next day. That wasn't too bad, and I didn't go hungry, either. There was plenty enough grapes and chinquapin nuts to keep me going."

"How long did the Rebels chase you?"

"Hell if I know. They caught the others, so maybe they thought they had us all. All I know is that by the third night, there weren't any signs of them, just me and the alligators. Ever seen a Georgia gator up close?"

"And Lord willing, I never will. Weren't you frightened?"

"I wouldn't want to snuggle up with one, but nah. There's frogs down there the size of gelded pigs, and the gators seemed more interested in eating them than this scrawny sack of bones. Kinda pleased about that, I must say. I did have fun annoying them, though."

"How does one annoy an alligator?"

"By throwing pine knots at their head."

"They probably should have eaten you. Did you make it to the coast?"

Mike scratched his beard, dislodging dried flecks of his last meal. "On the fifth day. But it was useless. When I looked out over the Gulf, the only sign of a ship I could see was the flag on top of a mast, clear out on the horizon. Must've been several miles out.

"Well, wasn't that just a kick in the balls? Here I come all that way, and I got nothing to signal the boat with. It was too far away to see a fire. I couldn't swim to it, and I don't know how to build a raft, even if I had the tools to do it. Which I didn't. What a stupid plan it turned out to be."

"At least you were out of the prison."

"I didn't escape just to say I did it. If I was gonna die anyhow, I might as well have stayed put in camp and saved myself the aggravation." He paused to catch his breath.

"Damned asthma. So I hunkered down for a couple of days, ate me some berries and clams, and made a better plan. Figured

I'd head back up the Flint and meet Sherman's army in Atlanta."

"You knew General Sherman?" Mariel said, pausing her scribbling.

"I knew where he was. Atlanta was the next closest place I could find Union men."

"All that time you were in Southern territory. I'm afraid I'm not that brave."

"Brave, my ass. I was close to pissing myself every step of the way." Mike stood up and stretched. He stopped looking at Mariel as he spoke, as if he were relating the story to himself. "After two days following the river, I turned east and came to a deserted plantation. No one there but two Negroes living in an old cabin on the property. When they saw me in the field, an old man on crutches came out to meet me. That was first human being I'd seen since Andersonville. With my torn clothes and long hair and beard, I must've looked like a wild man. He was plenty nervous about me, but I said don't worry, I'm a Lincoln man. Now, any Reb'd rather be shot than say a thing like that, and he knew it. He smiled at me with those old yellow teeth and said, 'Father Abraham's folk, they always welcome here.'

"That old man took me to his cabin, where I explained to him and his wife about my escape. 'Well, bless your soul,' she said. She cooked up everything they had on hand. 'Honey,' she said, 'you eat all you can. Got to make yourself strong. We don't need it like you do.' Then while I slept, she sewed my trousers. Cotton thread was fifty cents a spool in Reb money, way too expensive to waste on me. But she did."

Mariel thought of both of her encounters with the Crow. *You are kind*, Walks-with-the-Sun had said. *We do not forget.* "I suppose you'll always remember that old man and his wife with fondness."

Mike nodded. "I tell you, Mariel, I don't get it. Those

people? I never even learned their names, but they risked their lives for me, a white man. Rebs had caught them helping a Yank, they'd've slaughtered us all. And it wasn't just cooking and sewing. The old man said I was lucky I made it as far as I did. The roads near the plantation were usually patrolled. I probably wouldn't be so lucky when I went out again, so he led me through the woods, at night, on crutches, to a different plantation, where I met another Negro called Joshua. Younger fella. He was a trustee slave, who pretty much ran the place after all the white folks had left. The Negroes had some kind of network set up, with secret stations all over the place. It was for runaway slaves, but it served my purposes, too.

"I rested up the next day with Joshua. He took me out when the sun went down. The Rebs were thick that night, I can tell you! Likely they were out to shoot them some Negroes, just for fun.

"Me and Joshua were hiding in some pussy willows next to the railroad tracks when two soldiers passed by so close we could hear them talking. Something about wanting the war to end so they could go home. And I thought, well, amen to that. We listened till their voices died away, then crept over the tracks and dropped into another bunch of willows on the other side. This was a great relief, for it looked like we were in the clear. We got to the next station without much trouble."

Mike bent over double as he was seized by a coughing fit so violent Mariel feared he might expire before her eyes.

"Is there anything I can do?" she said.

He straightened up and hugged his sides as if the spell had torn the muscles under his ribs. "I'll have Phoebe rub some chloroform liniment on my chest tonight," he gasped. "Sometimes that helps. Anyway, I'm gonna go see my nephew G.W. down in Iowa next month. That rascal owns the town of Johnson's Landing and half of Waterton. Says he knows a good lung doctor."

Mariel hadn't memorized Iowa's geography, but she couldn't help but wonder how close Johnson's Landing was to Cedar Rapids, where Lottie and Theo were staying. She pretended to yawn. "I'm afraid my youth has fled me, Mike, and taken with it my stamina for late hours. Could we finish another day?"

"Feels like my chest is filled with pudding. Not much left of this part of the story anyhow. Every night I was taken to the next station, where another guide would lead me on. They all knew which roads were guarded and how best to avoid them, but even then we often found it necessary to wait as long as an hour before getting a chance to pass. Along the way, Negro women supplied me with generous midnight lunches."

Mike suddenly stopped talking. For a few moments he simply stared at her, causing her more discomfort than when he'd shared the bed. His face was red from coughing, his forehead wet with perspiration. The lamp's flame was in his eyes.

Mariel looked away, watching her toes again, the stars, the lamp—anything that wasn't Mike. Finally, the silence overwhelmed her, and she said, "This means so much to me. I've always desired to see my name in print. Now Mr. Goss can't refuse me."

Mike cupped her chin and lifted her eyes back to his. His fingers were hardened with calluses, his nails rough and stained gray from a lifetime of work. "There's one more story," he said. "It's the one you need to tell me."

Mariel felt her lip quivering. "You know."

He nodded. "I thought we were friends."

She broke away from his touch and buried her face in her pillow. "Forgive me, Mike. You and Phoebe could not be dearer to me. Lottie and Theo did tell me, but I didn't know what to do. The happiest I've ever been was when I was young and in love. I wanted them to know that feeling."

"And they wouldn't have it if you'd told me?"

Mariel rolled over to look at him. "I'm so sorry. They shouldn't have put me in that position."

Mike rose and walked to the door. Fighting to control his voice, he said, "*I* shouldn't have put you in that position."

CHAPTER THIRTY
WELCOME TO PARADISE
Friday, April 22, 1887

Herb Goss brought in a professional brass quintet from Yankton to play for the county seat ceremony. Two trumpeters, two trombonists, and a tuba player sat on the left side of the podium that had been erected in front of Goss's newly donated courthouse.

Clyde Hartwig and Hank Moehler performed preliminary songs, with Vicky Woolridge accompanying on piano. Hank perched on a stool on ground level, directly beneath the flags and banners, his violin lowered while he waited his turn. Mrs. Woolridge played the introduction to "God Bless Our Glorious Land." Hartwig stood behind the piano, facing the audience. He came in on precisely the right count and pitch, his powerful bass voice deep and luscious.

Governor Pierce's representative, whose name Mariel had already forgotten, occupied the chair of honor next to the Gosses in the center of the podium. While he smiled like a man pretending not to be bored, Goss beamed as if securing the county seat was the culmination of his life's work.

Mike Hammon, Frank Chamberlain, Marshal Woolridge, and Deputy Dalton, having been named official dignitaries for the occasion, sat on the other side of the Gosses. Mike looked alert, Frank pleased, Trippledy sleepy, and Woolridge like he'd rather be mucking an outhouse.

The weather had cooperated with a fine, sunny day, temperatures warm but not too hot. Mariel and Phoebe stood about halfway back in the audience. Randall, still hobbled, had been given a seat in front of the crowd, as had Peg Moehler because of her advanced age. The Blackfords were not present, nor was Liam's cousin Carter Cowan.

On the song's second verse, Hank played harmony above Hartwig's melody. It was lovely, and again Mariel marveled at how filth like Hartwig could produce such beautiful sounds.

Nobody is just one thing, she thought, and that idea nagged at her for the remainder of the song. When it was over, the audience responded with polite applause. Mrs. Woolridge waited for the clapping to subside, then launched into "The Battle Hymn of the Republic." The program indicated it was to be an instrumental featuring Hank on violin, but the crowd was unable to refrain from singing. As if attending a performance of "The Hallelujah Chorus," the dignitaries on the podium rose. The brass quintet came in with powerful rhythms, harmonies, and countermelodies.

Excitement pulsed through the crowd. Even Mariel, who couldn't care less about the county seat or the ceremony proclaiming it, was swept up by a feeling of good will. Her heart raced as she sang, her spirit soared. She'd heard and sung the "Battle Hymn" a hundred times before. She didn't know why it seemed so special today, but when its truth went marching on toward its rousing finale, she was overcome with emotion. Everyone was experiencing the same thing, and the last triumphant chord brought waves of cheers and applause.

"My goodness," Mariel said, "where did *that* come from?"

"I don't know," Phoebe panted, "but I wish it'd come around more often."

Mariel glanced at the program. The band was supposed to

play "The Gladiator March" before the proclamation was read, but any other music would be anti-climatic now. And indeed, when Goss looked back at the band, the lead trumpeter shook his head and shrugged, and all five musicians lowered their instruments.

After the dignitaries took their seats, Goss lifted a speaking trumpet to his lips and introduced the governor's representative, who rose and delivered an even shorter proclamation.

And then it was over. Goss Valley was once again the county seat. The band packed up their instruments without playing another note. The citizens shuffled off to their daily routines, their lives unchanged by the town's status.

"But," Mariel heard one man tell another, "it was a hell of a song, wasn't it?"

****

Mariel had typed the first part of Mike's tale after he left last night. Now, article in hand, she sought out Herb Goss. The ceremony had been over for hours. Hartwig was driving the Governor's man to Kimball to catch the train to Pierre, the podium had been stripped, the banners taken down. She just hoped Goss wasn't drunk yet.

In the post office Sadie shook her head and said, "Nah, he's snockered enough over his big triumph today. He had some errands to run. Should be back soon. Care to wait? I could show you the new hat I got from Silas."

Something about the suggestive way she dropped her voice when she said the milliner's name convinced Mariel that she didn't want to hear the story. "I saw it on the podium."

That seemed to please Sadie. "You noticed. What do you think?"

"Very pretty." Mariel looked at the stairs that led to Randall's office, and to Beryl's room. "There's something I've been meaning to ask Beryl. Is she in?"

Sadie's expression instantly dropped from grin to grimace as she realized Mariel didn't want to talk about either the hat or Silas. "She came in a few minutes ago. Knock on her door. If she throws something, you woke her up."

Mariel climbed the stairs. Randall likely wouldn't be in his office yet, which was good, because she wasn't ready to face him. His groveling could wait.

She heard the muffled sounds of Beryl singing in her room. "Battle Hymn," of course.

The singing stopped when she rapped on the door, but no one answered. She rapped again.

"What?"

"May I speak with you?" Mariel said.

The door opened a few inches, far enough for Mariel to see that Beryl was wearing nothing but a bath robe, which she hadn't bothered to close. "I don't serve ladies," the woman said.

Mariel didn't understand what that meant. "I could come back if this is inconvenient."

"Do I know you? No, wait, don't tell me." Beryl scrutinized her as she tried to recall. "I know I seen you before. Sadie-Lady's friend? Yeah, I remember, you're married to that Army fella that busted up his knee. What do you want?"

"That's what I need to ask you about, Miss Beryl. My husband."

Beryl rolled her eyes. "Oh, for Chrissake, Mrs. Whoever, you think he's been calling on me after hours?"

"Forgive me," Mariel said. "I didn't intend to begin our conversation like this."

She peered around Beryl into her room, which was neat and orderly. The bed was made, with pillows fluffed, curtains drawn, and pretty knick-knacks arranged in rows on a bureau. An iron was heating on top of the stove.

"Never seen a whore's room before, eh?" Beryl said. "Well, what did you expect? Looked even better when I had your husband's office. I was about to straighten my hair. You can come in, if you ain't gonna yell at me."

Mariel pointed at her robe. "Will you close that, please?"

Beryl laughed. "Prim and proper, eh? Can't say as I blame you. I don't much like looking at me, neither." She pulled the door fully open and stepped aside. "Welcome to paradise, honey."

Mariel felt nervous, as if crossing this threshold was entering a realm from which she could never escape. She hesitated, hugging the pages of Mike's story to her bosom. "I really can't stay."

"Then say what you came to say and go. I ain't holding you here."

"I just wanted to know about the day of Randall's accident. Mr. Hartwig said he saw him escorting you across the street when he fell."

"Clyde's an ass, a liar, and the worst lay I ever had, no matter how much he pays."

Mariel didn't expect such directness. However, it came as no surprise to her that Hartwig had availed himself of her services. "I just want to ease my mind. I won't be angry with you."

"Look, ma'am, your husband's a fine looking man. If he'd put money down, I'd've lifted my skirts for him. So what? Ain't my job to keep married men on the straight-and-narrow. Their wives don't keep them happy at home, that's their own fault. But your husband, he's never tried anything with me. I was with him that day, all right, only it was me escorting him, not the other way around."

"What do you mean?"

Beryl looked at her sympathetically. "When he fell off the ladder I heard him calling for help, my room being right underneath. He couldn't walk on account of his knee, so I let him put his arm around my shoulder. He wanted to go see Mike Hammon at the hotel. Only the street was icy. He's a stout fella. Long as he stayed on his feet, I could steady him, but when he slipped again and hit his head, only thing I could do was get out of the way. That's all Clyde saw."

Mariel lowered her eyes. She knew it was true. "I owe you an apology, Miss Beryl."

"Sounds like you owe your husband one, too."

For that, yes. She squeezed Beryl's hand between her own. "Thank you," she said.

"Don't you start crying on me. I hate it when women go weepy. If you don't mind, I'm kinda busy. The iron's hot enough, and my hair ain't gonna straighten itself."

****

Mariel paced in the lobby while Goss read her article at his desk behind the post office counter. He tilted his head back, with his bifocals pushed low on his nose. He was only a little drunk tonight, but he had an open bottle of whiskey on the desk, so it wouldn't be long.

After what seemed like an eternity, he pushed his spectacles up, sighed, and said, "You're certainly persistent."

Mariel stopped pacing. "You wanted something about Mr. Hammon's experiences in the war, and there it is."

"There *part* of it is. This has no ending. From what you have here my readers won't even know if he made it to Atlanta."

"That's next. It could run in installments to build up the suspense."

"I'm not committing to anything until I see the whole story.

221

What if I print this and then Mike decides not to tell the rest? Want to lose subscribers? Start something you don't finish."

"The only reason he stopped was because he didn't feel well."

"Look, Mrs. Erickson, I don't know what to say. You refused to write about hunting coyotes. Now you come to me with half of a story. Is this what I can expect from you?"

True, she'd failed him with the coyote, but it wasn't her fault Mike's asthma got the better of him before he could finish. "I am dependable," she whispered, feeling the hollowness of her words.

"You haven't shown it yet." He pushed the papers across the counter. "Get the rest of the story. Be a professional and clean up the language. If it lives up to the promise of this part, I'll print it. Your byline. Fair enough?"

CHAPTER THIRTY-ONE
YOU DROWN THEM
Sunday, May 1, 1887

A few minutes after six a.m. Mariel opened her door to a bustle of activity in the hotel. She'd decided to go home later this morning, but first she offered to assist Mike in his morning duties. He was expecting a full house, and Phoebe was in bed with a cold.

She found him in the kitchen, looking overwhelmed. "What do you need me to do?"

"Much obliged," he said, wiping his hands on a dish cloth. "If you cook, I'll set the table."

With that he was gone with an armload of tablecloths and silverware.

The hotel's usual breakfast fare included eggs, toast, and sausages, served with coffee or milk, with oatmeal and jam for the children. As soon as she rang the breakfast bell, guests herded into the dining area like pigs at a trough. She fried eggs until she saw yellow-and-white spots in front of her eyes. After that it was the meat and toast. Mike rushed in to collect the plates almost as fast as she could fill them up.

Half an hour later the ordeal was over and Mike called for her to bring a fresh pot of coffee. Church would be starting soon. Many of the guests were already filing out, but the dining area was still about a third full. A familiar man was seated at the first table, along with a woman, three boys, a toddler, and a babe in swaddling clothes. She recognized him as Carter Cowan, Liam's cousin. Mariel offered to refill the adults' cups.

"Sadly, your frontier brew's too bitter for my tastes," Cowan said, his Scottish brogue harsher than the Blackfords' Irish lilt, but enchanting nonetheless. "Have you tea?"

Mariel looked at Mike, who shook his head. "We do have sugar to sweeten the coffee if that will help."

"Thank you, ma'am, it will do," Cowan said. He leaned back in his chair and studied her. "We've met, haven't we? Aye, the woman with the dog at the pub."

She smiled. "Kind of you to remember me, Mr. Cowan."

"This is my wife Tara, and the rest of the Cowan clan."

My goodness, she thought, Irish or Scottish, Liam and his kin certainly know how to breed. "Pleased to make your acquaintance," she said, holding her hand out to Tara Cowan. "I'm Mariel Erickson. I teach school, but today I find myself conscripted as apprentice cook."

"Delighted," Mrs. Cowan said, although she didn't look delighted, and she didn't take Mariel's hand. Perhaps she was simply weary, but beneath her veneer of politeness, she seemed quite cold, even angry. "And a fine meal it was."

Mike brought a bowl of sugar and placed it on their table.

"Have you been in the hotel before?" Mariel asked. She poured coffee for Cowan, but his wife demurred by placing her hand over her cup.

"I've been staying with Liam while we finish our house," Cowan said. "Tara and the children only just arrived. I'm off to shingle the roof now. How much sugar does it take to dilute this poison?"

"Three parts sugar, one part coffee," Mariel jested, "then pour out the coffee."

She excused herself to attend to the other guests. By the

time she'd made all the rounds, cleaned up a child's milk spill, and replenished the outhouse with medicated paper, the Cowans were gone and work had slowed to a normal pace.

The last people to leave were a couple and their two small children, a boy and a girl. The boy was examining a sausage. He held it up and wiggled it, then said something to his sister, who squealed. "Yes," the mother said, "that is *exactly* what it is. It's what happens to little boys who misbehave."

The boy threw the sausage to the floor and fled crying through the door. Mariel smiled, stooped, and wrapped the meat in a rag to take to Bruno.

The dining area finally empty, she joined Mike in the kitchen to tackle the ponderous mound of dishes.

"I'll wash, you dry," he said.

"Mr. Goss has expressed an interest in your Andersonville story."

"'Course he has." He refreshed the hot water in the sink, then added a stack of dirty plates. Passing a towel to Mariel, he said, "Decided to go home, eh? It's about time you stopped being a damn recluse."

"I can't avoid him forever."

"You know Clyde's driving him back to the Jesuits today to have his cast removed? Probably won't be back till tomorrow."

"Seems everyone knows more about my husband's comings and goings than I do."

Mike swabbed the first plate and handed it to her. "Bobby'll help you with your things. I'll stop by sometime after I take Randy's two o'clock readings. We'll talk then. Gotta be this afternoon, 'cause I'm leaving for Iowa in the morning to see my nephew's fancy lung doctor."

She dried the plate, placed it on the counter next to the sink, and didn't inquire about the possibility of his seeing Lottie. "Will you be gone long?"

"No more than three weeks, I hope. Never did care much for G.W., if you want the God's honest truth. The son-of-a-bitch is richer than Croesus, yet he's jealous of me."

"Of you?"

"The war. I fought in it, he didn't. All he got to be was a drummer boy. Thinks he missed out on some big adventure. Like butchery's a thing to be desired. "

"This is difficult for you, isn't it?"

Mike shrugged and handed her another dish. "Talk about it or not, it happened."

"I appreciate your generosity. And after I failed you with Lottie and Theo...."

"Well, hell, if you ain't as much of a whiny-butt as Randy. You didn't fail anybody."

"I didn't know what to do."

"I know that, Mariel. So does Phoebe. Let it go. We hold no grudge in that regard." He stared into the dishwater as he continued scrubbing. "I got nothing against Theo. I just wanted to make sure he did right by my daughter. If I was paying attention, I might've seen how much distress I was causing them. But I had my head stuck south of my bowels."

"You just wanted what was best for them," Mariel said, "as did I."

"Still, it was good you didn't tell me right off. I'd've chased him down and shot him."

Mariel reached into the sink and flicked water into his face. "Oh, you would not."

Mike flashed his impish smile at her. "Maybe not. But I sure would've chewed a big chunk out of his ass. And hers."

"And then you would have embraced them both and offered to build a house for them."

By now Mariel's stack of dishes was growing dangerously tall. She moved it aside and started a new one.

Mike stopped washing for a moment and looked at her. "Is Theo the right man for my girl?"

Mariel touched his shoulder. "I don't know them well enough, Mike. She thinks so, and isn't that enough? Love is such a blessing."

Mike nodded and went back to washing. "You and Randy remember that when he gets home."

****

Bruno was no longer fat, but he still waddled as if he were. His nose recognized home, even if his eyes couldn't. He took his place next to the stove as if he'd never left.

Bobby carried in Mariel's possessions while Megan waited on the buckboard outside. Seemed like Mariel could never think about Lottie and Theo without also thinking of Megan and Bobby. The two made a darling couple. She just hoped two wouldn't soon become three. The way they openly nuzzled each other in public suggested a more enthusiastic canoodling in private.

Beneath her prim and disapproving façade, she envied them that affection.

She rewarded Bobby with a quarter.

"Thanks. Me and Megan are gonna—"

"Shhh. You don't need to tell me."

Bobby gave her a sly wink and a smile. "You're all right, Mrs. E."

Mariel closed the door behind them and listened as their horse clopped away. She'd been in the hotel less than a month, but it felt like ages. She didn't realize how thoroughly she'd missed her home until she returned to it. Dakota in general and this house in particular had become dearer to her in their nine months here than Chicago had in ten years.

She was disappointed to find the place as clean and tidy as when she left it. In that regard Randall had gotten by just fine without her.

Now there was just the matter of what to do about him. She hadn't yet decided what his penance would be, but she felt their disagreement had gone on long enough. It was time for a come-to-Jesus discussion. His daily notes to her seemed genuinely contrite. If nothing else, he'd already suffered in the court of public opinion. Certainly some of the men in town had no qualms about striking a disobedient wife—they claimed it was the natural order of things—but most of the women were vocal in their opposition to the use of violence. They had at their disposal the denial of marital privilege, leverage Mariel lacked. She and Randall hadn't been intimate since Chicago anyway, so she couldn't withhold what was already gone.

But there must be an accounting. Apologies weren't enough. Somehow, some way, she needed to make Randall understand not only intellectually *that* striking her was wrong, but emotionally *why*.

****

"Ever learn how to beat a pack of bloodhounds?" Mike asked. He sat with his elbows on Mariel's table, a mug of hot coffee in front of him. He inhaled the vapors as if their aroma and moist heat were a comfort to his ailing lungs. "The Negroes on the highway gave me a couple of pointers, but turns out their advice came to naught. The way it works is, there's usually three hounds together, one old timer and two younger ones in training. You wade halfway out into a stream, and when they catch up, you jump astride the old one and grab each of the young ones by the neck. Then you give them all a good dunking till they're finished."

Mariel set her pencil down and gaped at him. "You *drown* them?"

"You could, if you're mean enough. But usually they take off howling. There's a better way, though, that don't risk getting yourself bit."

"I should hope so."

"You keep a box of Scotch snuff on you. Drop a little here and there to cover your scent. When a hound gets a snootful of that, he'll never be a tracer again."

"You mentioned the Negroes' advice came to naught," Mariel said.

"Yeah, I got too anxious. I was within a few hours' walk to Sherman's troops that night, so I took the road. I'll be damned if a pack of hounds didn't sniff me out. Next thing I knew, they'd chased me up a gum tree. Their master was a man named Blank. After enjoying my predicament for some considerable time, he called out, 'What y'all doing up there?' and I told him 'I'm trying not to get eaten by your mutts, what's it look like?'

"Soon as he called his dogs off, I came down. He pointed a shotgun at me and asked who I was. I didn't see any point to lying, so I told him straight up, and he marched me over to his plantation. I figured he'd shoot me and be done with it, but he didn't, which I thought was mighty considerate of him. He introduced me to his wife and two daughters, all very handsome women. He had thirty-eight slaves, but not one team of horses or even an old mule.

"Don't think he knew quite what to do with me, but being it was late, they let me sleep in the storm cellar, with the hounds outside the shelter door to discourage my departure.

"The next day at breakfast he found out I could read. I told him I'd been a teacher and that most everybody up north had some schooling. Well, the missus's eyes damn near popped out of her head. That family couldn't read any better than a stone fence. Both parents lamented their daughters' lack of education. They offered me half their plantation if I'd stay and teach them."

"Why would they do such a thing?"

"Why did I give up my house for a school? They'd come to know the difficulties of ignorance, and meant to relieve their daughters of that condition.

"'Course, we all knew I couldn't stay, but before I left, I cut out the alphabet from the Macon newspaper and pasted it on a board for the girls to learn their letters. In one day they had it thoroughly memorized. Should've seen how pleased they were with themselves. They begged for more, but I said it would be impossible. I had to go back, even if it meant to prison."

Mariel sharpened her pencil with a table knife, letting the shavings fall into a waste bin. "Why did you have to go back?"

Mike stared out the window. "Think of it any way you like. Maybe because it wouldn't be right to accept such a generous offer. And maybe because I'd rather die in Andersonville than be shot by my own people for aiding the enemy."

"By teaching girls to read?"

"*Southern* girls. Passions were running high. You been a guest in Andersonville and then turn around and help the people who put you there? Lot of Northerners wouldn't look kindly on that."

"So you chose to go back to prison, after all the trouble you'd endured to escape?"

"Not before old Blank gave me the royal treatment." Mike chuckled. "He turned me over to Governor Orr. His plantation was about thirty miles away, down by Charleston. A thousand acres of the best land in the country, with a slave for every acre. He was sympathetic to my hard run, saying Wirz was probably too cruel for his own soul. Mr. Orr was a refined gentleman.

After a nice meal, he gave me a tour of the plantation. That was a sight I'll never forget. A cotton field big as the Dakota prairie stretched before us, where hundreds of slaves were pulling the cotton and putting it into baskets. The children ran around with glee, bare-assed as the day they were born. Governor Orr deplored their nakedness, but said they couldn't get clothing for them. There wasn't any to be had. The Union blockade was to blame.

"Anyway, I had three good days on the plantation, but then it was time to leave for the provost office in Macon. The governor took me in his personal carriage. He even gave me five Confederate dollars for necessities.

"In Macon I said my goodbyes to Orr and was taken to see the provost. That man sat like a king on the throne. He asked why I'd run, and I told him I thought I'd been in hell long enough. 'Apparently not,' he said, so smug I wanted to put a musket ball in his face. He had soldiers take me to the guard house, but there was no room for me there. 'Put him in the bullpen, then,' he said.

"There were fifteen prisoners there. Some had just come from Grant's army, two from Sheridan's at Shenandoah, and the others from Foster's division in Wilmington. Sheridan's men said they'd been two weeks on the way. They were all hungry. Soon after I had joined them, women came to sell us johnnycake and pies. How happy we were that the Governor had given me the five dollars. But the pies were made without salt or shortening. No wonder. Salt was a dollar a pound, and lard couldn't be bought at any price.

"The next morning the train came, and took me back to Andersonville. When we arrived we were marched in twos over to the gate, where we were searched. Then we were taken to headquarters, which wasn't nothing more than a little log cabin. Inside, Wirz sat behind a desk, shuffling papers around when I was set in front of him.

"A more cruel man I never did meet. His heart was as black as his beard. He must have figured out who I was, because he looked up and said in that foreign accent of his, 'You're the one that got away. You know what I think I'll do with you? I'll hang you, by God.' I just looked him in the eye and said right back, 'You've already killed fifteen thousand of us in this hellhole, so what's one more?' Oh, that set him off, all right. Those papers he was holding started shaking, he was so mad. He yells at me, 'I'll shoot you *and* hang you, goddamn you!'"

Mariel put her hand over her mouth.

"Well," Mike continued, "that convinced me I'd had it, so I said, 'Do it, then. I don't care. I can only die once. Might as well be now.'

"But what he did next surprised the hell out of me and everybody who ever met Wirz. He turned to his sergeant and said, 'Go up to the cookhouse and get a chunk of johnnycake for this son-of-a-bitch.' And then he sent me back into the camp. They hanged him after the war, and rightly so, but I'll never know why he spared me."

****

Mariel had never been a good typist, partly because the order of the letters on the keyboard confounded her, and partly because she was a perfectionist. She couldn't tolerate messiness. Striking through mistakes with a pencil or, worse, with x's, looked amateurish and only called attention to the errors she was trying to cover up. As a result, if she misspelled the very last word on a page, she felt compelled to retype the entire page. Mike's story wasn't lengthy, but her compulsion for clean copy wasted three pieces of paper for every one she completed. She worked until well after dark, finishing around eleven-thirty.

Before retiring for the night she allowed herself to admire her work. She had to admit it was an impressive document, but the best part was the title page. She could just see it splayed in large letters across the top fold of the *Goss Valley Sentinel*.

THRILLING ESCAPE FROM CONFEDERATE PRISON
A True Account
By Mariel Erickson

Proud of herself, she straightened the pages into a neat pile and put them into a folder. Tomorrow she would call on Herb Goss, and her writing career would be launched.

CHAPTER THIRTY-TWO
DEATH IN A PRAIRIE TOWN
Monday, May 2, 1887

No dreams troubled her slumber, and when the sun woke her in the morning, her body hadn't changed positions since she'd gotten into bed. At once fully alert, she looked out the window onto a fine clear day. Since Goss wouldn't yet be in the post office, she took her time dressing. She expected Randall home today, with all the emotional fireworks their reunion would bring. To avoid fretting over that, she concentrated on what she knew about the operation of printing presses, which wasn't much. In order to get the text to print properly, the letters were molded in reverse, as mirror images, then arranged in the machine right to left. Otherwise, the process was a mystery.

Mariel had never seen Goss's press, nor any other, beyond illustrations in books. There were several varieties, big and small, with gears and levers, wheels, plates, and frames, and God only knew what else. She imagined Goss's would necessarily be one of the smaller devices, as he reportedly did everything himself.

With visions of bylines in her head, she emerged from the bedroom humming the tune to "Fountains in the Park." May might indeed be a merry month, but mornings in Dakota were cold, so she put wood in the stove and turned up every lamp in the parlor. Before doing anything else today, she had intended to take Bruno for a nice brisk walk, but he had died in the night.

She knew it the instant she looked at him. He was curled up as always, but his left eye was partially open and reflected none of the light from the flames.

"Bruno," she said. She knelt and touched his side. He wasn't yet cold, but cool, not yet rigid, but stiffening. He hadn't been gone long. If he yelped in his death throes, she'd slept through it. She prayed he hadn't suffered, and indeed, there were no signs of writhing, no expression of pain.

Mariel scooped him up and sat with him in her lap on the sofa, scratching between his ears the way he liked.

She tried to hold in her tears. After all, he was only a dog. People were more important than animals. The Gosses had lost their little Alma. The girl had taken with her to the grave Sadie's happiness and Herb's sobriety. The Blackfords had lost Terence, and in their grief photographed him as if he were alive.

She herself had lost her father, grandfather, and so, so long ago, her mother. She'd cried for all of them. They were human. They were family. They deserved that much.

But Bruno—ugly, drooling, smelly Bruno—was more of a nuisance, constantly underfoot, barking, chasing creatures, costing her and Randall time, money, and aggravation. All he ever did was eat and excrete.

Mariel lowered her face to his fur and wept.

Ellie had loved him so.

She had loved him.

She didn't know how long she sat like that, but when Randall came through the door some time later, he looked at them and said, "Oh, no."

****

She felt silly insisting Bruno be buried in a wooden peach crate and given a proper funeral. She intended to keep his collar as a memento for Ellie. Truth was, her daughter was an adult now. She probably no longer felt sentimental about things she had cherished as a girl, even a beloved pet. It was Mariel who was nostalgic. She retained the keepsakes, believing that one day, as Ellie reached her middle years, she would come for them, seeking reminders of her youth. When she visited, if she visited, Mariel could tell her that this is where Bruno had come to rest, beneath the Dakota sky.

Randall grunted as he dug. The temperature was over eighty, but four inches down the ground remained frozen. "It's like digging through rock," he gasped. Since his right knee still couldn't bear much weight, he had to jump on the head of the shovel with his left foot to drive it into the earth. Mariel suspected that, given his choice, he would've been satisfied to deposit Bruno in the prairie and let the coyotes do their work. "If word if this gets out, we'll be the laughing stocks of the territory."

"Will you say a few words for him?"

"You're not serious." He leaned on the shovel's handle. He'd always produced an inordinate amount of sweat during physical labor, slimy salt mixing with dirt to produce a malodorous vapor.

"Doesn't he deserve some kind of prayer?"

"He was a *dog*, Mariel."

She touched her cheek where he'd struck her. "And I'm your wife."

Randall jumped on the shovel again to force it into the unthawed soil. "Forgive me if I seem uncaring," he said, his tone so neutral she couldn't tell if he was angry, flippant, or simply in pain.

They had much to discuss, she and Randall. Bruno, bless his

little heart, had delayed the conversation, and perhaps in so doing, given them a few minutes together to become accustomed to one another's presence again before delving into the "incident."

"He should be deep enough that other animals can't get at him."

"This isn't helping my knee."

Mariel sighed dramatically, but perhaps it was too much to ask. "Bobby should be finished with your afternoon readings by now. Shall I have him dig the hole when he brings the reports?"

"I'll give him a dollar."

"Until he comes, will you put Bruno in the storm cellar to spare him from the heat?"

Randall wiped his forehead. "I can do that." He bent to lift the crate.

"Wait." Mariel knelt and placed her hands on the crate. She had borne too many loved ones into the ground. There was something she wished to tell him, something profound, but Randall was right, what did one say to a dead dog? No eulogy would come, so she just shook her head. As she rose and turned toward the house, she said over her shoulder, "We'll need to talk, of course."

****

Randall was in the bathtub when Bobby arrived. He'd been weeping and appeared as if he might do so again.

"What is it, Bobby?"

"Is Lieutenant Erickson here?"

"Shall I get him?"

Bobby nodded. "Mr. Hammon left for Iowa this morning, so Mrs. Hammon sent me to get your husband."

"Is Phoebe all right?"

237

"It ain't her. Please hurry."

Mariel went into the washroom. She felt uncomfortable intruding upon Randall's bath, but it couldn't be helped.

He drew a towel over the tub to cover himself when she came through the door. "To what do I owe the pleasure?"

"Bobby's here. He's in tears. He hasn't told me why."

"What the hell," Randall said, rising and letting the towel fall to one side. He stood before her, forgetting modesty.

She turned her eyes away. "I'll wait outside."

Bobby paced between the front door and couch, pounding his fists against his thighs.

"Has something happened to Megan?"

The boy's eyes were bloodshot, his nose runny. He collapsed onto the couch.

"Oh, Mrs. E," he said once, and then again. "It's her father. He was attacked."

Mariel sat next to him and wrapped her arm around him. "Attacked, how?"

"With a baseball bat." Bobby sobbed onto her shoulder.

God in heaven, she thought, trying to remain calm. "Please tell me he's not dead."

The washroom door opened, and Randall emerged wearing only the towel. "What's going on?"

"Mr. Blackford was attacked," Bobby repeated. "He's alive, but Mrs. Hammon says the wound is... it's...." He gulped several times to steady his voice. "She says the wound is mortal. His skull is crushed."

Mariel's first thought was of Bridget and those thirteen children.

She drew Bobby closer. "Who struck him?"

"Who else?" Randall said. "Goddamn him. It's Hartwig."

TRIAL

CHAPTER THIRTY-THREE
THE CHARM OF DISTANCE
Monday, May 9, 1887

It was Mariel's forty-ninth birthday. As a present to herself, she'd bought flower seeds from Smith's store: larkspurs, cranesbills, phlox, coneflowers, marigolds, and black-eyed Susans for summer blossoms, and asters for fall. The prairie was beautiful, but it was wild beauty. She needed structure, a symbol that at least on her property, nature could be bent to her will.

Eventually she'd plant them around her house, but for now, what better place to start than at Bruno's grave? The sun was hot on her back as she knelt before his little cross. The epitaph etched into the wood was simple.

BRUNO, 1875-1887.

Ellie was fourteen when he was born, Alex eight. They'd both adored that silly dog, and would be distraught to learn of his death. She'd have to tell them soon, especially since she now owed Ellie a letter. Last Friday, after all this time, Mariel finally received a postcard from her.

She thought about her daughter's words as she turned her first spade of dirt. The charm of distance was that it was supposed to make communication dearer and reminiscence sweeter. But Ellie had been agonizingly brief, almost terse. She wished her a happy birthday, but neither sent nor asked for other news.

Mariel plotted a patch behind Bruno's grave to hallow his ground with color. She decided not to plant the seeds directly above his peach crate coffin, as they sprouted indiscriminate roots which took their nutrients wherever they could find them. Death sanctified the living, but this wasn't some wild creature buried here, it was her beloved pet. That was a bit too macabre.

The seed packages described the colors of the flowers. She chose bright yellow marigolds for the perimeter. The interior rows would be, in successively smaller squares, orange cranesbills, pink coneflowers, and red phlox in the middle, with purple larkspurs interspersed throughout. The black-eyed Susans would have a special row on either side of the cross, their yellow matching the marigolds and the black center disks serving as eyes to watch over Bruno's resting place. If the seeds grew true and she kept her garden weeded, it should be lovely.

Of course, if Bruno were alive, he wouldn't care how beautiful the flowers were. In fact, the little scamp would probably dig them up and eat the roots.

As she toiled, she wondered what kind of flowers Catholics preferred at their funeral masses. Or was it all candles and incense, holy water and hymns? Not that it mattered. Mariel's blossoms wouldn't be ready in time for Liam. The Jesuit doctor, Father Brandon, had declared no hope for his recovery. A week after the beating, somehow he was still holding on, but he hadn't regained consciousness, and never would.

Her back and joints ached, and her knees were filthy, but she kept digging, planting, and thinking. Liam's attacker, Clyde Hartwig, occupied a cell in Marshal Woolridge's jail, awaiting circuit judge Willard Larrabee, who wasn't due in this part of Dakota until July. It was an open-and-shut case, as five witnesses had seen Hartwig club the back of Liam's head into pulp.

Mariel finished with the phlox at the center, then used a hoe to cover the seeds and erase the footprints she'd made tiptoeing between rows.

Her first Dakota garden was in. She retrieved a bucket of water from the well for her new seedlings' first feeding. Planting around her house was a task for another day, for she intended to visit the Blackfords yet this afternoon. For that she'd need to bathe and change clothes.

Randall came up the path just as she was heading inside, carrying his weather charts. He followed her in and looked at her with amusement. She was filthy, bonnet to boots. "Have you been slopping the neighbor's hogs?" he said.

"Ha ha. I planted flowers for Bruno."

"You made an altar of a dog's grave?"

This would have been a good day for him to refrain from snide comments, given his recent fall from grace. He was mired in a deep hole, and had only just begun his climb out of it.

"This is a garden, not a cathedral."

"Vegetables would've been more practical, but I'm sure your flowers will be pretty." He dumped his charts on the table. "I received a message from Alex's commander this morning. He got his first demerit. He started a fight with another cadet after getting drunk."

First Ellie's letter, and now Alex—this close together, after having heard nothing for so long? What witchery was this? Mariel turned her back toward Randall. "Unbutton me? Was he hurt?"

He unfastened her dress. "They slept it off in jail, and were the best of friends the next day."

"I don't recall him having a taste for alcohol."

"He's a full-grown man now. I had my first drink when I was twelve. Tequila. That stuff was awful. But he's almost twenty. It was going to happen sooner or later."

A Killing Snow

Mariel pulled her arms from the sleeves and stepped out of the dress.

He seemed intrigued as he gazed at her in her skivvies. "Going to the Blackfords' again?"

"After my bath."

"Liam's taken a turn for the worse. Word is he won't last the day."

"That's been the word every night since Hartwig struck him."

"You can't save him, Mariel."

"I didn't say I could. Bridget needs me."

He shrugged and unrolled a map. "Do you want me to fix supper?"

"What do you have in mind?"

"I ordered a cake, for one thing."

Mariel smiled. *Well, what do you know, he remembered my birthday.*

****

The pleasant afterglow of Randall's surprise was short-lived. On the road to the Blackford house she fell in step with Father Brandon, an unusually tall and lanky fellow with crude features and a craggy face that belied his youth. Not yet thirty, he could pass for fifty. She supposed the appearance of maturity lent legitimacy to his dual vocations as both priest and doctor. It was a good thing he was a priest, for surely no lady would consider him matrimonial material.

"Mrs. Erickson," he said gravely. He was carrying the tools of his trade: a Bible, a large crucifix, and a small vial. "How's your husband's knee?"

"Still sore, but getting better. He told me about Mr. Blackford. Is today the day?"

"I only hope I'm in time."

"I'm sure God will wait for you, Father."

Father Brandon almost smiled. "You're a good-hearted woman, Mrs. Erickson, flawed only by misguided Protestantism. I pray one day you'll come to the true faith."

There was nothing Mariel could say to that, so she said nothing.

As they approached Liam's house, they encountered Carter Cowan, his wife Tara, and their five children. Mr. Cowan removed his hat to greet them. "Father," he said grimly. "Ma'am. A sad day, though not unexpected."

"*Dominus vobiscum,*" Father Brandon said, "*et dabo tibi confortari.*"

"Thank you, Father."

The infant in Mrs. Cowan's arms began to fuss. "Hush," she said, her face strangely passive. Perhaps she disliked Liam and felt no compulsion to manufacture false grief. Or perhaps she was simply stoic, like Randall.

Mariel surprised to see Herb Goss, stewed as always, slumped on his backside against the doorframe of the Blackford home.

"My goodness, word travels fast," she said.

"They wouldn't let me in," Goss said. Even from several feet away his breath reeked of whiskey. He slurred his words so badly he was nearly unintelligible.

"State your business here," Cowan demanded.

"*Sentinel.* I thought Blackford might want to tell his side of the story while he still can."

"He can't," Father Brandon said. "You are a disgrace, sir. Mr. Cowan, will you kindly remove this gentleman from the premises?"

Cowan grabbed the shoulder of Goss's shirt and the seat of his pant, jerked him to his feet, and propelled him as forcefully as he could. Goss landed on his face several feet away. He didn't attempt to get up. "I see you around here again," Cowan said, "and I'll load up yer arse with nitro and give you a strong boot. Begging your pardon, Father."

While Mariel had no sympathy for violence, she had none for inebriation, either. She knelt next to Goss. "You should be ashamed."

"Talk to Blackford for me," he whispered, and passed out.

Father Brandon knocked on the door. Megan answered, one arm wrapped around Bobby and the other around her younger sister Frances. Their eyes were puffy and red. Everyone inside was weeping, none more loudly than Bridget.

"Go away," Megan said. "I know why you're here, Father."

The priest touched her face with his fingertips. "Whether I stay or go, child, there's nothing more to be done for him in this life. What path would you have him walk in the next? Wouldn't you prefer him to be with the Lord?"

"I'd prefer for him to be with us," Megan sobbed, but she stepped aside and allowed everyone in. The parlor and kitchen were crowded with people. All the bedroom doors stood open. Mariel could see through the children's rooms into Liam and Bridget's. Bridget was praying beside the deathbed. Liam's face was only just visible above the blankets. The bandages around his head made him look like mummified. There was a small table with a white cloth next to the bed, upon which had been placed a crucifix and two burning candles.

"I must go to him now," Father Brandon said.

At that the Blackford children's weeping grew inconsolable. They looked to Mariel for guidance, their faces stricken with grief and confusion. She was their teacher, and they expected her to have an answer for them. "Bobby, take them back to kiss their father goodbye."

"I'm not Catholic."

"Father Brandon won't mind."

"We're afraid," the triplets said together.

"I know you are." Mariel recalled what should have been the final words in *Hamlet: And flights of angels sing thee to thy rest*. "Father Brandon will open the door for him, but your love will sing him to heaven."

The younger Blackfords resisted, but Megan and Bobby were able to herd them to the back. Cowan followed behind them, while his wife, their children, and Mariel remained in the parlor. She couldn't see the priest through all the tumult, but she could hear his deep voice intoning something mysterious and comforting in Latin. When he was done, there was a moment of silence. Then he said to the children, "Come, and be blessed."

Mariel sat on a kitchen chair and looked at the panoramic photograph above the fireplace. The picture now depicted two corpses, one before death and one after, but corpses nonetheless. If there was charm in distance, there was pain in proximity.

She'd never gotten the chance to say goodbye to her parents, in words or actions, but she had her grandfather. That was the most agonizing kiss since Judas betrayed Jesus, but she wouldn't trade it for anything.

Tara Cowan stood next to the door, cradling the baby to her bosom. The other four children moped about, wishing to be anywhere else. "What're these people to you, ma'am?" she said. "Surely Liam's brood is just another family of filthy immigrants."

The comment was rude, presumptuous, and unkind, one Mariel shouldn't dignify with a response. But she wiped her eyes and said, "I like them. I don't care where they came from."

Mrs. Cowan seemed skeptical, but said no more about it. Instead, she ordered her children to go outside and play. "Tell

Mr. Cowan where to find us, won't you?"

After she was gone Mariel closed her eyes and allowed the tears to come.

"It's my birthday," she whispered.

People were born every day. People died every day. But from now on the anniversary of her birth would forever be linked with the anniversary of Liam's death, and no amount of distance, in time or place, would change that.

CHAPTER THIRTY-FOUR
THE FOURTH ESTATE
Tuesday, May 10, 1887

"Well, I'm not drunk now," Goss said from behind the post office counter. "Correct me if I'm wrong, Mrs. Erickson, but isn't it your wish to write for the *Sentinel*?"

"Of course." Mariel gripped the package she'd come to mail, the photograph of her mother Claire that she thought Ellie might enjoy.

Goss poked a fountain pen at her, causing her to jump back. "I'm running out of patience with you. This is how it works. One: a newspaper reporter goes where the story is, no matter how unpleasant. Two: a reporter does what his editor tells him to do. *I* am the editor of this town's newspaper. *I* make the decisions. If you want to write for me, you need to understand that. Didn't I say I wanted a statement from Liam before he died?"

Mariel pounded her fist on the counter. "How *dare* you lecture me after the performance you put on at the Blackfords' yesterday? You should be ashamed, sir. Yes, you are the editor of the *Sentinel*. You're also a drunken fool. How can anybody trust you? Do you recall the story you demanded I get from Mike Hammon? You promised me you'd print it. Have you done so? Do you plan to?"

Goss was the first to look away. "You have spunk, I'll give

you that. And you're right. I did plan to run Mike's story. Still do. But then this trouble with Hartwig and Blackford came up. People want to read about Andersonville, but right now they're in lathered up over the murder. We've never had one in Goss Valley."

"I understand their excitement, but everybody already knows what happened."

"Do they?" Goss pulled up his three-legged stool and sat with his elbows resting on the counter. "Maybe the attack itself. But what they don't know is why. What was Clyde's quarrel with Blackford? Why'd he do it?"

"Why don't you ask him?"

Goss peered at her over the top of his spectacles. "Why don't you?"

"You want *me* to talk to Hartwig? I despise that man."

"Your point is?"

"Are you giving me an assignment?"

"If you want to write for me, then write for me. Five dollars per week plus a penny for every ten words. More if you learn to typeset." He stood up. "You have something to mail?"

"Yes, to my daughter." Mariel set the package on the counter. "If you could stay sober, you could speak to him yourself."

"That seems to be the problem, doesn't it?"

Interview Hartwig? How much did she really want the job? "When?"

"No one's bailed Clyde out yet."

"You mean go to the jail now?"

"No better time than the present, as they say."

Mariel glanced at the door. Her instinct was to bolt. "Will you accompany me the first time?"

"Nope. Go home, gather your thoughts. Then pick up a pad and pencil and get over there."

Mariel imagined Hartwig behind bars, unwashed and unshaven, as repulsive physically as he was morally. "What should I say to him?"

"'Hey, you no-good murdering son-of-a-whore, why'd you kill Blackford?'"

"You don't mean that."

"No." Goss put her package on a scale and checked a price chart. "Anything breakable?"

"Glass. It's a photograph."

"You'll need better packaging than this. The extra weight will cost you more."

Mariel fidgeted impatiently. "Yes, that's fine. How do I approach him? Just walk in and demand that he speak with me?"

"Why not? Knowing how much Clyde likes to talk about himself, it shouldn't be too hard. He's likely to tell you to go to hell a few times before you get through to him, but reporters have to get used to that kind of thing."

"And when he does that?"

"Have him tell you a story, like Mike did. Everybody's got a story, even Clyde Hartwig."

"And a sordid one it is, no doubt."

"Don't be so sure. He didn't just pop out of his mother's womb a nasty bastard. He got to be that way somehow. Find out. I'll be right back." He went into the office behind the counter and emerged a few moments later with a flat cardboard box. "I'll put a couple of rags on either side of your picture. That ought to give it some protection."

"You're determined not to come with me?"

"I work here until five, have a council meeting at five-thirty, and an engagement after that."

Mariel thought of Beryl. She raised a disapproving eyebrow at him.

"Save your salacious nonsense," he said. "My friend is of the potable variety."

In a way that was more disappointing than an extramarital tryst. But drinking was what Herb Goss did. "Whiskey will be the death of you," she said.

Goss laughed in an eerie, almost unhinged, manner. "Don't you know? I'm already dead."

****

By virtue of the town's status as county seat, the building once known as the Goss Valley Marshal's Office had been renamed the Buffalo County Jail. The office in the front half of the building was painted white, with windows on three sides to admit the sunshine and give the room a cheery look. However, there were no windows in the back where the cells were located. Hartwig's only light was provided by a candle on a small table. His cell was dark, hot, stuffy, and stank to high heaven. The thunder mug that served his bodily needs apparently hadn't been emptied for some time. Luckily it was early enough in the spring that the flies and maggots hadn't come out yet, or whole place would be teeming with them.

"Go to hell," Hartwig said. He was lying on a wooden cot, facing the wall. He didn't move when Mariel announced herself.

"I'd prefer not to do that, Mr. Hartwig," she said.

"I don't give a shit what you prefer. Get out of here."

"Mr. Goss sent me to—"

"He can go to hell with you. He wants to sell papers, least he could've done is come himself, instead of sending some Paddy ass-licker."

Mariel almost smiled. Hartwig was trying so hard to sound tough, a ridiculous stance from a man in an eight-by-six cage. "You don't intimidate me, Mr. Hartwig."

He turned on his cot and pushed himself slowly to his feet. He winced as his joints popped. "I don't like you, Mrs. Erickson. I never did, only now I don't have to hide it no more, 'cause I'm gonna hang anyway."

"And well you should."

Without warning Hartwig lunged at her. Although he couldn't reach her through the bars, she screamed and jumped back.

"Scared now?" he said.

A moment later Woolridge poked his head into the back room. "What're you hollering about, ma'am? Clyde behaving himself?"

"Just making a point," Hartwig said.

"I'm fine, marshal," Mariel said. "He can't hurt me."

Woolridge spit chaw into a tin cup. "Don't stay too long. I can't be late for supper. Vicky's frying chicken tonight. Best in Dakota."

"What about me?" Hartwig growled. "I ain't been hung yet. Till then, you gotta feed me."

"If you're nice to Mrs, Erickson, I'll bring you a drumstick. Otherwise it's whatever slop Trippledy's been giving you."

"Is there ever a time he's unguarded?" Mariel said.

Woolridge shrugged. "Not really. But I wouldn't mind if he escapes. Then I'd get to hunt him down and shoot him."

Hartwig laughed in his sneering way. Woolridge ignored him and returned to the front office.

"You're despicable, Mr. Hartwig," Mariel said. "Liam Blackford was a good man."

"Good, my ass. I could tell you things about that spud-nigger that'd blister your ears."

"Here's your chance. Mr. Goss wants to hear your side of the story. Personally, I don't believe there's anything you could say that could inspire my sympathy. Prove me wrong."

A Killing Snow

"Pay my bail and I'll talk."
"Don't be ridiculous."
"A bottle of whiskey?"
"You're not in a position to bargain."
Hartwig returned to his cot. "Then go to hell."

CHAPTER THIRTY-FIVE
A DAY AT THE RACES
Wednesday, May 11, 1887

At five in the morning it was raining hard. Randall sat at the table, reading through weather charts while Mariel cooked breakfast. She worried about him climbing that ladder to the post office roof. The rungs would be wet and slippery. He shouldn't even be doing it in dry weather, but try telling a man anything. Still, it couldn't be helped. Mike was in Iowa visiting his nephew, and Bobby rarely left Megan's side in her time of grief.

"Liam's funeral is Friday," she said.

"I know."

"Bridget wants him buried at the mission, in a Catholic cemetery."

"I know."

"I plan to attend."

"I know."

"Are you going?"

"Too much to do."

Mariel used the spatula to ladle hot grease over the eggs, keeping the yolks runny, the way he liked them. "You realize the reservation is on the way."

Randall looked up at her with anger in his eyes, but he kept his voice calm. "I'm aware of the geography. Go wherever you want. Just don't antagonize me about it."

"I wasn't trying to antagonize you. Are you ever going to tell me?"

Randall scrutinized a map a little harder. "Tell you what?"

"You know what. Mike said there was a reason you don't like Indians. Something to do with Fort Defiance."

"Mike's in Iowa."

"This was some time ago. I was afraid to ask." She delivered his eggs to him. "What did the Navajos do to you?"

Randall pushed the plate away, then stood up and walked toward the door. "They ended my career," he said, putting on his coat. "And all due to a goddamned horse race."

It seemed impossible that he could tantalize her like that without finishing the story, but that's exactly what he did. Instead, he limped out into the rain, leaving the door open behind him.

****

She found Trippledy leaning back in Woolridge's chair with his hat pulled over his eyes and his feet on the desk, snoring like a flock of quarreling geese. He didn't stir when Mariel entered the jailhouse, but his head snapped forward when she cleared her throat.

"What time is it?" he said.

"Nearly ten."

"I wasn't sleeping," he said.

Mariel smiled. "How long have you not been sleeping, Mr. Dalton?"

The deputy returned her smile. What teeth remained to him were a greenish-black hue. Mariel didn't know what was keeping them in his head. "Oh, 'bout half an hour, I s'pect."

"I should like to speak with Mr. Hartwig."

"Best not, ma'am," he said. "Louisa and the kids are with him."

Mariel listened at the door to the cells in back, but heard nothing. What would Louisa say to him? If Mariel were in her position and Randall were the assassin, what would she say? *I love you anyway? How could you do this to Liam? How could you do this to me?*

All of them, no doubt, with tears and shouting.

Perhaps Hartwig would be less disagreeable with his family present. "I'll just give my respects to Louisa, then," she said. "I'll not be long."

Trippledy covered his eyes with his hat again. "Keep it quiet. I'm working hard out here."

"I see that, Mr. Dalton."

Mariel peered through the door to the back room. Wayne and Jeannette were pouting on the dirty wooden floor, while Louisa slumped in a chair. Hartwig himself perched on the edge of his cot, head down, hands folded together, elbows resting on his knees. He looked up when Mariel entered.

"No," he said in a weary voice.

"Look," Wayne said, "it's the worst teacher in the world."

"Aah-oooo," said little Jeanette.

"Who the hell do you think you are?" Louisa said.

"I apologize for the intrusion—"

"You're friends with those Blackfords. Clyde's going to hang because of them."

The Fragment Society at its finest, Mariel thought. "Did Mr. Blackford attack your husband's baseball club with the back of his head?"

"How can you support them against your own people? They're *Irish*, for God's sake."

"I've come to listen to Mr. Hartwig's version of events."

"You've come to crucify him in the newspaper. Word's out.

Everybody knows it."

"Louisa, I assure you, I'll be fair."

"Oh, piss off."

"Did you bring whiskey?" Hartwig said.

"Of course not."

"Then write what you want. I got nothing to say to you."

"I'll punch you if you don't go away," Wayne said.

He'd do it, too. Mariel had had quite enough of punching, thank you very much. "Mr. Hartwig, if I get you whiskey, then will you speak with me?"

"Show me the bottle, and we'll see."

****

Mariel finally finished *Huckleberry Finn* and, finding its language as vulgar as she'd expected, chose fare more to her liking, poets from early in the century. She was reading Byron's scandalous but aesthetically superior *Don Juan* when Randall got home. It was still raining, and his clothes were soaked through. As soon as he came in he stripped to the waist.

Mariel fetched him a towel from the washroom and returned to the sofa.

"The war wasn't the only time I was a first lieutenant," he said without preliminaries. "The Army needed men with experience, so some officers got promoted above their rank for the duration. Custer was the most famous. He was a general in the war, but captain afterward."

Randall paused to hang his wet shirt and undershirt on the coat rack, then dried his hair and patted his chest and underarms with the towel. Although his body was softer than it had been in his youth, the outlines of his muscles were still visible beneath the padding. "There was no disgrace in being restored to my original rank after the war. But that wasn't my first demotion."

She leaned forward. He'd been a second lieutenant when they'd met in New York. Other than during the war, she had no idea he'd ever been anything but. "Fort Defiance?"

He nodded. "I was a first lieutenant just out of West Point in 'fifty-five. Captain Shepherd commanded the entire Third Infantry, but I was twenty years old and already in charge of Company E. This was years before Kit Carson came along.

"The Army built the fort in 'fifty-one on the Navajos' grazing grounds. They resented us for that, but over time tensions eased."

When he abruptly strode into their bedroom, Mariel was afraid he was going to leave her hanging again. But he'd just gone to remove his boots and trousers, and soon emerged in a robe. He hung his trousers and stockings on the rack to dry next to his coat and shirt. "One of their favorite traditions was horse races. By the time I arrived our relations had become friendly enough for them to challenge us to competition. I must say, it was enjoyable. We all looked forward to it."

He took the poetry book from Mariel's hands, looked at it with his usual disinterest, and gave it back. "Then in fifty-six one of our soldier's horses tripped one of theirs. It was an accident, but the Navajos accused us of cheating. They were furious enough that I feared an attack, so I withdrew my men into the fort." He lowered his head. "I finished ninth in my class, Mariel. I'd just been commissioned as first lieutenant when I arrived in New Mexico Territory. I had a future."

Randall sat at the table and gazed toward the window. She'd seen him in distress before, but never in defeat.

She waited as long as she could bear it before asking, "What happened?"

"I panicked and ordered the men to open fire. Killed thirty Navajos. That led to years of skirmishes and a bigger battle in sixty. We'd finally established a good rapport with them, and I ruined it all in a matter of seconds."

Mariel's reaction was one of dismay rather than surprise. He must have killed men—of course he had, he fought in the War—but she couldn't imagine how he'd hidden such a life-changing event from her for thirty years. Just over a month ago, before he'd struck her, she wouldn't have believed him capable of such actions. Yes, he could be arrogant. Yes, he could be callous. Yes, he could be stubborn, unemotional, and unromantic.

But impulsive? Never.

Now the revelation was less surprising. Still, she wondered how she could have failed to recognize this aspect of his nature. What else hadn't he told her?

On the other hand, she'd rarely questioned him about his life before her. Was that a lack of curiosity, or a premonition that he might tell her more than she wanted to know?

"Were the Indians armed?" she said.

Randall didn't answer directly. Instead, he said, "Shepherd didn't want a scandal, so my role in the bloodshed was never made public. I wasn't court-martialed or dishonorably discharged, but I was demoted from first to second lieutenant and shipped back to New York with the understanding I would rise no further. I wouldn't have, either, except that they hadn't foreseen the Civil War. That postponed their revenge on me for four years."

"First to second doesn't seem like much of a demotion?"

"After the war, no. That was just a reversion to original rank. Any other time, *any* demotion is humiliating. It was worse than being busted back to private. Privates can muster out. But the Army was my life, and they knew it."

For years the reason for Randall's unchanging rank had been of so little concern to her that it rarely crossed her mind, except on the occasions he alluded to his dissatisfaction.

She joined him at the table and took his hand, so large and rough against her own. "Yet you stayed in the Army. You faithfully perform your weather duties, rain or shine. I'm proud of you for that. Most men would have quit."

"Proud of a stupid kid who let thirty goddamned dead Indians wreck his career?"

Mariel jerked her hand away. Now it was all appallingly clear: Randall was willing to acknowledge he'd made a mistake, but refused to accept the consequences. Instead, he blamed the Navajos for having had the bad manners to die when he shot them.

"That's the reason you forbade me to go to the reservation?"

"Remember what I said about not antagonizing me?"

CHAPTER THIRTY-SIX
COFFIN SHIP
Thursday, May 12, 1887

Hartwig sat on his cot in the dark guzzling whiskey. Mariel could scarcely see him. The day was bright and sunny, but there was no window in the back, and he refused to light his candle. The only illumination came from beneath the door to the front office.

"Are you going to talk to me now?" she said. She had a pad and pencil in her purse, but hadn't taken them out yet.

"When I'm drunk enough."

"If I wanted to interview a sot, I'd speak to Mayor Goss."

"Piss on you. You came to me. You can wait."

"How long, Mister Hartwig?"

Hartwig burped. "Until angels shovel snow in hell, Mrs. Erickson. Until I can stand the disgust in your voice. Until I say so."

Lord, how she loathed this man. "Drink up, Mr. Hartwig. I've nowhere else to be all day."

"Ain't that funny, neither do I."

Mariel shifted on her chair. It was rough-hewn, and not particularly friendly to her bottom. Gradually her eyes adjusted to the darkness. Even so, Hartwig was black as a chimneysweep, silhouetted against the gray of his cell. As nearly as she could tell, he hadn't bathed or changed clothes since his arrest. "Will you light your candle, please?"

"I got no desire to look at you."

"I don't particularly care to look at you, either. But I need to see who I'm speaking to."

"For Christ's sake, you know who." He took several more swallows of whiskey, then struck a match and touched it to the wick. "Satisfied now?"

As the flame grew, she noticed the feral look in Hartwig's eyes, the gauntness of his cheeks and body. He'd never been a husky man, but now he appeared emaciated. His whiskers were as patchy as always, but they'd grown over an inch and tangled on his chin and neck like barbed wire. His hair was greasy. He probably had lice. *Hot wig*, as Reverend Dall pronounced his name, was in desperate need of a bath, a shave, and a week of hearty meals.

"You look dreadful," she said. "Don't they feed you?"

"Ever eat jailhouse food?"

"I've never been incarcerated, Mr. Hartwig."

"If you're gonna be a smart ass, we're done."

Mariel held his gaze. She would never forgive him for what he did to Liam. He deserved to hang for it, but his trial wouldn't be for two months, when the circuit judge arrived in Dakota. Until then, absent bail, Hartwig would remain in this bleak, stinking cage, like a dog quarantined for rabies. Like poor Bruno. She wondered if Woolridge ever let him see the sun. Unbidden and unwelcome, she felt the stirrings of pity. "Forgive me, Mr. Hartwig. I didn't mean to sound sarcastic."

"Never saw much use in educating females. I ain't impressed by your ten-dollar words."

She sat quietly as he continued to drink. When he'd emptied half the bottle, she said, "Have you had enough whiskey yet?"

"What d'you want to know?"

She retrieved the pad and pencil. "To begin with, *why*?"

"I was drunk and he was an Irish bastard."

"That's all there was to it?"

Hartwig broke wind loudly. He didn't bother to excuse himself, and she didn't expect him to. It was just another vulgar expression of his disdain for decency. "That ain't enough?"

"No, Mr. Hartwig, it isn't."

"Damn foreigners come to Dakota grabbing up our land, thinking life's gonna be easy. Well, it ain't, unless you got money. We have to work hard, scratching out a sawbuck where we can."

"I've heard you're not without resources."

Hartwig answered by slamming his fist against the frame of his cot. She didn't know why the comment upset him so, but it had certainly struck a nerve. "I'm still in jail, ain't I? You wanted me to talk, so shut up and let me talk."

"Of course. Go on."

"Winter's the worst. It's like them immigrant sons-of-bitches never heard of snow before. Instead of stocking up in the fall like sensible folk, they eat what they grow soon as they grow it. Then when winter comes and nothing's left, they think we oughta share what little we got."

Mariel interrupted again. "Is your scorn for all immigrants, or just the Irish?"

He returned to his cot. The candle was down to a nub now, its remaining flame casting his face in orange and black. He drank another quarter of the bottle before speaking again. "My mother was a Nolan. You know, *Nolan*?"

"An Irish name." A man of Irish ancestry who hated the Irish. Curiouser and curiouser, as Mr. Carroll would say.

"When Ma remarried over here, she didn't want nothing to do with being Irish no more. She knew what that meant. Almost killed her."

"When did she come to America?"

"Before I was born. Forty-seven, I think she said. Everyone was starving in Ireland, so her and her first husband sailed on the *Ajax* for Quebec. Immigrants was crammed below deck like pickles in a barrel. They shit and pissed their own britches. They hardly ate at all, and drank water full of sewage and typhus. People was dying faster than the crew could dump them overboard. Ma said the sharks took to following the ship."

Mariel winced at the grisly image.

"Two months of that," Hartwig said. "Then when they got to the Gulf of St. Lawrence, they wasn't allowed off the boat. The *Ajax* was stuck in a line of ships that had to be checked by doctors before anyone could come ashore. Coffin ships, they called them."

"What about your mother?"

"Goss teaching you how to ask stupid questions, or do you think of them all by yourself? If she died then, I wouldn't be here, would I?" Hartwig took another swallow of whiskey, and another. "But her husband did. He ended up shark food, too."

He spoke passionately, as if reliving the events himself. Perhaps that was an indication of the intensity with which his mother had related the story to him.

"A boat finally came," he continued, "and took her to the hospital on Grosse Isle. She was so sick with typhus she had to crawl down the gangplank. But she rode it out. Afterward she made her way to Detroit and married my Pa, who was German. Said she'd never be Irish again."

"I was born in Detroit," Mariel said.

"Good for you. It's a big town. Lots of people were born there."

Hartwig's tone was still hostile, but she got the sense that, as Goss had suggested, he was warming up to her, since he was the subject of the conversation. "When were you there last?"

"Why, you gonna put that in the paper, too?"

"I won't know what I'm going to write until I have the whole story."

"We moved to Pennsylvania in sixty-five, I guess, about the time Pa mustered out. I was still a boy. Never been back since."

"After my mother died," Mariel said, "my father took me to Ohio."

"What'd she die of?"

Mariel stiffened as she conjured the memory of her mother's face in the photograph, and those maddeningly unfocused—perhaps already dead—eyes. She'd been told Claire's death had been the result of an accidental fall, but she'd never been comfortable with that explanation. Both her father and grandfather seemed uneasy whenever they spoke of it, and that planted a suspicion that remained to this day: If her mother hadn't died in a fall, then what was so sinister that they felt the need to conceal the truth from her?

Her father, her grandfather, her husband. Had men always lied to her?

"I don't know," she said.

"Well, ain't that a hell of a thing?"

The stuffiness and nauseating vapors of the cell were starting to affect her. She felt light-headed. Do your job, she thought. Just do your job. "What was her name?"

"Ma? Kathryn."

"Mine was Claire."

Hartwig raised the bottle in salute. "To mothers."

"Indeed." After a respectful pause, Mariel said. "Help me to understand. Your mother was Irish, and she suffered because of it. I should think that would make you more sympathetic to their plight, not less."

"God *damn*, you're thick." He drained the last of the whiskey. "I'm sick of looking at your face. Go home to your husband and be glad it ain't you in here."

She rose and hurried to the door. "May we resume our discussion another time?"

He tapped on the bottle and said, "Suit yourself."

****

"Storms in Colorado, Wyoming, and Nebraska," Randall said, "heading this way."

"Your charts tell you that?" Mariel said. She sat reading on the sofa while he pored over his papers on the table.

"It's just a matter of deduction. Weather moves west to east. Over the past two days points west have reported thunderstorms. Tuesday they were in Denver and Cheyenne, yesterday Grand Island. They'll be in Rapid City by daybreak."

"So I should plant those vegetables tonight?"

"Or tomorrow morning."

"Liam's funeral is tomorrow."

"I forgot."

"You did not."

"You're right, I didn't. Ten-thirty? You'll be fine going. Getting home could be bumpy."

"Would you rather I not go?"

Randall looked up over his spectacles at her. "Does it matter what I say?"

"Not really."

CHAPTER THIRTY-SEVEN
HENCE, THE TEARS
Friday, May 13, 1887

Everybody in town not named Blackford chose to forego Liam's funeral, save for Mariel, Sadie Goss, Frank Chamberlain, and Bess Baughman, who was attending only out of loyalty to her son Bobby. Bess and Bobby rode in the Blackfords' wagons, which led the way, while Mariel and Sadie accompanied Frank in his open carriage.

Wednesday's rain had been followed by heat and sunshine on Thursday, allowing the muddy trails to harden enough to make passage possible. The party had left before dawn in order to arrive by ten-thirty, when the services began.

Frank's presence was a bit of a mystery. He was the only attorney in Goss Valley, but nobody had an inkling yet whether he would be Hartwig's prosecutor or defender. Whichever he chose, who would take the other side? If Frank himself knew, he wasn't saying.

"I dislike funerals," Sadie said.

"Can't think of anyone who doesn't," Frank said, "except the undertaker. Why go? I've never heard you express any great fondness for the Blackfords."

Quite the opposite, Mariel thought, although Sadie's prejudice against immigrants wasn't as virulent as those of some of the citizens of Goss Valley. She simply parroted the sentiments of the people around her, which most of the time was Peg Moehler, Louisa Hartwig, and the ladies of the Fragment Society. In Mariel's company she tended to echo Mariel. Maybe the woman had no opinions of her own, no essence at all beyond what she absorbed from others.

How sad.

"As mayor, Herb wanted to represent the town at the funeral, but he claimed the priest would've had him shot if he came anywhere near the mission, so he sent me as his proxy. I believe there was an incident at the Blackford home on the day the father died."

"It wasn't his finest moment," Mariel said.

"He was already working on a good drunk again this morning."

"He assigned the coverage to me," Mariel said.

Sadie shook her head. "Why write anything? Nobody will miss Mr. Blackford."

"His family will. I will."

"It isn't as if anyone *wanted* him dead."

"One person did."

"Clyde's version is what they're interested in, not the funeral."

"I'm writing that, too."

They were approaching the Crow Creek Reservation. Mariel wondered if she'd see Walks-with-the-Sun, her child Howling Dog and grandfather White Eagle. She hoped not, because then she'd want to stay and visit with them, and she couldn't. Simple decency demanded she be at the mission to offer support to Bridget and her family.

"You've spoken with Clyde, then?" Frank said.

"You know I have. The whole town knows."

"What's your impression?"

"My impression of Mr. Hartwig may not be spoken aloud by

a Christian woman."

Frank chuckled. "He is a scoundrel, no denying that. What will you write about him?"

She flashed a coquettish smile. "You'll just have to wait."

The sun was an hour above the horizon. There wasn't a cloud to be seen, but the humidity was high and the air heavy. Perhaps Randall's prediction of afternoon storms would come true.

"Do you intend to defend him?" Sadie asked.

Frank didn't answer. Instead, he said, "The Crow are coming out to greet us."

As the Blackford wagons entered the reservation ahead of them, several Indians gathered on the street to watch them pass.

"Do they always do that?" Sadie said.

"Probably hoping we're the supply wagons," Frank said. He clicked at the horses to increase their pace, and soon they were directly on the Blackfords' heels.

Mariel lowered her head, hoping she wouldn't be recognized if Walks-with-the-Sun was in the crowd. In her peripheral vision she noticed the Indians were only spread out along two blocks or so, after which they thinned and disappeared. Still, she didn't risk looking up until they had passed the remains of Fort Thompson.

"Someone you don't want to see?" Frank said.

"Someone I want to see very much," she answered.

****

The Cowans had brought Liam's body directly to the mission on the night he died, and had remained here since. His shrouded casket now rested on a bier by the altar, with candles burning on candelabras all around it.

It wasn't Father Brandon reciting the Requiem Mass. Keeping his back to the congregation, the unknown priest addressed the altar, and therefore, Mariel surmised, God himself. She wasn't entirely certain the man was a priest, for he looked too young to be shaving yet. However, he pronounced the Mass for the Dead with a deep voice that belied his choirboy appearance. She didn't understand Catholic practices enough to know if an ordained priest was required to perform the Rites, or if a monk or deacon was sufficient for the task. Perhaps all Jesuits were priests.

Whatever the young man was, he spoke in Latin. As always, Mariel luxuriated in the sound and rhythm of the language.

The first time she had visited the mission, on Palm Sunday, she had gotten the impression it was quite spacious. However, she'd been over the moon because of her visit with Walks-with-the-Sun earlier that day, so everything had seemed big and wonderful to her. This morning, in the somberness of Liam's funeral, she realized that the stone building was rather cramped, narrow and oblong, like a hallway leading to a cathedral that had never been constructed. Unadorned windows allowed shafts of sunlight to flow in unimpeded, which only served to highlight the mission's smallness. For the time being the structure probably had no need to be larger, as the only Catholics in this part of Dakota were the Blackfords, the Cowans, the Jesuits themselves, and whatever Crows they might have converted.

No Indians and surprisingly few Jesuits were present today. As Mariel had feared, the mourners consisted only of the Blackfords, the Cowans, and her traveling companions. Bridget and most of her children sobbed throughout the service. The exception was Sean who, being the man of the family, behaved with all the bravado and toughness a boy his age thought that entailed. Mariel wished he would cry—wasn't his father worth his tears?—but she knew he wouldn't.

Father Brandon sat between the Blackfords and the Cowans. He and Carter appeared agitated, exchanging red-faced whispers during the young priest's pauses. Tara Cowan was also distraught, although not, Mariel thought, by Liam's death, but by whatever it was Father Brandon and her husband were arguing about. The Cowan children fussed and fidgeted. She'd seen that before in Ellie and Alex when they were young. Impatient and bored with an occasion that didn't concern them, they simply wanted to go home.

Sadie nudged Mariel with her elbow. "Do you understand any of this?" she said under her breath. "Why doesn't he face us when he speaks?"

"It's their way."

"Well, he could at least speak English."

Frank Chamberlain was taking notes. Mariel had no idea why.

The young priest turned and invited the congregation to sing *Libera me, Domine* while he sprinkled holy water on the casket. When the song was finished, he said a prayer for Liam and made the sign of cross. Then Father Brandon and two other robed men stepped forward to roll the casket and bier out of the mission and into the graveyard. The priest walked in front bearing a crucifix and swinging an incense burner.

As they passed up the aisle, the families sang another hymn. The first line was *In paradisum deducant te Angeli*. Mariel deduced "paradise" and "the angels" from *paradisum* and *te angeli*, but couldn't think of any equivalent word for *deducant*. Latin grammar was different than that of English, so the words needn't be arranged in the same order.

The Blackfords were first in line behind the casket. Bridget, bleary-eyed and weary, glanced at Mariel and mouthed, *Thank you*.

The Cowans trudged behind them, the children smiling because they probably thought the ordeal was over. It wasn't. There'd be a committal service as Liam was laid to rest, with many prayers, blessings, and hymns yet to come.

Mrs. Cowan glowered at Mariel, Sadie, and especially Frank. Oh, yes, she'd been crying, too, but hers were definitely tears of anger. Whatever her reason for making the journey here, it was not to mourn Liam.

"Why's she mad?" Sadie said.

"How would I know?"

Frank was closest to the aisle. He said something to Mrs. Cowan, a single word, a word that elicited an instant outburst of real tears. Her husband overheard. He jabbed a finger at Frank, then dragged it across his own throat.

Mariel gasped. She couldn't quite make out what Frank had said, but it must have been powerful to have provoked two such strong reactions.

He wrote something in his notebook and closed it before Mariel could see what it was.

Something was going on here that she didn't understand. She was a reporter for the *Sentinel* now. Should she press Frank to reveal what was happening?

Maybe she didn't want to know.

Sadie wasn't as reticent. Everyone else was out of the mission now. "Mr. Chamberlain! What did you say to her to make her weep so?"

"I merely made an observation. Asked a question, really. I knew I'd be sorry for letting Liam talk me into making that real estate deal for Cowan."

"What did you ask her?" Mariel said.

"Something she didn't want to answer," Frank said. "*Hinc illae lacrimae.* 'Hence, the tears.'"

A Killing Snow

****

The storm Randall had foreseen broke just as they arrived at the Crow Creek Reservation that afternoon. The sky churned, unleashing a gale of rain, accompanied by hail half the size of silver dollars. The terrified horses bolted for the first shelter they saw, the remains of Fort Thompson. Although most of the buildings in the complex were in some state of disrepair, they weren't complete ruins. Most importantly to the animals, much of the fort's livery stable was still useable. There were holes in the roof and wood rot in the walls, but the boards of the haymow above blocked most of the rain and hail.

None of the Indians' horses were here, so the livery appeared to be used only for storage. At some point they'd been prudent enough to bring the hay down from the loft to protect it from the elements. If they were like town folk, they'd bought a large supply last autumn to see their animals through the winter. It was May now, and only a few stacks of bales remained. Except where the rain made it through, the hay was dry and brittle.

Frank had a kerosene lamp in his carriage. He, Sean, and Bobby dismounted the wagons to feed their frightened horses.

"Use the wet stuff," Sean said. "Otherwise it'll just get moldy anyway."

"You know horses," Frank said.

"Had to," Sean replied.

Megan hopped off the wagon to sidle up next to Bobby. He wrapped one arm around her waist as she leaned her head onto his shoulder. He used the other arm to carry hay back and forth, and Megan stuck with him as if she were embroidered to his side.

"Not too close," Bess Baughman said.

"Aye," Bridget agreed.

Bobby and Megan snuggled anyway. Judging from their mothers' resigned sighs, disobedience was normal.

Frank peered out the entrance and looked around to the west. "I didn't think we were going to be able to outrun the bastard. Still black as hell. Make yourselves comfortable. It looks as if we're going to be here a while."

"Randall's going to be angry if I don't come home tonight," Mariel said. It was inevitable in view of what had passed between them recently.

"Herb won't notice," Sadie said. "Sometimes I wish I'd married Silas."

"You both have husbands to go home to," Bridget said hoarsely. She didn't sound bitter, just melancholy. Before the funeral she'd probably been able to keep her mind occupied with the preparations. But now that was all over, and she must be wondering, *What will I do now*?

Once the horses were tended to, all they could do was wait out the storm. Young, sad, and in love, Bobby and Megan perched on a fence between stalls. Bridget and Bess were engaged in a quiet conversation in a corner. Bess embraced Bridget in a tender hug, a lovely, human gesture of comfort. Mariel didn't know how Bridget felt about Bess, but until now she'd not believed Bess was overly fond of Bridget. She supposed one wasn't required to like a person in order to behave decently toward them, and that in itself was an encouraging thought.

Sean paced in the back of the livery. He glanced often at Bobby, as if he feared that in courting his sister, the young man was trying to usurp his place as the family's rightful head.

Bridget's other children were physically exhausted and emotionally spent. They hadn't even left the wagons to stretch their legs or use the buckets Bridget had brought for chamber pots. They remained curled up next to each other, whimpering.

Frank leaned against the livery's entrance.

"What were you writing in your notepad?" Mariel said.

He clenched his jaw. "I've decided to represent Clyde."

Mariel's saliva tasted like bile. "You can't be serious."

"Well, shit," he said, gazing into the rain. Six Crow approached the stable. Thunder and lightning exploded continuously, the rain increasing its ferocity with every bolt. Despite this, they stopped outside, oblivious to the elements. All wore traditional garb, minus the headdresses, not the cast-off white-man's clothes Mariel had previously seen them in.

A young brave confronted Frank, who, as the oldest male, represented the greatest threat. He pointed his rifle directly at Frank's chest. "You have stolen our hay," he said. "We could shoot you."

Mariel wouldn't think an attorney had occasion to stare down the barrel of a gun very often, but Frank didn't flinch.

The same could not be said for the youngest Blackford children. They shrieked and scrambled down to hide beneath the wagons. Sean interposed himself between his mother and the Indians, although Bridget displayed no emotion whatsoever. She seemed numb beyond caring, as if Liam had taken the best part of her with him to the grave. Bess and Megan dived behind separate stacks of hay. Bobby clenched his fists for a fight, prepared to demonstrate that his manliness was equal to Sean's. Sadie fainted, landing with a splat on wet bales. Mariel ducked behind Frank's carriage and peered over the top. Her heart pounded from her temples to her belly. Walks-with-the-Sun and her grandfather would vouch for her, for all of them, if they were here.

But they weren't.

"As you can see," Frank said, "we have children with us. We needed shelter."

The brave bared his teeth in either a snarl or a malicious

grin. "Shelter," he snorted. He lifted his eyes to the sky, allowing the rain and hail to pummel his face. Bare-chested and backlit by lightning, the man's muscles crackled with fire and ice. He was magnificent. "This is our land. It is all you left us."

"We have no weapons."

"That is not our concern. You have stolen our hay."

"I'll pay you for it."

"Must pay first, then take."

"There was no one around."

"We are no one?"

Mariel noticed a few beads of sweat on Frank's forehead. "Are you the chief?"

"No."

After it became clear he wasn't going to elaborate, Frank said, "What happens now?"

The brave conversed with the other men in their native tongue. When they'd reached some sort of consensus, the brave turned back to Frank. Mariel didn't know much about guns, but the Crow all carried what appeared to be single-shot rifles. With six Indians, that was more than enough to dispatch Frank and the two older boys.

"You must go to our jail for two days. If you refuse, we will shoot you."

"Because of *hay*?"

"Because white men steal what is not theirs."

"The Army will come if you detain us," Frank said.

"What more can they do to us?"

"I know Chief White Eagle," Mariel blurted.

All eyes focused on her.

"He is dead," the brave said with dispassionate acceptance.

Good Lord, not the chief, too. She'd just seen him in April, but what did that matter? A minute was enough time to die. "How?"

"He was old."

She stepped out from behind the carriage. Not wishing to appear weak, she held her tears. "These children have just buried their father. We're returning from his funeral at the mission. Will you let us go?"

"How many Crow fathers have died?"

She wouldn't get into a debate about the white man's aggressions and transgressions. While mistreatment of the Indians was undeniable, there was nothing she could do about that. "Where is Walks-with-the-Sun?" she said.

For the first time the brave displayed an emotion other than controlled anger: surprise. "You claim also to know her?"

"She's my friend."

The brave spoke over his shoulder to the others, who laughed for two consecutive seconds before resuming their blank looks. He then barked what sounded like an order, and one of the men trotted down the street toward the shop White Eagle had managed. "We will see," he said.

"I have to make water," Caitlin Blackford whined.

Mariel looked at the brave. He shrugged and waved the girl on.

Ciara and little Caitlin emerged from beneath the wagon. Ciara reached into the bed to retrieve one of the buckets, then led the girl behind a stack of hay. Everyone dutifully averted their eyes, except the Indians, who expressed no interest whatsoever.

"What is your name?" Mariel said.

The brave responded in his own language.

"Your English name."

"I do not have a white-man name."

Sean stepped forward. "Don't you know us? You see us on Sundays on our way to Mass."

The brave scrutinized the boy, then the rest of the

Blackfords. "Fire hair," he said, nodding.

When Caitlin had finished, she returned to her place under one of the wagons. Meanwhile Ciara—valiant, silly, foolish girl—defiantly carried the bucket past the tribal police and dumped its contents in the street. Perhaps her father's death had inured her to fear and common sense. When she rejoined her siblings, they gaped at her with something like awe. Even Sean looked impressed.

Predictably, the Indians were nonplussed. Mariel thought she might even detect a glint of approval in the brave's eyes, as if he respected her spunk.

Moments later Walks-with-the-Sun appeared at the entrance to the livery. The Blackfords weren't the only ones who'd suffered a recent loss. Her grandfather's death must have weighed heavily upon her, because she looked a decade older, her face lined, her haired flecked with gray, her shoulders drooped.

Mariel wanted to rush to her, but the look in the woman's eyes stopped her. It wasn't cold or hateful, it was just... nothing.

"Yes," Walks-with-the-Sun said. She then turned, nodded to the brave, and walked away in the rain.

"You must leave in the morning," the brave said. "And pay us for the hay."

CHAPTER THIRTY-EIGHT
RANDYS WHIRLWIND
Saturday, May 14, 1887

Although the morning sky was clear, evidence of last night's storm was everywhere. The route back to Goss Valley was a quagmire. Mariel gazed over the prairie she had so loved when she first arrived. Large swaths of grass had been knocked flat by wind and hail. She hoped her flowers hadn't been washed out. The horses snorted and strained against the suction of the mud. Fortunately Crow Creek, which wound through the west side of the reservation, didn't intersect their path. Following last night's downpour, it would have been a torrent of raging current, impossible to ford.

This time Bess rode with her and Sadie in Frank's carriage so the Blackfords wouldn't have to go through town to take her home. Frank and Bess sat in the front of the carriage, Sadie and Mariel in the back. Nobody spoke. Bess was sullen because Bobby had again chosen Megan over her. Herb was probably too drunk to notice Sadie's absence. Mariel didn't know how Frank's wife Pearl might react, but Randall would be furious.

With the "incident" still fresh on their minds, Mariel's overnight refuge at the reservation couldn't have come at a more inopportune time. It was yet another sin in the ledger of Clyde Hartwig, without whom the journey wouldn't have been necessary.

She ached to ask Frank why he'd chosen to defend Hartwig, but if he chose to explain himself, which he wouldn't, she didn't want him to do so with Bess and Sadie present. Goss wouldn't want to print printed second-hand news. Mariel didn't know if Bess was a gossip, but Sadie? The best way to get anything known in town was to tell her it was a secret.

She held her tongue.

After a trip that took hours longer than it should have, their wagon finally pulled into the west side of Goss Valley. The roads in town were worse than those in the country, with just as much mud and water, but deeper ruts.

Bess's place was closest. As Frank hopped off the wagon to help her down, the horses guzzled from a puddle in front of her house. Their muscles quivered and their bodies foamed white with sweat. "Drove them too hard," Frank said.

Bess gazed at him forlornly and said, "At least their ordeal is almost over."

He patted her shoulder. "Bobby's a good boy. He knows his way home."

She nodded and went inside.

At the Goss house, Sadie gave Mariel a hug and a quick peck on the cheek. "We've had quite an adventure, haven't we? I'm sure my loving husband will come bounding right out that door with tears of relief that I've arrived safely."

For the briefest of moments Mariel thought she was serious. She and Frank looked toward the door, but it didn't open. Sadie snorted and shrugged. "Imagine that. Remember me to Pearl, won't you, Frank? And to Randall?"

Then it was Frank and Mariel and a wagon covered to its axels in slop. She climbed into the seat next to him. At first the horses resisted his shake of the reins, but when he leaned forward and tapped the rear one's rump with his buggy whip, the entire team lurched forward. "Just a little farther," he said, and it was almost as if they understood.

As the carriage turned south and plodded toward Mariel's house, she stared at Frank's face in profile. He was handsome enough, but his bushy eyebrows gave him an air of frivolity. He must have sensed her looking at him, because he said, "You wonder about Hartwig."

"It had crossed my mind."

"Do you remember that snake oil professor who was here last summer? Shot a chicken out of a cannon? While we were admiring the bird, his assistant was robbing us blind."

"I was in Kimball that day, but I heard about it."

"I don't like Clyde any more than you do. But Liam? He was selling us a bill of goods, just like that flimflam scientist."

"I don't understand."

"Shhh. Listen." They were passing the jailhouse. Inside, Hartwig's magnificent bass voice crooned a melancholy "Swing Low, Sweet Chariot."

For the second time since his crime Mariel allowed herself to pity him. Assassin that he was, he was also a man afraid of his own mortality. That chariot's not coming for you, she thought.

"One thing I'll say for him, that Clyde sure can sing."

"You were about to explain."

Frank turned to her and smiled. "Was I?"

"Is that the way it's going to be?"

Roy Duncan called Frank's name from the door of his tavern. He splashed through a puddle, soaking himself. Frank stopped the carriage.

"Hell, man," Duncan said, "you better have a *real* good story, because you could cook eggs on Pearl's head, she's so mad. She'll have your ass when she gets her hands on you."

"Sounds serious," Frank said, laughing. "I fear my backside will not be her first target."

"She's all in a dither thinking you got yourself killed in the storm. Howdy, Mrs. Erickson."

Mariel nodded. "Mr. Duncan."

"Say, your husband's a real smart man. Yesterday morning he told us something bad was coming. We didn't believe him. Maybe he's got all them fancy machines, but we've lived here longer. Cyclone weather don't start up in Dakota till June. But sure enough, a little twister spun up south of town and took the roof right off of Charlie Koerperich's smokehouse. Folks're already calling it Randy's Whirlwind. Guess we ought to listen to him, huh?"

"He's been at it a long time, Mr. Duncan."

"Best get you home," Frank said. "I've got a few storm clouds of my own to face."

"Been good knowing you," Duncan said before scurrying back to the tavern.

As they lurched forward, Mariel said, "I'm angry with you, Mr. Chamberlain, teasing me so."

"I wasn't teasing. How's Randall going to react to your tardiness?"

"I'm confident no body parts are in danger," she said, although she wasn't at all confident that the same could be said for their marriage. "I'll not stop asking you about Liam."

"Of that I am certain."

They didn't speak again until the carriage reached her house. "Do take care of those poor beasts, won't you?"

"I may be living with them once Pearl gets done with me."

Mariel smiled. "Good luck with your wife, Mr. Chamberlain."

"And with your husband, Mrs. Erickson."

She watched the carriage slosh down the street for a few moments. Then she drew a deep breath and went inside to face Randall's wrath.

He was seated at the table with his head in his hands. When he saw her, he hobbled to her as fast as his bad knee would allow. He threw his arms around her, lifted her off the ground, and wept, "Thank God you're all right."

CHAPTER THIRTY-NINE
INFERNAL DEVICES
Monday, May 23, 1887

Hartwig had refused to see her since Liam's funeral, leaving Mariel at loose ends for the past nine days. School, assuming her services were retained, wouldn't begin again until autumn. She'd already written Mike's story, and couldn't finish Hartwig's until she could speak with him again.

To avoid idleness, her activities of late had consisted of reading poetry, weeding her garden, cleaning house, weeding her garden, shopping for groceries, weeding her garden, visiting the Blackfords, weeding her garden, cooking, weeding her garden, planting carrots, beans, beets and peas—which would also need weeding—and weeding her garden.

Today was a fine and clear Monday, pleasantly warm with low humidity. Mariel walked to Smith's General Store to inquire if Goss had been sober enough to publish the *Sentinel* last Friday. Surprisingly, he had. She paid a penny for a copy and a nickel for a sarsaparilla.

By the time she got home, the morning dew had evaporated from the grass. She sat next to the cross marking Bruno's grave to enjoy the sunshine and read the paper. The leaves of her flowers poked through the ground, but the stems hadn't formed buds yet.

The newspaper was a single large sheet printed on both

sides, the bulk of which was filled with the next week's ads for local businesses. The only two brief items of news were both written by Goss. The first, five sentences long, appeared at the top of the front side of the paper, and bore the headline,

FRANK CHAMBERLAIN TO REPRESENT CLYDE HARTWIG IN MURDER TRIAL.

This correspondent has learnt that attorney Frank Chamberlain has agreed to defend Clyde Hartwig in his murder trial. When Mr. Chamberlain was asked why he would represent a man whose crime was witnessed by so many residents, he replied, "Every man has a right to counsel." Hartwig remains in the Buffalo County jail awaiting trial in July. The name of the prosecutor has been announced. He is Gregory Van Pelt, a Kimball man.

The second story, intrinsically related to the first, appeared at the bottom of the newspaper's verso. It was even shorter, with no headline:

The funeral Mass for Mr. Liam Blackford, late of Goss Valley, was conducted at the Xavier Jesuit mission at ten thirty on the morning of Friday, May 13, 1887, with internment immediately thereafter in the cemetery at that location. Mr. Blackford is survived by a wife and many children.

Mariel didn't like the placement of Liam's story, and didn't appreciate Goss's byline. He assigned her to write about the services, then, without consulting her, wrote the article himself. Goss was angry with her for not going forward with the

Hartwig interviews. But what could she do? As long as Hartwig insisted upon being pigheaded, the marshal wouldn't let her see him.

She gazed fondly at Bruno's grave. She missed his homely face, his fat body and stubby legs, even his disagreeable vapors.

"What should I do, old fellow?" she asked. "Once again I have failed as a reporter. Shall my aspirations never be fulfilled?"

An unexpected gust swept the *Sentinel* from her grasp and dislodged strands of hair from her bun. Mariel watched the paper flit away into the greening prairie. She brushed hair out of her eyes and giggled with girlish delight. "Was that you, Bruno? Surely you must know *that* wasn't the answer I had hoped for."

What did she hope for? Until arriving in Dakota she'd never had any realistic expectation to be a reporter. Chicago, a big town with big newspapers and hundreds of experienced male reporters, had been no place for an aging schoolmarm to make her mark in the field of journalism. Now that she was here, the dream had become a possibility. Yet one obstacle after another sprang up in her path to keep it from happening.

Unseen prairie chickens cackled in the grass. Hawks, or perhaps buzzards, glided above, scanning the earth for a meal. It was full spring in Dakota now, the air verdant with the aromas of new growth. The sun bathed her in its light. As she lolled her head to enjoy its warmth, she realized that she herself was the source of most of the obstacles holding her back.

She patted the ground above Bruno and said, "Thank you, little friend."

****

Marshal Woolridge and Trippledy were smoking pipes and drinking coffee in their rocking chairs in front of the jailhouse when she arrived with pencil and paper.

"I intend to speak with Mr. Hartwig," she said.

"Cowan's in there with him right now," Trippledy said.

"What could he possibly have to say to Mr. Hartwig?"

"Don't figure to be exchanging recipes," Woolridge said. "Clyde don't want to see you."

"Well, I want to see him, and I won't take no for an answer."

The men glanced at her with amusement. Woolridge gave her a mock salute. "Yes, ma'am."

"Good. May I wait with you gentlemen until Mr. Cowan finishes his business?"

"Sure," Wooldridge said. "Duane, give Mrs. Erickson your chair."

Trippledy nodded, but took his time moving. "Ain't it something how your husband predicted the storm that wrecked Charlie's smokehouse? Impressed a lot of folks. Mayor Goss asked him to write a weather column for the paper. Kinda funny, when you think about it. I mean, you wanting to be a reporter and all, but it's your husband who—"

"Duane," Woolridge said, "this'd be a good time to go inside and fetch a chair for yourself."

Goss had done what? And Randall hadn't mentioned it?

"Sorry, Mrs. Erickson," the deputy said. "I didn't mean no offense."

Mariel attempted a weak smile. "None taken, Mr. Dalton."

Trippledy looked at his feet awkwardly and muttered, "I'll just get that chair now."

When he opened the office door, Cowan was emerging from the cell area, but turned back toward Hartwig for a final word. In a voice loud enough for Mariel to hear, he said, "Your best hope is to hang, sir. Believe me, a rope is the kinder fate."

Cowan tried to squeeze past Trippledy, but the deputy slammed him against the doorframe with his forearm. "No one comes into my jail and threatens my prisoners. You got that? Hartwig ain't had his trial yet. Nothing's settled."

Cowan doffed his cap in a manner Mariel thought flippant. "Oh, indeed the matter is settled, constable. Indeed it is."

Woolridge pushed himself to his feet. "You might've noticed we got more than one cage back there. Maybe Clyde would like some company."

"On what charge?"

"Being a pain in my neck. Go home, Cowan. I don't expect to see you here again."

"As you wish, constable. But know that I'm not easily intimidated."

"Me, neither," Woolridge said, tapping his badge.

Cowan bowed his head to Mariel, and said, "Good day to you, then, gentlemen. *Adieu*, Mrs. Erickson."

After he was gone, Mariel said, "I no longer need your chair, Mr. Dalton. May I?"

Woolridge gestured her to go inside. "Try not to shoot him. Looks like he's had a bad day."

"I shall restrain myself, marshal."

Mariel found Hartwig slumped on his cot, face in his hands. His candle was burning.

He looked up as she approached and said meekly, "Why now?"

She was shocked by the depth of despair he squeezed into those two syllables. He had the appearance of a defeated man, quite unlike anything she'd ever seen in him before.

"Is there anything I can do, Mr. Hartwig?"

He stood up, and some of his usual belligerence flared in his eyes. "You can write the truth about them Irish bastards in Goss's rag."

"I believe Mr. Cowan is Scottish."

"Like it matters."

"I heard what he said to you. A rope is the kinder fate? What did he mean?"

"If I don't hang he's gonna dynamite my house with my whole family in it."

Mariel took a step closer to the bars, already scribbling furiously. "That was hyperbole."

"Hyper- what?"

"He was simply expressing his anger. Mr. Blackford was his cousin, after all."

"Cousin, my ass. And I tell you what, he don't give a damn that Blackford's dead."

"I'm afraid you're not making sense, Mr. Hartwig."

"You know what a Fenian is?"

"I've heard the word, of course. Some kind of movement for Irish independence? I thought that died out years ago."

Hartwig shook his head. "It started up again after the Civil War. You didn't bring whiskey?"

"Not today, Mr. Hartwig. What's our Civil War got to do with Ireland?"

"I talk better with whiskey. Maybe you should get some."

"Tell me what I want to know, and maybe I will."

"So it's blackmail, then." Hartwig laughed, a sound equal parts humor and desolation. "Well, *that* I understand. Have it your way. I can't do nothing about Cowan, but Blackford? I saved this town from a terrorist son-of-a-bitch."

Mariel snickered at the ridiculous assertion. "Please, Mr. Hartwig, I may be naïve, but I'm a little old for monster-under-the-bed stories."

"The Fenians liked how bombing public places in the war scared the bejeezus out of people."

"That was over twenty years ago. Mr. Blackford was a Traveller in Ireland then. You said so yourself. In any case, this is America. Why would they target us?"

"They ain't targeting us, but just because they came here, that don't mean they stopped hating their government."

Mariel sighed impatiently. "This is all very interesting, Mr. Hartwig, but could we get back to the subject? My hope was to record your version of the incident with Liam Blackford."

"Am I talking to myself? You deaf, or just dumber than usual today?"

"No need to be abusive, Mr. Hartwig. I'm listening."

"What's the word for people who don't want no government at all?"

Mariel recalled the Haymarket Massacre in Chicago a year ago, just before she and Randall departed for Dakota. What had been a peaceful labor protest ignited into a bloody riot when someone threw dynamite at the police. "Radicals? Anarchists?"

"Yeah, anarchists, that's it. That's what your friend Blackford was. And Cowan. Anarchists."

Mariel hesitated before asking the next question. "Was your mother also an anarchist?"

Hartwig shook the bars so violently they creaked and groaned in their moorings. Mariel feared the strength of his fury might be sufficient to shatter the iron. She gasped and dropped her notepad and pencil. "My mother was the best woman to ever walk the planet," he said. "This shit is over."

Mariel knelt on one knee to pick up her writing materials. "I sincerely apologize for casting aspersions, but I'm confused. You've said you're of Irish ancestry. I'm having difficulty reconciling that with your abhorrence for your own kind."

"*Reconciling. Abhorrence.* The hell with it, and the hell with you."

"Mr. Hartwig—*Clyde*—please tell me. I'll buy you that whiskey. I'll do anything."

"Pay my bail?"

"Except that."

"Pleasure me here on my cot?"

"Especially not that."

"Then there really ain't much you will do, is there?" Hartwig spit, missing her feet by inches. "If I finish, you'll get out and never come back? Swear it, or we're done."

She crossed her hands over her bosom. "I do."

He slapped the bars and turned his back on her. "Don't open your mouth again."

Mariel almost did, then didn't.

"I met Blackford before you did, even before his boy cold-cocked Wayne at the dance. I didn't have nothing in particular against him at the time, other than him being Irish. But I'll drink with any man till he gives me reason not to.

"So one night we're both liquored up over at Duncan's, and he tells me he knows how to build bombs. 'Infernal devices,' he calls them. 'You're a liar,' I say. And he says no, he went to dynamite school in Brooklyn. Learned how to make bombs from some fella name of Mezzeroff. Says there's good money in bombs. The Fenians used them in Ireland to blow up statues and police stations."

Mariel couldn't hold her tongue. "Liam hasn't been back to Ireland since he came to America."

Hartwig glared at her. "I didn't say he blew things up himself. I said he made the bombs that did. Do you wanna hear this or not?"

Mariel pressed her hand over her mouth and nodded.

"So he says he knows how to make dynamite, and I say, 'Prove it.' He says he can show me, but it don't come cheap. I take out seven ten-dollar silvers and slap them on the table. I tell him I got seventy bucks that says he's full of shit. He says it'll take him a couple days to get the stuff he needs, so we set up a time to meet later that week. Only he never shows. Wasn't till he came out to the field behind Duncan's that I ever heard anything more about it."

"Wouldn't that indicate he didn't really know how to make explosives?" Mariel said. "You killed him over the seventy dollars, didn't you?"

"Think what you want, but Roy saw him out north of town one day with a wagon full of dynamite. Said he was delivering charges for a well company. *What* well company? We dig our own around here, and we don't need dynamite to do it."

"That doesn't make him a terrorist."

"He was worse. He *trained* terrorists. The police in Ireland got wise to the Fenians in America. They started checking the docks to make it hard for anyone to ship bombs over there. So what's Blackford do? He teaches other Fenians how to make bombs here, then sends them to Ireland to build them over there. That kind of scum don't deserve to live."

"If this is true, why didn't you go to Marshal Woolridge?"

"With what? It ain't illegal to make dynamite. Anyway, Woolridge don't like me. He wouldn't've believed me if I did tell him."

"I don't believe you, either."

"Where else did Blackford get the money to feed that brood of his?"

****

"I didn't tell you because I haven't accepted his offer yet," Randall said, blowing on his hot coffee. "It isn't as if I've never gotten an indication right before. I predicted a bad storm and was lucky enough to get a little twister to go with it. Now suddenly I'm a wizard."

Mariel poured herself a cup and joined him at the table. "I'm just envious, I suppose. I've been trying to write for Mr. Goss for months, and so far all my efforts have come to nothing."

Randall looked down at the base of the stove, the spot where Bruno once slept, and her eyes followed his. "Still expect to see the little nuisance there, don't you?"

Mariel smiled wistfully. "I miss him."

"I hate to admit it, but so do I." He checked his pocket watch, then turned his gaze on her, his expression both stern and sympathetic. "I won't write for him if you don't want me to. But I have to ask you, have you done enough to earn the job? It seems to me you haven't completed any of the assignments Herb's given you."

"I got Mike to tell his Andersonville story."

"You did do that, although I understand Herb's reasoning for not printing it yet. Liam's murder was the biggest thing to ever happen in Goss Valley, even getting the county seat back. You still haven't delivered Clyde's story to him."

Mariel waved her notes at him and then glanced away. "As of today, I'm finished with Mr. Hartwig. He said the most dreadful things about Liam."

"What did you expect?"

She lowered her voice, as if someone were eavesdropping at the door. "He said Liam was a Fenian."

Randall was just taking a sip when she said the word. He laughed so hard he shot coffee out his nostrils. "*Clyde* used the word Fenian?"

"That's what he said."

"Please tell me you don't believe it. He's a murderer and a liar. He can't claim he didn't do it because there were witnesses, so he has to justify the killing somehow. Correct me if I'm wrong: Sometime in your interview today, Clyde claimed Liam deserved to die."

Mariel shook her head in amazement. "Maybe you really are a wizard. You can predict the weather and reveal people's thoughts."

Randall looked at the time again.

"Expecting someone?"

"Any minute now."

"Who?"

He only smiled. "Should I do the weather column for Herb?"

"That's entirely your decision."

"I think I will, then. Do we have any medicated paper?" When she nodded, Randall went outside to the outhouse. While he was gone there was a knock on the door.

Mike and Phoebe Hammon were standing on the porch when she answered. Mike beamed a magnificent smile through his beard. His hair hadn't been trimmed for some time, and his cowlick stood straight up like the horn of a unicorn. Phoebe appeared to have been crying, but not, Mariel thought, from sorrow.

"You're back from Iowa," Mariel said, stupidly stating the obvious.

"You gonna invite us in, or just stand there gawking?" Mike said.

"Good heavens," Mariel said. "Forgive me. Yes, do come in."

Randall came in just as they were settling at the table. "Told her yet?"

"Thought we'd wait for you."

"Your nephew's doctor cured your asthma?" Mariel said.

"The man was a quacksalver if there ever was one. Made me eat paste that tasted like cow manure. I near to died choking it down, and then again puking it up. Nah, that's not the news. I only stayed with G.W. a day. Figured since I was more likely to die from his doctor's cure than the asthma, I might as well not waste any more time there."

"Stop beating around the bush, Sergeant," Randall said.

Mike saluted, left-handed, as always. "Yessir, Lieutenant Shit-head, sir."

He paused just long enough to make Mariel nervous. She gazed from face to face to face. Phoebe sniffled, nodded, and squeezed Mike's hands. "Tell her."

"I took the train down to Cedar Rapids. Guess who I saw?"

Cedar Rapids? Lottie and Theo!

Before allowing herself to become too excited, she squinted at him and said, "You didn't shoot Theo, did you?"

Mike laughed a joyous laugh. "Now why would I shoot the father of our grandchild? Lottie's due this winter."

CHAPTER FORTY
POKING THE WRONG BEAR
Tuesday, May 24, 1887

"I know what word you said to Mrs. Cowan at Liam's funeral," Mariel said. She sat before Frank Chamberlain's desk, a pencil in her right hand and a notepad in her left.

"Indeed?" he blew on his spectacles, then cleaned the lenses with his tie. "It's a hot day. May I offer you something cool to drink, Mrs. Erickson?"

"No, thank you. It was *Fenian*, wasn't it?"

Frank smiled. "Still the reporter in training. You look so earnest."

"I am earnest, Mr. Chamberlain."

"Have you ever investigated anything professionally before? Did Herb teach you, or just throw you to the wolves?"

"I won't be deterred," she said. "Upon what did you base your decision to defend Mr. Hartwig?"

Frank put his glasses on. "I meant what I said after the funeral. I'll have no comment until the trial is over. I told Herb that every man is entitled to counsel, and I stand by that assertion."

"What about this prosecutor, Van Pelt?"

"I only know him by reputation. Judge Larrabee appointed him, so he'll do fine." Frank leaned forward and winked at her. "Besides, the case is open-and-shut, remember? Five witnesses.

How can I win?”

“You don’t even like Mr. Hartwig.”

“My personal tastes are irrelevant.”

“Even if he’s guilty?”

“Especially then.”

“You are infuriating, Mr. Chamberlain.”

“A character flaw my wife points out to me daily.”

Mariel shifted in her seat, crossed her legs, and tried a different tactic. “Forgive my impertinence. Mr. Goss didn’t send me to question your decision. He sent me to find out if the gossip is true.”

“About Liam being a Fenian?”

She nodded. “Something at the funeral convinced you.”

“Who have you spoken to about this?”

“That isn’t your concern.”

“A word of advice?” Frank rose and circled around his desk to help Mariel up.

“May I assume I’m leaving now?”

“You’re too blunt, Mrs. Erickson. Sometimes it’s more important to observe than to ask. If you aspire to be a good reporter, you’ll need to learn subtler methods. Devious, even. More so if the answer you’re looking for is dangerous. Has it ever occurred to you that you might be poking the wrong bear?”

CHAPTER FORTY-ONE
SANCTUM SANCTORUM
Sunday, June 19, 1887

Reverend Dall was hoarse with influenza today, but still managed to deliver a sermon damning the usual suspects to hell: anyone who didn't show up for church this morning. He didn't mention Hartwig, who already had a reservation in hell for killing Liam. Mariel assumed that once a man had been consigned to hell, he was stuck there, so it would be redundant for Dall to damn him every week.

After the service, she walked out into a hot and sticky day with Randall, Mike, and Phoebe. Mike and Randall took the lead, with the women following.

Once Mike returned from Iowa, he resumed responsibility for taking some of the weather readings. Randall's knee was so much improved that his limp was scarcely noticeable, but with Bobby spending most of his time with the Blackfords, he couldn't be relied upon to maintain a regular schedule. That left Mike to fill in when Randall needed a break.

"Ever thought about giving up the Corps and going into business for yourself?" Mike said.

"Making weather indications?" Randall said.

"Why not? I've been reading your column in the paper, and you've done pretty good so far. It's all over town how you predicted the twister at Charlie's place, right down to the minute.”

Randall shook his head. “I didn’t predict a twister *at all*. I said thunderstorms.”

“Well, the point is, you got it right. Why should only Hazen get to issue indications?”

“Hazen died in January. Fellow named Greely’s the boss now.”

“Same question.”

“Where’s the money in it? Goss can’t pay me what I’d need to quit the Corps.”

“You could get a real job to cover the difference. Hard work might make a man of you yet.”

Randall gave him a playful shove. “I’ll let that one go. How could I do it independently, anyway? I need the readings from out west. Those are taken by the army. If I resign my commission, they won’t send me the readings.”

“Time to set up a civilian weather service, then.”

“That’s a job for a younger man.”

“You *are* a younger man,” Mike laughed. “Supper at the hotel tonight?”

Randall looked at Mariel, who nodded.

They said their goodbyes to the Hammons. Neither Mariel nor Randall spoke as they headed home. He had his own thoughts, and she was too hot to think about anything other than changing out of the multiple layers of her Sunday best. Her gardens needed weeding, so she’d have to do that before she could take the bath she craved.

As soon as she entered the house, she rushed to their bedroom. She didn’t even bother to close the door as she stripped. Randall relaxed at the table, where he could watch her. As she got down to her underwear, she allowed herself to recall the fever in his blood at the sight of her nakedness when they were young. But that ship had sailed. She was forty-nine and stout, hardly the object of any man's lust. In any case, she wasn't entirely sure she would be inclined even if he was. He had struck her, and that blow had resonated in ways more significant than the injury to her cheek.

Yet he continued to watch. Was that a smile?

"Like what you see?" she said.

His eyes flickered at the sound of her voice, and in that moment she realized he hadn't been looking at her at all.

"You've been inquiring around town about Carter Cowan."

"Mr. Goss asked me to follow up on Hartwig's claim about Liam. He still doesn't understand why Hartwig's mother turned against her own people. He thought if she'd had encounters with terrorists, that might explain her hatred of the Irish. Perhaps she was ashamed to be one of them."

"What does that have to do with Clyde killing Liam?" Randall locked both hands behind his head and stretched his back until it popped. "I need coffee before I check readings."

"In this heat?" Mariel wiggled into her lightest cotton dress and joined him in the kitchen.

He lit the stove, put the pot on, and went outside to fetch water from the well. When he returned, he brewed the coffee. "You do understand, don't you," he said, "that if Cowan is a Fenian, the stupidest thing you could possibly do is confront him about it? You're no one special to him. If you pose a threat, why wouldn't he throw dynamite through our window?"

"Mr. Chamberlain suggested I might be poking the wrong bear."

"You shouldn't be poking *any* bears."

"But dynamiting our home? Really, Randall. Isn't that a bit lurid? It sounds like the plot of a dime novel."

"Why rile folks up against the Irish again? For now the Blackfords enjoy the town's sympathy. How long will that last if you start spreading this talk of terrorists?"

"Goss says my only concern should be the truth, wherever it takes me."

Randall liked his coffee strong. He sniffed the steam over the pot, then filled a cup and sat next to her. "Oh?" he said. "Tell him to snoop into Cowan's affairs."

"With his drinking—"

"That's his problem, not yours." Randall's voice rose only slightly in volume, but Mariel recognized the signs of anger. He steadied his cup with both hands and took several swallows. "Herb doesn't actually intend to print that drivel, does he? That Liam was some kind of international terrorist? If Hartwig had his way, they'd build a statue of him in front of the courthouse."

"I don't believe Liam was a Fenian, but shouldn't it be investigated, if only to disprove it?"

"Until you brought it up, nobody would have suspected there was anything *to* disprove." He reached for her hand. "Mariel, Clyde doesn't need an excuse to hate. He thinks the only way to avoid the gallows is by offering a reasonable excuse for the killing. You're helping him do it."

****

She met Beryl en route to the post office. Typewritten pages in hand, Mariel intended to confront Herb Goss and draw a line in the sand: Publish this, or else. There was nothing on the other end of that threat, however. She couldn't quit what she had never started.

Beryl, as was her custom, was returning to her room to drink herself to sleep.

Mariel was in a sour mood, and didn't feel like talking, but the woman asked to walk with her, since they were heading the same direction.

"How's your husband's leg?" Beryl said.

"Better, thank you."

"You don't seem happy about it."

"Just discouraged."

"You still fretting about him and me and his accident?"

"No, I believe you. It's just that after he hit me, things have been different."

She had no idea why she was confessing this. It wasn't even the blow that was bothering her. It was the failure of anybody to take her seriously as a journalist.

"Shit," Beryl said, "I got my knickers in a bunch every time a man knocked me around, I'd be too busy weeping to make a living."

"Perhaps you allow that kind of treatment. I do not."

"Then throw him out on his ass."

"I can't."

Beryl stopped in the middle of the street. "Make up your mind. Either keep him or don't. I'm not saying I know which is right, but Jesus, honey, you got to do *something*."

"I want to forgive him, but—"

"But what? What's stopping you?"

"I don't know how."

"How about you give him a nice tumble in bed?"

Mariel blushed. Was she truly listening to romantic advice from a prostitute? "I'm afraid, Miss Beryl, that intimacy isn't the answer to everything."

"No, Mrs. Erickson, *fucking* isn't the answer. That's what I do, and it's not the same thing at all. I don't get sloppy feelings for men any more, but used to be I did. I'm telling you, when it's for love, a tumble's the best thing for you. That, and some wine. The wine first. And candles. You can't just live in the same house together. Long as he doesn't hit you again, then sooner or later you got to start acting like he *never* did. Else it'll always be between you."

Mariel was shocked by the use of that word by a woman. But after speaking with Hartwig and Mike, strong language didn't have the power to shock that it once did. "We hadn't done *that* for years before he hit me."

"Then what's the point?"

Mariel didn't have an answer for that, but then they were at the post office, and she didn't need one. Sadie was behind the counter.

"Howdy, Mariel. Howdy, Beryl-girl."

"Hey, Sadie-lady. Straighten Mrs. Erickson out, why don't you?" That said, Beryl kissed her bottle as she might one of her clients and hurried up the stairs, singing, "Glory, glory hallelujah."

Mariel shook her head in amazed amusement. How could someone who lived as Beryl did be so cheerful?

"What am I supposed to straighten you out about?" Sadie said.

"It was just a couple of old hens clucking. Is your husband here?"

"In the cellar, working on that machine of his."

"The printing press?"

Sadie nodded. "Would you like to go down there?"

Mariel felt a rush of excitement. During all her time in Goss Valley, all her pestering, all her ambitious pursuit of literary glory, she had never been invited into Herb Goss's *sanctum sanctorum*, his holiest of holies, the site from which the *Sentinel* originated. "Do you think he would mind?"

"Not even sure he'll notice. Come on, it's back here."

Heart fluttering, Mariel walked behind the counter and through the mail room. Sadie led her to a door, opened it, and hollered down, "Herb, you got company." Then she turned around and headed back toward the counter. "He's all yours," she said.

The temperature dropped as she descended the stairs. One of the benefits of a cellar, beyond the storage of canned goods, was that it served as a refuge from the heat in the summer.

"Who the hell is it?" Goss called, and by the slurring of his words, Mariel knew he was well on his way to oblivion. "Oh, hello, Mrs. Erickson. Are you going to holler at me again today?"

Mariel was an observant woman. Normally she would try to note every detail of the cellar, but now her entire attention was captured by the machine to which Goss was attending. Constructed of metal and wood, it was a marvel of plates and cranks and bars, with buckets on the side. She was enthralled: her first printing press. The device was smaller than she had imagined, and yet the most beautiful thing she'd ever seen.

"Before you open your mouth," Goss muttered, "I'm committed to other things this Friday, but I'll be running the first installment of Mike's Andersonville story on the first. Your byline. As I said, a penny per ten words."

The vestiges of Mariel's bad mood disappeared. The lighting was dim enough that she hoped he couldn't see her tears from across the room. All she could manage to say was, "I'm grateful."

"Hartwig, though, I'm not sure about that terrorism shit. Nobody will believe he killed Liam out of the goodness of his heart. But whatever we run, it can wait. Closer to the trial will be a better time for that story."

Mariel looked at the reams of paper stacked against the wall. She noticed the ink roller and the metal types, upon which the letters were carved backwards. How confusing that must be!

"But first," Goss said, stumbling toward her, "Mike says I need to show you how to work this damn contraption. Methinks my profligate ways are coming home to roost."

CHAPTER FORTY-TWO
HARPIES
Monday, July 4, 1887

"I'm fixing to turn Catholic," Bobby said. "That's why Mama kicked me out."

He, Megan, Bridget, and Mariel were eating a late dinner at the hotel. Most of the town had gathered outside Duncan's Tavern to await the Independence Day fireworks, but the rest of the Blackford children had stayed home, the celebration being past their bedtime.

"He's living in our barn," Megan said.

Mariel scrutinized the girl for any sign of weight gain that might have been facilitated by Bobby. She was as lithesome as ever, though. If there was an awkward situation developing, it was in its earliest stages.

"Do you approve?" Mariel said to Bridget.

"I spoke with Liam about it," the woman whispered, looking around to make sure nobody else could overhear. "I know you must think me barking mad, but I talk to him all the time."

"I understand perfectly. After my father died, I did the same. If I had a problem, I'd ask his advice, just as I did when he was alive. I always got an answer."

She got answers, yes, but like praying to God, what she heard always coincided with what she wanted to do anyway.

"Liam thinks Bobby's a fine lad," Bridget said. "But Irish

don't marry outside our faith."

Marry, at their age?

Megan beamed a stunning smile at her. "No, mum, 'tisn't what you're thinking. It'll be a few years yet for Robert and meself."

Mariel found it adorable how the girl still pronounced her young beau's name *raw butt*.

"Then ... congratulations? So your mother's not happy about your conversion?"

Bobby shrugged his shoulders in the nonchalant way young people did when pretending they weren't bothered by something that bothered them. "Daddy was Catholic," he said.

"A mighty poor excuse for one," Megan said.

Phoebe interrupted Mariel's next question when she brought their food orders: potato soup for the Blackford women, a beefsteak for Bobby, and buttered toast and lemonade for Mariel. "Must be hard for you," Phoebe said to Bridget, "having to wait this long for the trial."

"At least we know our deliverance is at hand, mum. They'll hang that bridge-troll, and then we'll not have to think on him any longer." She took tasted her soup. "This is excellent, and we Irish know our potatoes."

Phoebe had never cared for Hartwig, and likely wouldn't lament his passing. "Mariel, can you come see me when you're done? I need a word."

"Of course." She returned her attention to Bobby, who was cutting into meat so rare it might not be dead yet. "May I ask what happened to your father? Did he pass away?"

"Far as we know, he's still taking up space above ground. But we killed him a long time ago, in here." Bobby pointed to his temple. "He never married Mama, you know."

"I had no idea."

"That's why she don't like Catholics. But I'm gonna do right by Megan. I think Mama'll come around."

When they'd finished eating, Bridget said, "Children, perhaps you'd enjoy going for a stroll for a moment?"

Bobby and Megan agreed, too quickly, Mariel thought, as if their exit had been arranged in advance. Bridget needed to talk, then. Seemed Mariel was popular today.

When they were gone, Bridget said, "I'll not beat around the bush, Mrs. Erickson. I'm aware you've been interviewing the beast in jail. Now, don't fret, I know you've simply been doing Mayor Goss's bidding, and I bear you no ill will for it. But I'd be obliged if you'd tell me what dreadful things he's been saying about Liam."

Mariel couldn't claim journalistic confidentiality, as she'd spoken to others about it. But this was not a conversation she'd ever intended to have with Bridget. Her mouth went dry. She sipped her lemonade and struggled to find the right words. "I put no credence in Mr. Hartwig's story."

Tears welled up in Bridget's eyes. "Aye, then I well know what he said. 'Tis a horrid word, a horrid word. I swear it's not so."

"I believe you."

Bridget lifted Mariel's hand to her lips and kissed her fingers. "Thank you, mum."

Mike looked in from the kitchen. "They're about ready for the fireworks."

"I've never seen an Independence Day celebration," Bridget said.

"This is my first time in Dakota."

"I must find the children." Bridget rose and scurried out into the crowd.

While the door was open Mariel heard a multitude of voices building in excitement. She started to follow, but Mike redirected her into the kitchen where Phoebe was waiting.

"What's this all about?" she said.

"Watch yourself," Phoebe said. "It's all around town that Peg Moehler and her Fragment Society women are trying to get your teaching contract revoked."

"Mr. Hartwig tried that last year. You saw how far that got."

"This ain't last year."

"What are their grounds?"

"Louisa claims you're trying to prejudice the jury against Clyde."

Mariel snickered. "He hardly needs my help for that."

"And they say it ain't proper for a married woman to teach. They think Randall ought to be supporting you."

"They didn't complain when I was offered the position."

"That was before they were mad at you."

"Bunch of harpies," Mike said.

"Yeah, but those harpies're vicious," Phoebe said. "Mariel, you gotta stop asking about Liam's past. Behind Louisa's back they'll say you support a murderer. In her presence they'll say you support terrorists. In between that you're trying to influence the jury. Any way you look at it, they can claim you ain't fit to teach their children."

"Ridiculous. What's that got to do with my ability to teach? Mr. Goss will support me."

"The election's coming up in November," Mike said. "Just back off, is all we're saying. Don't talk to Clyde, don't ask about Liam, and never say Fenian again."

"I'd no idea it could come to this."

"It has. There's a city council meeting Wednesday night. You're on the agenda. The harpies tried to hire Frank Chamberlain to represent them. He said no."

"Well, that's a relief. I'm done with Mr. Hartwig in any case."

Mike grinned. "Good, that's settled. By the way, word is

John's gonna bring him out to watch the fireworks. Clyde's always been the one who sets them off. I think Charlie's doing it this year."

"Is that wise?"

"Don't see how it could hurt anything. He'll be in shackles. Hell, the man's been in jail for two months. He needs the air."

"I should warn Bridget. Seeing him will upset her."

Outside, the sky had gone overcast since morning, but the humidity was low, and it didn't feel like rain. There was still enough light that she could clearly see people's faces, although the sun must be beneath the horizon by now. Everyone in Goss Valley was on the streets. Had they come just for the fireworks, or had they, too, heard the rumor of Hartwig's appearance?

Moments later it was rumor no more. Marshal Woolridge and Trippledy brought Hartwig out of the jail, his hands and ankles manacled. Woolridge had his pistol at the ready, while Trippledy carried a rifle.

Some in the crowd catcalled, but an alarming number cheered. A few even approached the marshal in a menacing manner. Woolridge raised his pistol. "Now goddammit, folks, I'm not going to put up with any nonsense. He's only out to watch the celebration. Just stay where you are and enjoy the show."

Mariel caught sight of Carter and Tara Cowan emerging from the crowd in front of Duncan's Tavern. Tara only took a step onto the street, but her husband rushed toward Hartwig. He had a sidearm, but it wasn't drawn.

"Mr. Hartwig," he yelled loudly enough to be heard by all, "you've one foot in hell already. Soon you'll complete the journey."

Before he could say anything else, Trippledy clubbed him in the face with the butt of his rifle. Cowan crumpled and lay still.

"Shoot him!" Tara cried. "Shoot him!"

"I ain't shooting nobody," Trippledy said, "but this sumbitch here's been warned before. Hartwig'll get what's coming to him, one way or another."

"Duane," Woolridge said, "I believe Mr. Cowan needs a place to recover tonight. There's a nice cell right next to Clyde's."

"I don't want that son-of-a-bitch by me," Hartwig said.

"Don't remember asking your opinion. Do you want to see the fireworks or not? Because I can take you back in now."

"I'll stay out here."

"Then shut your mouth." Woolridge called up to the roof of the post office. "Okay, Charlie, let them fly."

Mariel was certain Randall wouldn't appreciate explosives set up there with his weather equipment. But Woolridge hadn't asked his opinion, either.

As Trippledy dragged Cowan into the jail, his wife plopped down onto the street, her dress and petticoats billowing around her.

Mariel went to offer assistance. She knelt before the distraught woman and said, "Mr. Hartwig will hang soon enough. What would be the point of your husband shooting him now?"

"I was talking to the constable. I didn't mean shoot Hartwig, I meant Carter."

Mariel staggered to her feet. "*What*?"

Tara Cowan glared up at her, white showing beneath her dark pupils, her face contorted into a grimace of fury, agony, or madness. "I know what you think," she spat, "but Carter doesn't give two *shits* about the Fenians. My dear husband's for hire to anyone who'll pay him. He just likes to blow things up."

CHAPTER FORTY-THREE
AMEN TO THAT
Friday, July 8, 1887

An informal meeting was set to convene in the main auditorium of the courthouse at nine a.m., Mayor Goss presiding. The building was more like a barn than the restored seat of power for Buffalo County. There were no statues, no marble façades, nothing to indicate the grandiose purpose it served. However, the wood paneling Goss had installed inside was handsome, and the bench pads were comfortable enough. He had plans to hire a sculptor to carve some stone lions or buffaloes or Jesus for the edifice outside, but hadn't done so yet.

Mariel, Randall, and the Hammons sat on the left side of the front bench, nearest the podium. Peg Moehler, Louisa Hartwig, and most of the ladies of the Fragment Society occupied the right. Mariel wasn't surprised that Sadie Goss hadn't come. To support one faction, she'd have to oppose the other to their faces, and that wasn't in her nature.

The stated purpose of the meeting was to allow the Fragment Society to vent their spleen about Mariel. They had demanded her contract be revoked, based upon cleverly worded accusations which, when boiled down to their essence, claimed she had befriended undesirables —the Irish and the Indians. Although Goss had met two nights ago with the city council to assess the situation, their decision had yet to be revealed. Other than Mike, none of the councilmen was present today, an oversight Mariel found odd. When she asked him about it, he only smiled.

Louisa Hartwig approached her. Her voice was positively venomous. "You're a vile woman, Mrs. Erickson. You mean to see my husband hang."

"That is not my intention at all. I was trying to be fair and present his version of events. But as Mr. Goss has chosen not to print my story, I can't imagine what your objection could be. However, I do forgive you your insults, as I would expect you to support your husband."

Louisa jabbed a finger at her. "Yes, I do support him! Unlike you, who abandoned yours at the slightest provocation."

Randall stood up. He towered over Louisa. "I believe we've heard enough."

Herb Goss came in through a side door and assumed his place at the podium. Rather than interrupt the exchange between Randall and Louisa, he watched with amusement. For once, he appeared to be sober.

"Are you going to strike me, too?" Louisa said.

"No," Randall said, "but I'll be happy to escort you back to your seat."

"I know the way." She narrowed her eyes at Mariel. "The husband is the master of the house. If you disobey him, you deserve to be beaten."

Finally Goss cleared his throat. "Louisa," he said, "sit down. No, don't bother. This won't take long. Ladies, I presented your petition to members of the council Wednesday night. As their decision was unanimous, I didn't feel compelled to call them again this morning. We will be renewing Mrs. Erickson's contract. In addition, her salary will be increased by a dollar a week."

A Killing Snow

The Fragment Society erupted in protest. Goss listened to them with indifference, and answered them with a yawn.

Peg hmmphed her disapproval. "You won't even hear our case?"

"The council heard your so-called case on Wednesday. Your petition has been denied."

"We'll appeal."

"To whom? I'm the mayor."

"Governor Pierce, if we have to."

Goss massaged his temples. "I wish I could find a law to fine you for wasting my time."

"We won't have that woman teaching our children," Louisa said.

"Keep them home, then."

"Need I remind you that November is coming?"

"Why wait? Let's vote next Tuesday. If someone else wants the job, he's welcome to it."

"My Charlie's on the council," Nora Koerperich cried. "I told him how to vote."

"Shocking to learn you don't speak for everyone in Goss Valley, isn't it?"

****

"That'll be a dime for the pair of them," Lem Smith said.

Mariel and Randall were buying sarsaparillas to celebrate her victory when Carter Cowan burst through the door. His right eye was black and swollen where Trippledy had struck him, his upper lip split, and his nose pushed to the left, shattered by the impact.

"There you are," he slurred, his thick accent further distorted by his injuries. "Mrs. Erickson, I'd have words with you."

Randall interposed himself between them.

Her heart rate and breathing quickened, and her mouth went dry. "I'm quite sure we have nothing to talk about, Mr. Cowan."

"Don't we now? I know the things you've been asking."

"I'm not responsible for rumors."

"Mr. Cowan," Randall said, "I suggest you buy what you came here for and leave us alone. My wife said she doesn't wish to speak with you."

"That's right," Smith warned. "Don't make trouble, or I'll have the marshal on you."

"I've already been the guest of your constable, sir. I suppose his cage seems daunting to you, but where I'm from it's like a holiday on the beach."

"Is it true you enjoy playing with dynamite, Mr. Cowan?" Mariel said. Randall shushed her, but the damage had been done.

"'Tis you, dear lady, who are playing with dynamite. I know where you live."

"You'd threaten a woman?" Mariel said.

"We all heard it," Smith said.

Wincing at the effort, Cowan curled his damaged lip into a sneer. As he stormed out the door, he said, "You'd be wise not to trifle with me, the lot of you."

Randall and Mariel waited a few minutes for him to be safely away before they left the store. Randall wanted to work in his room at the post office until it was time for the two o'clock readings. Since the morning was pleasant, Mariel walked with him.

"See what I mean?" Randall said.

Mariel sipped from the straw in her bottle of sarsaparilla. "I do fear him. How could I not, when his own wife despises him? But let's not trouble ourselves with monsters on such a glorious day. The sun is shining and I shall be teaching again in the autumn."

Sooner or later you got to start acting like he never did.

She took his elbow and leaned her head against his shoulder. He'd never cared for public displays of affection, so she knew he wouldn't tolerate such an egregious breech of etiquette for long, but she couldn't help herself. Despite Cowan's threat, she was in a buoyant mood.

"Ahem," he said, gently lifting her hand from his elbow when he saw Marshal Woolridge and Trippledy emerging from the post office. Both men had red and angry faces, and Woolridge was muttering, "Shit, shit, shit, shit, shit!"

Mariel discreetly fell one step behind Randall.

"What's the matter, John?" he said.

Woolridge looked at him furiously, although Mariel knew her husband couldn't be the source of his anger. "Shit, goddammit, shit!" he said.

Trippledy nudged Woolridge along toward the jailhouse. "Come on, boss," he said. Peering over his shoulder, he called back to Randall, "Ask Goss."

Randall and Mariel gave each other a perplexed look. Inside, Goss was at the telegraph, still sober. "Need something mailed?" he said. "Just be a minute."

"No," Randall said. "What was that all about?"

"John and Trippledy?"

"They seemed rather upset," Mariel said.

"Wouldn't you be? Hartwig's trial's been delayed."

"Who in hell would do that?"

"Just got the telegram. Judge Larrabee got called out east for some big powwow there. He can't get here until at least January, if the weather cooperates."

Randall pounded his fist into his palm. "Shit, goddammit, shit!"

Mariel clenched her teeth. Amen to that, she thought.

CHAPTER FORTY-FOUR
THE SMART MONEY
Friday, August 5, 1887

"Lottie is four months along," Phoebe said, handing a three-by-five photograph to Mariel. "She had this made in Cedar Rapids. It arrived with Friday's mail."

The picture depicted Lottie wearing a light summer dress and standing in profile to the camera. Perhaps her midsection had become a bit stout, but she didn't appear all that different than last time Mariel had seen her. When she was pregnant, particularly with Alex, she'd expanded to the size of a grain silo. Sadly, after Alex, her body seemed to have grown fond of that shape and resolutely refused to change back.

Lottie still had five months to go, but she was several years younger than Mariel had been then. No matter how big she got, she'd regain her lean figure. This time, anyway. Her smile in the photograph was radiant, a new wife anticipating the years of happiness stretching out before her. A wave of maternal warmth flowed through Mariel, followed hard by a twinge of melancholy. She prayed that someday her daughter would bless her with similar tidings, and that Ellie, too, would experience the miracle of birth.

The thought was selfish, and she quickly banished it. "Phoebe, look at her. She simply glows."

Phoebe sniffled and poured them each a glass of milk, still

cool from the cellar. "She's my beautiful girl. I only wish the baby wasn't due in the dead of winter. Don't matter. I'll find a way. Won't nothing keep me from being there to welcome my grandchild into this world." Milk had painted a little white mustache. "Lottie's gonna send me a new photograph every month."

"Have they chosen names yet?"

"I think if it's a boy they'll name it after Theo's dad, Glenn. A girl, I don't know. Theo wants a boy, of course. Lottie don't care too much, but I think she's leaning toward a girl. You done with the picture? I'm gonna paste it into my diary."

Phoebe sprang up the stairs to her room, her linen dress swishing behind her. Mariel tried to convince herself she was overjoyed for the Hammons and the Parleys. Both couples were entering wonderful times in their lives. Mariel had had hers already, first with her father and mother, then with her father and grandfather, and finally with a youthful Randall and their own children. Perhaps they'd create more good years for themselves here in Dakota when Ellie, and eventually Alex, gave them the grandchildren she so dearly desired.

She set her glass on the table and watched the liquid swirl and settle. If only her mind would settle so easily. *We're always looking behind or ahead for our happiness, never suspecting that we might, at this very moment, be living in a golden age. The past makes us forget and the future makes us hope, leaving all of our problems to accumulate in the present to cloud our contentment.*

Oh, Mariel, how dreary you've become.

She got no further in her self-absorption. Fiona Bohnet rushed in the door, her hair fallen from its bun. Without so much as a hello, she blurted, "Clyde Hartwig made bail!"

Mariel nearly spit out her milk. "Who would do that?"

"No one knows. We've always thought he's got more money

than he lets on, but if he did, why would he have sat in jail for so long? Maybe someone took pity on him."

"Pity Clyde?" Phoebe said from the top of the stairs. "Sure, he's got friends, but bail is awful steep for murder. Nobody likes him that much."

Mariel didn't envy Hartwig the six additional months he faced in that dreadful jail cell. Others probably felt the same, but enough to pay his bail? "My Lord," she said, "Mr. Cowan's going to blow him up."

"If I was a betting woman," Phoebe said as she descended the steps, "I'd say the smart money's on Clyde loading up Louisa and the kids and hightailing it out of Dakota. How stupid would it be to stay? Cowan can kill him now, or a judge can hang him later."

****

Mariel rocked on her porch with the latest copy of the *Sentinel* spread out on her lap.

Herb Goss had finally kept his promise and printed the first installment of Mike's prison story, giving her the prominent byline she craved.

However, her article was upstaged by Goss's editorial, written before the fact, concerning possible scenarios that might emerge should Hartwig ever make bail. The coincidence seemed so prescient that she wondered if it was Goss who'd put up the money.

That brought up a host of disturbing questions she'd rather not think about.

She set the paper down. Randall had predicted rain for tomorrow, but tonight the sun was setting in a clear blue Dakota sky. The flowers at Bruno's grave had blossomed spectacularly, and her little vegetable garden was producing nicely. With natural light fading, she took in the lush aromas and peaceful sounds of life until it was time to go inside and change into her bedclothes.

CHAPTER FORTY-FIVE
SNAKE EYES
Friday, September 16, 1887

Carter Cowan was mailing a package in the post office when Mariel came in with Randall's lunch. She couldn't help noticing the suspicious size and shape of the box.

A sober Herb Goss stood behind the counter. He, too, eyed the package with consternation.

Cowan nodded to her. "Mrs. Erickson."

Even uttered in his lovely Scottish accent, her name sounded vile on his lips. "I'd prefer not to speak with you, Mr. Cowan."

"Nor I you, ma'am. I once thought I might want a word with you, but that time has passed."

"Where you mailing this to?" Goss said. "I can't read your writing."

"Why, to Mr. Hartwig's home, of course."

Goss jumped back as if the package were on fire. "I'll have no part of that—"

"Och, you damn fool. It's books and a map for my brother in Toronto." He drew his finger under the name on the paper wrapping. "See, Vincent Cowan?"

Goss visibly relaxed. "Well, I don't suppose you'd mail a bomb to your own brother."

Cowan sneered his awful smile. "Why not? I'm an evil man,

after all. Ask her."

He just likes to blow things up.

Mariel blushed, not because of anything Cowan said, but because she was still standing there, listening, when she should be on her way upstairs.

Cowan seemed to sense her thoughts. "Taking notes, ma'am? Milady is to be commended for her account of Mr. Hammon's travails. I very much enjoyed your work. But the cynic in me suspects old war stories are just a place-holder in the paper until you can find something more provocative to print. Eh, Mayor Goss? Waiting for me to give away my nefarious plans?"

"Forgive me. I didn't intend to eavesdrop. Mr. Goss is perfectly capable of taking his own notes, if he's so inclined."

"I know what you're wondering, the both of you. Why is Hartwig still alive?" He didn't wait for their response. "For now I'm content to allow your American justice to run its course, delayed though it may be. If your court reaches the appropriate verdict and punishment, no one in your quaint village need fear anything from me."

"And if it doesn't?" Goss asked.

Cowan pushed the package closer to Goss. "Is postage to Canada extra?"

"I'll have to weigh it and check my chart. Any truth to what Hartwig told Mariel about you and Liam?"

"Why, did he say something unflattering?" Cowan's arrogance was insufferable. He sniffed the air, then glanced at Mariel's basket. "A meal for your dear husband? Your devotion touches my heart, but 'twill be for naught if his food gets cold."

Embarrassed, Mariel nodded goodbye to Goss and headed toward the stairs. She heard coins being slapped onto the counter.

"That's too much," Goss said.

"Look, both heads. Snake eyes. I've forgotten—in America is that a good roll or bad?"

"Depends on the game."

"Indeed it does, sir. You may keep whatever remains after postage."

Mariel slowed her steps to wait for Cowan to leave, then returned to Goss. "You didn't really think it was a bomb, did you?"

Goss shook the package. It made the sounds one might expect of books and a map. "That's not the only reason I was nervous. For Christ's sake, Hartwig's upstairs with Beryl. He's got a quick trigger, if you get my meaning, so he won't be long. What if he'd come down when Cowan was here?"

"Was it you who paid his bail?" It was the first time she'd been brave enough to ask.

"Not even I could get that stupid drunk."

****

She'd fried pork chops for Randall, with bread, butter, and molasses on the side. He thanked her, but wasn't very talkative as he studied his charts and maps. In a few minutes he needed to go downstairs and have Goss telegraph his readings to St. Paul.

Mariel had hoped for conversation to drown out the sounds emanating from the room next door where Hartwig and Beryl were still transacting business. Bedsprings squeaked as Beryl emitted gasps intended to be construed as pleasure, but even from Randall's office Mariel recognized them as feigned. She remembered summoning similar gasps herself, back when she thought it important to reinforce Randall's sense of virility.

Hartwig grunted the sounds men made during such moments. She hadn't minded with her husband, but the idea of

Hartwig engaging in *the act* made her skin crawl.

"How do you tolerate the commotion next door?" she said.

Randall finished chewing a mouthful of pork. "Beryl? She's usually asleep this time of day. All I have to endure is her snoring—which isn't much worse than yours."

"I do not snore!"

He smiled and took another bite. "I wouldn't object if the walls were a bit thicker, though."

"It's Hartwig in there with her. Mr. Goss told me. I wonder if Louisa knows?"

"I wouldn't be surprised if she paid Beryl herself in order to keep Clyde away from her."

Mariel recalled Sadie once saying something like that about Goss. *If she can get him to raise anything but a glass, God bless her.* "Do all married men cavort with prostitutes?"

Randall pushed up his spectacles and looked down his nose at her. "This one doesn't. That's all that matters." Then he leaned back in his chair and chuckled.

"What's funny?"

"I never told you this, but shortly before we were married, Noah pulled me aside and asked if I'd ever had carnal relations with a woman before. Naturally, I was offended at the very notion and denied it. He said, 'Good God, man, you're going to *practice* on my granddaughter?'"

"He said that?"

"I was fond of that old man. I wish I'd had more time to get to know him."

She wouldn't have wanted Randall practicing on anyone else before her, but she had to admit that Noah's comment was amusing.

"Why do you suppose Hartwig hasn't left town?" she said.

Randall shrugged toward Beryl's room. "I don't know and I don't care. I have work to finish. Thank you for lunch."

Mariel stood up. "I can take a hint."

She noticed it had grown quiet in the next room. Randall must have noticed, too. "Hartwig's not busy anymore," he said. "Why don't you ask him?"

Mariel grimaced. "Knowing what he's been doing?"

"So? Have you wondered when you see Mike and Phoebe if they just got done doing *that*?"

"You're a horrible man, and I'll thank you to keep your obscene thoughts to yourself."

She hurried downstairs, then paced in front of the post office counter. She hadn't seen Hartwig since his release on bail, which was fine with her. Charlie Koerperich had been forced to replace him at the livery stable with Oliver Nielson, one of Augie and Caroline's boys. Therefore, Hartwig had little reason to go out in public—except, apparently, to visit Beryl.

"You waiting for Clyde?" Goss said.

"I don't know what I'm doing."

The whole situation confused her. Hartwig was a despicable excuse for a human being. Yet he didn't terrify her nearly as much as Cowan, whose only offense was being the subject of a rumor.

This didn't in any way imply that she was eager to see Hartwig, particularly after he'd just disgraced his wedding vows. A door closed above and Hartwig said something to Beryl, or perhaps to Randall. Then there were footsteps on the stairs.

The man looked remarkable. His face was still gaunt, but he was now clean-shaven, having scraped the patches of whiskers from his neck, chin, and cheeks. He'd also gotten a haircut and dressed in clean clothes.

"Mayor," he said, ignoring Mariel.

Goss acknowledged his greeting with a nod.

"You look quite dashing, Mr. Hartwig," Mariel said.

"Well, if it ain't old Scoop herself. Beryl likes her men spiffed up. Gonna put that in the paper?"

So much for pleasantries. "It isn't my intention to publically humiliate you, Mr. Hartwig, regardless how richly you deserve it."

"That's right, Clyde," Goss said. "All we want to know is why the hell you haven't left town. I bet you would. Figured you'd have rabbited out of here the minute your bail was paid."

He looked at them both with contempt. "Guess you jackasses don't know me as good as you think. Here's something for you to write down, Mrs. Erickson: Hartwigs don't run."

CHAPTER FORTY-SIX
HARBINGER OF WINTER
Monday, October 3, 1887

At seven in the morning, Mariel sat in the front of the classroom, awaiting her students. The autumn weather had been favorable, allowing Goss Valley's farmers to reap a bountiful crop of wheat, barley, corn, soybeans, and hay. The harvest was already being canned for the winter or stored in sheds and barns to feed the livestock. Whatever was left over was taken by wagon to Kimball to be loaded onto trains for the markets in Saint Paul and Chicago.

Released from the fields, the children could now return to school. Thirty-one names were on her class list, only six fewer than last year. Apparently the ladies of the Fragment Society had come to their senses, at least for this term.

None of the Cowan children were enrolled, nor was Wayne Hartwig, but all thirteen of the Blackfords were. Bobby Baughman was coming back for another year, too, although he was of an age that he should be considering college or seeking permanent employment. Megan Blackford had much to do with his decision.

Mariel couldn't be happier. Her stars seemed to be in alignment. Not only was she teaching again, but Goss had been instructing her in the intricacies of typesetting. She practiced reading text backwards in the mirror, so when it was time for her to set the types, it came naturally to her. And there'd be plenty of material with which to ply her new skills. Her article about Andersonville had proved popular, and Mike had agreed to provide more Civil War stories for the *Sentinel*.

The room was chilly, as there'd been a hard freeze overnight. Cold was the death knell for her gardens, although her hardy, fall-blooming asters might survive another two weeks. To calm her usual first-day jitters, Mariel decided to make a few "cats" to take the edge off the chill.

She draped her coat over her shoulders and strolled out into a glorious sunrise, the western sky still deep blue, the eastern ablaze with red and orange. The leaves on the Hammons' trees were at their peak colors, while frost blanketed the prairie in sparkling white. Of all the seasons, she loved autumn best, even if it was the harbinger of winter.

Mike always kept the shed padlocked, yet today the door stood open. A light burned within. The padlock wasn't broken, but hung on the hasp staple with a key in it. Expecting Mike, she was shocked to find Hartwig. She gasped loudly enough to startle him. He'd reverted to his slovenly look, unshaven and unwashed. The lantern's flame carved harsh shadows into the caverns of his face and set his eyes aglow with menace. Her first thought was that he must not have visited Beryl lately.

Her second was to run.

"Ah, the schoolmarm," Hartwig sneered. "Don't scream. I ain't gonna hurt you."

"What are you doing here?"

"What's it look like? Charlie hired Augie Nielson's boy to take my place at the livery stable. I gotta feed my family somehow. Mr. Hammon told me to make cats for you."

"Mike hired you?"

"I'm his handyman, ain't I?"

"That was before you murdered Liam."

"I ain't been convicted of nothing yet."

"A technicality that will soon be rectified, I hope."

"You talk pretty sassy to a man you think's a killer."

She took a step back. "You said you wouldn't hurt me."

"Maybe I'm a liar, too."

Mariel tabulated all the commandments he'd broken and decided to change the subject. He had a small stack of cats at his feet. "I'll just take what you have, thank you."

"Mr. Hammon paid me for a week's worth, in case the weather stays cold. I give him his money's worth."

Hartwig with a sense of honor? Seemed that whenever she convinced herself he was evil incarnate, he'd trip her up with something decent.

Swing low, sweet chariot, coming for to carry me home.

"You exasperate me, Mr. Hartwig."

"I don't even know what that means. Is it fun?"

"Would you hand me a few cats?"

"I'll bring them. Wouldn't want to muss your pretty dress."

"Thank you. Goss didn't pay your bail. Was it Mike?"

"How's that your concern?"

"It isn't. People say you have money from the grain market and your wheat seed."

"Been listening to gossip?"

"I dislike gossip, Mr. Hartwig."

"Like hell. You ain't no different than them hens in Louisa's sewing circle."

"I see no reason to stand here and be insulted."

"Would I have stayed in jail if I had money?"

"I can't imagine why. But then, many of the things you do are beyond my comprehension."

She turned and walked toward her classroom. As she approached the door, he called out to her. "It was Carter Cowan, Scoop. He paid my bail."

CHAPTER FORTY-SEVEN
FATHER OF JUSTICE
Tuesday, November 1, 1888

After dismissing school for the day, Mariel hurried to the courthouse to write a story about the election, since Goss, being a candidate, didn't feel it an appropriate task for himself.

A number of men were lined up outside, waiting to vote. Surrounding them, the ladies of the Fragment Society protested in the street. They hadn't forgiven Goss for denying their petition to terminate Mariel's contract. Fortunately, they couldn't vote, so all they could do was make noise and threaten their husbands with bedtime solitude if they didn't vote against Goss. With Beryl in town, Mariel didn't think that threat carried much weight.

Most of them were sending their children to school. That's all she cared about. She ignored their catcalls as she went inside to join Randall and Mike. She met Marshal Woolridge along the way.

"Good news," he said, when they found Randall and Mike in line. "Just got a telegram from Judge Larrabee. He arrives in Kimball the ninth of January, with the trial being held a day or two after that. I think he's got some legal stuff with land deeds to clear up with Frank, too."

"I'll make sure he has my best room," Fiona said. She'd come with her sons Phineas and Ned. Ned had just turned twenty-one, and this was his first election. By the sour look on his face, he didn't care who the mayor was and didn't want to vote. Mariel suspected it had taken some ear pulling on Fiona's part to get him here. Phinny, on the other hand, probably didn't mind. He'd been on a few benders with Goss in which the older man provided the liquor. Any man who plied him with drink was good enough for him.

Lloyd Koch was the other candidate. He'd allowed his name to be added to the ballot only so Goss would have competition, but said he didn't even plan to vote for himself.

Half the city councilmen were also up for re-election, but they were running unopposed.

"Where's your ballot?" Mike said to Woolridge.

"Courthouse is open till five," Woolridge said.

"Who you voting for?"

"I'm gonna write in your beard as a candidate. Not you, just your beard. Without your mouth behind it, it'd be a lot quieter around here."

Mike laughed and muttered a vulgar, seven-letter word for a specific body part. They all moved forward in line, inching closer to the ballot box.

"Do you know anything about this judge?" Randall said.

"Not much. In Cheyenne, three, four years back he hung six horse thieves at once from the same scaffold. Got two boys who are also judges, from what I hear. Guess that makes him the father of justice, eh?"

"That title," Mariel said, "belongs to God."

"Father of justices, then. Anyway, one way or another this shit's gonna be over with. I'm sick of keeping track of both Clyde and Cowan."

"Had a chance to talk to the prosecutor?" Mike asked.

Woolridge shook his head. "The marshal there asked me to make copies of the witness affidavits and send them down there for Van Pelt to study. Frank's gonna talk to the judge about reading my statement into the record so I don't have to testify."

"You're marshal. Why wouldn't you testify?"

"Nothing to say, really. I knew who did it, I knew where he lived, and he didn't resist arrest. Besides, I'm providing security at the trial. Can't be shooting rowdies from the witness stand."

"Mr. Hartwig claimed it was Mr. Cowan who paid bail," Mariel said. "Is that true?"

Randall sighed his impatience. "I told you not to bother John about that. Clyde's a liar."

"He surely is that," Woolridge said, "but not this time. It was Cowan."

"Doesn't that strike you as odd?" Mike's beard said.

Mariel giggled at the thought. The men looked at her curiously. She ahemed, coughed into her hand, and resumed a straight face.

"Sure as hell did, and I didn't like it one little bit. But what could I do? I asked Clyde did he want to stay in jail, in case Cowan was gunning for him, but he said no. I said fine, but if you try to run, you won't have to worry about Cowan, 'cause I'll come after you myself."

The Bohnet boys had voted, and were now on their way out. Ned still didn't look happy. "Quit your whining," Fiona said. "It didn't hurt you one bit."

"I was supposed to meet Tessa after she got out of school."

"I don't want to hear the girl's name again."

"I can do what I want. I'm a grown man."

"I got a pair of scissors and a bad attitude that can change that."

They exited the courthouse to more verbal abuse by the Fragment Society ladies. "Atta girl, Fiona," Mike said. "About time she gave those boys the what-for."

"Would you really shoot Clyde?" Randall said.

"Never shot anybody my whole career," Woolridge said. "I'd like to keep it that way. But yeah, if I had to."

"I wouldn't mind you kicking Cowan's ass right out of Dakota," Mike said.

"For what? Just 'cause I don't like his looks? Well, you're a homely cuss, too, but that doesn't give me the right to run you out of town."

"In my defense, my beard is cute."

They moved to the front of the line and received their ballots from Frank Chamberlain, who was also Goss Valley's election official.

Mariel watched Randall fill his ballot out for Herb Goss and the unopposed councilmen. She wondered how she'd vote if she could. As a dignitary Goss was a drunken embarrassment, yet he'd gotten the county seat back for the town—nothing Mariel cared about, but some thought it an achievement—and, more to the point, he was finally giving her chance to be a writer.

And with the other choices being Lloyd Koch, who didn't want to be mayor, or Mike's beard, which hadn't stated a preference, she'd probably choose Goss, too.

CHAPTER FORTY-EIGHT
YOU CAN KINDLY GO TO HELL
Saturday, December 31, 1887

"To the new year," Randall said, clinking his wine glass with those of Mike, Phoebe, and Mariel. Mariel seldom imbibed spirits, but on special occasions she enjoyed red wine diluted with water or sarsaparilla. Phoebe had also brewed tea, just in case.

"To the new year," they repeated. They were celebrating early because Randall had to work at midnight. Bobby's continuing preoccupation with Megan was keeping him away again tonight.

Despite agreeable weather for the past few days, the hotel had no lodgers, allowing Mike and Phoebe to spend a rare night in their own home. A large window occupied a third of the kitchen's west wall, and the moon, a sliver past full, was bright enough to illuminate the room by itself. Its light fell across the table, so white it leeched the color from their faces, prompting Phoebe to light a lamp.

"This weather gonna hang around till the judge gets here?" Mike said between coughing spells. Mariel hoped it was just the wine tickling his throat, but knew better.

"According to Salt Lake," Randall said, "it's cold upstream, but there aren't any big storms. It should hold through the beginning of the week, but ten days? No one knows that far in advance."

"If something delays the trial again, I think everybody's ready to say to hell with it."

"I already have," Phoebe said, favoring them with a grin so wide Mariel could count her teeth. "I'm leaving for Cedar Rapids on Monday. Lottie's doctor says the child should arrive around the middle of the month. First babies are usually late like that. Never mind the trial, just be sure the weather's good enough so I can get to the train."

Randall raised his glass again. "I promise there won't be any twisters."

"You sure you want to go out on a limb like that?" Mike laughed.

"Are you going, too, Mike?" Mariel said.

"Sooner or later."

"He'd just get in the way," Phoebe said. "Besides, this big tough man's scared to death of newborns."

"I'm always afraid I'll drop it and break it."

"See what I mean? I might let him visit when the child is twelve." She paused, then shook her head. "Can you believe it's gonna be eighteen eighty-eight already? Remember when the turn of the century seemed so far away? Our little grandbaby will be twelve then."

"Thirteen," Randall said.

"Twelve," Phoebe said.

"Twelve," Mariel said.

"Twelve," Mike said. "Even a damn officer ought to be able to add eighteen eighty-eight and twelve and come up with nineteen hundred."

"I can, and do. But the century doesn't change until January first, nineteen-oh-one."

"So the twentieth century don't start until a year after it starts?"

Mariel sighed. "We've had this discussion before. There's no reasoning with him."

"There wasn't a year zero," Randall said. He stood up and went to the window. The moon threw his shadow across the floor and over the table. Looking out, he said, "Our years are dated from the time of our Lord's birth."

"Here we go again," Mariel said.

"So?" Mike said.

"So the date went from one B.C. to one A.D., with no zero in between. A new century can't begin on a year ending with zero."

"Why not? By that logic, the eighteen eighties didn't start until eighteen eighty-one, and that's just plain foolish."

Randall turned to face them. "It doesn't work that way."

"You're saying decades start on the zero, but centuries on the one?"

"I didn't say the nineteen hundreds don't start until nineteen-oh-one, I said the twentieth century doesn't."

"They're the same thing!"

"They are not."

"Randy, get your ass back over here and drink some more wine. You are way too sober to be this aggravating."

"You wouldn't like me when I'm drunk."

"I don't like you when you're not." Mike stared sternly at Randall as he rejoined them at the table, but he winked at Mariel.

Phoebe tried to change the subject, but Mike saw the need for last word on the subject. "I get it. The first decade of every century only has nine years."

"No!"

"But that's balanced by the last one of the previous century having eleven," Mariel said playfully. She didn't exactly relish Randall's exasperation, but it didn't displease her, either.

"You're enjoying this."

Mariel took her second sip of the evening and didn't answer.

****

Mike and Randall wanted to discuss what interest Judge Larrabee might have in Frank Chamberlain's deed files, so Mariel and Phoebe used the opportunity to retreat to the bedroom and begin packing for Phoebe's journey.

Mariel held up a blue calico dress. "This is nice."

"Put it in the trunk."

"How long do you plan to be away?"

"At least April this time, but forever, eventually. Mike, too. His asthma's giving him fits. The only place he hasn't tried is the desert, and he won't go there. He figures if it's gonna kill him, he wants to be near family."

"Surely it's not that bad?"

"It'll never get better."

Crestfallen, Mariel plopped onto the bed. "You're really moving to Iowa?"

Phoebe folded a pair of bloomers and tossed them to her. "Won't be before fall. Mike'll be here most of the time till then, trying to teach Fiona's boys the ropes. I'll be back and forth."

What will become of my classroom? Mariel thought. Our social life? Had Randall known and not told her? "I was hoping eighteen eighty-eight would be a better year."

"We'd've had to leave anyway. You know our land's a military homestead exemption. That means wrangling with the government. Mike's been going 'round and 'round with Sparks for a couple of years now, arguing over when he mustered out. He says one time, Sparks says another. Also claims Mike didn't prove up the land."

"Sparks?"

"Land Commissioner."

"That's right. I recall Mike mentioning him.'

After Fort Defiance, perhaps Randall deserved his shunning by the Army, but as far as Mariel knew, Mike had served honorably. For goodness' sake, he'd gone to Andersonville in the service of his country. Now they wanted to expel him from his land? "He built this house. What more does Sparks want?"

Phoebe perched next to her and tied several pairs of stockings into a knot before packing them. "Crops, I reckon. Mike can't farm, on account of his asthma."

"It's disgraceful."

"We're sick of fighting it. It don't matter. Like I said, he wants to be closer to Lottie."

"It's the principle of the thing."

Phoebe smiled. "Last week he sent Sparks a note, saying 'Thanks for nothing, and you can kindly go to hell.'"

Mariel wrapped her arms around her. "I shall miss you."

Phoebe squirmed out of her embrace. "We ain't left yet, silly. And it's not like we're moving to the moon. Hardly takes any time at all to get to Cedar Rapids by train. We'll still see each other, just not as often. It'll get me in the habit of writing letters again."

"I wish we had a grandchild."

"Ellie will come through for you. If not, your soldier boy will. Girls love that uniform. He don't go to them, they'll come to him."

Mariel rose and selected another dress for Phoebe. Alex had received his first demerit at West Point, for fighting and drinking. He was growing up too fast. "He does have his father's good looks, and I know his children will be beautiful. I just hope there's a marriage between the courtship and the consummation."

****

Thirty minutes later they heard a female voice in the kitchen. Mariel and Phoebe looked at each other in bewilderment. What woman would come calling at this hour? Beryl, perhaps, but she usually entertained her clients at the post office. In any case, she had *no* business visiting the home of a married man after dark. Or ever.

Phoebe cracked open the bedroom door and peered out. "I'll be damned. It's Louisa."

"Hartwig?"

"Know any other gals named Louisa in Goss Valley?"

Mariel came up behind Phoebe and listened. Mike and Louisa sat in profile, their figures silhouetted by the moonlight. Randall was in the middle. He had his arms folded across his chest. Although his face was in shadow, she could just see that annoying expression of scorn and smug amusement.

"Clyde's scared, Mr. Hammon. He'd skin me if he knew I was here. He's over at Duncan's, drinking with Herb Goss and Phinny Bohnet."

"Who's with your kids?" Mike said.

"Wayne's old enough to watch over Jeannette."

"Would you like tea or wine?"

"Tea, thank you."

Mike got up, then disappeared briefly from Mariel's view. "Well, now, Louisa," she heard him say, "I don't mean to sound heartless, but don't he have good reason to be scared?"

"He was ready for the trial last summer, but I think all this waiting has got to his nerves."

Mike returned with the teapot and poured her a cup. "He gonna run?"

Louisa blew the steam from the top of the liquid. "No. He thinks that's why Cowan paid his bail. That way he can shoot him down and no one will call it murder."

Mike resumed his chair at the table. "That's kinda what I

figured, too. Why are you here tonight, Louisa? What can I do for you?"

She barely touched the brim of the cup to her lips, drinking as if inhaling vapors. "Nobody much likes Clyde. I know that. Even Herb can't stand him, except when he's drunk."

Then Goss is a true and constant friend, Mariel thought.

"You're the only one who's been decent to him. Charlie wouldn't take him back at the livery, never mind that there's still plenty of work to go around. Said, 'How'd it look if I hired an accused assassin?'"

Good for you, Charlie Koerperich.

"There were five witnesses," Randall said.

"I don't expect you to understand, not the way that wife of yours stirred up trouble."

"Herb didn't print any of that."

"Randy, shut up. Are you asking me to find him more work?"

"Not for the money so much, but just to give him something to do. When he's not working or drinking, he's driving us mad about Cowan. He taught Wayne to shoot a long time ago, but now he wants me to learn, too, and I think he'd even put a gun in Jeannette's hand if she was big enough to hold one. He hardly ever sleeps, just keeps looking out the window and door. About every half hour he circles around outside."

"The trial's in less than two weeks."

"I know."

"He'll probably be convicted."

"I don't think Clyde fears hanging. It's Cowan, him and that damned Blackford clan. They're a different breed. He says they kill people they don't even know, and they don't care if it's women and children. He's worried about us, Mr. Hammon. I know he can be mean and vulgar, but one thing I'll swear to: He loves his family."

Don't, Mike! Mariel wanted to cry, but he nodded, his cowlick swaying with the motion.

"I'm sure he does, Louisa. Listen, my wife needs to catch the train in Kimball on Monday. Think Clyde would drive her? I gotta pay someone to do it. Might as well be him."

"He's not supposed to leave town."

"I'll see if I can clear it with John. If he ain't skedaddled by now, I don't s'pose he's gonna."

"You'd trust a killer with your wife?"

"Oh, Clyde's not dumb enough to mess with Phoebe. Hell, even I'm scared of her."

"God bless you, Mr. Hammon."

"God *damn* you, Mr. Hammon," Phoebe whispered.

CHAPTER FORTY-NINE
INDICATIONS ARE GOOD
Tuesday, January 10, 1888

Mariel's students had been impossible to control all day. If their wild behavior was any indication of their parents' state of mind, the entire town was ready to burst. She felt it, too, although she harbored no illusions of attending the trial, since it would be conducted on a school day. In such a simple case, there was little chance it would extend into the weekend.

Everything was set. Eight days ago Hartwig, with Trippledy in tow, delivered Phoebe to Kimball and returned without incident. Five days later Woolridge rescinded his bail and locked him up to await Judge Larrabee, in case Hartwig should develop last-minute rabbit feet. On Sunday, when Randall announced in church that no precipitation was likely, there was a collective sigh of relief, for that meant the train bearing Judge Larrabee would get through to Kimball on schedule.

Yesterday Goss and Woolridge went to fetch the judge, along with prosecutor Gregory Van Pelt. They stayed overnight in Kimball and planned to arrive home late this afternoon.

At four o'clock Mariel dismissed school, bundled up against the cold, and walked to town. A crowd had already gathered outside the hotel. Hartwig was going to pay a life for a life, and everyone wanted to see the man who would impose the sentence. It was morbid curiosity, a despicable trait in humans, made more so by Mariel's own susceptibility to it. Still, her only regret, if it could be called that, was that Hartwig had waited an awfully long time to face the hangman. Liam had been unconscious in his bed for a week, unable to contemplate the inevitability of his condition. But Hartwig had had seven months to brood on his own mortality, to listen to the clicking of the clock, to grasp that the final darkness was but a gavel's thump away. On the other hand, unlike Liam, he'd been able to make his peace with God—if Hartwig was capable of a belief in God.

A hoop and a holler went up just before sunset as the delegation pulled into town and parked in front of the hotel. Mariel was able to catch a glimpse of the new arrivals. The man she assumed to be Van Pelt was young and handsome in his way, while Larrabee rather resembled photographs she'd seen of the late Ambrose Burnside, the former Union general, Rhode Island governor, and United States senator. Like Burnside, he was bald on top, with massive side whiskers which connected his mustache to the remaining crescent of hair. Unlike Burnside, whose close-cropped hair was white, Larrabee's locks were bright red and extended nearly to his collar.

He looked distinctly Irish.

Fiona put the judge up in her finest suite—which, but for the word suite, wasn't one stitch better than her other rooms. At least he got one, for the rest had already been filled by potential jurors and by out-of-towners drawn to the trial. Without Phoebe, poor Mike must be running himself ragged trying to keep up with all the guests.

If anyone expected a speech from Larrabee, they were disappointed, for he entered the hotel without acknowledging their presence. Immediately thereafter Woolridge dispersed the crowd, and Mariel went home.

Randall was scrambling eggs for both of them. He told her

A Killing Snow

Judge Larrabee was to meet with Frank and Van Pelt after supper to hear pre-trial motions in closed session.

And so it had begun.

****

Two hours later, she was reading Keats on the sofa while Randall worked on his charts at the parlor table. He brought some of them home from the post office almost daily now to prepare his weather column in the *Sentinel*.

She was in the middle of "La Belle Dame Sans Merci" when Herb Goss and Frank Chamberlain arrived unannounced at the door.

Mariel set down her book and showed them in. "To what do we owe the honor? May I take your coats?"

"We won't be staying long," Frank said.

"Is there a problem?" Randall said.

"Call it a request. Judge Larrabee wants your assurance of good weather this week. Assuming the trial takes no more than a day, he'd like to wrap up whatever business remains on Thursday,"—in other words, the sentencing—"complete the deed work with me on Friday, and leave on Saturday."

Randall looked at the men with annoyance. "My assurance? What kind of power does he think I have? I predict the weather, I don't control it. What's his hurry?"

"He's scheduled in Deadwood on the seventeenth. The marshal there has already telegraphed twice asking for confirmation."

"What happened in Deadwood?"

"Some cowboy opened fire in the street. Three dead, including a little boy." Frank wiped his boots on the welcome mat. "May I see your magic charts?"

"They won't mean much to you."

"I know a little something about numbers."

Goss followed without wiping his boots, trailing slush across Mariel's clean floor.

"What are Clyde's chances?" Randall said as Frank looked over his shoulder.

"Van Pelt's got a damn good case, I can tell you that."

"You could have been the prosecutor."

"I know," he said.

When he didn't elaborate, Goss slurred, "So what's your crystal ball say?"

Randall pointed to some symbols, lines, and shapes on his map. "It's thirty-six degrees and sunny in Salt Lake. That's what's heading our way. Did it take both of you to ask me that?"

Frank nodded toward Goss. "He wants a word with your wife."

"What can I do for you, Mayor?" Mariel said.

"I declared tomorrow a holiday. I'm canceling school and closing the post office. Any other business that doesn't want to open doesn't have to."

"You're shutting down an entire town for a killer? Children still need to learn. People still need to earn their livelihood."

"I'm not making anyone go, and I'm certainly not doing it for Hartwig. But nobody's ever seen anything like this in Goss Valley before. We've never even had a trial, let alone one for murder. The courthouse will be packed to the rafters."

"That's no excuse. The children can't attend the trial, so they might as well be in school."

"There won't be anyone to teach them. You and I are covering the trial for the *Sentinel*."

Mariel didn't need to ask why he needed her help. She could smell it on his breath. Her anger evaporated as her excitement built. Real news! Not stories from the past, not interviews that never saw print, but an actual event as it was happening.

She was ashamed to admit it, but she blessed the demons of Goss's affliction.

"I can assure the judge of fine weather, then?" Frank said to Randall.

"Assure? No. But tell him the indications are good."

Mariel was still trying to catch her breath when the men turned to leave. "Jury selection's set for nine o'clock sharp tomorrow morning," Goss said.

CHAPTER FIFTY
A SINGLE COUNT OF HOMICIDE
Wednesday, January 11, 1888

The trial was to be held in the main hall of the courthouse, but spectators weren't allowed in while the jury was being selected. Throngs of people waited outside, grumbling and rubbing their hands together for warmth. It wasn't a terribly cold day, as Januaries went, but it was still below freezing. Mariel stood at the door, pleading with the appointed bailiff Trippledy to let her in, but he wouldn't budge.

"There ain't but fourteen men to choose from," he said. "Won't take more than twenty minutes to seat them, I reckon."

"But I'm writing an article for the *Sentinel.*"

"Mayor Goss saved a seat for you, but not till the trial starts."

"I'd like to get started by writing my early impressions."

"Well, you can't be in the hall till the jury's been chosen. Judge's orders. But what say I put you in with some of the witnesses? They're in Herb's office. Maybe you can interview them."

She removed her pencil and notepad from her coat pocket. "That will be satisfactory, Mr. Dalton. Thank you."

He led her inside, interposing his large body between her and the lawyers questioning the prospective jurors in front. She didn't know why it was such a secret ceremony. She'd see their faces during the trial anyway.

But no matter. Trippledy was just doing his job. He opened a door for her and closed it behind her. The mayor's office was small, which probably didn't concern Goss, who rarely used it anyway, but it was a problem for the five people stuffed inside.

For one thing, there were only three chairs. These were occupied by Nora Koerperich and the Bohnet brothers. Charlie Koerperich and Augie Nielson stood in opposite corners.

Mariel knew the Koerperichs and Bohnets well enough, but had only spoken with Mr. Nielson a few times. He was the father of her student Constance. An unsociable man, he'd never said three words in succession to her.

"Hey," Ned Bohnet sneered, "you ain't a witness."

"I'm covering the trial," Mariel said, displaying her writing tools, as if that were proof.

"You gonna interview us?" Phineas said.

"May I?"

"No," all five said together.

"Don't think it's allowed before the trial," Charlie Koerperich said.

"Mr. Dalton said I could."

"Trippledy's a big fat idiot," Ned said.

Disappointed, Mariel put her pencil and note pad back into her coat pocket. Goss would tell her a real reporter didn't give up that easily. But he wasn't here, so he hadn't tried at all.

"Least you get to watch it," Ned said. "We can't."

"Of course you can. You're testifying."

"Nope," Charlie said. "Not till after we give our evidence. Frank says the judge don't want us influenced by what the others say. One of you boys get up and let Mrs. Erickson have your chair."

"By then all the good stuff's probably gonna be over," Ned said.

His brother elbowed him. "Quit your damn pouting."

Mariel had never seen a trial before and was unfamiliar with the procedures. When she thought about it, though, that made sense. "It's all right, Mr. Koerperich, I can stand."

Nora Koerperich, card-carrying member of the Fragment Society, glared at her. "You don't write any better than you teach."

Mariel took the high road and ignored her. "Did you see the jurors?" she asked Charlie.

"That lawyer from Kimball don't want anybody who knows Clyde," he said.

"Ain't nobody that don't know Clyde," Ned said.

"The judge called in mostly outlying farmers," Charlie said. "They don't talk with him as much. But Frank says it don't matter. Anyone who knows him is just as liable to convict as those who don't. Maybe more. No one's gonna vote innocent because they *like* him."

"What do you think, Mr. Nielson?" Mariel said.

The taciturn man stood staring at his feet and clenching his jaw. "About what?"

"Anything."

"No opinion."

"I got one," Ned said. "I hope it goes on forever. Phoebe's gone, so Mama's making me help out more at the hotel. Long as I'm here, I ain't there."

"Don't hurt you none," Phineas said.

"Like you ever do anything. I had to wash dishes."

"Poor baby."

"Shut up."

"You can't tell me what to do," Phineas said.

"I can say what I want."

The brothers rose and commenced a shoving match. No one intervened until Phineas knocked Ned against Mr. Nielson.

Nielson pushed the boy to the floor. "Enough!"

Ned rolled to his feet, fists at the ready. "Or what?"

"Else."

Apparently the tone in his voice was sufficiently threatening, because both boys backed down and returned to their chairs. "You wasn't even at the field that day," Ned said.

"Close enough," Mr. Nielson said.

"Next time," Phineas said to his brother, "I'll kick your teeth so far down your throat you'll have to suck your thumb with your ass."

Charlie yawned. "Thanks, fellas. That was entertaining. I needed something to wake me up." He looked at Mariel. "The prosecutor had us here this morning at five-thirty to tell our stories."

"You're up before then anyway," Nora said.

Trippledy poked his head in the door. People rushing into the hall behind him sounded like a herd of stampeding elephants—not that Mariel had ever experienced stampeding elephants, but she could imagine. "Mrs. Erickson, the jury's been picked. You can come on in. Herb's here, but even the mayor can't hold off these lunatics forever."

Ned Bohnet jumped up.

"Not you," Trippledy said. "I'll come get you when it's your turn."

The atmosphere in the main hall was charged with excitement. The population of the entire valley couldn't exceed a hundred, yet surely twice many were jostling for space in a room designed to hold fifty. Mariel watched in horror as the crowd surged past her. Anyone unfortunate enough to fall would be trampled.

Marshal Woolridge was on the stage with his hand on his six-shooter, watching.

Mariel picked out Randall, already seated, but he was

engaged in conversation with Bobby, and didn't notice her. Bobby was here representing the Blackford family, who'd already indicated they wouldn't attend. Mariel didn't blame them. How could they bear to hear the gory details?

She was surprised she didn't see Cowan's snarling face. He must be in the hall somewhere. She could almost feel his evil presence.

Goss waved from the middle of the back row. Mariel managed to cut between people without being injured. As she settled into the one remaining open chair, she noted he wasn't particularly drunk, but he did seem rather out-of-sorts, as if he were ill or sleepy. Maybe it was just the light, but his skin seemed to have a yellowish tint.

"Late night?" she shouted over the clamor of the crowd.

"Mind your own business." He said this with a grin, so she knew he wasn't being rude. "This will be the shortest trial in history. I don't know why Clyde doesn't just confess."

"You're supposed to be unbiased."

"You're writing the story. You be unbiased."

"Are we the only members of the press present?"

"This isn't Chicago, Mrs. Erickson. No out-of-town paper is going to send a reporter to Goss Valley to write about a dead Irishman."

The din in the hall was deafening. "We won't be able to hear a thing," she said

"They should've done this at the Masonic Hall."

"And let your fine courthouse go to waste?"

He leaned his head back against the wall and closed his eyes. "Wouldn't bother me. I only needed it to get the county seat, and now we have it."

"Are you all right?"

He half-opened one eye and glanced at her. "Late night," he smiled.

"Where's the jury?"

"Front row."

"Do I know any of them?"

"How do I know who you know? I'm sure you'll recognize some of them."

The noise grew louder as Frank, Van Pelt, and Hartwig entered from another side room. Hartwig rewarded the crowd with a theatrical bow.

Van Pelt stood an inch or two taller than Frank. He used too much grease to plaster his hair down, which accentuated the straight white part in the middle. Despite his good looks, he had an air of haughtiness about him which she found distasteful. She'd probably be confident, too, if she were presenting a case as ironclad as his.

Following behind them was a rotund little fellow Mariel had never seen before. She nudged Goss, startling him into alertness. "Who's that?" she said.

"Do you ever stop talking?"

"I thought reporters were supposed to ask questions."

"Not of your editor, imbecile." Goss blinked his eyes several times, shook his head, and tousled his own hair in an attempt to rouse himself. He scrutinized the stout fellow. "I don't recognize him, either. Probably Larrabee's stenographer. I'll wager *he* knows shorthand."

Two tables had been carried onto on the stage, one on either side of the podium, each bearing books, notepads, ink bottles, and a ewer with two glasses. An armchair had been placed to the right of the podium, and a large American flag adorned the wall behind it. Woolridge stepped aside as the men climbed the stairs. Frank and Hartwig sat at the table on the left, Van Pelt and the stenographer on her right.

Frank wore a gray tweed suit. But then, he always dressed professionally. Hartwig had on a pleasant blue suit and a string necktie. His hair had been cut short, and he was clean-shaven.

"All rise," Trippledy cried.

The same door from which the four men emerged opened again, and the crowd hushed. Judge Larrabee lumbered into the auditorium, plodded up to the stage, and assumed his position behind the podium. Sunlight poured in from the north windows, illuminating his magnificent side whiskers in a blazing tangle of red. The audience, as unfamiliar with trials as Mariel was, began to applaud. Larrabee slammed his gavel against the top surface of the podium.

"Y'all shut up and sit down," he growled. "There'll be no more of that foolishness."

Although his hair made him look Irish, his accent was pure Texas. *Y'all* was going to drive Mariel crazy. She'd just broken Bobby of the unfortunate habit.

The spectators took their seats. The courtroom became still.

"Here we go," Goss whispered.

Larrabee gazed about the auditorium with a look of disdain. As a circuit judge in frontier towns, he surely would have seen worse accommodations for a trial than this, so it must be the crowd he found wanting. Finally his eyes settled on Hartwig.

"You the defendant?"

Before Hartwig could speak, Frank said, "He is, your honor."

"All right. Let's get started. Deputy?"

Trippledy ambled in front of the stage, stopping beneath the podium. He'd probably never addressed a gathering this large before. Reading from a sheet of paper, he cleared his throat and said in a warbling voice, "The case of the people of Dakota Territory versus Clyde Eugene Hartwig is now in session, Judge Willard K. Larrabee presiding."

As soon as he was finished, he retreated to the foot of the steps and stood at uneasy attention.

"Git up from your chair, Mr. Hartwig," Larrabee said. Frank and Hartwig rose together. "This here's the complaint against you. You've been indicted on a single count of first-degree homicide in the death of Liam Blackford. How do y'all plead?"

Hartwig looked at Frank, who nodded.

"Not guilty, your honor."

That set the crowd a-twitter.

Larrabee raised his gavel again, but didn't need to bring it down to silence them. "Good," he said. "Mr. Van Pelt, as prosecutor, you get to talk first."

For some reason, Mariel had expected the young man to stand, but he remained seated as he spoke. "Gentlemen of the jury, good morning. My statement will be brief, as this is a straightforward case. On the second day of May, eighteen eighty-seven, the accused, Clyde Hartwig, did willfully and with malice aforethought strike Mr. Liam Blackford with a baseball bat, causing grievous head injuries, of which wounds Mr. Blackford subsequently perished. The prosecution will present the testimony of five residents of Goss Valley who witnessed this vile attack.

"In addition, we will prove motive by entering into evidence statements concerning the defendant's deep-seated hatred of Irish people. There is also the matter of seventy dollars Mr. Hartwig claims was paid to Mr. Blackford under false pretexts. Men have been killed for less."

Although he was commenting upon a vicious crime, his voice droned as if he were reading the ingredients of a recipe. Either he was a poor prosecutor, or he was so confident that he felt he need put forth no effort in his recitation.

"That all, Mr. Van Pelt?" Larrabee said.

"It is, your honor."

"Then it's your turn, Mr. Chamberlain."

Frank rose and strode around the table. Facing the

spectators, he said, "Your honor, the defense wishes to postpone its opening argument. We reserve the right to deliver it at the beginning of our case."

Larrabee scowled at him as if he were a madman. "This some kinda trick, Mr. Chamberlain? 'Cause I don't like tricks."

"No trick, your honor."

Mariel could hear the judge sigh from the back row.

"Damned if I know what you're up to. But have it your own way, sir. So stipulated. Bailiff, read Marshal John Woolridge's affidavit into the record, as agreed to by counsel for both sides. Then, Mr. Van Pelt, you can call your first witness."

CHAPTER FIFTY-ONE
THEY DON'T HANG HEROES
Wednesday, January 11, 1888

From the bottom of the steps, Trippledy read into the record Marshal Woolridge's account of his capture of Hartwig. Both sides agreed to accept the affidavit in lieu of testimony, freeing Woolridge for his security duties.

With the proceedings on a raised stage, Mariel thought it almost like watching a play. The first witness to be called was Father Brandon, who'd been sequestered apart from the five witnesses to the murder. After Trippledy swore him in, he ascended the stairs in his priestly robes and took the chair next to the podium.

Van Pelt again remained seated. "Sir, please state your name and profession for the record."

"Father Allen Brandon." Until this moment Mariel hadn't known his first name. He remained the oldest looking young man she had ever seen, thin and sepulchral, his features not at all a pleasant resting place for women's eyes. "I'm a Jesuit priest," he said, "and a trained physician."

"What was your relationship with the victim?"

"I was his spiritual advisor and his confessor."

"Were you also his doctor, Father Brandon?"

"I only served in that capacity the one time."

"Which was?"

"After the incident."

"Which incident?"

Father Brandon cleared his throat. "The attack on Liam. The murder."

"Objection," Frank Chamberlain said.

"Sustained," Larrabee ruled. "Murderous intent has not been established. The witness will confine himself to his area of expertise. Strike the words 'the murder' from the record. Gentlemen of the jury, ignore that remark."

"I withdraw the question, your honor," Van Pelt said. "Did you treat the victim?"

"I did, sir."

"And what was the nature of his injuries?"

Brandon lowered his eyes and shook his head. "I live at the St. Xavier Mission north of the Crow Indian reservation, so it took time for me to respond to the telegraph message. In Mr. Blackford's case, however, it wouldn't have mattered if I had been there the moment the injury was incurred. The blow was mortal, and no amount of medical intervention could have achieved his recovery. His skull was crushed, the cause of death massive hemorrhaging and swelling of the brain. It was God's own miracle he survived a week."

"What caused the injury?" Mr. Van Pelt said.

"The shape of the wound indicated a single blow from a heavy object such as a fencepost or the butt of the rifle."

"Could it have been a baseball bat similar to this?" Van Pelt now rose from the table and held up the offending weapon for the jury. Even from the back row Mariel could see was it stained with something dark.

"Absolutely."

"Your honor, I'd like to enter Exhibit A into the record. Father Brandon, in your expert opinion in your capacity as a physician, from which direction was the blow struck?"

Brandon glared at Hartwig. "From behind, Mr. Van Pelt. The wound was in the back of his head."

"Therefore the victim was facing away from his assailant?"

"Yes."

"Thank you. No further questions." He nodded to Frank. "Your witness."

Frank approached Father Brandon. "Would you consider yourself a friend of the victim?"

"As I said, I was his spiritual advisor."

"Yes, we all heard you say that the first time. But that's not what I asked. Were you and Liam Blackford friends?"

"Yes, I suppose you could say so. I was, and I continue to be, fond of the entire family."

"Indeed? No more questions at this time. However, the defense wishes to recall this witness during its case."

"So noted," Larrabee said. "You will make yourself available when called, Dr. Brandon."

****

A truculent Ned Bohnet was the next witness. He fidgeted in the chair next to Judge Larrabee's podium, picking at his nose and scratching as if he had fleas. Maybe he did.

"Mr. Bohnet," Van Pelt said, "describe the circumstances on the afternoon of Monday, May second, eighteen eighty-seven."

"Circumstances?"

"What were you doing when Mr. Blackford was struck?" Van Pelt said. "Where were you, and why were you there?"

"Oh. We was out in the field back of Duncan's. It was a nice day, so a bunch of the fellas talked about getting up a baseball match when they was off work. A couple years ago Ray marked off bases and foul lines back there. 'Cept no one showed up but me, Phinny, Charlie, and Clyde. Four people ain't enough. It still gets dark pretty early in May, so we didn't have much time."

"No one else was present?"

"Mrs. Koerperich came out to watch, I guess. I don't remember seeing Mr. Nielson."

"And Mr. Blackford?"

"You know damn well he was there, or he wouldn't've got hisself killed, would he?"

Larrabee pounded his gavel. "Young man, that kind of language is not acceptable in a court of law, unless it's a direct quote."

"I don't know what a direct quote is."

"That doesn't surprise me," Larrabee said. "Just answer the questions. Proceed, Mr. Van Pelt."

"When did the victim arrive?"

"I dunno," Ned said, "a little while after Charlie, I reckon."

"Did he say why he had come?"

"If he did, I didn't hear. It wasn't to play baseball."

"What happened then?"

"Clyde started right in yelling at him."

"What was the nature of their conversation?"

"Huh?"

"What did they talk about?"

Ned's eyes darted toward Hartwig. "Clyde says, 'You owe me seventy dollars, you spud-nigger son-of-a-bitch.'" He looked up at Larrabee in trepidation.

"That is a direct quote," the judge said.

"Did the accused ever tell you why he believed Mr. Blackford owed him money?"

"No, sir."

"How did Mr. Blackford respond?"

"He said something I couldn't make out, but I did hear him tell us baseball's a stupid game, like a bug."

"A bug, Mr. Bohnet?"

"That's what he said. Don't remember what kind right now, but it was a bug."

"Where were you in relation to Mr. Hartwig and Mr. Blackford during this conversation?"

Ned seemed to struggle with the question, but before Mr. Van Pelt needed to clarify, he answered, "I was sitting on home base, waiting for the other boys to come. Clyde, Charlie, and Phinny was tossing a ball across the infield. Mr. Blackford headed straight for Clyde."

"And?"

"And the yelling commenced. Then Clyde hit him."

"With a bat?"

"Yup."

Van Pelt showed him Exhibit A. "This one?"

"Objection."

"Sustained."

"Did it look similar to this one?"

"Yes, sir, just like it."

"How long have you known Clyde Hartwig?"

"About five years."

"So you could not be mistaken that it was the accused behind Duncan's Tavern that afternoon?"

"It was Clyde."

Van Pelt wrote something on a notepad. "Has Mr. Hartwig ever expressed to you a disdain for the Irish?"

"Has he *what*?"

Ned Bohnet had never been noted for his keen intellect, but Mariel found his inability to understand even simple words alarming. The prosecutor rephrased the question. "Did you ever hear him say he hates the Irish?"

"Yes, sir, all the time."

"Other than the seventy dollars, could that have been another reason he struck Mr. Blackford?"

Larrabee intervened before Ned could answer. "Aren't you gonna object to that question, Mr. Chamberlain?"

Frank smiled. "No objection, your honor."

The judge gave him a strange look. "All right, son, go ahead."

Ned shifted from one side of his bottom to the other. "I guess so."

"Thank you. No more questions. Mr. Chamberlain?"

Frank allowed Ned to squirm a few moments more. "Did Mr. Hartwig ever explain why he hated the Irish?"

"Not really. He just did."

"Don't you wonder?"

The boy shook his head. "Why would I? I don't like 'em much, either."

"I see. Had any of you been drinking that afternoon?"

Ned grinned. "Well, what fun is baseball if you ain't drinking?"

"What about Mr. Hartwig?"

"Probably, but he just got off work at Koerperich's, so he couldn't've been too drunk."

Frank paused as if he were about to make a dramatic pronouncement. Instead, he said, "Ned, have you ever seen a bug play baseball?"

The spectators snickered. Larrabee banged his gavel.

"I didn't say it *played* baseball."

"I certainly hope not. Nothing further."

"Will you need him back for your case?" Larrabee said.

"No, your honor."

"All right, Mr. Bohnet. You're excused."

"Hot damn!"

Ned burst past Woolridge, hurdled down the stairs, and found an open space against the wall of the hall where he could watch the rest of the trial.

A Killing Snow

****

Nora Koerperich appeared annoyed by the inconvenience of being subpoenaed. "I dislike baseball," she said to Van Pelt. "It's bad enough that Charlie plays the silly game, but he insists I come to his matches. He expects me to praise him when he does something good."

Van Pelt nearly smiled, the first time Mariel had seen a crack in his demeanor. "And do you?"

"I don't know the first thing about it. It's just overgrown children swinging a stick at a ball. But he needs me to tell him how wonderful he is, and I don't just mean baseball."

The women in the crowd laughed, and some of the men.

"Objection. Relevance."

"Sustained. Madam, leave the gutter humor outside the courtroom. Go on, Mr. Van Pelt."

The prosecutor poured himself a glass of water. "What did you see when Mr. Blackford arrived?"

"There was an argument, and then Clyde struck him with the baseball stick."

"Did you hear what was said to trigger the altercation?"

"I was sitting on the stoop out back of Duncan's, which is a ways from where the matches are played. All I heard was Clyde yelling something about seventy dollars."

"Did Mr. Blackford owe him money?"

"How would I know?"

"Don't answer a question with a question, Mrs. Koerperich," the judge admonished.

"Thank you, your honor," Van Pelt said. "What happened next?"

"Not long after that, Blackford turned around and Clyde did what he did."

"To be clear, you are referring to Mr. Hartwig's attack on the victim?"

"Yes."

"What did Mr. Blackford do?"

Nora's eyes narrowed when she located Mariel in the crowd. "Why, he fell down, Mr. Van Pelt. Then everybody started hollering and Clyde ran away. Mr. Nielson went to find Mike Hammon. He's as close to a doctor as we have in town."

"Did Mr. Hammon come?"

"He was out of town, so Phoebe, his wife, told Charlie and Phinny to carry Blackford to the hotel. Finally somebody telegraphed Father Brandon at the mission, but he was several hours away."

Van Pelt looked at Frank and then at the judge. "Were you aware of the defendant's hatred of the Irish, madam?"

"What's to like?" she said, glaring abhorrence at Mariel. "They're vermin."

"Just answer the question, Mrs. Koerperich."

"I was aware."

"Your witness, Mr. Chamberlain."

"Nora," Frank said, leaning back so far in his chair that Mariel feared he might tip over, "are you a member of the Fragment Society?"

"Objection. Relevance."

"Overruled. You may answer, madam."

"You know I am," Nora said.

"And what does this Fragment Society do?"

"We make and mend clothing for the less fortunate in our community."

"I understand that to be the Society's *stated* mission, but have you, in fact, ever aided a single poor family since the founding of Goss Valley?"

"Objection. Argumentative."

Frank sat forward. "I withdraw the question. Mrs. Koerperich, for what reason does the Fragment Society do what it claims to do?"

"It is God's work. 'Gather up the fragments, that nothing be lost.'"

"Yes, I know the quote. Tell me, then, was the death of Liam Blackford God's work, too?"

"All right, that's enough," Judge Larrabee said, slamming his gavel down hard. "Mr. Chamberlain, approach the bench."

Their discussion was conducted in animated whispers. Mariel struggled to hear what was being said, but once the trial was delayed, everybody in the courthouse started speaking, drowning out the conversation at the podium.

"What's that all about?" she asked Goss. His eyes had the same yellow hue as his skin.

"Larrabee's chewing Frank out."

"For what?"

"Haven't you been paying attention? He's working hard to prove his own client had plenty of reasons to kill Blackford. Why didn't he object to Van Pelt getting Ned's opinion into the record?"

"About the money?"

Hartwig had told Mariel the story about the seventy dollars. It didn't seem improper for Ned to testify about that if he'd indeed heard Hartwig mention it that afternoon.

"No," Goss said. "It's one thing for Van Pelt to ask Ned if he'd ever heard Clyde express hatred for the Irish. It's another to ask if he thought that was why he killed Blackford. Ned's a twenty-one-year-old kid with the mind of a child. He's not qualified to speculate about another man's motivations."

"Frank should have objected?"

"You're damn right he should. Larrabee even suggested it. But no, it was *no objection, your honor*. Then there's this business with Nora. Killing Blackford was a mission from God? Is he trying to place the noose around Clyde's neck himself?"

Mariel began to wonder if that was why Frank took the case in the first place, to sabotage the defense and insure Hartwig got what was coming to him. *Every man has a right to counsel.* Nobody more eagerly anticipated Hartwig's hanging than she, but surely this was unethical. She wouldn't have believed Frank capable of it.

But then she thought about Bridget and the children. The prosecution's case was strong enough without Frank's help, but why take chances? As long as justice was served, who cared if a few corners were cut in order to usher Hartwig into the everlasting?

"I'll be damned," Goss said. "I understand. Frank's trying to prove Clyde is deranged, and therefore not responsible for his actions. That sly son-of-a-bitch."

"Will it work?"

"Not one chance in hell."

When the discussion at the bench was over, Frank announced he had no more questions for Nora, and wouldn't need her again later. As soon as Larrabee dismissed her, she fled the courthouse.

****

"I got no idea why I'm here," Mr. Nielson said. Those seven words were the most he'd ever spoken at one time in Mariel's presence. "I didn't even see the blow. I'm at Charlie's livery talking to my boy Oliver when I hear Clyde's voice shouting something behind Duncan's. By the time I get out back to see what the commotion's about, Liam's already on the ground and Clyde's standing over him with a baseball bat."

"What did the accused do next?" Van Pelt said.

363

"Charlie yells, 'Clyde, you stupid shit, what're you doing? You killed him.' Then one of the Bohnet boys says, 'You better get out of here,' and Clyde takes off running."

"Which direction did Mr. Hartwig go?"

"Right by me and through the livery."

"Did he say anything to you?"

"'They don't hang heroes.'"

Van Pelt paused as if he expected an objection from Frank. When none came, he said, "Didn't that strike you as odd?"

"No odder than beating a man to death with a baseball bat."

"What did you do then?"

"Even that far away I can see there's blood all over Blackford's head, so I run to find Mike Hammon. I got the rheumatiz bad in my back and hips. It ain't easy getting these old bones moving fast like that. But I did it, only Mike's not home. I don't know what to do. Then I remember that one of them priests up at the mission is a doctor. He treated Randall Erickson's hurt knee last winter. I hurry over to Herb at the post office—"

"That would be Mayor Herbert Goss?"

"Yessir. I say to him, 'Does the mission got a telegraph machine?' Herbs says yes and sends a message to the priest."

"You did the right thing, Mr. Nielson. Thank you. Your witness."

Frank looked at Nielson, scratched his nose, and said, "No questions."

"Recall?"

"Nope."

Judge Larrabee excused the witness and said, "You're a perplexing fellow, Mr. Chamberlain. Mr. Van Pelt, how many more folks do y'all intend to call?"

"Just two, your honor, Charlie Koerperich and Phineas Bohnet."

"What say we recess for lunch first?"

Van Pelt checked his pocket watch. "Certainly."

"How about you, Mr. Chamberlain?"

Frank smiled. "No objections, your honor."

Larrabee tapped the gavel. "Back at one-thirty, then. Does this town have a decent place to eat?"

****

Few people left for fear of losing their seats. Goss did, though, with instructions that Mariel hold his. She wasn't sure how she was going to do that, but Trippledy rescued her by joining her during the break. Nobody was going to dislodge him.

"Get any good quotes?" he said.

"From the witnesses? No, Mr. Dalton, they declined to speak with me beforehand. I did see a shoving match between the Bohnet brothers."

"Both of them's gonna end up in jail someday."

"What do you think of the trial so far? As bailiff, are you allowed to express an opinion?"

"Larrabee never told me not to, but I don't think I should. Guess all I can say is I hope everybody's said their goodbyes to Clyde."

"It certainly looks that way." Mariel's stomach rumbled. She'd neither eaten nor relieved her bladder since before Randall's six a.m. readings. "Do you think Mr. Hartwig is deranged?"

"Mrs. Erickson, Clyde's an asshole, but he's no madman. Sorry for my language, but there's no nice way to put it. Sounds like you're hungry. Go ahead and get something to eat. The wife's bringing me lunch. Me and her'll save your chairs."

She smiled and nodded. "You're a kind man, Mr. Dalton."

Mildewed clouds were tinged yellow-brown by the weak winter sun. No snow appeared imminent, though, and the temperature was tolerable, just as Randall had indicated. Although most people remained in the courthouse, enough had come out that Mariel chose not to eat at the hotel. Fiona refused to close for the trial, and she and Mike were likely swamped. Instead she walked home to fix her own meal.

Randall wasn't there. She didn't know who would be taking weather readings this afternoon. He and Bobby were at the trial. Since the proceedings were to reconvene at one-thirty, perhaps business at the hotel would slow enough that Mike could get away at two to take them.

Mariel used the outhouse, then washed her hands under the well's spigot. Inside, she wasn't in the mood to cook, so she cut herself two slices of bread and ate them plain. As little food as she required, she ought to be thin as Father Brandon. But her body was plump as a rain barrel, and there didn't seem to be much she could do about it.

She placed a log into the stove and relaxed in her rocker. Bruno used to sleep at her feet, basking in the heat. A homely, stinky, slobbery chimera of a dog, the little devil was a nuisance if ever there was one. He chased chickens and skunks and probably would have eaten prairie dogs if he could have caught them. Oh, how she missed him.

An hour remained until the trial. She laid her head back and closed her eyes. Something about the courthouse reminded her of a church in Detroit when she was a little girl. She'd been sick, and her father had brought her all the way from Ohio to find a doctor. She couldn't remember why she was in that church, but she did know that's where she met her grandfather Noah for the very first time. He had been so angry with her father, so very angry. And yet, he'd cried tears of joy when he saw her. "An unexpected gift," he'd called her. Until that day, he hadn't realized he had a granddaughter.

He was her mother's father, and she'd always suspected his anger had something to do with Claire's death. But it was an accident. They both said so.

****

At one thirty-five her eyes popped open. In a panic she rushed out without her coat. She arrived at the courthouse to find Goss livid and Charlie Koerperich on the stand.

"What the hell?" Goss said, and she knew he'd had whiskey for lunch.

"Sorry. Have I missed anything?"

"Quiet!" hissed the man next to her.

"He was just sworn in," Goss said. "I ought to fire you."

Mr. Van Pelt, seated as always, got Charlie to repeat the baseball scenario the other witnesses had already testified to, before asking, "Where were you when Mr. Blackford arrived?"

"In the infield, warming up my arm with Clyde and Phinny."

"I understand the victim approached Mr. Hartwig. Did Mr. Blackford indicate why he had come?"

"Not that I heard. He seemed to think baseball's dull."

"What was said?"

"Clyde was spitting mad about some money he said Liam owed him."

"Were you a friend of Mr. Hartwig's?"

"I was his employer, and yeah, I s'pose, his friend."

"Did he ever tell you why Mr. Blackford owed him money?"

"Not in so many words. It was a wager, I think."

"What kind of wager?"

"You got me. Whatever it was, Liam lost."

"He certainly did."

"Objection," Frank said.

"Sustained. Keep your personal remarks to yourself, Mr. Van Pelt."

"Sorry, your honor. Mr. Koerperich, was there anything else you heard or saw that you can tell the court?"

"Liam didn't like baseball. He saw the bat laying next to Clyde's feet, and said, loud enough for all of us to hear, 'A quaint game, Mr. Pogue. Our cricket is something like it, only interesting.'"

"Mr. Pogue?"

"Don't ask me. That's what Liam called Clyde. Whatever it meant, Clyde hated it."

"Was anything else said?"

"Maybe, but Phinny was closer to them than me. You should ask him."

"I intend to, Mr. Koerperich. Describe what happened next."

"Liam turned around to leave. Clyde picked up the bat and swung it like he was aiming for the fences. Only Ray don't have fences. That bat sounded like a mallet crushing a melon. We all knew right then that Liam was dead. Nobody could've survived a blow like that."

"Objection."

"Sustained. You're not a doctor, sir."

"Well," Charlie said, "he died, didn't he? Tough son-of-a-gun hung on for a week, though, I'll give him that."

"Have you had occasion to speak with the defendant since his arrest?"

"I stopped in to jail once or twice. Had to tell him I gave his job to Oliver Nielson."

"How did he react?"

"Not well."

"Did he discuss the situation concerning Mr. Blackford?"

"Not with me."

"Thank you, Mr. Koerperich. Your witness, Mr.

Chamberlain."

Frank kept his eyes on his notes, never looking up. "Do you enjoy baseball, Charlie?"

"Objection. Relevance."

"Sustained."

Charlie broke into a wide grin and spoke anyway. "You like it, too, Frank, and if you'd come to play that afternoon like you said, you sure as hell wouldn't be sitting on that side of the podium today! You could've saved Mr. Van Pelt here the trouble."

The crowd laughed. Even Larrabee smirked before restoring order with his gavel.

Frank smiled. "When the judge sustains an objection, Charlie, that means you need to shut up."

Mariel glanced at Hartwig, who didn't appear to find the exchange funny at all.

"Can I go now?" Charlie said.

"One more question," Frank said. "Was Clyde Hartwig a good employee for you at the livery?"

"No complaints. He could be—well, you know how Clyde is —but he always did what he was told, and got it done right."

"Would you consider him a good family man? A man who cared about this town?"

"Objection."

"Sustained."

"That was three questions."

"So it was. Go on home, Charlie, I'm done with you. I won't need to call him for the defense, your honor."

"Home, my ass. And miss the rest of the trial?"

****

Phineas Bohnet confirmed the testimony of the other

witnesses, with one additional detail. Being the closest to Hartwig and Liam, he'd overheard the one exchange everyone else had missed.

"And what was that?" Van Pelt said.

"Mr. Blackford said, 'I don't owe you a thing, you bloody bastard. I did what you asked, and I might just deliver it to your house some night while you're sleeping.'"

"Those were his exact words?"

"Near as I recall. I don't always understand his foreign accent so well, but that's about what he said."

"What was to be delivered?"

Phineas shrugged. "Damned if I know. But it sure set Clyde off. He picked up that bat and knocked Mr. Blackford into the middle of next week."

"Was the victim physically threatening Mr. Hartwig in any way?"

"No, sir. Looked to me like he was leaving. Least he turned his back on Clyde."

"And that was when the blow was struck, when his back was to the accused?"

"Yes, sir."

"He's all yours, Mr. Chamberlain."

"No questions at this time, but I want this witness back this afternoon."

Finally Van Pelt stood up. "The prosecution rests, your honor."

Larrabee pounded the gavel. "There'll be a thirty-minute recess before the defense starts its case."

CHAPTER FIFTY-TWO
IN SPIRIT, IF NOT IN BLOOD
Wednesday, January 11, 1888

"Clyde Hartwig killed Liam Blackford," Frank said, strutting back and forth across the stage as he spoke. "That fact is not in question, and I will not attempt to prove otherwise. But was it murder, gentlemen? Was it premeditated, cold-blooded homicide? My opponent, Mr. Van Pelt, would have you believe that the incident was a vicious and unprovoked attack upon an innocent victim, fueled by the lust for seventy dollars and a hatred of all Irish people.

"Vicious? Certainly, but it was a blow struck in the name of fear and love for his family, a blow each and every one of us would have made had we been in Mr. Hartwig's position.

"Unprovoked? Balderdash. I intend to reveal the circumstances behind those mysterious seventy dollars. I will explain the meaning of the cryptic words Phineas Bohnet heard Mr. Hartwig speak on the baseball field, and what he meant when he told Mr. Nielson that they don't hang heroes."

He paused for dramatic effect, then resumed his speech with the impassioned voice of an evangelical preacher. "When a country is at war, we do not hesitate to defend ourselves and our land. We shoot, and we shoot to kill, in order to protect our homes and families, our way of life. What was the Civil War fought for? When we kill our enemy, is that murder? If we are threatened and we fight back, is that murder? If a thief comes in the night—"

"Objection," Van Pelt said. "Relevance? We are not at war."

"I didn't object during your opening argument."

"He's got a point there, Mr. Van Pelt," Larrabee said. "Overruled."

"We are not at war, you say? I agree, sir, *we* are not. But Mr. Hartwig was, or believed he was, and I intend to prove his actions were a matter of self-preservation for himself and his family.

"Do you know who else was at war? Liam Blackford. He was at war with Ireland, and he brought that war here, to the monoliths of New York City, and to these green prairies of Dakota.

"Do we grieve for his widowed wife and orphaned children? Of course we do. Of course we do. But their plight is not due to the strong arms and mighty swing of Clyde Hartwig. No, gentlemen. Responsibility for their plight lies at the feet of Mr. Blackford himself."

Whether or not the audience believed Frank could deliver on this outrageous claim, they were swept up by his oratory, and gave him a rousing round of applause.

"Objection, your honor," Van Pelt cried.

"Sustained," Larrabee said, hammering his gavel several times. "Knock it off, or I'll throw y'all out of the courtroom."

****

Father Brandon was hostile. He was a friend of the Blackfords. Mariel understood his reluctance to testify for the defense of the man who killed Liam. But there he was, in all his righteous fury, seated in the witness chair once again. He wore a cross and rosary beads, the latter of which he rolled between his fingers.

"Dr. Brandon," Frank said.

"I prefer Father."

"I'm not Catholic, but as you wish. *Father* Brandon, what nationality are you?"

"Objection. Irrelevant."

"I agree," Larrabee said. "Sustained."

Frank walked around to sit on the front of the table. "You have stated that Mr. Blackford was your friend. How long have you known him?"

"I met him on a visit to Ireland. They had just lost one of their sons, and I happened to be acquainted with the priest who performed the funeral mass."

"Were you aware the family were Travellers?"

"I was—the operative word being *were*. They'd given up the life by then."

"Objection," Van Pelt said. "Your honor, I don't know how this is relevant. Of course the Blackfords traveled...."

Frank smiled condescendingly. "'Traveller' is the word for a kind of Irish gypsy."

"Objection overruled," the judge said. "Carry on, Mr. Chamberlain, but I do hope y'all intend to get around to talking about your client before the day's out."

"Just coming to it, your honor. Father Brandon, aren't the Travellers known to be people of low moral character?"

"Certainly some have that reputation, but I form my impression of each man by the man himself, not by the group he's associated with."

"And what was your impression of Liam Blackford?"

Father Brandon studied Frank suspiciously, as if he felt he were being led into a trap. "Hard-headed but hardworking."

"Did he struggle to feed his family?"

"That's no sin."

"Would you have helped him if he'd asked?"

"He didn't."

"Did he ever speak to you about what he did to make ends meet?"

"I was his confessor. As you know, the sanctity of the confessional is absolute. I can reveal nothing of our discussions in that regard."

"I'm only asking—"

"Mr. Chamberlain, if, in his confession, he told me what he had eaten for breakfast his last morning, I could not break that trust."

"I see. When Mr. Blackford died in his home, did you perform Extreme Unction?"

"I did, sir."

"Did you pray for his soul?"

"As I pray for everybody's, including yours."

"Good to know." Frank stood up and moved a few steps closer to the witness chair. "Did you know that I attended Mr. Blackford's funeral?"

Father Brandon shrugged. "If I noticed you then, I've forgotten."

"On the other hand, sir, I noticed you, and I remember everything very well."

"Your point being?"

"You were Mr. Blackford's friend, yet you were not the priest who performed his funeral mass. Why is that?"

The question clearly took Father Brandon by surprise. Before he could answer, Van Pelt objected again, and Larrabee overruled him.

"That doesn't concern you," Father Brandon said.

Frank stormed to the chair, looming over the defiant priest. *"That doesn't concern me*, sir? Need I remind you a man's life is at stake here? Did Mrs. Blackford request a different priest?"

Father Brandon gazed up at the judge. "Do I have to answer, your honor?"

"Not as long as you don't mind spending a few nights in jail for contempt of court. I just overruled Mr. Van Pelt's objection. That means y'all have to answer."

"Did Mrs. Blackford request a different priest?" Frank repeated.

"No."

"Then what is the reason you refused to perform the service?"

"Objection. The witness didn't say he refused."

"Sustained. And Mr. Chamberlain? Don't hover over the witness."

Frank stepped back a few paces. "Father Brandon, did you choose not to perform because you learned of disturbing information concerning Mr. Blackford, information that conflicted with your Christian beliefs?"

The priest hesitated before responding. He gazed at Larrabee, as if pleading with the judge to intervene on his behalf. When Larrabee simply stared back, Father Brandon shook his head and said, "It was an internal decision at the mission. That's all I can say about that. Your honor can send me to jail if he so chooses."

"That won't be necessary, Judge." Frank returned to his chair. Hartwig looked at him and smiled. Frank folded his hands together, and spoke in a calm voice. "Father Brandon, have you ever heard of the Fenian Brotherhood?"

Hands trembling, the priest held his rosary to his lips and kissed it.

Van Pelt sprang to his feet again. "I vigorously object, your honor! There is no foundation for this question. It's completely irrelevant."

"Be quiet, you pompous ass," Frank said. "I didn't tell you

how to conduct your case. Don't tell me how to present mine. I'm laying the foundation, if you'd stop objecting long enough to pay attention."

Judge Larrabee struck his gavel. "Maybe y'all want to take this out back and settle it like men?" He didn't wait for an answer. "Mr. Van Pelt, your objection is overruled. Mr. Chamberlain, I'm not bashful when it comes to tossing counselors into the pokey, either. Another comment like that, and that's just where you'll find yourself. We clear?"

"My apologies, your honor."

"Good. Father Brandon, it's your turn to talk again."

"Of course I have," he whispered in a strained voice. "They're terrorists."

"And what do Fenians do, Father?"

"They terrorize."

"Don't try to be clever, Father. *How* do Fenians terrorize?"

"They blow up buildings and monuments in Ireland."

"Why?"

"They don't like British rule."

"What do they use to accomplish their dirty work?"

"Pipe bombs and dynamite, from what I've heard."

"Dynamite, you say? Do people die in these attacks?"

"Unfortunately, yes."

Frank's dramatic pauses were becoming tiresome, but this one was effective. "Father Brandon, was Liam Blackford a Fenian?"

"Objection!"

"No ruling necessary, your honor. Your witness, Mr. Van Pelt."

The prosecutor should have been prepared for this line of questioning, but he seemed flustered. He riffled through papers. Mariel got the impression he was just pretending to look for something while he figured out what to say next.

"Father Brandon, I withdraw my objection. Within the constraints of your holy office, tell the court if you were personally aware of any connection Mr. Blackford may have had with the Fenians."

"I was not, sir."

"To the best of your knowledge, was Clyde Hartwig a member of the British government so hated by Fenians?"

"Of course not."

"Therefore, even if Fenians had been present in Goss Valley, they'd have no quarrel with Clyde Hartwig?"

"Objection."

"Sustained."

"No more questions."

****

Mariel was taken aback when Frank called Carter Cowan as his next witness. She knew he was going to be trouble when he refused to say, "So help me God" as Trippledy swore him in.

The judge had to intervene. "Just affirm to tell the truth, and leave the Lord out of it."

"So affirmed," Cowan said, his Scottish accent rattling like a viper's tail. He took his time sitting down. Everything about him radiated arrogance and contempt.

Frank had him confirm his name for the record, then said, "Do you know why you're here, Mr. Cowan?"

"Because you subpoenaed me, *tú fear dúr*."

"You were Mr. Blackford's cousin, is that correct?"

"In spirit, if not in blood."

"What does that mean?"

"It means what I said."

"You were not actually related to him?"

Cowan sighed with annoyance. "We had a bond."

"More like brothers than cousins? *Fenian* brothers?"

Cowan glared at him. "That's what this is about, then? Sorry to ruin your performance, sir, but I never heard of Fenians."

"And so you don't know who Gaspodin Mezzeroff is?"

"Is he Russian?"

"Perhaps I can jog your memory. He runs a school in New York that teaches young dissidents—young Irish dissidents—to make bombs and gunpowder."

"I wouldn't know about that. I'm Scottish."

"Have you ever manufactured dynamite, Mr. Cowan?"

"Objection. This witness is not on trial."

"Sustained."

Cowan leaned toward the judge and said, "Mr. Van Pelt is mistaken, your honor. I am on trial. Liam is on trial. This man"—he pointed to Frank—"is putting everybody on trial to deflect the blame from the bastard that did the bloody deed."

Predictably, Larrabee pounded his gavel. "Remove that statement from the record. The witness will confine himself to answering questions he's asked."

"All right, Mr. Cowan," Frank said. "Let's back up a bit. I have sworn statements from people in this town that you've told them Mr. Blackford was your cousin. Have you, in fact, done so?"

"I suppose I have. At least I didn't contradict them if they made that assumption."

"But by blood or by law, he was not your true cousin?"

"No."

"So that was a lie?"

"Lying is a sin, Mr. Chamberlain."

"Just answer the question," Larrabee said.

"A harmless lie, then. As I said, we'd a bond stronger than family."

"Do you often lie?"

"Often? No."

"Were you and Liam Blackford members of the Fenian Brotherhood?"

"I told you, I never heard of them."

Frank thanked him and turned him over to Mr. Van Pelt.

Mariel admired the way he exposed Cowan as a liar, and then forced him to lie before the court on the most important issue.

Van Pelt stood up and said, "Your honor, this line of questioning is absurd. No questions."

As soon as he was excused, Cowan left the stage and found a place among the spectators.

"Call your next witness, Mr. Chamberlain."

"Your honor, the defense calls Mrs. Mariel Erickson."

Mariel almost screamed. She'd had no advance warning she'd be called to testify.

"Objection. She isn't on your witness list."

"Mrs. Erickson is a reporter for the local newspaper," Frank said. "She interviewed Mr. Hartwig in jail on a number of occasions." He held up some handwritten papers. "I have here the notes Mrs. Erickson submitted to the editor, Herbert Goss. I wish them read into the record. My only purpose in calling her is to confirm that this is indeed what she wrote, and does accurately represent the conversation she had with Mr. Hartwig on May the twenty-third, eighteen eighty-seven."

Larrabee looked at something he had lying on the podium. "Take a gander at the evidence list, Mr. Van Pelt. The lady's statements are right there. If that was objectionable, y'all should have tried to keep it out in pre-trial motions. Too late now."

"Perhaps I didn't notice it, your honor."

"I can't do your job for you, sir. Objection is overruled. I see no reason why she can't confirm her own words."

"But she wasn't sequestered with the other witnesses!"

"Mr. Van Pelt, I overruled your objection. If she's covering the trial for the paper, she can't very well be locked out of the courtroom, can she?"

"This is not how a trial is works in this Territory."

"I'm the one holding the gavel, counselor. Objection *overruled*." Larrabee scanned the spectators. "Mrs. Erickson, I assume you're in the courtroom?"

"Good heavens," Mariel whispered to Goss. He was more or less awake, but feeling the effects of the whiskey. "You gave him my notes?"

"Don't work yourself into a state," he said. "Frank asked for them. Get up there."

"I'm here, your honor," Mariel called. She rose and clambered past the people sitting in the back row. Every eye was on her as she approached the stage. She was terrified she might fall, but she made it without incident. Trippledy stopped her at the bottom of the stairs and held up a Bible.

"Place your right hand on the Good Book, ma'am. Do you solemnly to swear to tell the truth, the whole truth, and nothing but the truth, so help you God?"

"I do," she squeaked.

"You'll be fine," he whispered.

Frank greeted her above and escorted her to the chair. Marshal Woolridge nodded encouragement as she passed.

"Hello, Mariel," Frank said. "State your name for the record, please."

"You know who I am, Frank. Oh. Sorry. Mariel Erickson."

He showed her the notes she'd taken during one of her interviews with Hartwig. "Is this your handwriting?"

In the second row, just behind the jury, she saw Louisa Hartwig. For a moment Mariel lost her train of thought.

"Mrs. Erickson?"

She glanced at the papers. "It is."

"Would you read it into the record for the court?"

"Me?"

"If you don't mind."

If Louisa's eyes could spout fire, Mariel would be ablaze. She took a deep breath. "I had typed a better report. I don't know why Mayor Goss didn't give you that. These are so disjointed."

"Just tell us what you wrote."

Mariel recounted Hartwig's and Liam's conversation in the bar involving Mr. Mezzeroff's bomb school and the subsequent seventy-dollar challenge from Hartwig to prove it. "In expressing his skepticism, Mr. Hartwig used a vulgar term, Mr. Chamberlain, that I do not choose to repeat."

"Full of shit, Mrs. Erickson?"

"That's it."

"So Mr. Hartwig didn't believe him?"

"Not at that time."

"And he specifically said seventy dollars?"

"Yes, sir."

"That wasn't the end of the interview. What did Mr Hartwig tell you then?"

After explaining Liam's failure to appear at the agreed-upon time, she said, "I pointed out to Mr. Hartwig that missing an appointment didn't make him a terrorist. Mr. Hartwig claimed he was worse, because he trained terrorists."

"This is the conversation as you remember it?" Frank said.

"Yes."

"And you're certain Mr. Blackford told Mr. Hartwig he knew how to make dynamite?"

"I'm certain Mr. Hartwig claimed that's what he said."

"Thank you," Chamberlain said. "That's all there is to it."

"Not quite," Van Pelt said. "Mrs. Erickson, did you believe

the defendant?"

"I did not."

"Why did you conduct the interview in the first place?"

"I'm beginning to wonder about that myself. It was at Mayor Goss's suggestion. In any case, the interviews were never printed."

"This was three weeks after the murder?"

"Objection."

"Sustained.

"After the incident?"

"Yes."

"Plenty of time for Mr. Hartwig to concoct a story."

"Is it, Mr. Van Pelt?" Frank said.

"Address the court, not each other, gentlemen. Don't make me tell y'all again."

****

Phineas Bohnet was recalled to the stand, but before questioning could begin, Sadie Goss sneaked in a side door, handed Trippledy a note, and quickly departed. With her husband at the trial, post office and telegraph duties had been delegated to her.

The judge noticed the interchange. "What's that about, bailiff?"

"Telegram for you, judge."

"Bring it here, Mr. Dalton."

Trippledy did as instructed. After reading the note, the judge checked his watch. "Ah, good. This concerns another matter that will require my attention tomorrow. I don't s'pose you gentlemen can wrap this thing up this afternoon?"

"My closing statement will be brief," Van Pelt said.

"Mine may be a bit more lengthy."

Larrabee sighed. "All right. Question your witness, Mr. Chamberlain."

Frank turned to Phineas. "Sorry to make you come back, Phinny."

"The trial's a lot more fun from down there than up here," Phineas said.

"I daresay," Frank chuckled. "I won't keep you long. Phinny, I want you to repeat what Mr. Blackford said to Mr. Hartwig there in the infield, right after Mr. Hartwig claimed he was owed seventy dollars."

"He said, 'I don't owe you a thing. I did what you asked, and I might just deliver it to your house some night while you're sleeping.'"

"And this was said on May the second, the day of the incident?"

"If that was the day Clyde hit Mr. Blackford, then yeah."

"Tell me, Phinny, what do you think Mr. Blackford meant by that?"

"Objection. Calls for a conclusion."

"Sustained."

"To your knowledge, did Mr. Blackford ever handle dynamite?"

"He sometimes delivered it for a well company."

"What well company?"

"Dunno. That's what Clyde told me Roy Duncan told him."

"He said this before May the second?"

"Must have. I ain't seen much of him after."

"Did Mr. Blackford make the dynamite himself?"

"Objection."

"Sustained."

"How come he don't let me talk?" Phineas said.

Frank smiled and patted him on the shoulder. "It's not you he wants to shut up, Phinny, it's me. Let me ask you this, then.

Did you ever hear Mr. Blackford threaten Mr. Hartwig?"

"They got in fights all the time."

"Who won?"

Phineas peered at Hartwig. "Sorry, Clyde, but I gotta tell him. Mr. Blackford did, every time."

"So Mr. Hartwig had good reason to fear for his life?"

"Objection," Van Pelt said.

"Withdrawn," Frank said. "Phinny, you know Mr. Hartwig. Why do you think he told Mr. Nielson they don't hang heroes?"

"I didn't know he said that," Phineas answered before Van Pelt could object.

He objected anyway, and Larrabee sustained it.

Frank turned toward the jury. "Phinny, you and the other witnesses have established that Mr. Hartwig was concerned about the seventy dollars on May the second, so we can be sure he didn't concoct the story after he was arrested. Now, let me ask you: What if it was dynamite Mr. Blackford was threatening to deliver to Mr. Hartwig's house while he and his family were sleeping?"

"Don't bother to object, Mr. Van Pelt," Larrabee said. "Sustained. I see where you're going with this, Mr. Chamberlain. Save it for your closing arguments."

"Thank you, judge, I will."

"Speaking of which, it's getting late, counselors. Mr. Van Pelt, your cross-examination of this witness will have to wait—"

"Again, your honor, this theory is nothing but a desperate gambit by Mr. Chamberlain to free his client. No questions. Go home, Mr. Bohnet."

"Then the defense rests," Frank said.

"Unfortunately, there's no time your summations today. I got other business tomorrow, so I'm afraid I got to recess these proceedings till Friday morning. Gentlemen of the jury, I can't see a reason for sequestration, but y'all're admonished not to talk about the case with anyone. Not even your wives. If you do, I'm gonna have to declare a mistrial, and that will make me angry. I need to be in Deadwood on Tuesday. If I'm *not* in Deadwood by Tuesday, y'all rest assured the Buffalo County jail will have twelve guests for every day I'm late. Understood? Good. Have a pleasant night, and enjoy your day off. Nine a.m. sharp on Friday, everybody. Except you, Mr. Chamberlain. We'll meet in your office first thing tomorrow."

The spectators were aggravated, but Frank didn't seem surprised, so he obviously knew the content of the judge's telegram.

Before everyone left, Mariel rose to her feet and shouted, "Parents, I will be holding class in the morning."

CHAPTER FIFTY-THREE
DAY OF RECKONING
Thursday, January 12, 1888

Bright sunlight slanted in through the south windows, validating Randall's prediction of fine weather. Just back from his morning readings, he was in the kitchen pouring two coffees when Mariel emerged from the bedroom.

"Is it as nice as it looks out there?" she said. This was the first she'd seen him since the trial recessed. He hadn't come home between the evening recess and his midnight readings, and when he did, he went straight to bed.

"It was already twenty-eight at six o'clock."

"Magic Randall, at your service."

"People make too much of that. I just read my charts and do the math."

He handed her a cup. As they sipped their coffee in silence, Mariel planned her school lessons. She'd start with penmanship, then reading, then geography, and finally arithmetic before lunch. Nothing motivated children to complete their ciphering like the prospect of food.

"What do you think of the trial so far?" Randall said.

"I'm afraid Frank is being a bit too effective."

"Give him credit, he's putting up a surprisingly good

defense. But when all's said and done, it's all malarkey. If you crush an unarmed man's skull as he's walking away from you, that's murder. Even if he took Liam's statement as a threat, he was in no danger at that moment. You can't kill somebody now because you fear he might hurt you later."

"I hope you're right. Hartwig needs to hang."

He drained his cup and poured himself another. "You've never been a vengeful person."

"I was fond of Liam, and I grieve for his family."

"Would you think so highly of him if he was a Fenian?"

"He wasn't. You said so yourself."

Randall returned to the table. Folding his charts and maps, he said, "Whatever he was, hanging Clyde won't bring him back."

"That's not the point."

Randall didn't argue. "I was surprised Frank called you as a defense witness."

"*You* were surprised?"

"And a little jealous. I've never even been a juror at a trial, let alone a witness. I'd like to someday, just for the experience."

"Next time you can go in my place."

"You handled yourself well." He set his cup down and looked out the window. "What a job I've got. By Thanksgiving we'd already seen thirty below. There's December ice out there that won't thaw until April. And then we get a day like this. Twenty-eight degrees. I won't be shocked if the temperature hits forty."

"It sounds like a lovely day for a walk, then." Mariel was running a few minutes behind schedule, so she didn't take time to finish her coffee. She donned her coat, said her goodbyes, and headed out the door.

The trek to the schoolhouse was invigorating. Along the way, she saw barn doors flung open to welcome in sunlight.

Chickens scratched and pecked through snow in the yards. Farmers who were busy chipping ice off the cattle's troughs paused to wave as she passed. Even at this early hour, wives were taking advantage of the relative warmth to hang laundry on the line. Their husbands, up to their knees in snow, fixed shutters, mended fences, and loaded wagons. Children emerged from homes, carrying books and lunches.

When she arrived at the Hammon home, she found several boys and girls already in the yard playing tag and tossing snowballs. Most still had their coats on, but had either removed their mittens and scarves or had neglected to bring them at all.

She grabbed the bucket hanging near the front door and fetched water from the well. "Good morning," she said. "The first person who throws at someone's head will wear the dunce cap."

Inside, she slipped out of her coat and fired up the burner. There were only two hay cats in the house, but with the prospect of forty degrees this afternoon, that should be enough to keep the room warm all day. She moistened the cats to extend the length of time they'd burn. Their coal embers would continue to emit heat for another an hour or two after that.

It was still chilly inside, however, and the ink wells were frozen, so she moved them to a shelf closer to the heat. She'd have to wait until after reading to have the students do their penmanship.

Satisfied the room was in order, she stepped outside and rang the bell.

Once the boot stamping and general jostling abated, the children remained standing next to their chairs while she took attendance. She counted fourteen, less than half, but that was expected, considering the chaos caused by the proceedings at the courthouse. Only two of the Blackfords were present, Sean and Megan. Perhaps they were the only ones old enough to truly understand what was happening at the trial, so Bridget sent them to school to distract them from brooding.

"You may be seated," Mariel said. "Open your *Fourth Readers* to page one-twenty. Sean, tell us the title of this reading."

The boy was understandably sullen. "Number forty-three. *The Winter King.*"

****

At one o'clock Mariel stepped outside to ring the children in from recess. To her surprise, most of them had stopped playing to stare slack-jawed at the northwestern sky. When she followed their gaze, she was stunned. A wall of black clouds roiled toward them at appalling speed. They churned like a massive thunderstorm, except that Dakota didn't have thunderstorms in January. She could hear the ominous rumble of wind, but it hadn't arrived yet.

"Get inside, everyone!" she yelled.

No sooner had the last child entered when the storm slammed against the schoolhouse with the force of a hurricane. Rafters groaned under the pressure. The blast of wind roared down the chimney and whistled through tiny gaps in the wall's planks.

Mariel had experienced windstorms before, but nothing that had risen as quickly and ferociously as this one. It was eerie, almost unnatural. Spreading frost on the windows indicated the temperature was dropping fast. She considered moving the children to other rooms, but the north and west walls of the house were taking the brunt of the gale, so they'd be colder than the classroom. One of her walls also faced west, but the hay burner was here. It could generate more heat than the Hammons' wood-burning and cooking stoves combined.

That was small consolation as she felt the entire structure rattle.

"What's happening?" Suzy Osman cried. She was one of Mariel's older students, perhaps fifteen or sixteen.

The rest of the girls and some of the younger boys screamed, while the older boys hurried to the windows. In the few seconds it took them to get there, a torrent of white obscured the view of the outside world. By the clatter on the roof, the snow might also contain sleet or hail.

"It's a twister!" Bobby laughed, but he was clutching his rosary beads. A bit of Divine intervention might be useful right about now, but Jesus, Joseph, and Mary notwithstanding, she couldn't have him frightening the children more than they already were.

"Robert Baughman, you stop that kind of talk this instant!" Mariel said.

"'Tis the devil's breath," Megan said.

"Coming to blow Clyde Hartwig to hell," Sean said.

"It's not the devil," Mariel said, though she wasn't as confident as she was trying to sound. "It's simply weather. We've all seen snowstorms before."

A terrific crack outside was followed by something heavy crashing against the roof. Mariel assumed the Hammons had just lost a limb from one of their trees.

"Make it stop, Mrs. Erickson," Emil Klindt whined. He was one of the students whose parents never came to church or other social events. Mariel had only met them a handful of times.

She scanned her pupils' faces. Even the older boys showed the beginnings of panic. She forced a smile. "I'm sure it'll pass quickly. Shall we get back to work?"

They tried, but an hour later the wind had increased, the snow intensified, and the temperature plummeted further.

Attempting to teach was futile while the tempest raged. Even indoor games of Hot 'n' Cold and Cupid's Coming did nothing to ease the children's anxiety.

"I want to go home," sobbed Constance Nielson, a darling blond five-year-old. It was her father August who'd heard Hartwig's comment about hanging heroes.

"Be patient, honey," Mariel said, thinking it might be time to pray. "Your parents will come for you as soon as they're able."

"I want my mommy now."

Mariel turned to Megan, who was nearly as frightened as the little girl. "Will you take care of her?" Megan nodded and lifted Constance onto her lap.

Bobby joined her at the front of the classroom. He spoke softly, so others wouldn't hear. "Lieutenant Erickson told us in church on Sunday that it was gonna be nice this week."

"He certainly didn't see *this* coming."

Someone jerked on the schoolhouse door. Snow had piled up in front of it, making it difficult to open more than a foot. Two men forced their way through the crack.

"Daddy!" Elaine Koch cried. "Danny!"

Mariel knew Elaine's father Lloyd as a fine tenor and recent disinterested mayoral candidate, and her brother Daniel as an occasional, and equally disinterested, student. Both were tall and thin fellows who, bundled in several layers of clothing, appeared almost corpulent.

"We're down the road less than a quarter mile," Lloyd said, "and it was only by a miracle that we found our way here. You can't see the horses in front of the wagon. We come for Lainy."

As the Elaine put her coat on, Lloyd peeled back his scarf. Snow fell off in clumps. Beneath, his beard was frozen into a ball of ice, covering his mouth and nose.

"Won't you stay and warm yourselves first?" Mariel said.

"No time. It's piling up fast," Daniel said.

"The stuff's turned fine as sifted flour," Lloyd said. "You can't hardly breathe it if you're going into the wind. It comes right down into your lungs and chokes you. We better get moving."

"What about the rest of the children?" Mariel asked. "Are their parents coming?"

"I hope they got more sense than us. It's bad out there. I'd say plan on staying put overnight." As he pushed open the door, Lloyd looked at Elaine and said, "Where's your cap and mittens, girl?"

"Didn't need them this morning," she said.

"Dammit, what have I told you?" He wrapped his own scarf around her head. Daniel gave her his gloves.

"I can't see," Elaine complained.

"Neither can we," Lloyd said, then slammed the door shut behind them.

****

Monumental drifts piled against the north and west sides of the house, nearly reaching the windows. Enough snow had been forced through gaps between the boards that small piles were even accumulating inside. Light in the schoolroom grew dim. Mariel lit the lanterns and placed one in the middle of the room and the other in the south window to make the schoolhouse more visible. She also set up a routine with the older boys to keep the snow cleared away from the front door where the school bell hung. She planned to have one of them ring the bell every few minutes to guide any parents who may be trying to reach them.

This became increasingly difficult, as the storm showed no signs of abating. Yet within a period of an hour, the Osman,

Nielson, and Spencer fathers managed to make their way to school to collect their five children. All three men told harrowing accounts of impassable roads, snow blindness, bitter cold, and frostbite.

"Wouldn't it be better for you all to remain here than risk the weather again?" Mariel said. "Mike won't mind."

"Wind'll be at our back heading out," Mr. Spencer answered. He'd come for his girls, Hannah, Hailey, and Hope. "That won't be as bad. Besides, kids need to be with their own at a time like this. We'll be fine. Godspeed, Mrs. Erickson."

"Godspeed," she said, doubting there'd ever *been* a time like this before.

After they left, the remaining smaller children gathered into a circle around the hay burner. When they cried for their mothers, Megan sang them the song that Mariel herself had made up years ago. How appropriate it seemed now.

> *"When winter comes to call,*
> *and snowflakes start to fall,*
> *Just raise up your voices*
> *And lift up your eyes,*
> *Sing to the heavens*
> *And laugh at the sky."*

Nobody felt like laughing at the sky or anything else, but Megan did manage to get some of them to sing along.

Mariel took the opportunity to search the rest of the house for blankets, winter clothing, wood, and food. She'd been right to keep the children in the classroom. The other rooms were freezing. Thankfully, Mike and Phoebe had extra blankets in the linen closet. She took these and pulled the spreads off the two beds as well.

They'd left no winter clothing. Phoebe had taken hers to

Cedar Rapids, and Mike's must be in his room at the hotel. He had left behind some of his warm-weather shirts, trousers, and undershorts, which were too big for everyone save the two older boys and perhaps herself.

She was less fortunate locating wood and food. With Mike virtually living in town, he hadn't stocked the fireplace or the pantry. He was usually so considerate about seeing to her classroom necessities, but perhaps he'd been distracted by the excitement of their impending grandchild and Hartwig's trial. In any case, only a stale loaf of bread and a few jars of canned vegetables remained. God only knew how long they'd been sitting there. Even if they were edible, there wasn't enough to feed the eight children who were still here.

She did, however, find a bull's-eye lantern full of oil and several buckets in a closet.

Mariel distributed the blankets and bedspreads. Since nobody would be able to get to the outhouse, she set buckets in both bedrooms to serve as chamber pots.

The hay burner was beginning to cool, enough that the children were squabbling over the blankets.

"Huddle together," Mariel said. "Share the blankets. You'll stay warmer that way."

She leaned against the front of her desk and wondered how they would get through this. Sean approached her and whispered, "We should've stocked up on hay this morning, mum. We've no more cats to burn. I'll have to go out to the shed."

"You'll do no such thing. It's too dangerous."

"What difference if I freeze to death inside or out?"

"We'll burn books if we have to," Mariel said. The very thought made her stomach queasy.

"Mum, you need your books. Anyway, there's not enough of them to last the night. Someone's got to get to the hay, and that someone'll be me."

He was correct about that. If, God forbid, she had to burn her *MacGuffey's*, they'd be ashes in less than an hour. Still, she couldn't allow him to set foot into that maelstrom.

"The furniture—?"

"Even if we cut it apart, it wouldn't fit into the burner's cylinders. The thing was made to burn hay, not wood."

"The situation isn't that desperate yet."

"If not now, when? The temperature will only keep falling. If I don't go now, I mightn't be able to later."

"I said no."

"Will you condemn us all to freeze, then? It's but a short ways."

Mariel dreaded the next words she had to say. "Your father would be proud of you, Sean, but I'm the adult. I should be the one to go."

"You *are* the adult. That's why you're needed inside. And I wager I'm stronger than you."

Bobby joined them at her desk. "But you're not stronger than me, you tow-headed *Pavee*. What're you whispering about?"

"We need hay from the shed," Mariel said.

"And you're gonna let this squab get it? Might as well send a girl."

"Don't call me that," Sean said. "I can carry as much as you."

"Like hell. I'm going with you."

There was no anger in either boy's voice, just bickering patter between friends.

"Nobody's going anywhere," Mariel said.

"No disrespect, mum, but you've no longer any say in this."

"You heard what the men told us," Mariel said. She went to the south window and scraped a circle in the frost with her fingernails. "Look at this. You can't see the shed from here. The snow is up to your waist, the path is gone, and the wind is still howling. You'll get lost."

"How can we get lost?" Bobby laughed. "It's what, fifty feet?"

"It wouldn't matter if it was ten. There's no way to get your bearings. Go off course and you could die."

"I got an idea. Mike keeps a couple rolls of baling twine in the parlor."

Sean understood immediately. "Aye, tie a line around ourselves and anchor it to the house. Then if we don't find the shed, we can still get back here."

Mariel was impressed. She never would've thought of that.

She noticed Megan was watching them and straining to hear over the children's voices.

"The shed door's made of cheap wood," Bobby said. "Wind like this probably busted it to pieces. Don't know how many times I helped Mike fix it when a thunderstorm blew through."

"The hay will be frozen and buried in snow," Sean said. "That'll make it hard."

"He's got shovels and pitchforks in the back of the shed. We'll chop the ice off and bind up the hay in stacks. We can roll the cats in here."

Bobby went to fetch the twine. When he returned with two rolls, Megan launched herself at him before he had a chance to put his coat on. Nuzzling her face against his shoulder and kissing his neck, she said, "You come back to me, Robert Baughman."

"Don't fuss," he said. "It's embarrassing."

Her public display of concern colored his face an endearing shade of red. Mariel couldn't help but smile. The children laughed at his discomfort, too, a welcome sound on this dreadful day.

"*I'll* come back, too," Sean said, rolling his eyes. He took one of the rolls of twine from Bobby and handed it to Megan, along with his penknife. "Let him go, you *dearg-due*. Make yourself useful for once and cut off pieces to tie the hay with."

"How long?"

"Three feet?"

Bobby nodded. "Cut a half dozen."

Both boys bundled up for what Mariel hoped would be a successful sojourn into hell.

Bobby took the lengths of twine from Megan and put them in his coat pocket. He reached outside to tie one end of the second roll to the rail, then looped the other end around Sean and himself. The loop would allow them to alter the distance between themselves while still being connected. Finally, he coiled the twine in the middle and gave the roll to Sean. By the looks of it, they had well more than the fifty feet they'd need to get to the shed.

"Just let the rope out as we walk and reel it in when we come back."

"You think I couldn't've figured that out for meself?" Sean said. He winked at Mariel and added, "If you've not heard from us by dinner time, mum, then you can burn your books."

"What dinner?" she muttered.

Sean leaned toward her and murmured, "Then perhaps you should *eat* the books."

She insisted they take the bull's-eye lantern she'd found. Small and completely enclosed in metal and glass, it shouldn't be affected by the wind. She opened its little hatch and lit it, allowing its meager light to spill out.

Sean took the lantern, and the two boys forced their way out into an otherworldly landscape. Mariel tried to watch their progress, but within a few feet they'd disappeared in the driving snow. Even the little halo of light from their lantern was swallowed by darkness.

A Killing Snow

CHAPTER FIFTY-FOUR
CHILDREN OF THE SNOW
Thursday, January 12, 1888

With the two oldest boys gone to fetch hay, only six children remained inside: Megan, Norman and Christopher Wulff, Emil Klindt, and Sally and Cynthia Grabin. Their wailing created a dissonant harmony with the shrieking wind. Mariel sat at her desk, closed her eyes, and pressed her hands against her ears. Nothing could drown out the maddening cacophony.

Emil Klindt tugged on her sleeve. "Yes, Emil, what is it?"

"Someone's kicking at the door."

"What?"

"The door, ma'am."

Mariel rushed to answer. Bobby and Sean had returned, but they weren't alone. They were lugging the body of a child. They collapsed to the floor, the unknown boy lying motionless on top, his face obscured by scarf and hat.

"Found him in the shed," Bobby gasped. His face was ghastly gray, as was Sean's. The exertion had made them sweat, and the sweat had frozen.

"Jesus Christ," Sean moaned. He didn't apologize for taking the Lord's name in vain, and Mariel didn't ask him to.

"Who is he?"

"Don't know," Bobby wheezed. "He dug a hole in the hay. God *damn*, it's cold out there. I can't move my fingers."

Their clothing was white with snow and rigid as corroded iron.

"Megan, bring me blankets."

The girl did as she was told, then dropped to her knees and wrapped her arms around Bobby, heedless of the cold and snow. "You're so brave," she sobbed.

"Megan, get off him," Mariel said. "We have to get them out of those clothes."

"Can't," Sean said.

"We gotta go back for the hay," Bobby panted.

"Not until you warm up."

"If we don't go soon, the snow'll cover our tracks. We might not find our way again."

"Nevertheless," Mariel said.

She pulled the scarf from the young boy's face. It was Wayne Hartwig.

Horrified, Megan backed away as if Mariel had uncovered a serpent.

"Ah, shit-in-the-bed," Sean said. "Throw him back outside."

Bobby tossed off his blanket and struggled to his feet. He helped Sean up. They both loomed over Wayne as if they meant to do just that.

"No!" Mariel snapped. "Are you murderers, too, then? It was Wayne's father who killed Mr. Blackford, not him."

"He called me a whore," Megan said.

"That's not a nice word for young ladies to use."

"It's not a nice word for young ladies to be called, either."

"You don't like him yourself," Bobby said.

"Carry him closer to the burner."

When the boys didn't move, she dragged him herself. The device wasn't emitting much heat now, just the residual energy of the morning's hay embers. Mariel removed Wayne's wool stocking cap and rubbed his cheeks, trying to draw blood back into them. His skin was frigid, with the texture of sculpted marble.

"Is he dead?" Sean said, a bit too hopefully.

"What was he doing out there?" she said.

"I know," said Norman Wulff, a freckle-faced seven-year-old. "His daddy's in jail, so Wayne's the one that's gotta look after his mama and sister. Sometimes he comes over to help out my Daddy on the farm, feeding and watering the cows. I saw him this morning."

Mariel felt Wayne's neck for a pulse. If there was one, it was little more than a quiver. Likely even that was wishful thinking. "Why didn't he take shelter with your family?"

"It was still warm at lunch," Norman's younger brother Christopher said. "Maybe he was on his way home when the snow came."

"I want to go home, too," Sally Grabin said.

"I know you do, honey," Mariel said. "Why would he settle for the shed, when the house is right here?"

"Mum" Sean said, "it's worse out there than everybody said. This *leathcheann* probably didn't know where he was, and went to the first place he found. He couldn't *see* the house. Good riddance, I say. Let the devil take all the Hartwigs."

Megan wrapped a blanket around the shoulders of Bobby and Sean, who had come to stand next to the burner. Then, in an astonishing gesture of grace, she placed one on top of Wayne, too. When Sean gave her a disapproving glare, she said, "Mrs. Erickson's right. If we let him die, we're no better than his father."

Mariel pressed on Wayne's wrists, but there was no hint of movement. Open your eyes, she thought. Call me a hag. Smoke your cigarette. Make me want to slap your face again.

Open your eyes.

Wayne Hartwig didn't open his eyes.

Mariel's body and mind went numb.

"It's too late, dear," she whispered to Megan, needing to weep but unable to summon tears. "Bobby, take him to Mr. Hammon's bedroom."

"Is he—?"

"*Now.*"

Her tone brooked no argument. Bobby, himself frozen and battered, scooped Wayne's body into his arms and carried him away from the children's sight.

Afterward, he and Sean waited as long as they dared, then made another foray to the shed. They were back within fifteen minutes with five circular bundles of hay. Bobby carried two in each hand, while Sean had one. Being the light bearer, he needed the other hand for the bull's-eye lantern.

Perhaps knowing what to expect this time, they seemed to have held up better, although they were still intensely cold. After the boys dropped the stacks of hay, they took off their gloves and blew on their fingers. "Hay was frozen," Bobby said, "but not as bad as we thought."

"We tied the other end to the shed," Sean said, "so we've an anchor to both places."

"You're not planning to go back out?" Mariel said.

"Indeed we are, mum. We don't know how long we'll have to stay here. Five bales'll see us through the night, but no longer."

"Anyway, I think the snow and wind let up some," Bobby said, "but the temperature's falling bad. I bet it's twenty below."

They cut the twine with Sean's penknife, broke apart the stacks, and spread as much hay as they could in a single layer on top of the burner. "When this thaws," Sean said to Megan, "put some more on. Then you and the kids get to making cats. We'll be right back."

He and Bobby took deep breaths, opened the door, and plunged into the storm again.

Mariel wished that Reverend Dall would come to provide guidance. Even the Catholic counsel of Father Brandon would do. But they weren't here, so all she could do was pray for the boys' safe return and hope she could find the strength to bring everybody else through this disaster.

Praying gave her a measure of solace, but couldn't divert her thoughts from Wayne. Other than Megan, the children probably didn't understand the situation. When Christopher asked, she told him Wayne was asleep.

She didn't like the Hartwigs. But how tragic it was that the father's death would fall so hard upon the heels of the son's. Louisa didn't have thirteen children like Bridget—in fact, now she didn't even have two—but she'd have to go it alone. Bridget had Sean, Megan, and Bobby to support her, and Connor and Patrick were already older than Wayne. Carter Cowan was probably giving aid to the Blackfords, too, after his own nefarious fashion.

She didn't even have two....

Good Lord. Louisa didn't know about Wayne. Her husband was in jail, waiting to be hanged, and now her only son was missing during the worst blizzard Mariel could recall. The woman must be heartsick with worry. She'd had time to prepare herself for Hartwig's fate, but couldn't have foreseen Wayne's death. The pain of that news still awaited her and little Jeannette.

Mariel berated herself for her uncharitable thoughts. Her life was blessed compared to those of the Blackfords and Hartwigs. Ellie and Alex were safe. Randall, despite "the incident," was steady and hardworking. He trusted her intelligence, as she trusted his. He knew she wouldn't rashly try to get home. She would protect herself and her students by staying put.

Still, his confidence in her also meant he wouldn't be

coming for her tonight. That was the proper and sensible decision. She'd never forgive herself if something happened to him while attempting to rescue her. And yet, and yet....

The hay had thawed enough that Megan had the children weaving cats. They'd made four of them while Mariel was lost in her reverie. The familiar activity had a calming effect on them, for they'd stopped crying.

"Mrs. Erickson," said Sally Grabin, "I'm hungry."

"Me, too," agreed her sister Cynthia.

Before answering, Mariel stuffed a cat into each cylinder of the burner and lit one of them. The heat that rose from the flame felt wonderful and raised goosebumps on her arms. The growing flames fascinated her, drawing her down. She wanted to immerse herself in fire.

"Mrs. Erickson?"

The poor children must be famished by now. She'd not feed them the moldy bread in Mike's pantry. The canned vegetables might be all right. Then it occurred to her that since the weather had still been pleasant at their noon recess, most of them had been more interested in playing than eating. Their own lunch pails should still be full, as would those of the children who'd left with their fathers. She was relieved to find jerky, dried apple slices, peas, corn bread, and squash cake. "You needn't wait for my permission. Remember to share, but save something. We may be here for a while."

She got cups from her desk and filled them with water from the bucket she'd brought in this morning. She delivered them two by two to the children.

"We want to go home," Sally said, popping apple slices into her mouth.

"Try not to think about it," Mariel said. Electing not to take any food for herself, she sat at her desk and watched the children eat. It was going to be a long and excruciating night.

The weather fooled everyone today, making them forget how quickly Mother Nature could change her mind. Did we really believe, she thought, that we could conquer the prairie, armed with only our books, traditions, and culture? Megan had called the storm the breath of the devil. Undoubtedly Dall and Brandon would say it was God's punishment for sins the townspeople had committed.

But this was not the devil's doing.

It was not God's punishment.

It was Dakota's wrath, natural and impersonal, yet unforgiving. The settlers who had sewn the wind were now reaping the whirlwind.

Wayne Hartwig had already fallen victim to that wrath. How many other neighbors were still out searching for their loved ones, seeking a way home through unimaginable darkness? "Oh, my God," she cried.

Megan had been preoccupied with feeding the children, but now the same horror must be occurring to her, too. Her head snapped toward Mariel, her eyes already tearing up.

Bobby and Sean hadn't come back.

CHAPTER FIFTY-FIVE
DO ANGELS LOOK DOWN FROM HEAVEN?
Thursday, January 12, 1888

Megan frantically tried to button her coat and lace her boots at the same time. Both her sweetheart and her brother were outside in the tempest.

"No," Mariel said.

"I have to find them!"

"No."

"Damn your eyes, mum, they'll die!"

"So will you. I will not lose another child. I will *not*." Mariel's body trembled. She was terrified, for the boys and for herself. "I'll do it. I have to be the one."

"Let me go with you," Megan said, her face smeared with tears and nose mucus. Seeing her distress, the other children started in crying, too.

"Someone has to care for them," Mariel said. She removed her coat from the rack and put it on. In her entire forty-nine years she'd never known such dread. Despite her panting, she couldn't take in enough air. Her heartbeat was so furious she felt she would faint.

Megan jerked her mittens on. "You can't make me stay. I won't just sit here while—"

Mariel turned and, deliberately and without force, slapped

not go. I can't tell your mother a story like that." She gripped Megan's shoulders, then pulled her to her bosom, kissing her cheek and stroking her hair. The physical contact seemed to draw Megan's energy from her body and into Mariel's. "Your courage surpasses me, Miss Blackford. Your spirit overwhelms me. I am so, so proud of you. But you can't do this. I'm begging you. Let me go. I have to know that you and the children will survive this night, or I won't have the strength to try. Promise me that, and in turn I swear—I *swear*, Megan—that if it's within my power, I'll bring Bobby and Sean back to you."

Megan nodded and slowly removed her mittens. She slumped into the chair at Mariel's desk. "God bless you, mum," she said, her eyes glazing over, "but know that if you fail, I'll hate you with all my soul."

Fair enough, Mariel thought. She stretched Wayne's wool cap low over her ears, put her bonnet over it, and tied the strings around her chin. Then she wrapped her scarf around her face and neck several times and tucked the ends into her coat. She was wearing a dress and several layers of underclothing, but knee stockings were all she had to protect her calves. Mike had summer trousers in his bedroom. They were a thin cotton weave, but better than nothing, and they'd prevent the wind from rushing up her dress and freezing her thighs. Since he wasn't a large man and she was a stout woman, the fit shouldn't be too unreasonable.

As she went to retrieve the trousers, she realized she'd have to see Wayne's body again. The room was bitterly cold. Much as she didn't want to look, her morbid human nature drew her eyes to him. She'd taken the bed sheets earlier, so Bobby hadn't had any way to cover him. Unlike the romantic cliché, he didn't appear to be merely sleeping. Nor did he look like a dead child posed as if alive, like Terence in the Blackfords' photograph. More than anything, he resembled a statue that had never *been* alive. And yet, the metaphorical artist had had a sense of humor, for Wayne bore the same perpetual scowl he'd worn in life.

She hoisted the trousers up over her boots and under her dress, and buttoned them. They were snug enough at the waist, although too wide at the ankles. They might slow the wind, but they wouldn't keep the snow from creeping up her legs.

What a preposterous vision she must have presented, a woman in coat, dress, bonnet, scarf, and boots, wearing a boy's cap and a man's trousers. When she re-entered the school room, the children giggled. Even Megan managed a weak smile.

"I'm depending upon you," she said to Megan. "Don't let the fire go out."

Then she walked out into a scene even Dante couldn't have fathomed.

Wind forced snow through the woolen cap. Inhaling brought sharp pain in her throat and chest. Although she was facing south, the house, trees, and shed caused the wind to swirl, allowing it to unleash its frigid attack from every direction. It had already obliterated the footprints the boys had made a short while ago.

Thankfully, the rope was still attached to the rail. Beyond that, Mariel saw nothing but snow and darkness. Clutching the twine, she inched forward. All she had to do was hold on, and it would lead her to the shed. The drifts were too high to step over and too wide to go around, so she had to kick her way through.

Fifty feet.

The boys were only fifty feet away.

Please, Lord, let them be in the shed.

She counted her steps. Fifty feet equaled perhaps forty paces. She could make it that far. One, two, three....

"Bobby, Sean," she called into the howling gale, knowing it was futile. They wouldn't hear her if they were standing next to her.

Mariel plowed forward, eight, nine, ten.... Each step was agony, requiring more effort than the one before. The snow was powdery, sucking at her like quicksand, yet resisting like walls of stone. Her muscles screamed beneath frozen skin. The sweat under her clothes felt like pellets of ice.

The intense cold seemed to cauterize her flesh. Snow melted on contact, then refroze, creating an icy crust over her bonnet, cap, and scarf. Only her eyes were unprotected, and she had to blink continuously to prevent them from freezing shut.

Within minutes she lost sensation in her fingers, and could no long feel the rope. While she was still able to move them, she balled her left hand into a fist around the twine. If her hands were going to lock in one position, she wanted to make sure she maintained contact with her lifeline.

Mike's trousers were useless. As she feared, snow pushed up inside the hems and seeped through her stockings. Her left leg was the first to go numb, though the right wasn't far behind.

Fifteen, sixteen....

Less than halfway, and her body was already sluggish. The struggle to walk sapped not only her own energy, but whatever she imagined she'd drawn from Megan. Surely nobody could succumb to exposure this quickly... except that the number of footsteps didn't equate to the amount of time needed to take them. They'd cost her, what, fifteen minutes already? Thirty? In the end, the movement of the clock was meaningless out here. She either had time to get to safety, or she didn't.

She lifted her boot and set it down incrementally ahead of where it had been.

She lifted her other boot.

Twenty-three steps, twenty-four....

Or was it twenty-eight now?

Or nineteen?

It was difficult to remember. Her brain was dulling, too. She managed another call to Bobby and Sean, or thought she did.

Where was the shed? Even in this blackness, she should be able to see it by now. There was nothing but snow in every direction. Snow on the ground. Snow in the air. Snow on the trees. Snow on her clothes.

Snow in her soul.

Sing to the heavens and laugh at the sky.

Mariel stumbled. With herculean effort she rose, like a phoenix from bitter ashes. The rope had gone slack in the direction leading back to the house. Somehow her mind registered that it must have broken when she fell. She tugged on it but found no resistance.

Huh, she thought. At least it was still attached to the shed. Wasn't it? Or had she gotten herself turned around and was now facing the house?

Whichever, the rope was still attached to something. She'd have to go where it led her.

She thrust herself forward.

Thirty-six?

All she had to do was keep lifting her boots.

Why?

Her determination waned. Her life shouldn't end this way, but if it did, so what? Her father had drowned not long after her wedding, a careless fishing accident. She'd been inconsolable, haunted by the terror he must have felt as he thrashed about, breathing water, knowing he was going to die. But her grandfather Noah, an old sailor, said, "There's panic at first, but it only lasts a little while. Once you let go, once you accept, it's very peaceful, like going to sleep. That's the moment when you see the face of God."

Maybe freezing to death would be like that.

Sorry, Megan. Sorry, Bobby and Sean. Sorry, Randall and

Ellie and Alex. She wasn't cold anymore, but she was weary, so very weary. Mariel untied her bonnet and gave it to the wind. The snow beckoned like a soft bed, like the one in her home. Perhaps if she lay down for a moment, just long enough to catch her breath....

But then a fuzzy patch of un-darkness materialized before her in the distance, like the lamp on her nightstand where she kept Shakespeare and Twain. It was tiny, a yellow-gray hole in the black fabric of the storm.

She leaned toward the light.

And fell.

****

It was odd seeing her mother like this: No gossamer robes, no heavenly backlighting, simply a smiling young woman, not much older than Ellie, focusing her eyes directly on her. Mariel had not remembered them being so blue. She did remember the wavy hair, though, and the way it held the sun in a summer breeze.

Her mother. Claire. Such a pleasant name, warm and comforting.

Claire.

How do I address you, now that I'm nearly twice your age?

The woman tilted her head as if in amusement. She needed no heavenly backlighting. Her love generated its own light, radiating outward, bathing Mariel in its incandescence.

Seeing her like this here, wherever *here* was, she felt her old suspicions melt away. However her mother had met her end, it wasn't by her father's hand. Mariel wanted to speak, but had no voice. She wanted to embrace her, but had no sense of her own body, nor of the distance between them.

Claire rose elegantly and blew her a kiss.

Awake, my child.

CHAPTER FIFTY-SIX
SONS OF MERCY
Tuesday, January 17, 1888

"I couldn't save them both," a man said. A familiar voice, but not intimate.

"God in heaven." That was Randall. "What was she thinking?"

"Bless her heart for trying."

"At what cost?"

"She'll be the judge of that."

Mariel opened one eye a slit. She recognized the ceiling of her bedroom. Almost as quickly she noticed something on her nose. Gauze?

The next instant she felt the pain, sharp, horrific pain, like rats inside her chewing their way out. Her face, her skin, her fingers, her legs—every part of her felt as if it were being ripped open. She cried out and closed her eye, inhaling the numbing darkness like chloroform.

****

She knew time had passed. Father Brandon had prescribed laudanum to ease the pain's intensity, but the potion often made her incoherent, and always made her sleepy. It also gave her vertigo so debilitating she felt as if the bed were spinning in the funnel of a cyclone. She was in a constant daze, only marginally aware of what was going on around her, although at the moment, she sensed she wasn't alone in the room.

"How are the children?" she croaked.

"From school?" Bobby said. Even delirious, she'd know that Virginia drawl anywhere. "We all made it, Mrs. E, excepting of course Wayne."

"Why are you here?"

"Lieutenant Erickson told us what happened. Thought maybe you'd like a visit."

"That was sweet. What *did* happen?"

"You don't know?"

"I remember falling in the snow. What time is it?"

"You mean what day. It's Tuesday. About three o'clock."

Mariel risked peering up at him. The oil lamp next to her bed was burning, but that was the only light. Bobby's face was haggard and blotchy, his nose bandaged like hers. What she could see of it was the color of rotting fruit. Frostbite. Did she look like that, too? "You didn't come back," she said. "I went to find you."

"Everybody says you're a hero for trying to save us. Me and Sean think so, too. Not many would've done that for boys that wasn't their own kin."

"I did nothing but fall down in the snow. Where did you go?"

"We made it out to the shed all right, then that stupid *Pavee* slipped on ice and twisted his ankle bad. I thought it was busted. He couldn't put any weight on it. In summer I could've carried him back to the house, but in that storm.... Well, I wasn't about to leave him out there by himself. So we just decided to hunker down and cover ourselves with hay. Anyway, I figured two of us could stay warm better than one. And we had that lantern you gave us. It wasn't much, but we could wrap our hands around it to keep them from freezing."

"I remember calling your names."

Bobby glanced toward the foot of her bed, but quickly looked away. "Funny thing, Mrs. E. I heard your voice, but you wasn't calling for us. You was calling for your mama. Sean said it was just the wind, but I swore someone was out there, so I followed the rope and there you was, sticking out of the snow." His battered face crinkled into a smile. Good Lord, the boy looked like he was fifty years old. "Promise you won't tell Megan you and me spent the night in the hay together. I mean, you and me and Sean. In the morning Mike Hammon hooked a sled up to some horses and came looking for folks to rescue. You been asleep most the time since."

Mariel shifted in her bed, an effort that caused intense pain. From that angle she could see the west window. Snow outside had drifted above the top of the frame, completely blocking out whatever sunshine there might be today. How did anyone survive? "Are you and Sean all right?"

"Messed up my face pretty bad, like you can see. Sean lost some toes. They were black as coals. Father Brandon was still here from the trial, so he amputated them. You should see that mick strutting around on his crutches now, acting like he saved the world 'cause he lost a few toes."

Mariel experienced another wave of vertigo. "Is the trial over?"

Bobby became sullen. "Sure as hell is, but Lieutenant Erickson asked me not to talk about that till you're back on.... Till you feel better."

"Why?"

"Look, I gotta go, Mrs. E. Sorry for what happened."

Before she could ask what he was sorry about, he bolted out the door. She rolled over on her side and vomited into a bucket. Judging from the amount of bile already there, this wasn't the first time she'd thrown up, although she had no memory of having done so before. Her stomach must be nearly empty, for not much came up this time.

****

Mariel screamed.

And screamed.

And screamed.

She didn't scream in fear, although she was afraid.

Or in anger, although she was furious.

Or in pain, although she was in agony.

Lying on the wooden floor of her room, haven fallen from the bed, she screamed in despair. With her mind befuddled by drugs, she had tried and failed to stand up. The impact jarred her senses enough to realize why she fell. No amount of laudanum could dull the devastation of that sight.

Her left leg ended in a stump just above the knee. It was wrapped with a thick layer of white gauze. Trickles of blood still seeped through, almost black.

I couldn't save them both.

Father Brandon. Jesuit priest. Doctor. Surgeon. *Butcher*....

"No, you didn't!" she cried with a voice more terrible than last week's wind. In panic and disbelief she reached for her left knee, shin, ankle, and foot.

Gone. All gone.

Randall rushed into the room and saw her on the floor. "What the hell?" he said. "What did you do?"

She slapped at his shoulders as he lifted her back into bed, but her arms were too weak for her blows to be effective. "How could you let him do this to me?"

"He had no choice. You would have died."

Hysterical, she tried to vomit again, but all she managed

was dry heaves. "Why? Why?"

"Mariel," he said calmly, and she affixed her mind on his deep baritone. "Stop this nonsense. Gangrene had set in. You could live with one leg or die with two. I wanted you to live."

"You didn't ask what *I* wanted."

"You're behaving like a child."

"When you hurt your knee, he put your leg in a cast. Randall, he *cut mine off*."

He sat next to her on the bed and pulled her into his embrace. "Listen to me. I can't imagine what you're going through. But it could have been so much worse. You know Wayne Hartwig died. He's not the only one. Herb Goss found Sadie in the snow the next morning, not ten feet from their house. *Ten feet.* She didn't realize how close she was."

There'd been too many shocks today. Between her grief, revulsion, and the lingering effects of the laudanum, Mariel struggled to comprehend. Sadie Goss was dead?

"Alma grew up in heaven," she mumbled.

"What are you talking about?" Randall laid her back on the bed and stroked her forehead. "You still have a fever. I'll send for Brandon."

"No!"

"He saved your life, Mariel."

Now was a time Mariel wished she wasn't opposed to cursing. "He made me a monster."

"He took a leg, that's all," he said. "You're not a monster."

"That's *all*?"

"Goddamn it, Mariel, you're alive. I'm furious with you, almost as much as I'm proud. Even if you'd found the boys, how did you think you could help them?"

"Don't yell at me."

"I'm not yelling. But I came so close to losing you." Was that emotion she heard in his voice? "Wayne and Sadie weren't the only casualties. Lloyd Koch got his girl home safely, but the cold caught up with him, too. He died Sunday. Danny's still touch and go. Hank had a heart attack trying to clear a path to the barn to feed his pigs. Don't know yet how many outlying farmers were lost."

Perhaps tomorrow Mariel would weep for the dead, but today she wept for herself. "It's too soon for all of this," she sobbed. "You didn't give me enough time."

Randall nodded in acknowledgment. "I'm sorry. You know how blunt I can be."

"How will I teach?"

He patted her hand and stood up. "The same as you always have: very well."

****

She pushed herself into the corner of her bed, huddling against the junction of the north and east walls of the bedroom. Father Brandon had brought in a chair so he could sit while he spoke. She didn't want him near her, not in her bedroom, not in her house, not on her property.

"We can make a prosthetic," he said.

"That a fancy word for wooden leg," Randall said. He stood behind the priest.

"I know what a prosthetic is."

"We'll need to measure the circumference of your leg."

"My stump, you mean. I don't have a leg."

Brandon looked at Randall, who shrugged. "Mrs. Erickson, I need to warn you that the prosthetic will be painful to wear at first. All your weight will be pressing down on the skin and muscle between the end of the bone and the prosthetic. You'll be on crutches for as long as you need them. That will help, but you're still likely to bruise and blister. Sometimes the skin splits and has to be re-sutured.”

The priest removed a cloth tape measure from his pocket.

“Don’t touch me.”

Brandon appeared annoyed, but she didn’t know if that was because of her resistance, or because she assumed he would touch her in the first place. Probably the former, since by necessity, he’d had to lay his hands on her when he sawed off her leg.

“Lieutenant Erickson?” he said.

“Of course,” Randall said, but he looked squeamish.

Was that the way it was going to be from now on? Was he— was everybody—going to see not her but her disfigurement?

****

That night Randall brought supper to her. She’d refused to take the laudanum this afternoon, so her body ached, but her mind was clearer.

“You were wrong,” she said. “Your maps and charts didn’t warn you about the blizzard.”

Randall lowered his eyes. “It happens.” He was trying to sound nonchalant, but Mariel could see he was deeply upset. Behind his stoic demeanor, his eyes looked more abject than when he’d told her about the incident with the Navajos.

And her own mutilation.

“You don’t control the weather,” she reminded him.

“It came out of nowhere. You almost died.”

You should have let me, she thought. “I didn’t know you cared.”

“That’s unkind. You know I....” His voice failed him before he could end the sentence. He was no longer the virile and romantic soldier of their youth. What once came easily to him was difficult now. But that was all right. Old age didn’t demand the constant reassurances of youth. Mariel understood what it was he was unable to say.

"I know," she said. "I'm sorry. What did you cook?"

"Bacon. Biscuits. Careful with those. I never did get the hang of yeast."

Mariel sat up in bed, trying to find balance with her unbalanced body. She couldn't bear to look at the empty space her leg once occupied, so she piled the sheets and comforter high on the left side to make it level with the right.

The biscuits hadn't risen properly, but they had good flavor. The small movement of the muscles in her face as she chewed caused discomfort, and she remembered that her nose had also been injured. Maybe she should be grateful Brandon didn't take that, too. "It's odd," she said. "My left leg itches. *Below* the knee. How can that be?"

"Residual effects of the laudanum?"

"How does my face look?"

"Better, I think. Your nose is more gray than green now. Brandon says it should heal completely."

Mariel ate a slice of bacon. Despite the pain, she was hungry. "I don't like that man."

"He didn't cause the storm."

"He didn't have to take my leg."

"Yes, he did. Stop feeling sorry for yourself."

She finished her bacon. "I've never been the kind of woman who feels sorry for herself."

"My dear," he said, his voice soft and gentle, "you've never been anything but. Do you want more to eat? Coffee?"

She didn't argue. Could she be morose? Absolutely. But there was a difference between melancholy and self-pity, a distinction Randall had never understood.

Her more immediate concern was that the nonexistent itch in her nonexistent leg was driving her to distraction. She reached down to scratch it, but felt only the insubstantial material of her bedding. "Ow-w-w," she cried in frustration. It came out, "Aah-oooo."

Was that what the mother coyote was trying to tell her? *Ow. It hurts.*

"It's not there, Mariel," Randall said.

"Laudanum," she said. "Put it in my coffee."

He slouched out of the room. He was hurting, too. She wondered if he'd had to face Herb Goss, Peg Moehler, the Koch family, or Lousia Hartwig yet. Did they blame him for the death of their loved ones? Did he blame himself?

Randall returned with her coffee. Even its rich flavor couldn't mask the bitterness of laudanum. "There is some good news," he said, sitting next to her on the bed.

"That would be pleasant."

"The reason Frank and Larrabee met Thursday morning. You knew it concerned land deeds?" She nodded, and he continued. "Frank and Woolridge had been doing some research. They uncovered a federal regulation that said homesteading claims could only be made by the people settling the land, or in some cases by blood relatives. As Frank so brilliantly proved in court, while he was under oath, Cowan isn't really Liam's cousin. That claim was illegal."

Mariel set her cup on her nightstand. So that's what that line of questioning was about. Frank appeared to be exposing Cowan as a liar, when in fact he was getting him to admit he wasn't related to Liam. "The Cowans have to leave?"

"Oh, it gets better. In looking for one thing, they also found another. Seems Cowan has a warrant out. Bank robbery and attempted murder."

"What's going to happen?"

"Woolridge arrested him Thursday morning. Cowan got to watch as he and Larrabee signed the eviction notice in front of him."

"And Tara and the children?"

"She couldn't be happier. She hates Cowan as much as she hates Dakota. I don't think she'll even look back."

Mariel glanced at the bleak wall of snow blocking her window. "What was the hurry? Why did the judge have to delay the trial?"

"He ordered a federal marshal in Kimball to take Cowan into custody. The marshal was leaving for Denver Saturday. He telegraphed that he wanted Cowan in Kimball by Thursday afternoon, so Frank and Larrabee had to get the deed business out of the way Thursday morning. Of course, that was before the storm hit."

"Well, that puts a nice little bow on things, doesn't it?" Mariel said. "I do have one more question. Bobby said you didn't want him talking about the trial with me."

Randall stood up and walked toward the door. "Not now."

"Don't you dare leave. When did the trial finish?"

Randall leaned against the doorframe. "Yesterday."

"And?"

"I said not now."

"Yes, now. Did Larrabee set an execution date?"

Randall approached the bed but didn't sit. After a long pause and a series of sighs, he said, "Do you remember back on election day in November, what Woolridge said about Judge Larrabee?"

Mariel tried to scratch her itch again. The laudanum had better take effect quickly. She gritted her teeth and said, "Vaguely."

"Larrabee's sons are also judges, so John called him the father of justice."

"What's that got to do with Hartwig?"

"If Larrabee is the father of justice, then the men on the jury are the sons of mercy."

Her mind snapped into perfect clarity. "What are you saying?"

"As you might expect, not many people came back for the verdict. Everybody lost something. Livestock, wagons. Some barns caved in from the weight of the snow. Tree branches broke and landed on houses.... Clyde just learned about Wayne yesterday morning before the trial. I've never seen a man carry on like that. Frank delivered a rousing closing argument, but I don't think Clyde heard a word of it. He just sat at the table with his head in his arms, weeping."

"The jury believed that nonsense about Fenians?"

"No, I don't think they did. Van Pelt spoke last and destroyed that argument. The jurors decided to stay in town Wednesday night and then couldn't get home after the storm. As of yesterday, most of them didn't know yet what had happened to their own families. They felt *sorry* for Clyde, Mariel. Wayne's death broke him, and they knew the same news could be awaiting them about their own children. After that, the verdict didn't seem to matter much anymore. They just wanted to go home."

Mariel began feeling lightheaded, a clear indication the laudanum was doing its work. No drug could dampen this outrage, though. She knew the truth but had to ask anyway. "My God, Randall, they *acquitted* him...."

He stooped and kissed her tenderly on the cheek.

"Chalked it up to an old feud fueled by drink."

CHAPTER FIFTY-SEVEN
THE ACCUMULATION OF DAYS
Sunday, October 7, 1894

Once Mike and Phoebe moved to Iowa, the real estate agent in charge of selling their property refused to allow Mariel to teach classes in his house anymore, fearing the children might do damage and thus decrease the home's value. Herb Goss had kindly allowed the courthouse to be used for that purpose.

For that she was grateful, but she was apprehensive when he summoned her to the post office after church for important business. Of course Goss was late. Mariel had long since grown accustomed to her wooden leg, but still preferred to sit whenever possible. She looked about the place while she waited, noting how disheveled it had become since Sadie's death. After Beryl retired as post office special, she assumed the duties of maid-by-default. However, so far she hadn't shown the same diligence in bringing order to the entire building as she always had to her own room.

When Goss staggered in, his eyes and skin appeared more jaundiced than usual. He was drunk, of course. Without so much as a hello, he announced, "I've resigned my position as mayor. Brandon says I'll be dead within a year if I don't move to a warmer climate. The *Sentinel* is yours."

With that he started to leave. He'd never recovered from the death of his daughter Alma so many years ago, let alone Sadie's in 'eighty-eight.

"Wait," she said.

His feet got tangled as he slowed, and he fell. He made no effort to get up. He simply lay there staring upward, tears flowing. "Don't help me," he said. "I've soldiered on for six years without her."

"Has something happened? What triggered this?"

"Nothing. Everything. It's just the accumulation of days. Eventually they were going to collapse under their own weight. This was that day. I can't do it anymore. You know as much as I do about operating the press."

Suddenly Mariel had a hundred questions. "Where will you go?"

"New Mexico Territory. California. It doesn't matter. I can die in the desert as well as here."

"You don't mean that."

He inclined his head toward her and laughed. It was a horrible, bitter sound. "Hepatitis, cirrhosis, cancer.... Whatever I've got, my liver's gone. I don't care."

Mariel rose from the chair. Her artificial leg didn't hurt much anymore, but she hated, *hated*, the clopping sound of wood on wood as she crossed the floor. "Who'll be mayor?"

Goss looked away. "You better sit back down. The council appointed Clyde *mayor pro tempore*."

Mariel was appalled but not surprised. Since his acquittal, his fortunes had taken a dramatic upturn. Whatever his monetary situation had been before, there was no doubt about it now. In late 1888 his grain market investments paid off handsomely, making him the wealthiest man in Goss Valley. Wealth bought influence, and that influence had gotten him named to the governor's delegation that went to Washington D.C. in 1889 to witness President Harrison sign the proclamation transforming Dakota Territory into the states of

North and South Dakota.

Hartwig then tried, but failed, to parlay that prestige into supporting the movement to name Huron the capital of South Dakota, because of its close proximity. Pierre was accorded that honor.

"Why him?" she said, standing over Goss. "Can money even buy political offices now?"

"No one else wanted the job."

Mariel considered the implications of living in a town with Hartwig as mayor. She retreated to her chair. "Surely he'll terminate my teaching contract."

"He can't. He's a changed man, but the council didn't trust him not to revert to his old ways. To keep him from anointing himself king, we put a lot of conditions on him. One of them was to keep you as teacher."

That was flattering, but....

"What about the immigrants? The Indians? How can you be sure what he'll do once you're gone?"

"The council can veto any bonehead stunt he tries to pull. He's there mostly to sign official papers when necessary. Hell, that's all I ever did. Anyway, the only immigrants he really hated were the Irish, and they're gone."

That was true enough. Despairing at the failure of American justice, Bridget Blackford had taken twelve of her children and returned to Ireland. Before she left, she pleaded with Mariel to accompany her to Liam's grave one last time. Once there, though, Mariel remained at the mission while Bridget knelt before his crucifix. She couldn't hear individual words, but by Bridget's loud voice and angry gesticulations, she was furious with her husband.

That seemed a tragic way to say goodbye forever, but Bridget didn't explain and Mariel didn't ask. For some time she harbored suspicions, before deciding she was better off not knowing.

The one Blackford who remained in the States was Megan, who had married Bobby Baughman in 1891. They, too, decided to leave the valley to make their home in St. Paul. Mariel still received occasional letters from them. Their first child was already two, four years younger than her own grandson, Stephen.

"And my classroom?"

"Will remain at the courthouse until a real school can be built," Goss said.

She was relieved. Hartwig as mayor was galling, but a *powerless* Hartwig as mayor was almost... sumptuous. She looked at Goss on the floor, gasping like a fish on a pier, the last of its struggle against oxygen spent. Throughout her years here, she couldn't say she'd ever acquired much affection for the man, but her heart broke for him now. He was her mentor, after all, an editor who, through many twists, turns, and delays, had nevertheless allowed her to fulfill her dream of being a writer.

"Do you believe you'll see Sadie and Alma again?"

He emitted a morose sound from his throat. "I don't know. But I do know that once I'm gone, I'll never have to *not* see them again."

CHAPTER FIFTY-EIGHT
WHITE CROW

Tuesday, January 2, 1900

Despite Randall's foolishness about the year zero, today was not only the second day of 1900, but of the twentieth century. Mariel put on her coat and gathered her school supplies. She considered teaching a lesson in which she'd have the children speculate about what the new century would bring. That ought to annoy him, since he'd claim she was being a year premature.

It was seven a.m., and he was still in bed. He'd retired from the Army Signal Corps in 'ninety-five, so he didn't have to take his thrice-daily readings. Although he'd never quite lived down his failure to predict the blizzard of 'eighty-eight, for two years after he retirement he'd been employed by the new civilian weather service. He quickly tired of that, though, and now used his contacts there only to write his weather forecasts for the *Sentinel*.

He'd adapted to his retirement entirely too well for Mariel's tastes. He always seemed to be underfoot. With no weather devices to monitor, no charts to make, no maps to read, he rarely left the house anymore. But he was good to her, so she couldn't complain.

She opened the door onto a pleasant January dawn. The sun wasn't quite up yet, but the sky was clear, with a purpling of the darkness in the east. It had been a mild winter, with above normal temperatures for most of November and December. Except for a few defiant drifts, what snow that had fallen was now melted.

However, Randall warned her to expect a blast of reality tomorrow, as a storm was already being reported in the western stations.

Even in the worst of conditions, the trek to school was so much easier these days, as the new schoolhouse had been erected on the plot next to theirs. Also, the path took her directly past the little cross that marked Bruno's grave. Although he'd been gone nearly thirteen years now, she still fondly recalled his homely face and smelly ways. It was too dark to see his grave on winter mornings, but she did enjoy stopping by in the afternoons and having a chat with him when weather conditions allowed. Like so many things, his presence both comforted and saddened her. Of all her dead, melancholy loves, he was the only one rooted here in the South Dakota prairie.

Her bicycle was in the barn. Randall had bought it for her a few years back, specially fitted with a basket for her wooden leg and crutches. The terrain was flat, so pedaling with one leg wasn't difficult. She needed to push downward with the ball of her foot, then hook the top of her foot beneath the pedal and pull up. It was invigorating work. She was tempted to ride it to school today, but the blizzard of 'eighty-eight had taught her to never, never trust warm January mornings.

Mariel limped to her classroom, her wooden peg punching holes in the frozen ground. She appreciated the solitude of the fine morning, but looked forward, as always, to the arrival of her students. She had fewer than in the old days. The town had lost a third of its population in the past decade. Many of the original families had moved away after the storm. The final member of her first class in Goss Valley, Constance Nielson, graduated last year. Most of her students had married and produced children of their own. Like Bobby and Megan, like Lottie and Theo all those years ago, young couples would rather experience the excitement of bigger cities than toil away in this vast expanse of ennui known as Goss Valley.

Mariel herself had spent several years in Chicago. She understood the allure. However, she understood the pitfalls, too, and didn't regret their retreat to a simpler life.

A lamp was burning in the schoolhouse window. Electric lights, gas furnaces, and indoor plumbing were still a dream of the future in Goss Valley. The post office, now run by Daniel Koch, did have a telephone, which was impressive but impractical, since no one else in town did. They would soon enough, though, and when that happened, Daniel would be ready.

As usual, thirteen-year-old James Bohnet was already at his assigned desk, deep in his studies. James preferred to go by the first and middle names given him by the Jesuits, James Peter. He was a full-blooded Crow Indian. Since he dressed and spoke like everyone else, he seldom suffered abuse because of his heritage anymore. His mother Rebekkah had married Phineas Bohnet in the early 'nineties. Phinny had developed into a responsible young man, and had raised James as his own. The boy, who'd been in her class since he was seven, was an excellent pupil, a sterling example to the other students.

He was everything she hoped Alex's son Stephen would grow up to be. Ellie had stubbornly refused to produce a grandchild, so Mariel had been mighty pleased when Alex and his wife Nicola had filled that void.

"Good morning, James Peter," she said.

"Morning, Mrs. Erickson."

"What are you studying today?"

"Arithmetic."

"Good for you."

Mariel watched him with admiration and regret. It was good he was getting along so well, and yet, on some level she'd always lamented the lifestyle his people had been forced to abandon in order to assimilate into white society. The Wounded Knee Massacre, over nine years past but still fresh in everybody's mind, had crushed any hopes of the Indian tribes regaining their former independence and glory. Their Ghost Dance was over. Physically James had the beautiful dark skin and eyes, high cheekbones, and black hair of the Crow people, but socially he was as white as any other child.

Mariel found that unfortunate. Perhaps if living in town didn't give him the freedom of the prairie, at least it was better than the reservation. She didn't know. It wasn't her choice to make. Since James seemed happy, and his mother content in her acceptance, it wasn't her business, either.

She'd never told James she'd met him just before Christmas 1886, when he was still a babe in his mother's arms, or that she knew his Crow name was Howling Dog. Rebekkah, who was born Walks-with-the-Sun, preferred he not be reminded of those days.

"Mrs. Erickson," the boy said, "did you hear the news?"

"What news is that, James?"

"You know Father Brandon's still trying to teach Dad the catechism? He stays with us every Monday night. Trippledy came for him at five this morning."

"What happened?"

"Mr. Hartwig died. Looks like a heart attack."

Mariel staggered backwards. "You're sure of this?"

"I heard him say it."

She turned toward the window. The sun had broken the horizon. Its rays slanted across the barren prairie. In a few months spring would return. Crops would rise from winter's desolation, and flowers would restore beauty to her frozen gardens. As always, death sanctified the living.

But what did Hartwig's death sanctify? These days he was neither at the pinnacle of his influence nor at the depths of his villainy. The jury hadn't hanged him when he most deserved death, melancholy hadn't claimed him when he most desired it —in the months following the loss of his son—and irony hadn't brought him down when he was riding highest.

She gazed into the blue expanse of the South Dakota sky. "Why *now*?" she whispered.

END

ACKNOWLEDGMENTS

Anyone interested in learning more about the blizzard of 1888 should read David Laskin's excellent book, *The Children's Blizzard*. It provided some of the source material not only for the storm itself, but for weather forecasting practices of the day.

Another primary source was Thomas Pirnie's unpublished memoirs of Michael Hileman, Jr. More about that later.

****

Variations of tales recounted in three of the chapters in *A Killing Snow* have been previously published online as flash fiction pieces. These were written by co-author Dave Hoing.

Chapter Eight, "Do Children Grow Up in Heaven?": The incident related by Mike Hammon involving a Union soldier shot trying to escape Andersonville prison was published in slightly different form in the ezine *Frontier Tales* as "The Dead-Line."

Chapter Fourteen, "Fowl Weather": The essay written by Bobby Baughman was published in the ezine *Flash Me Magazine* under the title "Indications."

Chapter Twenty-Six: "In Here They're Just Men": The entry in Phoebe Hammon's diary was published in the ezine *Frontier Tales* as "Mercy."

****

The authors would like to acknowledge the people whose input has helped make *A Killing Snow* possible: Lu Hileman, Rachel Hileman, Carol Kean, Karen Nortman, James Roberts, Bob Schott, Bill Tate, Edythe Thompson, and of course the wonderful folks at Penmore Press. A special shout out goes to Hal Hileman, whose efforts in recovering and preserving the memoirs of Michael Hileman, Jr. were extraordinary.

Thanks, too, to Diane House for taking the author and other publicity photographs, and to Jerry Grier for his assistance in that endeavor.

Virtually all of the fictional characters in this book get their names from friends and relatives. With one exception, we use a real person's first or last name for a character, but not both. Of course, many of these names are not uncommon, but since we had specific people in mind when deciding what to call our characters, we'd like to thank them here. Our use of their names does not in any way reflect our opinions of the actual people. In fact, in some cases the character is not even the same gender as his or her real-life namesake. Special thanks, in alphabetical order, go to Carter Anderson; Megan Blackford; Marlee Bockhoven; Wayne and Jeannette Clayton; Dave Dall; Paul Finch; Tessa Hanlon; Willard Hoing; Shawn Hollingsworth; Alex Kean; Hannah, Hailey, and Hope Koerperich; Steven Kunkel; Doug Larrabee; Ciara Lewis; Brandon McDuffie; Nora Meierotto; Lorraine Moehler; Becca Bohnet Phillipson; Cindy and Greg Reyst; Bob Spielbauer; Clyde Van Pelt; and Kathy Williams. Thanks, too, to co-author Roger Hileman's wonderful grandchildren Ellye and Everett, who are still too young to take much interest in novels.

We also borrowed the names of family members who are no longer with us: Roger's brother Randy and mother Elaine, and Dave's mother Peg and grandparents Glenn and Beryl Kelley.

****

The names of historical people found herein include Civil War officers Burnside, Custer, Foster, Greely, Hazen, Lucas, Rosencranz, Shepherd, Sherman, Thomas, and the infamous Captain Henry Wirz. Others one may find in American history books and Google searches are Cora Hatch Richmond, Land Commissioner Sparks, Governors Pierce and Orr, and President Harrison. A man calling himself Professor Gaspodin Mezzeroff really did teach Irish dissidents to make "infernal devices" (bombs) in a dynamite school he operated in New York City. Unknown to history, but actual people nonetheless, were the plantation owner Blank and his family, the slave Joshua, and the unnamed slaves mentioned in one of the stories told by our character Mike Hammon. And finally, we would be remiss if we didn't mention Bruno, a bulldog who did ride that train into Kimball, Dakota Territory, in the 1880s.

AFTERWARD:
FICTION AND HISTORY

At least fourteen people in South Dakota, as of the most recent census (2010), may recognize our fictional town of Goss Valley as bearing similarities to the very real Gann Valley in Buffalo County. Gann Valley has the distinction of being the smallest county seat in America.

Our fictional Goss Valley is not laid out in the same manner as Gann Valley. Although it shares some of its history, the dates for events don't match the real thing. For instance, there was a struggle between Gann Valley and Buffalo Center—Buffalo Prairie in this book—for the right to be the county seat. However, in our depiction that situation occurs later than it did historically. This is the case with many of the details we relate. We researched the history of Gann Valley, and found many of the events interesting and relevant. However, for the purposes of our novel, we needed them to happen at different times. Rather than offending American historians, we simply made the whole town, the dates of its history, and the people in it, fictional.

One of those people in our book is the mayor of Goss Valley. Our Herb Goss is loosely based on Herst Gann, who founded Gann Valley in 1883, but our character's lack of character, if you will, has nothing to do with the flesh-and-blood man. Sadie Goss takes a form of her name, and that only, from Herst's wife Sada.

Of course, historical fiction wouldn't be historical if it didn't contain some true events along with the fiction.

Some of these include:

1) The weather. Sadly, the tragic blizzard that occurred on Thursday, January 12, 1888, was not a product of the authors' imagination. Over a century and a quarter later, it is still

referred to as the Children's Blizzard. Throughout the Midwest, the storm claimed some 400 lives, many of whom were children who froze to death trying to get home from school. Other than that storm, no attempt was made to research actual weather conditions on particular days. Unlike Randall, we *do* control the weather in this book. For the most part, we made it rain, snow, or shine as suited our needs.

2) Mike Hammon's story. Another significant weaving of fiction and history in *A Killing Snow* may be found in the character of Mike Hammon. He is based on Michael Hileman, Jr., who was the great-great uncle of co-author Roger Hileman. Michael lived from 1820-1915 and witnessed many important historical events, including the Lincoln-Douglas debates and the infamous blizzard depicted here. We have a first-hand account of his life in the form of his memoirs, as transcribed by son-in-law Thomas Pirnie and preserved by Hal Hileman. This document is a fascinating look into 19th-century America. For a time Michael was a resident of Gann Valley. His second wife's name really was Phoebe, and their daughter was Lottie. As in this novel, Michael did allow his home to be used as a school. He was involved with the hotel in Gann Valley, albeit later than depicted here, and as its owner, not employee. In 1861 Michael enlisted in the Army at the age of 41 to fight in the Civil War with the 96th Illinois infantry (in this story the 92nd Illinois). The account here of his escape and subsequent return to Andersonville prison, although not verbatim, is a close approximation of the wording from his memoirs. The story recounted by Phoebe in Chapter Eighteen, "The Thieves of New York," was also experienced by Michael Hileman, Jr. However, as some parts of his memoirs relating to that incident seemed a bit contradictory, we altered it slightly to make it more consistent.

3) The murder. There is a kernel of truth in the murder of Liam Blackford, although the actual killing occurred in a different place (Iowa) and a different year (1847). It was the

first recorded murder in Marion, Iowa. In that case, a farmer named James Carnagy was clubbed by James Reed in full view of several witnesses. Carnagy died a month later, and Reed was charged with murder. The circuit judge was delayed, so the case didn't go to trial for over a year. In the end, despite the witnesses, Reed was acquitted by a jury that determined the incident was simply "an old feud fueled by drink."

4) The Fort Defiance horse races. Chapter Thirty-Five, "A Day at the Races," recounts an 1856 horse racing mishap at Fort Defiance, New Mexico Territory, involving the Navahos and U.S. Army soldiers. This unfortunate incident sparked two Battles of Fort Defiance, and many smaller skirmishes.

5) The Haymarket Massacre of May 1886, mentioned a couple of times, was real.

6) And, sadly, so was the massacre at Wounded Knee in December 1890.

7) And the Irish Travellers.

8) And the Fenian Brotherhood.

9) And the Fragment Society. It truly was a charitable organization, and its members were not the mean-spirited ladies depicted in this novel.

10) The chicken and the cannon. Even that wacky experiment was actually performed, although the name, date, and location were changed, and the event wasn't meant to scam anyone. The experiment was performed in 1842 by Professor Elias Loomis of Western Reserve College in Ohio. Thankfully, that unfortunate chicken was already dead when it was fired from the cannon!

****

A Killing Snow is related to two previous books we've written. It's a pseudo-sequel to our as yet unpublished novel *Shun the Heaven*. In that book Mariel is a nine-year-old child, living with her father on a farm in Ohio. We liked her character enough that we decided to bring her back as an adult in this one. In *Shun the Heaven* the answer to the mystery surrounding the death of her mother Claire, only alluded to in this book, is revealed.

A Killing Snow is also an inadvertent prequel to our first book *Hammon Falls*, which was published in 2010. *Hammon Falls* was inspired in part by the life and death of Roger's grandmother Cora, whose last name we changed from Hileman to Hammon for purposes of that book. While planning *A Killing Snow*, we originally intended no connection to *Hammon Falls*. However, Michael Hileman, Jr.'s memoirs are extraordinary, and for some time we had wanted to find a way to use them in a work of fiction. When it was decided to make him a character in *A Killing Snow*, it only seemed natural to give Michael the same fictional last name we used in *Hammon Falls*, as both novels contain true elements of the lives of Roger's ancestors. Ironically, perhaps, the only character the two novels share in common, G.W. Hammon, doesn't actually appear in either book. He is simply mentioned as the deceased father of one of the characters in *Hammon Falls* and as Mike's nephew in *A Killing Snow*. But through him the connection is made....

About The Authors

Roger Hileman

Roger Hileman writes nonfiction for a testing company by day and fiction by night. Naturally, the biggest challenge for Roger is keeping them straight. He and writing partner Dave Hoing collaborated for many years by mailing reams of paper back and forth through the US mail. Then one day someone invented this thing called the Internet. There was much rejoicing.

Through the years, Roger has been involved with numerous musical theater productions on stage, in technical roles, and as orchestra director. He gigs around Iowa with groups such as the New Venue Big Band and CR Jazz. He began his writing career as a playwright, but Dave eventually turned him to the dark side of prose. Roger loves history, especially the family kind, so his ancestors frequently become fodder for his fiction.

In his nonfictional world, Roger and his wife, Lu, live in Iowa City. They have three daughters, Andrea, Rachel, and Carlye, and three grandchildren, Everett, Ellye, and Zachariah. No pets, but he plays a bass trombone he named Eddie.

About The Authors

David Hoing

In real life, **Dave Hoing** is a library associate in the Special Collections and Archives unit of the University of Northern Iowa Library. His tenure there can be measured on a geologic time scale. He lives in Waterloo, Iowa, with his wife, Joni, a dog named Doodle, and a cat named Itzy. His adult stepchildren, Jon and Jovan, have emigrated to the fantasy land known as California.

In his other life, Dave is a member of Science Fiction and Fantasy Writers of America who no longer writes science fiction or fantasy. He pokes his fingers into a lot of other creative pies. In addition to writing, he dabbles in composing, drawing, painting, and sculpting. Music is his first love, but he concedes that he's better at stringing words together than notes, so there are times when he must tear himself away from one kind of keyboard to work at another. He also enjoys traveling—42 states and 27 countries to date —and collecting antiquarian books printed before 1800.

WINDMILL POINT

BY

JIM STEMPEL

Gripping historical fiction vividly brings to life two desperate weeks during the spring of 1864, when the resolution of the American Civil War was balanced on a razor's edge.

At the time, both North and South had legitimate reasons to conclude they were very near victory. Ulysses S. Grant firmly believed that Lee's Army of Northern Virginia was only one great assault away from implosion; Lee knew that the political will in the North to prosecute the war was on the verge of collapse.

Jim Stempel masterfully sets the stage for one of the most horrific battles of the Civil War, contrasting the conversations of decision-making generals with chilling accounts of how ordinary soldiers of both armies fared in the mud, the thunder, and the bloody fighting on the battlefield.

"We must destroy this army of Grant's before he gets to the James River. If he gets there it will become a siege, and then it will be a mere question of time." – General Lee.

PENMORE PRESS
www.penmorepress.com

WILDFIRE IN THE DESERT

BY

BRUNO JAMBOR

Action Adventure, Crime, Mystery,
Southwest History

Highly entertaining, well researched and original:

A Navy veteran returns home to his ancestral land to escape the pace of modern life. His nephew begs him to hide the drugs he is transporting to escape his pursuers.

An astronomer trying to find a replacement for his estranged wife finds solace in his work with the stars.

Police and the drug cartel try to recover the missing shipment, regardless of consequences, ready to sacrifice any opponent.

The antagonists crisscross the desert of Southern Arizona in a chess game where the loser will be eliminated.

Unexpected help comes from a famous missionary who blazed new paths through the same desert three centuries ago.

The climactic resolution will captivate readers of this thriller with deep spiritual undertones.

PENMORE PRESS
www.penmorepress.com